THE PRE-LOVED CLUB

Also by Sue Teddern

Annie Stanley, All at Sea

The Pre-Loved Club

Sue Teddern

MANTLE

First published 2022 by Mantle
an imprint of Pan Macmillan
The Smithson, 6 Briset Street, London EC1M 5NR
EU representative: Macmillan Publishers Ireland Ltd, 1st Floor,
The Liffey Trust Centre, 117–126 Sheriff Street Upper, Dublin 1, D01 YC43
Associated companies throughout the world
www.panmacmillan.com

ISBN 978-1-5290-2508-8

1 3 5 7 9 8 6 4 2

A CIP catalogue record for this book is available from the British Library.

Typeset by Palimpsest Book Production Ltd, Falkirk, Stirlingshire
Printed and bound by CPI Group (UK) Ltd, Croydon, CR0 4YY

Visit **www.panmacmillan.com** to read more about all our books
and to buy them. You will also find features, author interviews and
news of any author events, and you can sign up for e-newsletters
so that you're always first to hear about our new releases.

For Edward

Ned, 2017

Ned and Tanya were on a wardrobe recce. The kind of weekendy, couply thing couples do at weekends. Dora had been invited to her cousin's birthday party in Haywards Heath so it made sense to drop her off, nip to Ikea in Croydon and try out drawers and doors on the wardrobes Ned had researched so thoroughly online.

He was sure he could convince Tanya that the Songesand was the one for them, if she could just see it full-size and in situ: he loved the Ikea room settings. Not to mention the meatballs.

They were in a faux bedroom. It was all a bit too Scandi for Ned: at least twelve artfully scattered cushions in various shades of beige on the king-size bed; too many framed monochrome prints of dried-up leaves – and he kept walking into the low-slung lampshade, seemingly made from tea-stained serviettes.

'Is this what they mean by "hygge"?' he asked as he bumped his head. Again.

'Hygge's Danish. Ikea's Swedish.' Tanya knew stuff like that.

The Songesand definitely looked the business: ample hanging space, somewhere for shoes, plus there was also a chest of drawers and bedside tables, if they ever went full-on matchy-matchy.

1

He opened the door, then closed it, then opened it again. Nice smooth action. Tanya leant, arms crossed, against a fake wall that was trying hard to look like paint-flaked old bricks. Funny the details he'd remember, years later.

'Come on, Ned.' Tanya sighed. 'I promised we'd collect Dora at six.'

'Flatpack stuff can be flimsy, though. Especially when I put it together.' He opened and closed the wardrobe one more time. 'Which do you prefer: Songesand or Visthus?'

No reply.

'Earth to Tanya. Are you okay? Hey, why don't we have lunch first, then decide?'

She frowned, took a deep breath and composed her thoughts. She had to get this right. 'I'm so sorry, Ned. I can't do this any more.'

'Fair enough. I suppose I could restore that pine wardrobe your mum gave us. New handles or a nice matt paint job? Cream, say, or dark blue to complement the curtains.'

He perched on the bed, patting it for her to sit beside him, but she stayed standing. Comfy bed, he thought. Comfier than theirs, which dipped in the middle. 'Maybe we should treat ourselves to a new mattress too?'

Tanya shook her head in close-to-tears frustration. 'You don't get it, Ned. What I'm trying to say is: I need more space or I'll explode.'

'The Songesand has extra storage at the bottom.'

'Forget the bloody wardrobe.'

He knew not to ignore that tone of voice. 'Sure. Absolutely. Ready for meatballs?'

Then she said it. In Ikea of all places. 'I think we need some time apart. From each other. I feel suffocated. You must know what I mean.'

2

She searched his face for a frown of understanding. But he didn't understand. Not then. Not now. 'We're just not, I don't know, we're not who we used to be. We've changed.'

'I haven't!'

'Exactly! We're in such different places. Surely you can see that?'

Ned shook his head. It made no sense.

'Mum and Dad will put us up for a bit, me and Dora.' Her voice cracked. 'Until we know if we've got a future.'

'I've got a future,' he said, louder than he'd intended. 'With you and Dora.'

He tried to find his Tanya in her eyes but she wouldn't look at him. She was clearly upset but at least she'd known what was coming. She wasn't the one who'd had the rug pulled out.

She let him reach out and take her hand. She reciprocated his squeeze of her fingers. It felt familiar but it was different. Everything was different.

Gemma, 2017

Gemma couldn't bring herself to enter Rocksy's Fish Bar for a good nine months after the break-up, even though it was way better than the chippie by the bus stop. Rocksy's felt cursed. So she avoided it. In fact, she avoided fish and chips full-stop: just the smell of batter was an emotional trigger and she had to gouge her palms with her nails in order not to cry.

Then she decided that, okay, Joe had screwed up her life but no way was he going to change her choice of takeaway. She reclaimed the fish supper, telling herself it was a turning point. One of many. Two steps forward, none back.

Win-win, me! Lose-lose, Joe!

Gemma's life had changed for good (for 'good'?) on an uneventful Wednesday in March. Cold. Drizzly. Not showing Bevendean's best side, if it ever had one. They were parked outside Rocksy's, waiting for Kelvin to return with cod, chips and mushy peas for three, and Gemma was telling Joe what a crap day she'd had.

'Then she accused me of not being a team player. I so am, compared to her.'

'This is Janine, right?' He knew it was Janine. It was always Janine.

'I should have applied for that job.' Gemma sighed. 'That

way, I might have stopped her *getting it. Why didn't I? What was I thinking?'*

Joe's silence spoke volumes.

'I know! I know you said to go for it. I didn't want the responsibility. I didn't want to be the one bossing my mates around. But, I swear to God, Joe, I could do that job in a coma, compared to Janine.'

Joe squeezed her hand. 'Course you could, hun. You're clever and smart—'

'Clever and smart are the same thing.'

'And *brilliant and kind. They're lucky to have you. I know* I *am.'*

He kissed her reassuringly, just as Kelvin clambered into the back seat with their fish supper and told them, as he often did, to get a room, not that he was entirely sure what that meant. Eleven years old and minutes away from an event that would reshape his life.

'Where's my change?' Gemma asked, waggling her fingers behind her head.

'You said I could keep it. Didn't she, Dad?'

'Did she, mate? Must have missed that.'

'And you *still owe me pocket money.'* Kelvin didn't miss a trick.

'Pay *the pushy little herbert.'* Joe chuckled. 'Wallet's in there.'

Gemma clicked open the glove compartment as Joe edged the car into the early evening traffic. And that's when it all changed. Everything.

Lime green sunglasses. Tucked under his wallet, half hidden by an empty Haribo bag and a parched chamois. Lime green with gold arms. She held them up.

'Whose are these?'

'Must be yours, hun. I don't suit green.' Gemma couldn't fault his swift response.

'I think I'd know if I had such bad taste.' She tried them on and checked herself out in the vanity mirror, shuddering at the lurid reflection staring back at her.

'Seriously, Joe. Who do they belong to?'

'I told you! No one!'

They drove on for a minute, turning into Dean Avenue, passing Carole from two doors down walking her arthritic Jack Russell. She waved. Gemma waved back. Kelvin was messing about on his phone, utterly oblivious to the tectonic shift in the front seats.

'Just tell me, Joe. Whose are they?'

'For Christ's sake, leave it, will you? And give the lad his fiver.'

'Tenner,' Kelvin muttered, still distracted by his phone. 'You owe me for last week too.'

Gemma opened Joe's wallet and pulled out a note, a combination of slow motion and autopilot. The smell of cod curdled deep in her stomach.

Chapter One

Ned

Waitrose car park is the usual Friday-night scrum: trolleys dumped in prime parking spaces for a patient employee to retrieve; pairs of comfortably-off sixty-something couples blocking the store entrance as they chat smugly about their skiing holidays. 'No, no, we went to Andorra actually.'

I grab a trolley, briefly distracted by an abandoned shopping list clipped to it that reads 'rosemary + kindling'. Hove Waitrose is a haven for 'rosemary + kindling' types. Tanya took against a certain kind of self-absorbed, self-important customer and would get in their way on purpose. Once she sneaked three Pot Noodles into a particularly smug trolley.

I know what's in my fridge and what I need to buy, which is pretty much everything. If I can just feed and water Dora tonight and have the correct breakfast cereal, we'll eat out for the rest of the weekend. I grab some trimmed broccoli and scrubbed baby carrots; Tanya can feed her veg-box kale covered in mud Monday to Friday. I even find her a trio of kiwi fruit that I'll no doubt forget about and they'll live at the back of the fridge until they grow goatees.

My phone pings. A text from Tanya, probably with updated instructions about what Dora and I can/can't do this weekend.

For a ridiculously long time, I had to keep her away from hand dryers. Now it's spiders.

'Can U come round 30 mins early? Give us chance to talk. Hope ok. C U later. Bye.'

I stop in my tracks, inadvertently getting in the way of the skiing couple, who are after olive oil. So, Tanya wants 'to talk', eh?

She's been really sweet lately, not like in the early, acrimonious months of our separation. Back then, she had a very short fuse and everything was my fault. Obviously, I didn't agree, but it was easier to take the blame than challenge her. However, paths of least resistance can turn into cul-de-sacs if you're not careful.

These days we reminisce over a cuppa after I drop Dora off: that camping holiday in Cornwall when I got food poisoning and we had to dump my sleeping bag in someone's skip; my predisposition to Springsteen; our much-missed cat Ronnie.

I think the thought I haven't allowed myself to think for a week or two. She's softening. Eighteen months apart has shown her that, yes, I'm an idiot, but I'm *her* idiot. I really, really think she wants us to try again.

I finish shopping at double speed, rush back to the flat to fill the fridge and spray my over-eager armpits. I put on the one clean shirt that's also ironed. Tanya bought it for me, daring me to wear primary-coloured flower print. I won't lie, I hate it. But she'll see by my shirt that I'm up for a rapprochement.

Andy would tell me to play it cool, keep my cards close to my chest. But Andy has 'Arsenel' tattooed on his forearm and calls women 'babes', so I think I can trust my superior instincts.

Tanya opens the front door. I painted it boring brown when we moved in. Now it's a tasteful dark red. She gives me a quick 'hiya' kiss without prompting as I stroke the door's silk finish.

'Looks really good. Let me guess . . . Oxblood Sunset?'

'Tuscan Plum.' She flashes a Tanya smile. My heart does a turn. 'Come in.'

I sit in what used to be my armchair – maybe it will be again – and Tanya takes the sofa, legs folded neatly under her. She's still doing the yoga then.

'Thanks for coming early, Ned.'

I shrug. 'No problem. Dora does still eat broccoli?'

'She loves broccoli. We must have done something right.'

I see where she's going with this. I don't want to jump in too soon but perhaps I should be the one to broach our reconciliation, to take the pressure off her.

'That's because we were a team, Tan,' I suggest tentatively. 'Maybe we still are.'

Then we do that thing they only do in movies. We speak over each other and don't hear what the other one's saying. We laugh. Like we used to.

'Do you reckon we want to say the same thing?' I ask, convinced that we do.

'Oh, that would be so great, Ned. You go first.'

I kick off, a little rambling and muddled, because I've forgotten what I rehearsed in the car. 'I just thought, maybe we could go out some time. You know, you and me. Call it a date, call it an excuse to try that new Thai place in Kemptown, whatever.'

Tanya looks uncomfortable. The truth *is* uncomfortable. I've started so I'll finish.

'We shouldn't be apart, Tanya. We're grown-ups now. You

9

definitely are. It could work. I could be different. We can pick up where we left off. Can't we?'

A loaded silence the size of Scotland. Then she replies. 'Ned, I . . . I met someone. I hoped you were going to say you'd met someone too.'

I want to lie but you can practically inhale my disappointment. I can't believe I've got it so wrong. It's just like Ikea. Again. I try to muster my thoughts but all I can say is: 'Who?'

'His name's Julian. Matt's best friend. Remember Matt?'

'The dentist. Did we ever return his strimmer?'

'You broke it. We got him a new one. Anyway, I met Julian at Matt and Jane's housewarming and, well, we've been seeing each other for a few months now.'

She looks to me for a response which I somehow summon from somewhere. . 'Okay. Right. Well, um, congratulations, good for you,' I stutter. Inside, I'm wondering how it came to this – how I'm congratulating Tanya on her new relationship when all I really want to do is beg her to take me back. Or cry. Or both.

'I thought you should know because it changes things. That's why I painted the front door.' There's another pause, but this time I don't – I can't – fill it. 'I had the house valued, Ned. Dora and I are moving in with him. Julian. So we'll need to sell up and split the proceeds, unless you want to buy me out.'

I manage a hollow laugh.

'Okay then, use your half as a deposit on a proper home. You can't rent that horrible flat forever. It isn't fair on Dora.'

'And she's okay with all this?'

'Why wouldn't she be? Julian's an amazing man. They get on really well.'

For a totally sussed woman, Tanya can be quite naive. As

Dora's dad and a responsible adult, it falls upon me to ask. 'Have you checked him out? You know, his past? You hear stories.'

'Oh, I see. I've met someone, so there must be something wrong with him!'

I shake my head vehemently, as if that isn't what I meant at all.

'Julian loves Dora,' she continues, 'and he loves me. That's all I need to know.'

I'm still processing this when she adds: 'Oh, and she's got a temperature so she can't come to yours for the weekend.'

'I got broccoli!'

'Pop up and say hi before you go.' She unfolds her beautiful long legs and stands. Meeting over. Jog on, loser. 'He loves me, Ned. He makes me happy. I'd really appreciate it if you could *try* to be pleased for me.'

An hour later, I opt not to tell Andy every nuance of my 'chat' with Tanya. He'll just get angry with me, tell me I played it all wrong. When I find him at his usual table in the Anchor, he's busy on his phone, sealing the deal with his latest conquest. He looks up with a satisfied grin as I return from the bar with two pints of Sagres.

'So that's four voicemails she's left me. Plus two texts and a shedload of WhatsApps. Keen as, or what?'

I pretend I know who he's talking about. 'Katie, right? From the queue in Tesco?'

'Lara. From the party in Fiveways.'

'At what point do you respond?'

'Thursday.'

'You really are a throwback, Andy. "Treat 'em mean, keep 'em keen."'

11

'Oh, and you're the alternative,' he sneers. '"I'm a doormat. Please stamp your crap all over me." That's you, Nedward. With knobs on.'

'It was mutual.'

Andy gives me a pitying look. Not for the first time. 'Mate. Tanya dumped you.'

'Doesn't stop me wanting her back. I honestly thought she was up for a reconciliation a couple of hours ago.'

'Seriously?'

'She said to come over early because we needed to talk.'

Andy looks genuinely horrified. 'You wouldn't!'

'I miss Dora. I miss me and Tanya being a family. But she just wanted to tell me she's met someone else.'

'Has she now? Poor bugger. Who is he?'

'An architect called Julian. Lives in a big, fuck-off house on Dyke Road.' My forlorn sigh comes from deep within my solar plexus. 'Okay, she doesn't want *me* any more. I get it. I do, Andy. But why did she have to meet someone else?'

He nods sympathetically. 'Time to turn a page, my friend, and look to the future.'

'I'm trying, I really am, but you can't just turn off your past like it never happened. Anyway, why would I? I was really, really happy then.'

'I can,' he boasts. 'I do it all the time. Right now, my only focus is whatsername from Fiveways . . . Lara. And whether I want crisps or nuts with the next pint. And that promotion at work. It's a shame we're in competition but I won't gloat when I get the gig.'

He knocks back the rest of his lager and burps. 'Peanuts. Definitely peanuts.'

And with that, Andy whips out his phone to check if the latest ping is another text from Lara. He chuckles to himself as he reads, then nods to me and crows triumphantly: 'Get in!'

I'm fond of and grateful to Andy. When my world fell apart, he got me back on my feet. When I needed somewhere to stay, he put me up on his lumpy sofa bed. When I needed someone to vent to, he listened. He and Tanya had never got on, so I knew I'd get 100 per cent loyalty from him.

Andy's a good mate. But I don't want to be nursing a pint in the pub with him. I want to be home – *my* home – with Tanya and Dora. If she's met someone else, how will we ever get back together? The thought that we might be a family again kept me going these past few months. Now I know it's not going to happen.

I want my house back and my life back. I want us to be 'us' again. I've had it with being 'me'.

Chapter Two

Gemma

All day, I get by on strong black coffee, plus two apples for lunch. By half three, my work is quite literally done. And it's a Friday. And Janine has the afternoon off, so who's to know if I skedaddle ten minutes early? Only Felipe, and I covered for him on Tuesday when he had a gig in Lancing.

In reception, Monica sits in coat and slippers, smelling of Avon talc and stale wee, waiting as always for the long-dead husband who will whisk her away from Willowdene Care Home. She beams at me, a smile full of hope and someone else's dentures.

I perch beside her. 'They're watching *Pointless* in the lounge, love. Why don't you join them?'

'Barry's late today. I expect he got stuck on the Old Shoreham Road.'

Felipe is passing with a vacant wheelchair; I gently hand Monica on and she winks at him. They all love Felipe here. Last week a couple of the more mobile ones even booked a minicab to see his Bangkok LadyBoy tribute act. Judy lent him her dangliest earrings.

'Are you doing the humpty-dumpty with Idris Elba

14

tonight?' Felipe asks as he settles Monica in the wheelchair. It's a running gag that's well past its sell-by date.

'Idris was last night. And I keep telling you, it's "rumpy-pumpy". No, Kelvin's got a mate sleeping over, so I've put my wild social life on hold.'

'Have a good weekend.' He pushes Monica into the lounge and I buzz myself out.

I don't *need* to meet Kelvin at the school gates, but it doesn't take me out of my way. He leaves the building, sees me and scuffs up. Literally. He can get through a new pair of school shoes in one term. 'I'm 12. I don't need walking home,' he snaps.

'What if *I* do? Where's Mohit?'

'I told him not to come.'

'Oh, Kel. I got two kinds of pizza and that disgusting cheesecake you like. You need to make an effort with your mates. It's how friendship works.'

That's when I see Joe walking towards us.

'What are *you* doing here?' I say, not even trying to sound friendly.

He ruffles Kelvin's hair, which I'd never be allowed to do. 'We've got a date. Haven't we, champ? I'm buying him some Adidas Predators. Top scorers need serious kit.'

So that's why Kel cancelled Mohit. 'Is that his belated birthday or Christmas present?'

'Does it matter? He needs new boots. And he may as well stay at ours tonight. Save me picking him up tomorrow morning. Okay with you?'

Kelvin looks keen so I'm obliged to agree. He has a big bedroom, an over-attentive stepmum and all he needs in Woodingdean.

'I want him home at half eight latest on Sunday night and his homework done. I mean it, Joe.'

They get in his car and Kelvin waves as they drive off.

So now I'm a free agent. The world is my oyster. I can go where I want, do what I want, be whoever I want to be. I decide to swing by the big Sainsbury's and stock up on bog roll, bin bags and cereal. Live life on the edge or die trying.

Once through checkout, I treat myself to a salted caramel latte and a slab of carrot cake in the instore cafe. I'm checking Facebook while dragging my thumb through the frosting when I see Hayley packing a stack of shopping into two new bags for life. I bet she buys one every time she does the weekly shop. She never got the 'dog is for life' thing either.

Or the 'best friend' thing.

I duck down, hoping she won't see me. She does. She waves, gathers up her bags and comes over. She's as curvy, bronzed and lush as ever, with a cleavage you could rest a cocktail in.

She plonks herself beside me, exuding matey-ness and her amazing double Ds. She's really pleased to see me. 'Hey stranger,' she gushes, planting a big 'mwah' on my cheek.

Before I can reply, she's off. 'Ooh, carrot cake. I love carrot cake. I'm on the 5:2. Five days eating for England, two days sniffing oven chips. Red velvet's my favourite. Cake, I mean. Did you know they make it from dried beetles?'

'You look well. Nice tan.' I set my conversation to cool, but not friendly.

She admires her brown, bangled arm. 'Fortnight in Turkey. Mid-thirties every day.'

'With Joe and Vicky. I know. I saw the photos on Facebook.'

Hayley reddens, caught out. She's always been world class

at putting her foot in it. 'It was Vicky's idea. The holiday. Us four going together, plus the kids, obviously. So we could share the babysitting and whatnot. My Scarlett adores little Amelie.'

'Aw, "little Amelie". Has Vicky learned how to spell that yet?'

Hayley laughs, even though she knows it's a dig. Then there's an awkward silence which she's unable to keep. 'Got any plans for the weekend?'

'Kelvin's at Joe's; I'm a free agent.'

I slowly lean forward in my armchair and force her to return eye contact. She braces herself for what's coming.

'It's brilliant that Scarlett and Amelie are best mates. It's important to have mates, isn't it? Friends you can rely on, whatever, whenever.'

Hayley nods guiltily. 'I'm sorry, Gem. I really, truly am.'

I've wanted to hear these words for so long but when they finally come, they're just air. 'Be honest, Hayley. Would you ever have told me, if I hadn't found out? Would it ever have occurred to you that your best friend deserved to know her husband was shagging around?'

'Lee made me promise.'

'Ah, and "husband" trumps "best mate" every time.'

'I wish I'd told you. I really do, Gem.'

While she searches for a scrunched-up tissue in her bag, I find Vicky's Facebook timeline on my phone and scroll down to the Turkish holiday snaps. There are hundreds of them. I thrust them under Hayley's nose.

'Vicky in three different bikinis and no stretch marks. You four, dressed to kill, out for dinner on the hotel terrace. Joe in pink shorts. I wouldn't have let him in the back garden in pink shorts! How can I not feel hurt and excluded when you four are buddied up literally for all the world to see?'

Hayley blows her nose hard. Her mascara is in wet clumps.

I'm not finished. 'Anyway, how do you know your precious Lee isn't screwing his PA every lunchtime in the cleaners' cupboard?'

'Gemma, that's a horrible thing to say! And he isn't.'

'You hope. The difference is, I'd tell you. Because we are – we *were* – best mates. And what's to say Joe doesn't cheat on Vicky? Christ knows, he's got form. Then she'll see just how it feels to be lied to, to have her heart smashed into tiny little bits.'

Hayley tries to take my hand. 'I'm so, so sorry, Gem. Can we be friends again? I miss you.'

'Hmm, let me think.' She looks hopeful. 'Don't be daft, Hayley. You ruined my life. Of course we can't be friends. Ever again.'

I gather my shopping, ready for the big finish. 'Oh, and while we're clearing the air, did you know Joe can't stand you? "Chicken drumstick in stilettoes." That's what he called you. "Voice like nails on a blackboard and thick as a frozen dog turd."'

Hayley looks horrified.

'And now you're best pals with Vicky and he's lumbered with you all over again! I call that a result.'

I stomp out of the cafe, feeling like Russell Crowe in *Gladiator*. It lasts until the bus stop, then I auto-reboot back to 'normal' and feel like shit again.

Joe and I had friends, good friends, when we were married. We were never short of party invitations, people to see, mates to meet for a spur-of-the-moment curry.

But Hayley was *my* friend, from the moment we clapped eyes on each other on the first day of secondary school. It probably wasn't an equal friendship: I led, she followed.

Okay, she was never the sharpest knife in the drawer, but she was funny and daft and loyal and I assumed that loyalty was unbreakable. You do with your best friends. That's why her siding with Joe hurt so much. What had he done to earn that? Nothing!

I still see 'our' friends and, God knows, I'm not the only single mum in our social circle. Certainly not the only one on our street. But now I'm awkward to have around. Not because I'll lunge at all the husbands or corner people in the kitchen at a party to whinge about Joe, but because I've fallen through the net. I've stopped being what's normal, what's accepted. I've become the elephant in the room, and losing my oldest friend was tough. Maybe not her specifically – a little of Hayley goes a long way. I lost a major part of my past, a shared history, back when I was just starting to find out who I was. I don't make friends easily and, anyway, who in their right mind would want to hang out with a wet weekend like me?

Chapter Three

Ned

I don't know how he did it, but Andy has persuaded me to go clubbing with him and we're queuing up to get inside a place on Brighton seafront called the Vault. The January wind whips through my coat and I'm still wearing the flowery shirt that was going to win Tanya round a few hours ago. Now it's all crushed and pointless. Just like me.

Three pints of lager has numbed the pain of my conversation with Tanya this afternoon, but I know it'll be my first thought when I wake up tomorrow. What on earth made me think she was going to suggest we try again? She's a massively attractive woman and just as gorgeous as she was the first time I saw her, at Sarah Hearne's party. Of course she's going to move on, turn a page, meet someone new. How did I not see that coming? Probably the same way I didn't see the split coming. That's how I am – terminally unobservant – and I'm not proud of it.

'I feel old,' I whisper to Andy.

'I bloody don't. In my head, I'm still 18.'

'Look at me! I'm all wrong here.'

Andy shakes his head wearily. 'Listen, Nedward, you're a bloody sight better-looking than me. I'd kill to be tall and have your hair. But what it is, is: I *know* I'm a catch and you don't. You've got no idea, mate.'

I shrug and he thinks he's getting somewhere.

'As I see it, you have two options. You can either feel sorry for yourself for another year, another five years, and turn into a weird, cranky old man. Or you can get back in the saddle and have a bloody good gallop. We are hot to trot, my friend.'

Andy has spotted four giggling women who pass us, in search of the back of the queue. He can't help himself. 'Hey, ladies, looks like your party just got started. Let's squeeze you in here.'

They hoot at his cheesy approach but join us anyway.

The door staff let us both in – despite our advanced years – and within twenty minutes Andy's on the dance floor with the giggly women, who turn out to be a hen party from Crawley. For a bloke edging towards a portly 40, he's an amazing dancer, and that's why he's surrounded. I don't dance. Tanya disowned me whenever I did. When he catches my eye and gestures to join them, I shake my head vehemently.

Andy keeps giving me pointed looks. I have no idea what he's so animated about. Then I realize I'm standing next to a woman. Late twenties, stylish, beautiful thick hair and big eyes that she won't stop flashing at me. He is telling me to go for it. I smile at her and she smiles back. Crikey, does this mean I've pulled?

Her name is Nancy, she lives in Seven Dials and she crossed the dance floor to say hi. Even if it's a bet from her mates, I go along with it. This is me getting back on the horse, ready for a gentle canter.

We try to talk but it's impossible. Were clubs always this loud? Nancy suggests we go outside. Andy is now kissing one of the Crawley women – probably the bride – and doesn't see me leave. Good. I can do this better without any patronizing thumbs-ups from him.

We sit on a wall and look out at the brightly lit pier. It's too cold to linger for long. Now what?

'I know it's tacky, but I love this view, don't you,' Nancy says. 'Chuck in the smell of doughnuts and it's perfect.'

I need to show an interest, ask insightful questions. 'Are you a native Brightonian?'

'Born and bred. You?'

'We moved here after Dora was born. Eight years ago. Me and Tanya. From London. We couldn't afford a rabbit hutch in Highbury but we just scraped enough together for a house in Hove.'

'Oh. Right. You're married, then?'

'God, no. We couldn't see the point. Well, I could, but Tan wasn't keen.'

'How does she feel about you going out clubbing?'

I'm an idiot. She thinks Tanya and I are still together. 'We split up. Just over a year ago. Thirteen months and one day, to be precise.'

'Oh, that's a shame.' Nancy seems genuinely concerned.

'She said we grew apart. I couldn't see it myself. Still can't, if I'm honest.'

'That's sad.'

'I thought she wanted us to get back together earlier tonight, actually. That's why I'm wearing this shirt. I was so up for giving it another go. I could do things differently, be different. But oh no, that wasn't what Tan had in mind at all. Guess! Go on, guess why she wanted to see me.'

'Not a clue.'

'She's met someone else. An architect called Julian. You

22

know those big houses on Dyke Road? All Arts-and-Craftsy with massive front gardens? She's moving in with him. Her and Dora. How can I compete with that?'

I gaze out to sea because a combination of Nancy's sympathy, the fresh air and too much lager has made me a little maudlin. I don't want her to see me like this. Besides, there's nothing wrong with silence. Silence is good.

I give it sixty seconds, then turn to ask Nancy if she'd like another drink.

She's gone.

I had so many plans for the weekend with Dora. I usually start thinking about it midweek and do some major googling of what's on at all the local museums and cinemas, from Worthing to Hastings: I don't want her going back to Tanya on Sunday night saying we just watched Netflix.

It was my idea to have her over every weekend, rather than every other, which was the initial arrangement after our break-up. I was dossing down on Andy's sofa bed and I wasn't in a good place – literally and emotionally. I didn't want Dora to see me like that.

As soon as I got myself sorted, with a place of my own and a spare room for her, I suggested to Tanya that we try out every weekend, with room for flexibility if we needed it. She agreed without any argument, possibly out of guilt, possibly out of a desire to have two days out of seven when she isn't just 'Mummy'. I get that. And, so far, it's working out for all three of us.

But it's hard to keep Dora occupied at my place. So, in a way, it's a relief that she's not here – or at least, that's what I tell myself to feel better. I can bin the kiwi fruit, and I don't have to tidy or put those fairy lights up in her room. I bought them months ago but they're still in the carrier bag.

When Dora's here, we get up early. I make eggy bread and hot chocolate, which she's not allowed to have for breakfast at home. We're usually out by ten, in search of something to do. The best Saturdays are when there's a kiddies' creative event at a museum: painting, writing poems, potato-printing. If it isn't raining, we do a kite festival or Drusilla's Park Zoo or we visit a castle. Dora in a good mood is the best company ever.

But she's not here. So I have a lie-in. I'm not used to drinking and those lagers have given me a fuzzy head. I think about yesterday. Tanya's news about her new chap totally knocked the stuffing out of me. It's made me feel sad, stupid and raw, all over again. I fast-forward to meeting Andy at the pub and then the club . . . and Nancy . . . Jesus! Okay, I may have talked too much about Tanya but I *was* all set to change the subject. Politics, maybe. Where she stands on Ed Sheeran. She didn't give me a chance. Note to self: banging on ad infinitum about your ex is not the most winning chat-up line. I really must file Tanya in my 'that-was-then' archive. I have to forget about her. Or at least to stop thinking about her so much. She's a chapter. A book. She's a book I've finished. I have to move on. Starting today.

At half nine, I get up and make myself some toast and coffee. An hour later, I wake up when the plate falls off the bed. I must have turned the radio on because the Reverend Richard Coles is interviewing Ken and Betty Reynolds who met in the playground in 1965 and haven't spent one day apart since.

By noon, I'm up and showered and ready to get some sea air. I stroll down George Street and hang a left. I may as well do the seafront walk from Hove to Brighton.

It's as busy as usual for a sunny Saturday. Runners and skateboarders thundering past. Over-excited dogs chasing balls. There are even one or two wetsuited swimmers, braving the winter waves. When we moved here, I thought I'd swim every day, but I must have gone in three, maybe four times. When you've got it on your doorstep, honestly, what's the hurry?

I see I'm approaching Marrocco's. Tanya and I could never pass that place without buying a scoop each of dulce de leche. Marrocco's was our favourite restaurant, with seafood pasta to die for. If I hadn't scared Nancy off, we could have gone there on our first date. I sit on a bench and my mobile rings. Maybe it's Tanya: Dora's feeling better and wants to stay over for the rest of the weekend. I could pick her up within the hour if I hurried. I have broccoli.

It's Andy. 'Well?' he asks.

'Fine, thanks. And you?' Sometimes even *I* can be obtuse on purpose.

'Well, how did you get on with Nancy?'

My blood runs cold. I was right to be suspicious. It *was* a set-up and Andy was in on it. How else would he know her name?

'Why don't you ask her yourself?'

Andy gasps. 'She's still with you? Way to go, Nedward. That's made my day.'

'What I meant was: if you know her so well, *you* bloody ask her!'

'Hey. Mate. Keep your hair on. She's a friend of Nick Watson. I chatted her up once but she didn't want to know. She wanted to know *you* all right though.'

'Yeah.'

'Women can't resist your sort. Good-looking but you don't

know it and all vulnerable and sorry for yourself. They like that in a man.'

'Women pity me?'

'They want to take care of you. And? Did she?'

'Did she what?'

'Take care of you! I was *well* taken care of. Kayleigh from Crawley. Matron of honour from that hen-night gang. Insatiable, I'm telling you.'

I can't tell him that Nancy talked to me for all of ten minutes, realized I was a twat and did a runner. So I lie. 'She wanted to meet tonight but I've got Dora, after all. In fact, I'm just picking her up now. Got to go. Bye.'

I walk along the seafront as far as the Grand Hotel, then up to Churchill Square. I end up in WHSmith and buy a *Guardian* for the TV guide, and a birthday card for my sister. At the queue to pay, an impatient woman harrumphs behind me. I ignore her.

'Did you need to push in like that?' she mutters accusingly.

'Me?'

'Yes. You. You pushed in. Typical man, not even noticing.'

I don't want to cause a scene so I step back. 'Please. You go first.'

She shakes her head. She's made her point.

At the till, the shop assistant waves her hand across a display of chocolate. 'Would you like any half-price chocolate at all?'

I spot a Toblerone. 'Ooh, I love these. My dad used to get them for me and my sister whenever he came through duty-free. I haven't had one in years.'

Or maybe the slab of Fruit and Nut. Tanya and I always bought a bar for long car journeys. Toblerone or Fruit and Nut? Tough call.

From behind, another harrumph. 'In your own time.'

I settle on a Toblerone and thank the assistant. 'That's brilliant. Cheers.'

'She didn't pick you out specially, pal,' snarks the woman behind me. 'She asks everyone.'

I ignore her. I don't respond to rude people. Bloody cheek, though.

Later that night, after I've eaten a Lidl pulled pork ready meal which wasn't too bad actually, I hunker down in front of the telly and channel-hop between a daft game show and an even dafter movie on Netflix about zombie crime fighters. I suddenly remember the Toblerone in my jacket pocket and knock it back in four mouthfuls. Tanya loved Toblerone.

This isn't good. It can't go on. Andy says draw a line, move on. Move on where and to what? I love Tanya. I loved our life together. Maybe she's right; we *were* in a rut and I was too bedded-in to notice. Maybe I wasn't the most exciting or dynamic partner ever – but it was *comfortable*. I was happy. And now? I've settled into singledom just like I've settled into this depressing flat. I go to work. I come home. I eat rubbish and I watch rubbish. I come to life at weekends when Dora's here, and I'm lost when she isn't.

This is no good. This is no life.

Chapter Four

Gemma

Normally on a Saturday, I'm rushing round the house, stuffing Kelvin's backpack with homework, clean football kit, clean pants . . . even though he has loads of clothes at Joe and Vicky's. I don't want her ever to assume she's in charge of what Kel wears. He's *my* son, and that's *my* job.

And normally on a Saturday, Joe rings my doorbell at ten, then scoots Kelvin off to soccer. But this Saturday, Kelvin's already at his dad's, tempted there yesterday by a new pair of football boots. Typical Joe. Why earn your son's love when you can buy it at Sports Direct?

So no hurry getting up. I can stay in bed all day, if I feel like it. What's to stop me? Everyone deserves 'me' time and this is mine.

By twenty to eight, I'm showered, dressed and I've plucked my eyebrows. I eat a wedge of cold pizza for breakfast and by nine I'm standing on a kitchen stool, removing all jars, packets and tins from my cupboards. I've been meaning to deep clean the kitchen for ages; I hate sticky rings. Joe always found my compulsion to scrub slightly unhinged, but then, he never met my nana. We nearly buried her in Marigolds.

I turn on the radio for company and hear about some old

couple who haven't spent a day apart for fifty years. Apparently they're sitting in the studio like a pair of lovesick kids. And that reverend who was so shit on *Strictly Come Dancing* and used to be in The Commodores wants to know their secret. No ta very much. I re-tune to Radio 2.

Once I've finished wiping down all the ketchup bottles and Branston jars, I decide to declutter the very top cupboard, the one too high to use. Right at the back, I come across a long-forgotten mug. It has a lairy cartoon of a grinning man wearing a huge medal that reads: 'Best Dad Ever'. A present from Kel when he was a toddler. In other words, I bought it.

I nearly tip backwards off the stool and have to sit down quickly to catch my breath. I feel winded and raw. Best Dad Ever. He was, then. We were so happy in those early years. We reckoned we were happier than anyone we knew because we'd found each other and we'd be together forever, bringing up Kelvin and all the brothers and sisters he was sure to have.

Inside the mug are some safety pins, a button, four euros, a stubby pencil and an ancient photo of the three of us on Brighton Pier, not long after Kelvin was born. Together forever, my arse. I tear off Joe's head and turn it into confetti. It shouldn't hurt this much any more but it bloody does.

On the spur of the moment, I decide to go to Bevendean Rec and watch Kelvin play soccer. Why should Best Dad Ever be the one to see him score the winning goal? I've been too accommodating, letting it be Joe's treat. Sod that.

There are packs of opposing parents lining the pitch, screaming at their kids and the ref and each other. Loudest is Joe.

'Oh, for pity's sake. Come on, Bradley, pass it back to Kelvin.'

I make a point of standing as far away from him as possible but he's too caught up in the game to see me anyway. Now Kelvin has the ball and he's streaking towards an open goal. My heart beats in my chest. Joe wasn't lying, he's amazing. I try to blot out his dad's shouty running commentary.

Suddenly a big lad from the other team trips him and Kel thumps to the ground. He isn't hurt but he looks deflated. I will him to get up but I won't shout.

It doesn't stop Joe. 'Oi ref, where's your guide dog? Blatant foul right in front of your nose.'

The ref glares at Joe while Kelvin gets to his feet and sees me for the first time. I give him my best reassuring smile.

'Get back in the game,' Joe bellows. 'Well, go on, son. What are you waiting for?'

Kelvin rejoins the match and I march over to Joe. 'Give it a rest, will you? Stop bullying the poor lad.'

Joe looks fazed. Give what a rest? He taps his temple. 'That lad needs to start thinking like a winner.'

'How can he, with you on his case the whole time?'

'You just don't get it, do you? Winning.'

'Because I'm so obviously the loser?'

'I didn't say that.'

The ref blows his whistle. Half time. The pressure's off.

Joe turns down the volume as we both watch Kel leave the pitch. 'I didn't say that, Gem. No way are you a loser.'

'Gemma nil, Vicky one. She gets the trophy. I get the pitying looks in Sainsbury's.'

Joe kicks a bit of turf, shoves his hands deep in his jacket pockets. The bastard can't even look me in the eye. 'It wasn't a game, Gem.'

'I bet it was at the start, you and her. The thrill of the chase. The little white lies. That's bound to be a turn-on. Then it got serious.'

'Swear to God it wasn't meant to.' He pushes a hand through his hair. 'You were in a state about your job and your dad and losing half a stone before your birthday. I couldn't help it. I lost the plot.'

'Are these excuses?'

He tries a disarming smile. 'Probably. They're a bit shit, though.'

'That Christmas. With all the snow. When Dad was so poorly and Kelvin broke his wrist. You were with Vicky, weren't you?'

'I wasn't!' he replies. There's a pause. 'Well, only on Boxing Day.'

I bloody knew it! '"They're half-frozen, Gemzy. Lovely old couple. I'm the only heating engineer they trust to fix their boiler and it's packed up again. He's got Parkinson's, she's got angina. I can't just ignore them." And I'm thinking, my husband the hero. Gives up his precious day off to stop a Christmas tragedy. I really take the prize for stupid, don't I?'

He has no words because he knows he's banged to rights. So we both watch Kelvin at the far end of the pitch, mucking about with a couple of teammates.

Eventually Joe breaks the silence. 'I hate us like this. Couldn't we at least be civil in front of the boy?'

'I am!'

He does a 'yeah, right' laugh. 'I can't change what happened. I wish I could but I can't.'

I won't reply. I won't give him an inch.

'You're so strong,' he says, not for the first time. 'You're a survivor. If I'd stayed with you, Vicky would have been in bits.'

My jaw drops. Can he even hear the crap he's coming out with?

He moves closer. 'I miss your laugh.'

'Hyena on steroids, you used to call it.'

'I never said that.'

'You bloody did!'

I hear how daft I sound and can't hold back a chuckle. He turns full-on and gives me his best Joe smile, the one with added twinkle. The look he gave me when I was 17 and he was 20 and we slow-danced to 'Truly Madly Deeply' by Savage Garden at John Hamilton's twenty-first. My heart does a somersault, like it did twenty-one years ago, like it always will.

'Stop it!' I hiss and look away.

Kelvin approaches, sucking on an orange segment.

'Tidy little player, our lad,' Joe says, ruffling his hair. 'Here he is. Man of the match. You slay 'em, son.'

And, for one brief moment, we look like a happy family again.

I don't stay for the second half. When Joe starts winding up the ref again, I give Kelvin a little wave and slope off. I can't be near Joe for long because it messes with my head. If he's within heartbeat distance, I can't hate him properly, the way I'm meant to.

I catch a bus to Churchill Square. I could check out the art books in Waterstones, try to look like I have hidden depths. I could get some new bras in M&S or replace Kelvin's torn cagoule. I could even walk down to the seafront and count the windmills on the horizon. I've promised Kel we'll take a guided boat trip to see them up close for his birthday.

Instead I find myself in WHSmith, flicking through gossip

magazines to see which C-list celeb has had a disastrous boob job. I know I shouldn't enjoy other women's bad decisions, but it's one of my guilty pleasures. My tits never got their bounce back after Kelvin but my tummy's flat and I've yet to have to hide bingo wings.

There's an article in *Grazia* about Sporty Spice – who I've always had a girl crush on – so I decide to treat myself. I can pass it on to Felipe. And then I think, why do I even have to justify this? When did I turn into such a killjoy?

At the till, there's a man dithering about change and chocolate as if this is the first time he's ever been allowed out shopping. Why do people have to be so slow and annoying? It's chocolate, pal. Just engage your brain and decide which one you want. Jesus!

When I get to the front of the queue, the girl at the till – who can't be much older than Kelvin – asks with zero enthusiasm if I'd like any chocolate.

'Do you see me buying any?' I snap. Seriously? Does she?

'But these ones are half price.'

'Because they passed their sell-by date before you were born.'

'No, they're safe to eat and everything.'

I snatch up a Toblerone to eat in front of the telly.

'Your bosses should be ashamed,' I tell her as I pay. 'Pimping chocolate to a captive audience. No wonder there's an obesity crisis.'

I have cereal for supper and start watching a stupid movie on Netflix, something to do with zombies. It's *so* stupid that I'm forced to zap over to an even more stupid quiz show. I polish off the Toblerone in four bites.

I feel slightly sick when I go to bed and Joe dominates my dreams, as usual. I wish he'd leave me alone, even in my sleep.

Chapter Five

Ned

Usually, after a weekend frantically keeping Dora entertained, I'm ready to be bored at work. That's what Mondays are for. But I did that yesterday. It was the worst kind of Sunday: no one to see, nowhere to go, nothing to do. I don't like my own company and if I go for a walk or pop into the Anchor – or anywhere, really – it's impossible to ignore all the happy families.

In the park, there'll be hordes of parents and kids vying for the swings, learning to ride the birthday bike or kick a football. In the pub, the big table is always taken up with a massive extended family, enjoying a noisy Sunday lunch. We used to take Tanya's mum and dad out for a pub roast when we were too knackered to cook. More often than not, Geoff would pick up the tab and Tan didn't have to slave over crackling or make gravy.

I miss all that. My old life. My *real* life. The one where I had a purpose and was happy. Where I was a father and a husband and I was *needed*.

Andy swings by my desk to see if I fancy a coffee. He wants to know how my weekend went. I won't lie but I don't need his pity either. I tell him I don't see a future for me and Nancy.

'Good thinking,' he agrees as I get two clean mugs out of the dishwasher. 'Great girl and everything but way out of your league. No reason why you can't see her for a week or two, though, have a bit of fun, then clear off before things get messy.'

'You really are a bastard.'

'I'm honest, that's all. If people just cut to the chase, didn't fanny about with *maybe*s and *possibly*s, we'd all be better off. Honesty is key, I'm telling you.'

He really believes this stuff. Before he can elaborate, Karen pokes her head round the door.

'Hey, Ned. Can you spare five minutes to catch me up on Welby-Daniels. Like now. And mine's a camomile. Leave the bag in.'

Saved by the boss.

Karen has the office next to the much-sought-after corner office. She's worked her way along the executives' corridor and it's only a matter of time till she's ousted the present incumbent. I admire her drive and ambition but she also scares the hell out of me.

I sit opposite her as she flicks through a report on her desk while she sips her tea. I made sure she got the Cath Kidston mug and I scrubbed away the grunge at the bottom. I'm a suck-up, I admit it.

'This looks good, Ned. Thanks,' she finally says, tucking a thick curtain of conker-brown hair behind her ears. 'And East Anglia?'

'Wednesday latest,' I reply, aiming to sound on-it. 'Sam's department went on a team-building awayday and got a bit behindhand.'

'God save us from paint-balling and zip wires and group hugs.' She sighs, rolling her eyes.

'And karaoke. Remember Sanjeev from Accounts doing his best Nicki Minaj!'

We laugh. This is going really well. 'I'll give Sam a nudge. Tell him we need that report asap. Leave it with me, Karen.'

She scribbles something in a Smythson notebook. My presence is no longer required. I make to leave but she waves me to stay seated. Eventually she looks up.

'So. We've made our decision. About the promotion.'

'Oh.'

'It's not official till Monday. But, hey, you and I did a mean Dolly and Kenny on "Islands in the Stream", so it can be our little secret. It's a yes, Ned. Congratulations.'

My jaw drops. Not a good look.

'It has to be said, you gave a rubbish interview. You really need to work on that going forward. Too many ums and ahs. Not enough passion. But your strategy overview was the clincher. Top work. We all thought so.' She holds out a hand for me to shake. 'So. Well done you.'

I still haven't taken it in; I only put my hat in the ring on deadline day because Andy said I shouldn't bother.

'Try to look pleased, Ned: 10 per cent pay rise, your own office. Eventually.'

'No, it is. It's great. I just wasn't expecting it.'

As I head for the door, she calls after me. 'How about a drink tonight to celebrate? But do keep it zipped till Friday, will you? We need to tell the unsuccessful applicants.'

After work, I head for Bar Rosso, across the road from the office. It's not a particularly welcoming place and the cocktails are pricey. Its saving grace is that the equally underwhelming

Queen's Head is a ten-minute walk away. As a result, all office socializing happens at Bar Rosso.

Andy falls into step as I leave the building. 'I can only stay half an hour, mind,' he warns me, as if I'd actually asked him along.

Karen's by the bar as we enter and gives us a wave. 'Aye-aye,' whispers Andy. 'D'you fancy a threesome?' She scares the hell out of *him* too, only he'd never admit it.

Karen spots an empty booth and nabs it sharpish, beckoning us over to join her. While Andy eyes up the barmaid, she gives me a 'who invited *him*?' look.

'Let's have some fizz,' she suggests, patting the leather banquette next to her and smiling at me conspiratorially.

'Not on *my* plastic,' scoffs Andy.

She pulls £20 from her purse. 'Get us the finest Prosecco this place can find.'

He looks puzzled. 'Why? What are we celebrating?'

Karen and I keep schtum.

Andy won't let it lie. 'The promotion? Hey, did I get the gig?'

'You'll hear on Friday,' Karen says, giving nothing away.

Somehow it's lost in translation and Andy does a victory fist. 'Get in! Hey, no hard feelings, bro. You gave it your best shot.'

He heads for the bar to buy the round. Karen smiles at me. Our little secret. I allow myself to feel victorious.

Andy stays for a couple of glasses of Prosecco and the lagers that follow, also paid for by Karen. Then he checks his watch, drains his glass, pulls on his jacket.

'Loving you and leaving you, boys and girls.'

'Hot date?' Karen asks.

'Room temperature, I'd say.'

I waggle my beer glass, trying to tempt him. 'My round.'

He pauses, mid-sleeve, and thinks about it.

'You'd stand her up for a free pint, wouldn't you?' Karen laughs.

'Karen, love, you've got me all wrong.'

Her expression says: Oh no, I haven't.

He heads for the door, shouting, 'Laters!' over his shoulder.

We both watch the door swing after him, then she turns to me, shakes her curtain of hair out from behind her ear and says, 'Alone at last.'

Obviously she's joking and I laugh quickly to acknowledge that we're merely two colleagues having a post-work drink together. No biggie. We talk shop for a while. The Welby-Daniels contract . . . head office politics . . . the apocryphal tale of the head of finance and the brothel in East Croydon.

Karen's nice. I finally see that she's human and far less scary than I thought. Once we've covered all aspects of QGT Logistics, we start talking families. She's a single parent too. I had no idea.

'My partner was a bully,' she tells me. 'What was yours?'

'A control freak. It suited me, actually. At least you know where you are.'

'Patrick was your typical alpha male. If I didn't go along with him, he'd slap me around. Nothing serious. He did this.'

She flashes me a sparkling smile. 'Chipped tooth. You can't see it now. Top-of-the-range veneer. In fairness, he only nudged me but I lost my balance and hit the worktop. It totally freaked him out.'

'Bloody right. Did he come to his senses?'

'Kind of. It was just verbal stuff after that. Coercive control, telling me I was a waste of space. And it still took me six years to leave him. Best thing I ever did, though.'

'Good for you.'

'I'm older, I'm wiser and I've got great teeth. How old's your little girl?'

'8, going on 35. Yours?'

'20. Doing Ecology and Conservation at UEA. And now you're meant to say: "You don't look old enough to have a 20-year-old daughter."'

'Oh. Sorry. Well, you don't.'

She pats my hand. 'Relax, Ned. I'm joking. So, do you do much dating?'

I think of Nancy and how I blew it but Karen doesn't need to know that. 'You have to get back into the saddle, don't you? Before you forget how to gallop.'

She gives a throaty laugh. 'Oh, I was in full gallop the second my decree nisi came through. I booked myself a week in Calabria. Waiter called Paolo. Ride 'em, cowboy.'

I know I look shocked. Is she trying to embarrass me?

She's still holding my hand. She gives it a squeeze. 'I like to take the reins, Ned. That way, I get what I want.'

Which is why, half an hour later, I'm at her place, on her bed. She's ripped my shirt open, my trousers are round my ankles and I'm 'cantering' as I've never cantered before. With my boss. Who has just promoted me. Bloody hell. Andy would be proud.

Tanya suddenly pops into my head and nearly puts me off my stride. What would she make of me 'moving on'? Is that what I'm doing – here, now – with Karen? I want to believe I am, so why must my ex invade my thoughts like this? Two assertive women are pulling at me, like a wishbone, and I really don't like how it feels.

Chapter Six

Gemma

A frail old man called Mr Allnutt, who could easily be a resident himself, has come to the care home to give a talk about Dubrovnik. He has a slide show so it takes a while to set him up, find the right extension leads and a little table for his notes and some souvenir ornaments.

Last month he gave a talk about Sussex wildlife. The month before that, he told us all he knew about the Royal Pavilion. He needs two of us on hand to fetch and carry and we like his visits because he sends nearly all the residents to sleep. Except Evelyn, who has Pick's disease, and shouted: 'Oh sod off, you silly sod!' last time.

Janine wants Mr Allnutt back next month to repeat the wildlife talk. She reckons the residents won't mind hearing it again. 'The ones who are still alive at least.' Typical Janine.

So Felipe and I get everyone in their seats, close the curtains and leave them to it. It's a welcome half-hour to grab a coffee and catch up.

Felipe has news. He's engaged. He and Martin have just moved into a rented flat in Peacehaven and decided they're ready to settle down. He's so excited.

'When do you tie the knot?'

Felipe looks puzzled. Every day a new bit of English slang floors him. Yesterday I said I wished Janine would wind her neck in. He loved it, once I explained, and instantly added it to the list on his phone.

'I *mean*: when do you get married?'

'Ah, I see! We don't have plans. This is to show Martin's parents we're serious.'

It's best I don't say anything. It's not for me to piss on his chips, not that he'd know what that meant anyway.

'It's good, isn't it?' he asks, picking up on my silence.

'Felipe, if you're happy, I'm happy. You two are made for each other. The rest's just a lottery.'

Felipe's a great one for fate and karma and destiny, whereas I'm too cup-half-empty for my own good. Always have been; even before Joe dumped me for Vicky. I'm hardly the poster girl for happy-ever-after and I can't fake it for the sake of it.

From next door, I can hear Evelyn telling Mr Allnutt to shove his slides of Dubrovnik up his arse. Coffee break over.

In the afternoon, I'm doing the tea run. I stay for a few minutes with a favourite resident, Alfie. He's sharp as anything for 84 but the pancreatic cancer is eating away at him and he gets scared. I know he likes someone in the armchair next to his bed when he's dozing. Sometimes I stroke his hair like his late wife used to. He's a sweetie.

As he snores, I have a quick scroll through Facebook. I like to visit Vicky's timeline. If the daft cow's too thick to secure her privacy settings, what's to stop me? Or maybe she *wants* me to see what a great life she has with Joe: her barbecues and coffee mornings, a gazillion photos of her with Amelie, Joe with Amelie, her and Joe with Amelie . . . my Kelvin with bloody Amelie.

I hear the clack-clack of stilettos on laminate flooring. Janine is on the prowl. Before I can put my phone in my pocket, she appears in the doorway.

'Tea break?' she asks, all fake chummy and supportive.

'It's my first proper sit-down all day.'

'Families go past, see you playing *Candy Crush Friends*, it reflects badly on all of us.'

I'm not having it. Not again. 'Okay, I'll wake Alfie up and make him drink his tea. Whether he wants it or not.'

'Maria *said* you were in one of your moods.'

'I'm not!'

Janine beckons for me to join her in the corridor so she can give me a proper bollocking.

'I can't keep making allowances, just because of your various emotional upheavals, Gemma. Other people have marital problems, messy break-ups, whatever. But they don't bring them to work.'

'I'm doing a good job. You tell me when I'm not.'

She lowers her voice to a hiss. I think she went on a management course where they were taught to do this. 'My advice, and I speak from experience: find some common ground with your ex, something you still enjoy doing together.'

Like what, I want to ask her . . . Arguing? Sniping? Shagging?

'I'm not being funny but we can't afford to keep un-cooperative, moody care assistants at Willowdene. Not with cuts on the horizon. Don't force my hand, Gemma.'

She clack-clacks away, probably to find some other care assistant daring to take the weight off for ten seconds. As she disappears around the corner, she says: 'Oh and once

Alfie's had his tea, I need you to "freshen up" Brenda before her son arrives.'

I revert to childhood and wave two sets of Vs at the space she's vacated.

Back home over tea, I try to find out about Kelvin's weekend. He's going through a monosyllabic phase but manages to grunt 'yes' when I offer to tip my unwanted oven chips onto his plate.

This was the weekend according to Kelvin:

How was the football? 'Yeah, good.'

How was *Doctor Who*? 'Yeah, not bad.'

Did you finish your history project? 'I said I did! Stop nagging!'

I try a different tack. I'm always curious to know what Joe and Vicky's house is like. You can't get the full picture from Facebook.

'So Amelie's nursery is next to the master bedroom?'

'Yeah.'

'Have they got a baby monitor?'

'Yeah.'

'You used to cry so loud, we could hear you in the next street. Not that your dad ever got up. I bet he leaves the baby to Vicky.'

Shrug.

'And your room's down the corridor? Near the family bathroom?'

Kelvin throws his fork down. 'Do you want me to draw you a map? So you don't have to ask me this like every week?'

'I don't, love. I'm just interested.'

As I fetch him a yoghurt from the fridge, I try to broaden the conversation. 'Modern houses are terrific on utility rooms and en suites, but they lose big time on character.'

He rips the foil off his yoghurt and digs in.

'Is Amelie's nursery fifty shades of pink? Vicky's quite traditional, isn't she?'

Kelvin pushes his chair away, grabs his yoghurt and charges up to his room. I really need to talk to him about his temper. I think he gets his short fuse from his dad.

Talk of the devil, I'm just settling down with *EastEnders* and a box of mint Matchmakers, a gift from Alfie's daughter-in-law, when Joe rocks up at my door with one of Kelvin's schoolbooks.

'Vicky found it. I thought he might need it for that history project.'

'Dozy article. He'd forget his own head.'

I take the book. End of.

Not according to Joe. 'Cuppa would be nice.'

It was good of him to bring the book round. He needn't have done, I suppose. I wave him into the kitchen.

'Does Vicky know you're here?' I ask, flicking the kettle on.

'It was her idea. And your point is?'

'Nothing.'

Joe surveys the kitchen. Not much has changed. The same B&Q Shaker-style units that were fashionable fifteen years ago. The same checkerboard lino that never looks clean, no matter how hard you scrub. Nothing like the bespoke oak units, Neff double oven and riven slate worktop he bought for lucky old Vicky.

He squints at the washing machine. 'Is that new?'

'The old one died. After it leaked gallons of sludge all over the floor.'

'Why didn't you say? I could have called Mikey.'

'Mikey got me the old one. "Reconditioned" my arse!'

I make tea. The 'Best Dad Ever' mug went in the bin. He'll have to make do with one commemorating the 2012 Olympics. As I dunk the bag, he looks into next-door's garden.

'That decking looks nice. We always meant to, didn't we.'

'I still could. You were the one dragging your heels.'

He blows on his tea, takes a tentative sip. 'This is good, Gem.'

'The tea?'

'Us talking. Quietly. Not biting each other's heads off.'

'You reckon it's all good now. I've turned a corner?'

'Have you?'

'Have *you*?'

He pretends to study the mug as he replies. 'Not really.'

I can't help myself. It's been niggling me for days so I cut to the chase. 'You shouldn't have said that on Saturday. About my laugh.'

'Hyena on acid, you mean?'

'On steroids. That you miss it.'

'I do.'

'Well, *don't*!'

'I even miss your custard. That you could slice with a bread knife. Vicky gets readymade from Waitrose.'

'You should have thought about missing me when you were sneaking off to see her on the side!' I hear myself losing control. 'Did it even occur to you that you were about to smash up our family and break my heart? And would it have stopped you? Course not.'

I turn away from him. Only losers cry in front of their exes. I am 'Best Loser Ever'. He puts his mug down and comes over, gently putting a hand on each shoulder. I want to shrug him away but I can't.

I can't stop him kissing me either. I don't want him to stop. Our lips fit together like they always did.

'No, Joe. Kelvin's upstairs.'

He puts a finger to my mouth to 'sshh' me. We don't even leave the kitchen as we undress and screw noiselessly.

We fit together like we always did.

Chapter Seven

Ned

Karen is at head office the day after our 'encounter', so I don't have to suddenly schedule a bunch of fake site visits and client catch-ups in order to avoid her. By Wednesday, however, she's back, so all I can do is act cool and pretend nothing happened. I have no option.

I hunker down at my desk as much as possible, only breaking for cover to nip to the loo. At one point, I gaze vacantly into space, trying to remember the name of the guy I deal with at the Taunton branch. Tom? Tim? Jamie? And I see Karen sipping coffee and smiling at me from her office door. I flash back a friendly nod, then look down again, flushing red from forehead to shins. I give it a moment, then look up again to see if she's still smiling at me. Oh sod it, she is.

Andy works at a nearby desk. I hiss his name and his head pops up from behind the dividing row of filing cabinets. 'You okay, bro?'

'Help!' I hiss weakly.

We go for an early lunch at the cafe around the corner. We sit at our usual table, alongside a randomly pinned noticeboard advertising Man + Van, FunkFit classes, dog walkers, house sitters and chakra locators. We tuck into our

47

usual: pasty, beans and chips. Andy takes all of five seconds to wheedle it out of me: I shagged the boss.

'I am seriously impressed, Ned,' he says between mouthfuls. 'How was she?'

I don't dignify his question with an answer.

He shrugs. 'Can't pretend *I* haven't thought about it.'

'Andy, you'd shag that pasty, once it had cooled down.'

'True. I'm like Kirk Douglas. It's an addiction.'

'Michael.'

Andy looks round. 'Where?'

'Douglas.'

'Sorry, mate. I have no idea what you're talking about.'

He shovels in more pasty and speaks as he chews. 'Fair enough, she's no Scarlett Johansson. But a shag's a shag. And it can't hurt your career prospects.'

'Uh-uh,' I reply without thinking. 'My promotion came *before* the shag!'

Andy looks genuinely crestfallen. 'You got the gig! *You* did!'

'I know. Even *I* don't believe it.'

The penny drops. 'Oh, I get it. That's what we were celebrating in Bar Rosso.'

'You'll be promoted next time.'

'Yeah, sure. So it counts for bugger-all that I've been at QGT longer than you.'

'You didn't present a strategy overview. You didn't mute your phone. Your tie had gravy on it. And you need to stop calling Karen "love". I'm only telling you for your own good.'

'I really needed that pay rise. No way I'm paying for lunch now.'

'When have you ever paid for lunch?'

'Congratulations, Nedward.' He clinks his Pepsi against

my tap water. 'Well, try to look pleased, you jammy bastard. You're on the up.'

Even so, I shouldn't have slept with Karen. What was I thinking? Andy sees my worried face. Time for a talking-to. The world according to Andy Muir.

'As I see it, you're a pig in poo. 1) You and Tanya are terminally over, move along please, nothing to see here; 2) you are now Senior Logistics Analyst, South-East Region; and c) you've just had a seeing-to by a woman of the opposite sex. Single, like you. With needs. Who can "mentor" you big time. Which bit of that's a problem?'

'Getting over Tanya isn't all about notches on the bedpost.'

'It's a start. Or . . . hey, you could join that lot.'

He jabs his ketchupped knife at a flyer on the noticeboard beside me. It reads: 'Single Parents' Advice Network'. They meet in the function room of the Anchor, every Wednesday, 7.30 to 9.00.

I shake my head. I don't bloody think so.

Andy, however, is pleased with his suggestion. 'Plus it's our local, bro. If that's not a sign from God, I don't know what is.'

'No. Capital N, capital O.'

'Well, *I'm* tempted if you're not.' Andy registers my shocked reaction. 'Why not? I'm single. I've nearly been a dad. They might benefit from my insights.'

'A room full of single women "with needs"?'

'No going on expensive dates, paying for popcorn at the pictures or Aperol frigging spritzes. Plus an odds-on chance of copping off. They'll be gagging for it.'

He sees my horrified face.

'What?' he asks, genuinely oblivious.

*

Karen finally corners me as I'm leaving work. I'm on the front steps doing up my coat when I feel a presence beside me. It's her. I redden all over again but she can't see that in the half light.

'Hiya,' I squeak. 'Is it really only Wednesday?'

'Thanks for the Welby-Daniels figures, Ned. I'll read your email properly tomorrow.'

'No worries. Anyway, I'd best be—'

'—Nice weekend coming up?'

I start gabbling. I always gabble when I'm nervous. Tanya would punch me in the arm to make me stop. 'Dora. My daughter. We do stuff. Burger and a film probably. That's what we usually do. Or a trip out somewhere. She likes Eastbourne. It's up to her, really.'

Karen puts a hand on my arm to shut me up. At least she doesn't punch me. 'Look, Ned. I'm cool if you are. About what happened.'

'Absolutely.'

'Bit of a laugh. No strings.'

'Oh, I couldn't agree more, Karen.' Phew, that's the end of it, then.

Not quite. 'Maybe we could go for a drink some time, take it from there.'

'Um, right. I don't know if . . . I'm a bit busy with stuff right now.'

'Next week then.'

'Absolutely.'

She spots a passing cab and hails it assertively before we can fix a date. And then she's gone.

I stand there for a moment, taking in what just happened. Andy said I should get back on the horse and I have, even though it's the wrong horse and I need to dismount before I get chucked off.

There again, I can hardly play the field from the safety of my sofa. How do I move on from Tanya if I'm not 'out there'? Karen is progress . . . of a sort. And that has to be a good thing, right?

When I reach home, there's a man hovering nervously on the doorstep. I know not to buzz him in, in case he's a burglar. (That's an error of judgement you only make once.) He's late forties, stylish, balding. I mentally file the description, just in case I'm needed as a witness, like last time.

He approaches as I find my keys. 'Ned, isn't it?'

'Yes?'

'I was just passing. I thought I'd say hello. I'm Julian Haig.'

Julian? Julian? I don't know any Julians. Then I remember. Tanya's new bloke. This is him. On my doorstep.

'Oh, Julian. Right. Hi.'

'I know Tanya's talked to you about me. Us. Our plans.'

'Moving in with you? Absolutely.'

'And I was thinking: if I was Ned, I'd be feeling a bit out of the loop right now. So I thought, if we met and you saw that I love Tanya and Dora and I only want them, all of us, to be happy, well, I thought it might help.'

'O-kay.'

'Obviously we can't be mates from the off. That would be weird.'

Too bloody right it would. I'd have to be pretty desperate to buddy up with the man who's stolen my life, my wife, my daughter. If there was no Julian, me and Tanya might be back together again and happier than ever. Why would I want to hang out with the man who's stopped that from happening?

Oblivious, Julian ploughs on. 'We can be grown up about all this, can't we? Then we can get on with our lives. Right?'

My brain says: I don't think so, you arse. My mouth comes out with another non-committal 'o-kay'.

Julian looks relieved. It's all sorted, as far as he's concerned. 'Phew! I'm so pleased you're on side with me here. Fancy a pint, mate?'

Seriously? He thinks we can be best pals after he's ruined my chances of being a family again. Oh, no-no-no! There's magnanimity and there's asking to be humiliated. I can't be magnanimous and I won't be humiliated. You're out of luck, mate.

'Sorry, Julian. I've got a thing. You know, to go to. And I'm running late . . . mate. Bye, then.'

If there was a passing cab, I'd hail it assertively like Karen did. Instead, I head briskly for the Anchor, texting Andy as I walk. Two awkward conversations within one hour. I need a drink.

Andy's propping up the bar when I get there. 'I didn't think you fancied it,' he says, catching the barman's eye. 'Two Sagres, Toby. Ned's paying.'

'Didn't fancy what?'

'Upstairs. The function room.'

I'm none the wiser.

'The Single Parents' Information Thingy. No, that can't be right – it spells SPIT!'

I realize what he's on about. No sodding way.

'I thought you must have changed your mind about going,' he says, watching Toby fill the first glass. 'That's why you rang to meet me here.'

'It's our local. We always meet here. Plus I needed to

escape Tanya's new bloke. He only came round tonight! He wants us to be best buddies. Yeah, like that's going to happen, you twat.'

'It might help. SPIT, SPOT . . . whatever they're called.'

'You said it yourself. I'm doing okay. My promotion, my shag. He was a complete arse, Andy. "Julian". The clue's in the name.'

'Absolutely, Nedward.'

'Un-bloody-believable.'

Andy does a concerned face. 'You know I'm here for you, bud, 24/7. Haven't I always been a shoulder to cry on? But you really need to share stuff like this with people like you. Other single parents who've been spat out, shat on. Go on, mate. Just give it a try.'

Our pints arrive. We both take a slurp.

'Not. A. Chance.'

'We'll do a runner at the break if it's not for us. What have you got to lose?'

Like an idiot, I start to come around to the idea. What harm can it do, exchanging tips and support with other single parents? This could be what Andy meant by moving on. I'm ready to climb out of my comfort zone and give it a go.

That's my first mistake.

Chapter Eight

Gemma

Judy missed her Wednesday pedicure because she slept in. So I volunteer to paint her toenails after lunch. She's another of my favourite residents at Willowdene. I suppose they all are, apart from the occasional whinger. And if I was living with chronic pain, lost memories or double incontinence, I might moan a bit too.

Judy woke up for lunch but hasn't got out of bed. She *has* put her face on, though. I've seen her without, but it isn't the real Judy. The real Judy has blue eyelids, false eyelashes and pink blusher on top of a thick layer of foundation and powder. She's currently going through a salmon-pink phase, lipstick-wise, but only fire-engine red will do for her toes, even though they're hidden in bed or tucked inside fluffy purple slippers.

She lounges on her bed like Cleopatra and I'm at her feet, like Cleopatra's maid. While I trim, file and varnish, she scrolls down yet another dating website on her tablet. I wish she wouldn't.

'Here's a good one. GSOH.'

'Great sense of humour,' I explain. Well, she *is* 89.

'I know *that*! What if this chap means something else though? Um, let's see . . . got sweaty old hands. You wouldn't find out until it was too late.'

'True.'

'Great sex over here . . . grubby sheets, oh hell!'

'Yeah-yeah, Judy, I get the idea.'

She enlarges his photo and gives him the once-over. 'He looks nice. Gentle Jeremy. Got his own picture-framing business. Widowed with two kids. Loves romantic nights cuddled up with someone special in front of a roaring fire.'

I have a quick squint at him. My heart doesn't race.

'Eyes too close together?' she asks. 'Ears too far apart?'

''I'm fine as I am. I'm not interested.'

She shrugs. I'm a lost cause, but she carries on scrolling because she can't resist. 'Please just tell me you've had an *interlude* lately, darling. That's all I need to know.'

I ignore her.

'This month? This year? Was the Queen Mum still alive?'

So I tell her, because it's been weighing on my mind all day. 'Okay then, I had hot sex on my kitchen worktop just last night. Believe me, do you?'

She hoots with laughter. As if!

'I bet I've had sex more recently than you,' she says with a false-eyelashed wink.

I look up wearily from her big toe. She needs no encouragement to spill the beans.

'You think we just play bingo in here, don't you? Have sing-songs, watch slide shows about effing Dubrovnik.'

She lowers her voice to a throaty whisper. 'Charlie on the first floor, with the Johnny Cash collection and the quiff. All I'll say is it's not just his radiogram that's king-size.'

She beams proudly, satisfied that she's shocked me. I can't help laughing. I want to be like Judy when I grow up.

I haven't been to a SPAN meeting for weeks. I know it's good for me to socialize with other single parents but I usually come home annoyed with everyone except Ros. Kelvin's round at Mohit's tonight, and there's nothing on the telly so I pull a brush through my hair, change into tomorrow's jeans and T-shirt and catch the 49 across town.

I wish SPAN met closer to home but Hove's more likely to hold self-helpy type bollocks than Bevendean. Round my way, we don't analyse why life's tough or unfair because we're too busy with gas bills and new school shoes and noisy students who've moved into the shared house next door.

Ros is on the phone when I find her at the bar. 'No, Rianna. Just tell Gabriel night-night firmly and leave the hall light on. He's winding you up, hun.' She sees me and waves the bottle of house red we'll need for the night ahead.

'Sorry, got to go. Ring if you need me.' She hangs up and sighs. 'New babysitter so Gabriel's testing her, little monkey.'

I scan the men in the bar. 'He's not here yet, then?'

'Who?'

'The Chris Hemsworth lookalike divorcee with the cute kid and the nice bum and the villa in Mallorca who falls me as soon as he walks in.'

Ros cocks her head at one of the SPAN regulars, Robin, who's got the zip pull of his fleece caught in a chair. 'When I start flirting with Robin, just shoot me.'

Upstairs, Gail, who runs the group – although I don't

remember anyone asking her to – has laid out half a dozen chairs in the usual semicircle. She's brought her flip chart and four different coloured marker pens so she must have some sort of group work planned.

The SPAN exercises and discussions are mostly pointless, but every few weeks I realize something about why my marriage failed. Something Joe didn't do that he should have. Something I did that I shouldn't. Water under the bridge now, of course, but I hope that at some stage in the future, it might come in handy.

It's the usual suspects tonight: Gail, Robin, me, Ros, Meryl and Loretta, who knits sweaters for her grandkids and barely says a word. Meryl, however, is like a cracked record. Every week, it's the same story. I can't blame her. I'd be in bits too.

'You tell me,' she says to no one in particular. 'How can it not be a slap in the face? Seventeen years together, then he suddenly turns round and "finds himself".' Her lip curls at the very idea.

Gail asks what she always asks. 'And you had absolutely no inkling, Meryl?'

Meryl shakes her head, too upset to speak.

'It hurts. Of course it does.' Gail puts on her best agony-aunt voice. 'Plus you can't help wondering what his new partner—'

'Danny,' Meryl spits.

'What this Danny's got that you haven't.'

Ros can't help smiling and Gail glares at her to behave.

'Sorry, Meryl,' Ros says, pulling herself together. 'It must be tough. But if I was you, I'd be like: Hey, it's not me personally he's gone off. It's my hoo-hah. Well, lady hoo-hahs in general.'

Robin shifts in his seat. He doesn't do below-the-waist topics.

Gail continues. 'We're twice as raw, twice as bruised when we're the ones who are left. For another woman, another man, whatever.'

Suddenly the function room door bangs open and two men enter, carrying pints. There's a bit of kerfuffle while the shaven-headed one helps Gail add two more chairs to the semicircle. Ros catches my eye and nods approval: Robin's been the only male attendee for weeks, but he doesn't count.

'Welcome to SPAN,' Gail says, once the two men are settled and seated. 'We started ten minutes ago; you just take your time and join in when you're ready. I'm Gail.'

She uncaps the black marker pen and writes on the flip chart in big letters, 'Most common reasons for breaking up.' She usually does little daisies over the i's but the late arrivals have distracted her.

Ros rolls her eyes. She hates stuff like this. (She's a widow so she can't join in.)

'I'll kick off, shall I?' volunteers Gail as she writes 'Money' in red. 'My ex wanted our children to be privately educated but we couldn't afford it. It tore us apart. Anyone else?' she asks, pen at the ready.

She looks to the two new guys. The nicer-looking one – he's got a Benedict Cumberbatch vibe, although I don't go a bundle on skinny men – shakes his head frantically. His mate's up for it, though.

'Could you write "Disrespect", please, Gail?' he suggests. 'If your other half doesn't respect you enough to be honest with you, you have to cut your losses. Am I right or am I right, ladies?'

Gail is impressed with this reply and writes "Disrespect" under "Money". Meryl and Robin nod in agreement.

He's only just started. 'My mum brought me up single-handed and she never got the thanks she deserved. But I knew how much she did, how much she gave 24/7, 365 days a year. You lovely ladies are amazing and you deserve medals. You all have *my* respect, for what it's worth.'

He does a little emotional gulp and gets his breath back. 'Sorry, I didn't mean to share like that.' His friend looks like he wishes he was somewhere else.

Gail is moved too. 'Thank you, um . . .?'

'Andy.'

'Thank you, Andy. That was lovely. Now, anyone else? Gemma? What was the reason you and your partner broke up?'

They all know my story, except for the two newbies, but I'm happy to get them up to speed. 'He was a dick.'

Gail hesitates with her marker pen.

'He was. He cheated on me. Dick!'

While Gail reluctantly adds "Dick" to the list, Andy turns to Ros. 'I can't imagine any guy cheating on you.'

'He didn't. He died.'

Andy tries to turn his face from flirty to sympathetic while his mate cringes and looks heavenward. Gail jumps to the rescue.

'Robin? Any thoughts?'

He shakes his head. He's not getting involved, thank you. She turns to Meryl, who's happy to oblige.

'Well, obviously in my case, he was batting for the other side.'

Gail looks unsure what to write. I look at my watch. I could have stayed home and done the ironing.

Then, out of the blue, Andy's mate opens his mouth. 'My ex wanted more space.'

'That can happen, um . . .?'

'Ned.'

Gail writes "More space". 'That can happen, Ned. No one's fault.'

'I was gutted,' he goes on. 'I literally didn't see it coming.'

'Welcome to the club,' I hear myself saying. 'Literally.'

Andy glares at me. 'It was bloody tough, actually, *love*. I had a ringside seat. She really wiped the floor with him.'

'How are you coping, Ned?' Gail asks.

'Oh, you know. One day at a time.'

'No, that's AA,' I tell him. 'They meet at St Luke's.'

He doesn't hear me and carries on. 'I was doing fine. I even thought we might get back together again. Then she suddenly announces she's moving in with the new boyfriend. People say, get on with your life, get back on the horse. I tried that. I went for a drink with someone from work, another single parent, as it happens. And then, well, I went back to hers. It was supposed to make me feel better but I still feel bad. Worse, even. So this back-in-the-saddle thing turns out to be a load of crap.'

Bloody men! I can't take any more of this self-pitying 'poor little me' bullshit. I let rip. 'So you confess your sins to a roomful of strangers, say a few Hail Marys and everything's fine again. Is that how it works?'

'Ned's being open and honest, Gemma,' says Gail, trying to smooth things over.

'No, Gail. He's being a bloke. A typical, self-obsessed bloke. He took advantage of a lonely, vulnerable woman because he could. All she wanted, I expect, was a little bit of human contact—'

He jumps in. 'It wasn't like that.'

'So you go round to hers, turn on the old charm. And she

falls for it, poor cow, because it might make her stop feeling like shit for five whole minutes.'

Ned looks down. I've clearly scored a bullseye.

'Here's a suggestion from me,' I tell him. 'Next time, try keeping *that* –' I point to "Dick" on the flip chart. 'Try keeping that inside your trousers. If it's possible. For a man.'

I know for a fact that I'm speaking for all the women in the room. Of course I am. That's why you can hear a pin drop. Then there's a scraping of his chair as he stands. He's not about to reply, he's about to leave.

'You know what?' he says as he reaches the door. 'You are a bitter, nasty woman and I really don't need this shit.'

Andy turns to me. 'Nice one, love. Straight through the heart.'

I stand by what I said. If he can't take the truth, that's his problem.

Chapter Nine

Ned

What makes some women so angry? I know Tanya and I are estranged but at least we can still be civil. That woman at SPAN was just horrible. Andy said he left soon after me, in solidarity, but I know he'd taken a shine to the blonde widow so I bet he'll be back next week. Not me. I'd rather pull my fingernails out.

The weekend comes around again and I'm instructed to pick up Dora from Julian's. I wait in the hall, trying not to drip rain onto the parquet flooring. I've already left soggy footprints on the Kilim rug. I don't know where else to stand, save for suspending myself from the Arts & Crafts coat rack. I spot Dora's daisy-patterned wellies, lined up alongside Tanya and Julian's his-and-hers Hunters, the sort that set you back £80 a pair. Tan and I never had matching wellies. Maybe that's where we went wrong.

I check my soles for dog poo. That would be the *pièce de résistance*, as if I don't feel awkward enough already. No. (I have an uncanny knack for treading-in all manner of turdage: cat, dog, fox, cow, horse – from Shetland pony to Suffolk Punch. If there's a virgin pile, I'll invariably flatten it with my foot.) Oh well, maybe I can tread some into Julian's doormat when I drop Dora off tomorrow night.

I hear stamping and shouting upstairs. I can't make out the words but it sounds like 'Don't want to!' followed by a stern 'Well, you've got to!' from Tanya.

Oh brilliant. So I'm a 'duty' now. A chore Dora has to get through before returning to her much nicer life with Mummy and Julian. I regard my widowed mother as a 'duty' but she's over 70 and a cow, so that's to be expected. Lucky for me, she lives in Guernsey. *I'm* only 35 and already I'm being tolerated by an 8-year-old.

Tanya appears first. Dora holds off for a loaded, little-madam moment, then flounces down the stairs in artfully mismatched polka dots and stripes. Tanya purchases complete accessorized outfits for Dora from Boden, not getting that the cutesy catalogue photos are just serving suggestions; Dora, on the other hand, pretends not to know that she looks utterly adorable. This is one thing Tanya and I can agree on: we have produced possibly the most beautiful child ever born. *Ever.*

'Where are we going?' Dora demands as she buttons her spotted cardy.

'It's your call, Adorabubble. You are in charge.'

Tanya frowns. 'No, Ned. *You* are in charge. You are the grown-up around here. Dora is in your care and I know you'll be responsible and sensible. Won't you?' It's not so much a question as a threat.

'Will I need my wellies?' Dora asks. 'My purple shoes got all ruined last time.'

'Can't hurt,' I tell her.

I pick up her Kidston-print overnight backpack, Dora grabs her wellingtons and we head to the front door. Julian pokes his head out from his study as we pass.

'Hey, Ned. How you doing, mate?'

Julian is *not* my mate. Julian will never be my mate. Mates are blokes you have a pint with and make Spotify playlists for. Julian is a brilliant architect who 'can't move for commissions', according to Tanya. He is the man she wants to spend the rest of her life with. The man she'd prefer my daughter to be brought up by. How does that make him any kind of mate?

'Oh, hey, hi Julian. Yeah, great. Not bad at all, actually.'

I visualize the big dollops of sloppy dog crap I will jump in before returning Dora tomorrow afternoon. I can't wait . . . mate.

We lunch on over-priced burgers at a new 'artisan bar & grill' in the Lanes, served by a waiter who doesn't seem to appreciate that tips are earned, not added automatically. I decide to leave him 40p in small coins as a protest gratuity. Ha! Pay off your student loan with *that*, punk!

I'm not the only Saturday dad here. I spot one by the window with a sulky Goth teen, and another two tables away. It looks like he's introducing his son to The New Girlfriend. Going well so far. That gives me hope.

Dora beams at the arrival of her full-size cheeseburger. She doesn't hold with kiddie portions. I tip some of my chips onto her plate.

'No, Daddy! I want my own,' she whines, testing me.

I fail the test and beckon to the waiter for a second portion. My bad? Too bad! Dora tucks her serviette under her chin and chows down.

'You like coming here, don't you, Bub?' I ask her when she comes up for air.

'When I have my own chips.' She grins greasily.

'We could go out other days too. How about every other Wednesday?'

'I do ballet on Wednesdays.'

'Tuesdays, then. You sleep over and I drive you to school the next day. How does that sound?'

'No, it's all right like we do it now.' She eyes a boy at the next table, standing on tiptoes in order to plunge his spoon into an elaborate ice cream arrangement. 'Can I have a Saturday sundae after this?'

I can't pretend I'm not hurt. She's *my* daughter but she sees more of Julian than she does of me. All I can do is spoil her and she knows I'm a soft touch.

'Yeah, sure,' I reply. 'With extra chocolate sprinkles but no flaked almonds.'

Then we amble round Churchill Square, with Dora looking longingly at expensive things that Julian can – and probably does – buy her by the shedload. Eventually I relent, pull out a tenner, and Dora emerges from Claire's Accessories, sweaty fringed and thrilled, with a carrier bag of flimsy, glittery tat. Tanya will probably bin the lot and Dora will go all stompy and grumpy. Job done.

There's a loud, bangy film, full of 3D SFX and merchandising opportunities, at the Odeon at 4.35. Dora's keen to see it and I'm just relieved that we have plans, because that means there's only one random hour to fill before we head for the multiplex. We can walk along the seafront for a bit, have another ice cream and watch the i360 go up and down.

That takes all of fifteen minutes. Now what? Dora knows what and my heart sinks. She needs to wee, of course. Every bloody week. Why does it never get easier? If this isn't the worst aspect of single-dad-and-daughter-dom, it's certainly in the top five.

The last time Dora needed the loo, in Hove Park, I waited anxiously on the path outside. She said she was grown-up enough to go in by herself and I believed her. She was wrong. I was wrong. She dropped her glove in a puddle of (fingers crossed!) leaky-pipe water, couldn't flush or open the door, even though I'd distinctly told her not to lock it. She was in there for what seemed like hours.

Worst of all, a jobsworth park keeper approached, as I loitered, and told me to move on as there'd been complaints from some mums in the nearby play area. I don't even *look* like a kiddie fiddler. Granted, my raincoat was a bit dirty, but only because we'd used it as a picnic blanket.

The park keeper's finger was hovering perilously close to the '9' button on his phone when Dora emerged from the ladies', not a happy bunny. She vouched for me and we scarpered. 'Yep, that's definitely leaky-pipe water, Bub,' I reassured her after a reluctant sniff of her damp glove. Even so, I chucked it away and told Tanya I'd lost it.

This time I have no option. I go *into* the ladies' with Dora, which is going to look 100 per cent less pervy than hanging around outside. Fortunately we're the only customers so the coast is clear. Dora wees in record time, while I stand outside her unlocked door, willing her to flush and finish.

'It's not very nice in here,' she shouts.

It seems we've got away with it. But, just as we exit, we walk headlong into a horrified young mum with a double buggy. I know what she's thinking. God knows, if I saw me, I'd think it too.

'Dora, tell this lady who I am.'

Dora obliges. 'My daddy.'

I stare the woman out. See! Perfectly normal. Have a nice day.

*

The film is full of explosions and cars screeching and some nauseatingly cute cartoon kids. The 3D glasses sit badly over my horn-rims and give me a cluster headache. Dora loves it and has room for a mega box of popcorn, on top of the lunchtime burger, sundae and sea-front cornet.

Maybe that's why she doesn't fancy anything for tea when we get back to the flat. I've stocked up on her favourite frozen pizzas and bought some salad veg. I don't want Tanya to think I survive on frozen peas – even though, in actual fact, Jamie, Nigella and Hugh all agree with me on their versatility and high nutritional value.

I splat some ketchup on to Dora's plate. That always worked with me and Brussels sprouts. Not my daughter. I try to distract her by showing an interest in the ridiculous film we've just seen.

'Was that funny robot in *Astro Boot Camp 1* as well?'

She pushes a bit of pizza around in the ketchup to make a pattern. 'Yes, because he can't die because he's a robot.'

I stop myself from telling her not to play with her food. I don't want to upset her. This to-ing and fro-ing between parents is tough on *her* too. Not that Julian's a parent. Not even close . . . mate!

I want her to understand that *I'm* her proper daddy, not him. Will she remember that if she only sees me at weekends? Children live in the 'now'. And now there's more 'now' with Tanya and Julian than there is with me. Will she forget all the years that *we* were a family? It will be hard for her to keep hold of all that stuff in a year's time, five years' time. When she's older, will I be in her life or just part of her past?

Dora will always be my little girl. But now she has Julian. (As does Tanya.) I'm slowly learning to accept that. There's still so much to adapt to, live with, grow from. Maybe, day by day, I'm imperceptibly adjusting to being without Tanya, but I couldn't bear it if Dora didn't see me as her daddy any more. 'Julian doesn't have kids of his own, does he?' I ask.

Dora shakes her head. 'And Mummy's his first girlfriend in yonks. Uncle Matt said.'

'Well, I'm happy if they're happy. And I'm super-happy if you're happy, Bub. And what makes me happiest of all is that I will always be your daddy, and I will always love you to the moon and back, via Jupiter, Mars and Venus. That will never, ever change because I won't let it.'

Dora nods. She gets it. Then she totally sideswipes me. 'Will it change when I'm in Oman?'

'What's that, Bubble?'

'When we live there. Me and Mummy and Julian.' She sees my confusion. 'Julian's going to win a prize for the best hotel. It's so beautiful, Daddy. It looks like a palace. Can I watch *Frozen* now?'

I nod, shell-shocked. Dora gets down from the kitchen table and runs into the living room as I absorb this news. I hear her turn on the TV and pump up the volume.

'Watch it with me, Daddy,' she bellows above the din.

My daughter's moving to Oman? I don't think so! Outrage competes with despair, fury tussles with an aching thud in my chest, as if someone punched me, out of the blue and for no good reason. If this is how I feel *now*, how will I feel when they actually leave? It's not somewhere I can pop to in the car like, I don't know, Reading or Ramsgate or France. I'm not even sure where Oman is, so I google it. I'm just buying time, putting off the moment when the reality of this will truly sink in.

I've lost Tanya and, yes, I'm getting the hang of us not

being together any more. I am. Slowly. This is *far* worse. Tanya was my past; Dora is my future. How can I watch her turn into a teen, grow into a woman, when she's – I google *this* too – 3,616 miles away as the crow flies and 4,548 miles by land transport, with a journey time of four days, five hours and forty minutes.

And, to put the tin lid on it, Tanya didn't bother to tell me. Or *wouldn't* tell me because she knows how wrong and unfair and impossible it is. I feel sick with anger and loss. I can't let this happen.

Dora doesn't like the little box room that's her bedroom whenever she stays over. I've bought a jolly yellow duvet cover and put a sign on the door saying 'Dora's Room' but, for the rest of the week, it houses a rack of washing and smells of damp socks. (I really should put those fairy lights up.)

I must have done something right today, because she's spark-out as soon as her head hits the pillow. Still trying – and failing – to digest her bombshell, I nod off on the sofa, in front of whichever US crime series features the Cher lookalike cop with the great tits. I wake up, dribbling down my cheek, at five past one and go to bed – not before checking on Dora.

Snoring gently, in her Boden jim-jams, she's my adored little Adorabubble. The best thing in my life; past, present and at this bloody rate, future. I can't lose her. *I can't.*

Chapter Ten

Gemma

All week, I've fobbed Joe off with texts to avoid talking to him. I delete his voicemails, unlistened to. Well, obviously I listen to them three or four times, just in case they're urgent. But I delete them after that. Well, most of them. I've kept one. I will delete it. I mustn't let myself fall for his bullshit again. I won't let myself.

I can't stop him picking up Kelvin for the weekend, though. And I can hardly hide in the garden like I do when I can see Jehovah's Witnesses working their way up the street. Or when Carole from two doors down invites herself round for a 'cuppa and catch-up'.

I'll be civil to Joe, course I will. I won't invite him in *or* slam the door in his face. Because nothing's changed. He's still with Vicky and I'm still The Loser. Only now I'm an even bigger one for sleeping with him. No wonder I bit the head off that poor sod at SPAN last week. He deserved it, but even so . . .

I take Kelvin's footie kit from the dryer and pack it in his sports bag as he chomps through a mountain of Cheerios. I try not to lay into him. *He's* done nothing wrong.

'Got your homework?' I ask, in my nice voice. 'Don't

forget to tell your dad you absolutely have to do it tomorrow afternoon, before you come home.'

He gives me his best put-upon groan and scuffs upstairs to fetch it. The doorbell rings. I jump.

'Kel, your dad's here,' I bellow.

I push a hand through my hair – even though I know it looks fine because I've checked half a dozen times – and open the front door.

'Morning, gorgeous,' Joe says, leaning cockily against the porch wall.

'Kelvin's nearly ready.' Cool as a cucumber or what?

He gives me a meaningful stare. 'You all right?'

'Kel, your dad's waiting,' I shout, determined not to understand his question.

Kelvin thumps down the stairs with schoolbooks and screeches into the kitchen to get his kit bag.

Joe lowers his voice. 'Why haven't you answered my calls? Anyone would think you had a guilty conscience.'

'Speak for yourself. *I* don't have a Vicky, do I?'

'The other night. It's all I can think about.

'It shouldn't have happened. It won't happen again.'

Kelvin appears with all his stuff, ready to go.

'Got your phone charger?' I ask as he joins his dad on the front path.

He pulls it out of his pocket to show me he hasn't forgotten and lets me kiss the top of his head. He pulls a 'yuk' face at Joe but I know he doesn't mean it.

I watch them head for the car. While Kelvin puts his bag in the boot, Joe fiddles with his phone. As they drive off, my phone pings. I read the text.

'Still want U, Gemzy.'

*

Another weekend with no scuffing, slamming, thumping or grumping. So now what? I could climb the north face of the ironing. And the oven needs cleaning after Kelvin made us mac 'n' cheese. I could hunt for his lost hoodie. (How can you lose a hoodie?) Or I can go back to bed, stick my head under the duvet and have a little sob. I go for the final option because I know I'll feel better afterwards. Kelvin can find his own hoodie.

I close the curtains and lie there for a while but I don't cry – or sleep. I can't stop thinking about Joe and me on the kitchen worktop and how good I felt just for that brief moment – even though I've felt terrible about it ever since.

Joe's always had that effect on me. Right from when we first met, we couldn't keep our hands off each other. Joe had had girlfriends before he met me; I was a virgin, despite a few close encounters with local boys. And yet we fitted together, right from the start.

It's like an unspoken language, I suppose, between two people. Joe and I . . . connected. Okay, sex isn't everything but, if it's good, it keeps the relationship strong. I don't want to know how 'connected' Joe and Vicky are, or how often. What I *do* know is that he still wants me. I don't miss Joe. Not one bit. But I miss what we had, and he knows it.

I hate that he has this power over me still, that he can click his fingers and I come immediately. In both senses of the word.

It's pathetic. *I'm* pathetic.

I can give myself grief like this 24/7 . . . why am I so weak willed and useless? What was I thinking? When will I learn? Eventually, I give myself a good talking-to. You can't lie here all day. Get your arse in gear. Don't waste your 'you' time feeling sad. Pull yourself together and *do* something.

The 49 bus to Brighton is full of loud, larky, over-made-up young girls going into town to hang out at the shops in Churchill Square and ignore the boys they're hoping to see there. Hayley and I were just the same when we were their age, always on the lookout for Derren O'Malley and Mark Rawsthorne.

'Hiya, love. All right?' Carole thuds into the seat beside me. 'You off to the shops too? I'm after a birthday present for Doug's mum. Not a clue what to get her. She's a very difficult woman.'

No response is necessary from me between Bevendean and the city centre. Carole can conduct both sides of a conversation.

'How's Kelvin? He's getting big, isn't he? Paul's 17 now, would you believe? That apprenticeship was a non-starter but then I never saw him as a plasterer. He can't even butter toast. He might try for *The Voice*. He sings just like Lewis Capaldi. Paul's no Lewis Capaldi, but they train them up, don't they? When they win.'

I gaze out of the window as Carole chunters on. I hope there'll be more opportunities than *The Voice* when Kelvin's Paul's age. The worse things get, the more kids round here think will.i.am, Lord Sugar or Jürgen Klopp will save them. How depressing is that?

Carole fades back into my consciousness. 'I saw Joe last week in Wahaca. With that Vicky. Are they married yet? He's looking well. Sometimes two people just aren't meant for each other till death do they part. Joe found Vicky and you'll find someone too. Lovely girl like you. Ooh, here's my stop. Nice to chat to you. Bye love.'

I watch her get off the bus and head off down London Road. She's right. Joe is looking good, despite a few extra pounds. I shake my head to delete the image.

I treat myself to a new lipstick in Boots. Strawberry Brûlée. I have six more in exactly the same shade in a drawer back home, one of them as old as Kelvin. The beauty consultant is all for flogging me an exciting new skincare system plus an on-mic makeover. No ta. I don't need the whole of Boots hearing about my open pores and messy brows.

I could go to Starbucks, have a chai latte and a low-fat (ha!) muffin. I could try on shoes, jeans, tops I have no intention of buying. I could catch a matinee of whatever's on at the Odeon. I could go to Brighton Museum and look at the china teapot with wheatsheaves on it that my nana had.

Instead, I get on a bus. The number 2 to Woodingdean. This is *really* silly. I haven't done this for weeks, and shouldn't be doing it now. I could get off at the next stop but I know I won't. I go upstairs and find a seat on the left. I wipe condensation off the glass with my sleeve in preparation, even though I'm a good twenty minutes away.

The bus nudges through the Saturday traffic, turns left before the hospital and heaves up the hill towards the big garden centre and the racecourse. Then more trees, more space. Great views of the marina and the sea. I like this part of town, which just makes it worse. I wanted to move here after Kelvin was born but Joe said no. Too far out. Too snobby. 'Out of our league, love.'

That was then . . .

The bus empties. People get off with armfuls of shopping: Pound Shop, Primark, Sainsbury's treats to eat in front of the telly. I'm going to the end of the line: Rottingdean car park, where I'll stay on the bus and head back into Brighton again. And on the way back, I'll move to the other side of the bus. That's the drill.

I wipe the window clear again for Glimpse Number One. The bus stops right outside Joe and Vicky's house. I see Vicky, with Amelie on her hip, taking shopping out of the boot of the Picasso while Joe and Kelvin kick a football on the front lawn. It goes into next-door's garden and, as Kelvin's fetching it, Joe happens to glance up at the top deck of the bus. Our eyes lock as the bus pulls away.

Half an hour later, the bus passes the house again, on its return to Brighton. But now blinds are closed and lights are on at Joe and Vicky's. When does Vicky start getting the tea on? Will Kelvin remember to tell her that he doesn't like tuna or will he suffer in silence as she whacks a big blob of it onto his baked spud? Mixed with sweetcorn, which he hates even more.

I let the bus window steam up; I don't need to see any more. It doesn't help. It just makes me feel worse. It has to stop.

When I get home, two very slow buses later, Joe's Picasso is parked outside my house and he's waiting on the doorstep. I'm barely up the path before he starts.

'What the fuck were you thinking? Vicky could have seen you. Or Kelvin. Promise you won't do that again, Gem.'

'Do what? Catch a bus?'

I unlock the front door and he follows me in.

'Don't go all bunny-boiler on me. That's the last thing I need.'

'You don't *need* anything, Joe. From what I can see, you've got it all.'

'Why were you going past my house? Are you stalking me or something?'

I laugh. It's funny. Sort of. 'Oh, and you're not stalking

me? Leaving messages and texts, popping by for a quick one. And now rocking up here in a strop.'

'We need to be careful.' He frowns. 'Seriously.'

'You do. *I* don't!'

He knows the buck stops with him. He must do, surely? None of this is down to me. And then I open up. I don't mean to but I do.

'It's like when Kel grazes his knee,' I tell him, trying to keep my voice level and calm, 'and he knows he shouldn't pick the scab. But he does anyway. And then it's bloody and raw and it has to heal all over again. Why can't you just bugger off and let me heal?'

He tries to put his arms round me but I push him away. 'You always want to be in control, call the shots. You do, Joe. Ever since we met. Well, maybe it's my turn to take control for a change.'

I kiss him so hard that he steps back at the force of it. Then we fall onto the sofa, pulling each other's clothes off. At least this time we don't have to be quiet because Kelvin's in Woodingdean with Vicky.

And even that thought doesn't stop me.

I'm snapped back into reality with a jolt when Joe's phone suddenly starts vibrating in the tight space between our groins. I take it out of his pocket and chuck it on the floor. Let it ring.

But it's put Joe off his stride and he has to answer. 'Hi love . . . Yeah, nearly done . . . Just getting the pilot light going again. Lovely old couple. No hot water. I'm the only heating engineer they trust to fix their boiler. He's got Parkinson's, she's got angina . . . Half an hour, forty minutes tops. Kids okay? . . . Well, you kiss her goodnight *for* me then! Okay. Bye.'

After he hangs up, he thinks we can just pick up where we left off. He genuinely can't understand why I turn away from his kiss, pull my bra back down over my breasts and tell him to go home.

Chapter Eleven

Ned

Sunday passes uneventfully. I take Dora to a kids' craft event at Bodiam Castle. It's a longish drive but I've uploaded a bunch of audio books to keep her entertained. We don't talk about Oman again. I'll take it up calmly and coolly with Tanya because she's the one who kept it from me. Maybe Julian told her to. I find my dislike of him growing incrementally as the weekend goes by.

By the time we get back to the flat and Dora is eating a Tunnock's tea cake in front of *Moana*, my loathing's nearly off the scale. What possessed Tanya to take up with him, apart from his amazing house and award-winning career?

At five on the dot, Tanya rings my doorbell and I buzz her up. She rarely comments on my flat but you can tell by the way she hovers in the hall that she thinks it's highly inappropriate for weekend parenting. We're civil with each other, as always.

When we split up, she accused me of never losing my temper, as if this was a serious flaw in my personality. She reckoned I might benefit from getting angry once in a while. I thought staying calm was a good thing. It's always been my way. Even when she got furious with me for not losing it, I didn't lose it. I'm rather proud of that.

While Dora gathers her things, I can see Tanya silently passing judgement. Yes, there's a pile of unironed shirts on the kitchen table and I should have emptied the swing bin. I could be tidier, I know that. But I don't see why I should make a special effort for her any more.

She gives Dora a big hug and takes her overnight bag. I hate these Sunday-afternoon handovers: passing my daughter back to her mother for another week, like I'm the pretend parent and Tanya's the proper one. I feel extraneous, peripheral, surplus to requirements. They could carry on perfectly well without me because I serve no purpose.

'Got your iPad, Pipsqueak?' Tanya says. 'Remember when you left it under your pillow and Daddy had to pop it round the next day?'

'It's on the coffee table, Bub.' And off Dora goes to fetch it.

Once she's out of earshot, I can't *not* ask. 'When were you going to tell me, Tanya? From Oman passport control? Better still, get Dora to, so you wouldn't have to?'

She shakes her head, more in sorrow than anger, as if *I'm* the one who's out of order. 'Now you're being paranoid.'

'When do you leave? Am I allowed to ask that, as Dora's father?'

'Who says we're leaving? It's all up in the air, Ned. Julian's holding fire until he sees it in writing. We might not even go with him. That's why I didn't tell you.'

'Oman, for fuck's sake. Dora gets heat rash on the Isle of Wight.'

'He beat twenty other architects to reach this stage. From all over Europe. I'm really proud of him.'

'Good for Julian.'

Dora returns with her iPad and Tanya switches from weary to chirpy. 'Like I say, it may not even happen. We'll have a proper talk if it does. So how about we just chill, okay?'

I give Dora a big, needy hug. I don't want to let her go. Now or ever.

'Julian's doing his special lemon chicken with roasties for supper,' Tanya tells her as they leave. 'Plus rice pudding for afters because he knows it's your favourite.'

I smile inwardly. Three Tunnock's tea cakes and a mango smoothie should put a decent dent in her appetite.

Karen is at a big conference in Stirling on Monday and Tuesday and I have a couple of site visits on Wednesday. So I manage to avoid her and any talk of our 'date'. I know I can't hide from her for ever and she's not someone you can say no to. Andy thinks I'm mad, but not getting involved with Karen might be the one sane thing I'm capable of at the moment.

Looking at my life through Tanya's eyes is always a chastening experience. She picks up on the clutter and chaos, the inability to plan ahead or see things through. Okay, I got that promotion at work but not because the best man won. I just didn't have gravy on my tie. Tanya has never had high expectations of me and it's left a permanent mark.

When we were together, Tan was the bringer of calm, the sender of birthday cards, the filer of bank statements, the replacer of loo roll. She was in charge. I took her for granted and now, when I see myself as she sees me, I inwardly cringe.

But if I can just make sense of what went wrong and finally acknowledge how much I slobbed around in my comfort zone when we were together, maybe we can try again. I honestly don't see Julian as a serious rival. Tanya and I share a history, a timeline, an archive of 'us'. I know more about her than anyone else and that's my USP. She thinks she can start a clean page with Julian. She can even move to sodding Oman. But she *can't* delete our 'us', and if I can get her to see that, I know I can make things right again.

I toy with going back to SPAN. I need somewhere to articulate these thoughts out loud. Mind you, what if that bitter cow's there again? I need sympathy and support, not a smack in the teeth. Who gave her permission to judge me, as if she's the one who's got it all sorted. If that's the case, what's she even doing there?

Before I decide, I check if Andy is planning a return visit. I can't pour my heart out to a roomful of strangers if he's sitting next to me, chatting up the hot widow. I text him, even though he's only sitting ten feet away: 'Got any plans for tonight?'

He doesn't text back, preferring to pop round and perch on my desk. 'I certainly do, Nedward the Curious. I'm hoping to hook up with Kayleigh from Crawley.'

I'm none the wiser, so he reminds me. 'From that hen-night crowd. We've been FaceTiming. I'm planning to spontaneously rock up at her local tonight, see how the land lies.'

'No SPAN then.'

He's none the wiser, so I remind him. 'Single Parents' Advice Network. Upstairs at the Anchor.'

He looks horrified. 'Don't tell me you're going back, bro. After that cow laid into you? You wouldn't.'

I shake my head emphatically. I don't need his pity. 'God, no. No way. I just wondered if you were tempted.'

He looks relieved. 'I only went to get you across the

threshold. Hey, come to Crawley. Kayleigh's got a mate called Debs and the trains are shit so we can go in your car.'

A gracious invitation but I decline.

After work, I'm not ready to go home. There's only eggs, Branston and frozen peas in the fridge, plus some luminous kiddie yoghurts Dora turned her nose up at. I could murder an Anchor burger, maybe even go to SPAN afterwards if I can be 100 per cent sure Toxic Woman isn't there. The other single parents seemed okay and the Oman business is seriously messing with my head.

It's 2-4-1 burger night and that makes me sad all over again: I don't have anyone to bequeath my second burger to. Toby takes my order and doesn't make a thing of it, but I can see the pity in his eyes.

I position myself at a small table by the loos so I can spot SPAN folk as they arrive. The woman in charge is first; I don't offer to help her get her flip chart upstairs to the function room because I'm loath to make myself known.

The next to turn up is the one whose husband is gay, and then the one with the knitting.

I'm spotted by the only other man – Robin – and he makes a beeline. 'You *are* coming, aren't you?'

'I don't know yet.'

'It's grim being the only bloke,' he says with a haunted look. 'A teacher called Geoff came for a while but then he met someone. And they froze poor Mike out. Well, Gemma did. Very bitter, that one.'

'Why do you bother?' I genuinely want to know.

'I fancy Meryl. Oh, go on, mate. Safety in numbers.'

I'm tempted. Why should I let that bitch Gemma freeze *me* out too? My mum always told me bullies should be confronted, not avoided. (Which is how I got seriously duffed up by Ollie Walker on the way home from Scouts. Cheers for that, Mum.)

I let fate take its course. If there are an even number of chips on my plate, I'll go. There are eight. I nip to the loo before heading upstairs, and find Gemma coming out of the ladies'.

'Well, that settles that,' I tell her, surprisingly fearless. 'If you're going to SPAN, I'll stay down here and watch the footie.'

'Fine with me,' she snaps. 'If you can't stand the heat.'

'Don't flatter yourself.'

'I don't need to. I just have a very good bullshit detector.'

'It wasn't bullshit. I was speaking from the heart. You didn't need to lay into me. You don't even know me.'

'Oh, I do. Every man who comes to SPAN "speaks from the heart" but it's the same old same old. "I didn't mean to screw around, honest. I just needed somewhere warm to park my prick."'

I am genuinely horrified. How dare she? And then I say out loud what should really have stayed in my head. 'Jesus, no wonder he dumped you!'

We're both surprised and shocked, standing in the little lobby outside the loos, beside a big poster for the Monday Quiz Night with its £275 accumulator. Then she bursts into tears. I've made a woman cry. I didn't even manage that with Tanya. I feel terrible but I can't hug her. I don't know her. I don't like her.

'Oh shit,' I say, sounding like the twat I am. 'I didn't mean it. Please don't cry.'

'I don't have a hankie.'

I nip into the gents' and return with a trail of loo roll. She does three unfeasibly loud nose-blows for such a slight woman.

'You *did* mean it,' she says, dabbing her eyes. 'And you're right. I'm a cow and a loser and I deserve everything I get.'

'Steady on,' I tell her and tentatively pat her arm. 'You can't be that bad.'

That starts her off again. We decide – well, I decide for us – that neither of us are in the right frame of mind to go to SPAN. We also decide – well, she decides for us – that a bottle of house red and some sticky toffee pudding might make us feel better. We grab the booth at the back of the pub so we won't be seen by any late-arriving SPANners.

'Thank you, um . . . Sorry, I've forgotten your name,' she says, slugging back a big mouthful of Merlot.

'Ned.'

She nearly spits her wine out. 'Of course it is. Bloody perfect.'

I'm not sure what she means by that. 'And you're Gemma.'

'Although I'm sure they've got other names for me upstairs.'

'Robin thinks you're bitter.'

She clinks my glass. 'No shit, Sherlock.'

I need to make amends. 'I'm sorry about what I said. It wasn't very nice.'

'That Joe was right to dump me? No, it bloody wasn't. Or even true. This may be hard to believe, but I wasn't a cow back then.'

'What happened?'

'To turn me into one? Where do I start, Ned? You really *are* a Ned? Not Ed or Eddie or Ted?'

'My folks called me Ned when I was a baby and it stuck.'

Our puddings arrive. She eats hers with gusto, then the last bit of mine.

'So,' she says, licking sauce off her hand. 'This woman

from work. The one you shagged. How's *she* feeling about it?'

'She says she's cool. She probably is. It's all a bit awkward.'

'Bound to be. Look, me giving you that bollocking – it wasn't personal.'

'It felt like it, though.'

'I wasn't having a go at *you*,' she explains, not really helping. 'I was having a go at Saturday dads in general.'

'Is that what I am? Who am I the rest of the week?'

'You tell me.'

'I'm Dora's daddy, 24/7, 365 days a year. Google-sodding-calendar can't change that.' I know I'm coming over a bit shouty but that's how I feel.

'All right, all right. I said I'm sorry.'

'Actually, I don't think you did.'

'I'm sorry.'

She's unwittingly put her finger on the one thing I'm most afraid of: not having a purpose, not being needed. When Tanya and I were together I knew where my life was going. I understood the point of it all. Now, apart from the days I have Dora, I don't know *who* I am. Yes, I've got a job, a good job. But that isn't the real me. That isn't what I'm here for. Dora's what I'm here for and, when she's four thousand miles away, I'll be a purposeless, pointless, daughter-less no one.

'My ex has Kelvin Friday to Sunday. All the pleasure, none of the slog. Plus he's got a lovely obedient wife to do it all for him. How often do you have yours?'

'Most weekends, now that I've got my own place. We try to keep things flexible so we don't unsettle Dora. What about you?'

'Every weekend. My boy's desperate to be fair, to share

himself out between me and Joe, bless him. Plus Kel and Joe are big Seagulls fans so I could hardly stop them going to matches together. Has yours got a new partner?'

'Yep. He's a twat.'

'And you're not?'

'Course I am. I've got a degree in it. Tanya wore the trousers in our relationship and she got tired of it. I can't blame her for pulling the plug.'

'Do you still fancy her?'

Good question. 'You can't just turn it off. Do you?'

'Dunno. I've never met her.' She chuckles to herself, pleased with her little joke.

'Ha bloody ha! I meant, do you still fancy yours?'

'Joe was my first boyfriend. The only man I've ever slept with.' She tops up her wine glass, ignoring mine. 'So you wouldn't, you know, sleep with your ex if it just sort of happened?'

'I don't want some pity shag out of sympathy,' I reply. 'I'd feel even more shit than I do now. Would you?'

'Ned, mate, I hardly know you.' She laughs again and this time I do too.

'You haven't answered my question,' I remind her. 'Would you sleep with your ex?'

'Course not. No way. Absolutely not.'

'Well, that's pretty definitive.'

As I pour out the last of the wine, I remember what I wanted to bring up at SPAN. 'They might be going to Oman. Tanya, Dora and the new guy. I wouldn't have found out if Dora hadn't told me.'

'And you'll just let them go? Without a fight?'

'How can I stop them?' I shrug. 'Hide Dora's passport?'

'What if she wants to stay in Brighton?'

'Hove actually.'

'What if she wants to stay here, be with her dad? Did you even ask her?'

I shake my head. It hadn't occurred to me.

'Bloody hell, Ned. You need to dig your heels in. Put up a fight. Your ex can't just take her halfway round the world.'

'I need to grow a pair, don't I?'

'Or you can borrow mine.' She drains her glass. 'This wine's finished. Fancy another?'

I let her words sink in; Tanya can't take our daughter halfway round the world without my say-so. I can dig my heels in, put my foot down, make a stand. I'm Dora's dad and I say 'no way'. Tanya wore the trousers in our relationship, now it's my turn. And maybe she'll like the new, commanding, confident, decisive me. Maybe she'll see that she's made a big mistake. And not just about Oman.

'Sure,' I say. 'Why not?'

Chapter Twelve

Gemma

Another Wednesday. Another exciting night at SPAN to look forward to. Reasons why I go:

1) It gets me out of the house. It's a chance to wear lippy.
2) Listening to some of the others rabbiting on – especially Meryl – makes me realize I am not alone. We might all be losers, but we're losers together.
3) Ros. I've made a friend of my own after my divorce. I didn't think I could but I did.
4) SPAN gives me perspective, shows me ways to process stuff and listen to others. It helps me to find strategies, angles and options, to be open, honest and fair. Plus the Anchor does awesome nachos with guacamole and melted cheese.
5) SPAN makes me look to the future, not keep picking at the past.
6) SPAN reminds what a total shitbag Joe was, how he hurt me and trashed Kelvin's childhood. I can't forgive/forget that.
7) Men at SPAN. I get to see them trying really hard not to sound like total shitbags. Then I get to tell them they are.
8) Definitely the nachos . . . and Ros.

To be fair, I don't think Ned's a total shitbag. He's too wet, too weak. I wonder how that happened. Was his mum a single parent? Was he an only child? And then I wonder if *I'm* condemning Kel to a life of weak wet-dom because *I'm* a single parent. Ned's a nice enough guy, easy to talk to, easy on the eye. So weird that he's got no idea how good-looking he is: cute smile, great hair, ten-out-of-ten arse. He'd have every box ticked if he could just find some self-confidence. But no backbone, no fight.

I suppose I keep returning to SPAN because, right now, it's my only social life. It gives me a break from being a parent. And Kelvin likes it too. Going to Mohit's, having proper cooked-from-scratch food and playing Minecraft on an enormous flat screen, rather than our modest little telly. It's a night off from Grumpy Mum who shows him how much she loves him by doing his head in 24/7.

Ned's problem, and I'll happily tell him if he asks – and even if he doesn't – is that he's too comfortable in his victim-hood. He wallows in it. Okay, I might beat myself up at home, in my own space, in my own head, but I won't wallow to the outside world. As soon as you show you're weak, you've lost. And I can't keep losing.

I certainly won't let anyone mess with my emotions again, especially Joe. What happened that night in the kitchen was a blip, a lapse, a weakness. Okay, I nearly let it happen again on Saturday. The fact that it didn't feels like progress. I will not be vulnerable, ever. Joe makes me weak, in every sense, and he mustn't have that power. He expects it, he gets off on it and he shouldn't. I won't let him.

I tell myself it's because I'm better than that. I know how it feels to be cheated on and I won't do it to Vicky, even though she obviously didn't give a stuff about doing it to me. Actually, it's self-defence, pure and simple. I'll only stay sane and strong if I keep away from Joe.

At work, Janine's also getting off on her power. She finds it physically impossible to thank any of us when we go the extra mile. Or just do our job. For someone who's chosen a career in the caring profession – and made it to manager – she has all the charm of a blocked sink. Every day I kick myself. I should have applied for that job. Why didn't I? Three people told me I should and I didn't believe them.

Most of this week, I manage to slip under her radar, but she's got it in for poor Felipe. Okay, he's not the hardest worker on the team. Even so, the residents love him, especially Judy. She'll tell anyone she 'adores the gays' and likes dragging him into her room to talk frocks and face cream. I swear Janine's installed a tracker in his trainers because she always knows when he's not where he's meant to be and where to find him. Every time.

Today he's looking through Judy's extensive earring collection for something turquoise to go with his new Mariah Carey stage outfit. He's just pinned a discreet orange dangler on his left ear and a big clip-on number that looks like a diamante sprout on his right ear, when she stomps in. I'm in the next room, checking on Vivien, so naturally I scoot to the door to catch the kerfuffle.

Felipe loses all his English when he's flustered and Janine knows it. He takes her shit silently and with a weird sort of dignity. But Judy doesn't.

'Who asked you to stick your nose in?' she demands.

'I don't need anyone to ask me. It's my job.'

'And it's Felipe's job to keep me happy so I can forget for

five bloody minutes that I'm at death's door. Which he's doing quite brilliantly, as it happens. So you can just bugger off.'

Janine gives one of her fake-tolerant smiles, as if Judy's senile, which she *so* isn't. Plenty of patients tell us to bugger off in the course of a day and I can't blame them. There's nothing dignified about some stranger sponging down your privates when you've been brought up to be modest, or perching you on the loo even though you're sure you've just been.

When I'm as old as Judy, I might finally learn to keep my gob shut, not to muscle in on someone else's row. But I keep a lot of anger stored inside, mostly directed at Joe, and every so often, it has to burst out. Plus I like needling Janine, and Felipe doesn't.

'Oh, definitely the clip-ons, Felipe,' I say as I swan in, all casual and matey. 'Don't you think, Janine?'

'I'm not here to choose earrings. And neither are you, Felipe. Perhaps you could help Rosena serve the teas in the Primrose Room. And don't forget to sing "Happy Birthday" to whatsisname, the chap with the toupee.'

'Derek,' we three reply as one.

Judy shoos us all out. She naps so much these days, which is understandable; her meds are heavyweight. Janine and I head down the corridor together, her click-clack heels drowning out my squeaky Tesco trainers.

'I'm watching you,' she hisses as I bob into Bob's room to see if his son's arrived.

'And when you find something to report me on, you just let me know. Catch you later, Janine.'

I fume all the way home. I didn't lose my rag with her. I was nice as pie. And still she likes to hint that my card's marked, because she knows I don't respect her. Well, so's hers. If I ever find out that she swore at a resident or stole one of the new leather armchairs from reception – someone actually did! – I'll be happy to whistle-blow her all the way to the Job Centre.

And even though I like catching up with Ros and maybe seeing Ned again, I suddenly decide I'm not in the mood for SPAN this evening. Okay, it might be my only chance to get out all week, but I just can't face it. Anyway, who needs the Anchor's cheesy nachos? I'll bung a stack of tortilla chips and Cheddar in the microwave, take off my bra and enjoy a night of nonsense on Netflix.

Joe *keeps* texting. He claims he's just firming up arrangements for Saturday. Or he'll send me a You Tube link to 'Vindaloo' by Fat Les which was very nearly 'our song' when we first got together. He makes it look like we're just mates having a laugh, a bit of fun, that's all. He isn't remotely trying to get inside my pants and pick up where we left off. Not a bit of it.

Ha!

I don't respond or react or say anything to encourage him. We sort out the Saturday pick-up and Sunday drop-off, then I let him stew. Maybe I do have the power after all. I'm cool as you like when he swings by for Kelvin. I pretend I'm on the phone so I don't even have to speak to him and he acts like it's no biggie.

But of course, he still has the power because he has the fun weekendy bit of being a parent: soccer, treats, Saturday burger, Sunday breakfast. While I rattle round the house, not knowing what to do with myself. It never gets any easier, whatever I tell myself about it being my moment to be me. I've forgotten who 'me' is and I don't much like 'her' whenever I *do* remember.

On Saturday, I finish tarting up a chair for Kelvin's room. I bought it in a junk shop weeks ago, so he wouldn't have to do his homework at the kitchen table. Last weekend I sanded it in the back garden and painted it Albion blue and white. (His idea, not mine.) Now I give it a second coat and re-upholster the seat with a remnant of blue fabric I bought from a stall in the Open Market. I wouldn't want it in *my* room but I've done a brilliant job, if I say so myself. I might even get a grunted 'Thanks, Mum,' if I'm lucky.

Felipe's invited me to the pub in Kemptown tonight where he's premiering his Mariah act. God knows, I've seen him rehearse it every day for weeks to Judy or in the staff room. I say I'm going but I don't. I do that a lot since the divorce. Better not to go at all than get somewhere and leave after ten minutes. Felipe won't mind. He won't even notice.

Sunday looms, just like it did when I was Kelvin's age. Not having to get up early is the best bit. Then it's all downhill. How do I fill my day? Fortunately, Ros rings and I have a reason to put on some clothes and leave the house.

'I need to up my steps,' she explains, 'and it's easier with company.'

Some people measure their lives in Slimming World syns. Some say it's been a good day if they've only had one unit of alcohol or got fifty likes on Facebook. Ros will sit at SPAN meetings, silently marching on the spot in a desperate attempt to hit her ten thousand steps.

'It's exercise. It's discipline,' she reckons. 'It keeps me moving and it releases my what-do-you-call-it . . .?'

'Your inhibitions? Your mortgage? I have no idea what you're talking about.'

'My endorphins. It's a natural high. You should try power

walking some time, Gemma. You might unclench those shoulders and actually breathe out for a change.'

We're hoovering up garlic bread and olives in Bella Italia at Brighton Marina, before we hit the coastal path and see how many steps we can clock up.

'I'm not clenched,' I tell her, a bit too defensively. 'I know how to relax.'

Ros laughs. She actually laughs and my shoulder blades scrunch together on autopilot.

'Go on then,' she says, licking olive oil from her fingers. 'How did you relax yesterday? Defrosting your fridge? Hoovering your sofa? Sorting out your sock drawer?'

No need, clever clogs, I did all that *last* weekend. Sock sorting is very satisfying if you listen to a real-crime podcast while you do it. Nor do I admit that I finished doing up Kelvin's chair, and I resist the urge to show her six photos of it on my phone.

'Actually,' I say, 'I *was* out last night. Felipe invited me to his drag show at the Horn of Plenty. I had a great time, as it happens.'

Ros looks impressed. Briefly. 'Good for you, Gem. Brilliant. You're bound to meet Mr Right and put that bastard ex behind you hanging out in a gay pub all night.'

'Joe *is* behind me. I've turned a corner. He doesn't rattle me any more, Ros. Honestly, I barely give him a second thought.'

She doesn't answer but her face says: Yeah, right.

'Or Vicky. I couldn't give a stuff about her either.'

Ros bites her tongue. Good. I don't want to fall out with her.

She does that writey-fingers thing for the bill and a waiter instantly rocks up. If you're tall, slim and blonde, you're never ignored. When Hayley and I were best friends, I was the one who got served super-quick in busy pubs or made cars screech to a halt at zebra crossings because I still looked pretty hot back then. Not sure when it stopped. When I had Kelvin, probably. Anyway, who needs the attention? I don't want anyone to admire me or validate me. I'm doing just fine as I am, thanks all the same.

We set off along the undercliff. Joe and I used to take Kel here when he was learning to ride a bike. It's quiet and calm, with the occasional jogger whizzing by or dog and owner out for a stroll. Ros walks at quite a pace in her paint-splash-look leggings, purple hoodie and super-clean Skechers.

I'm the poor relation: Sunday jeans, faded fleece, an old black T-shirt of Joe's and my trusty Tesco trainers. Designer labels are for airheads with more money than sense. Any high-status brands I own come from the charity shop. Kel always pulls an 'eeuw' face whenever I show him my latest finds.

'So,' Ros says. 'Those two guys who rocked up at SPAN. Ned and Andy. What do you reckon?'

'Reckon how? On the bullshit chart? The bastard chart? Which one's got the biggest willy? My head says Andy. But I reckon the other one – Ned – he might surprise us. Down there.'

Ros giggles. 'Gemma, you're outrageous.'

'Men judge us. All the time. Best boobs. Best legs. Joe was a 100 per cent boobs man. What about David?'

Should I have mentioned his name? Have I been insensitive? Have I upset her?

'Oh, David didn't care.' Ros keeps walking, staring hard at the waves crashing against the sea wall on our right. 'He did call me Bambi, because of my long legs.'

Then she speaks so quietly I can hardly hear her. 'Sometimes, when I answer for him, I can hear him saying: "Bloody hell, have you forgotten already, Ros? You *know* I preferred Pepsi to Coke." Or, "Duh, I *hated* button-down collars." I try so hard to keep it all saved in my head but bits fade and then I feel so guilty.'

I don't know what to say so I don't say anything. We walk for a while, passing an abandoned, deflated football. I know the feeling.

'Oh, I reckon Ned's definitely got the bigger willy,' she says with a grin and, hooray, Ros is back in the now. 'What did you think of Andy?'

'Hard to say. Anyone could see he was dead keen on you.'

'D'you reckon? Not my sort in a million years. Not a looker but he didn't have a problem sharing his feelings. He seemed more sensitive than the usual "shag-em-and-scarper" types I come across.'

'Would you?'

'God, no. I'm not ready for that, Gemma. Would you?'

'God, no.'

'Don't you miss sex? I do. Not the in-out, grunty stuff. I miss the intimacy, the sharing, the silliness. With someone who knows you, every part of you. I really miss that.'

'Yeah.' I sigh, hoping we can change the subject. Joe and I two weeks ago was 100 per cent in-out, grunty and over in minutes. There was no intimacy or sharing. Or love. I need to remember that.

'I miss you too, Gem. Why've you stopped coming to SPAN? Isn't it helping any more?'

I shrug, feeling bad. 'This week I was just too knackered. And last week I had a massive argument with Ned in the Anchor, just before the session. And, well, we never made it.'

Ros stops dead in her tracks. 'What do you mean, you "never made it"? Where did you go? What did you do?'

'We stayed in the bar, had some wine and got over it. I told him he needed to grow a pair and he agreed. Simple as. End of. We're not engaged or anything.'

'Wow. Why didn't you tell me? Like the next day.'

'It was no biggie. I forgot.'

Ros checks her Fitbit to see how her step count's going. 'Okay then: Ned who needs to grow a pair. Would you?'

'No, I flipping wouldn't!'

I won't lie, though, he does have a cute smile.

This is good. Walking's good. I should do it more often. We get as far as Rottingdean and Ros is up to speed on her steps. She even has 615 to spare but apparently you can't carry them over to the next day. Daft, if you ask me.

We find a cafe and celebrate with mugs of tea and fish finger sandwiches: flabby white bread, big fat dollops of salad cream, plus crisps as a garnish, instead of ridiculous rocket.

'My mum gave us fish finger sandwiches when there was nothing else in the house,' I tell Ros between mouthfuls. 'Who'd have thought they'd be on the menu in hip cafes? And macaroni cheese. When did *that* get trendy?'

We share a millionaire's shortbread and check our watches. Ros has to pick up Gabriel from her mother-in-law's soon. I've still got two hours to kill before Joe drops Kelvin off and I'm expected to feed him and strong-arm him through the homework he won't have done at his dad's. Like always.

Then my phone rings and my plans go tits up.

'Hello, is that Gemma?'

'Yes. Who's this?'

'It's Vicky. Joe's, you know, partner.'

I sigh and look heavenward.

'Hi, Vicky,' I reply for Ros's benefit. 'I hadn't forgotten you're Joe's partner.'

'I wouldn't have called you myself, Gemma. I know it's . . . awkward. The thing is, Joe's driving home right now and he's running late. Him and Kelvin. They're not back yet. They went to an indoor rock-climbing place near Haywards Heath, I think.'

'And you're telling me this because . . .?'

I know I'm making Vicky nervous. I shouldn't, but I can't help myself.

'We're off out to friends tonight. Me and Joe and Amelie. And he won't have time to drop Kelvin off at yours like he said he would because—'

'—because he's running late. Yeah. Got that.'

'So I was kind of hoping, if you don't mind, if it's no hassle, whether you could come to ours and fetch him. They should be home by five. Half five latest. Would that be okay, Gemma?'

'It's not exactly convenient. But, okay, yeah, why not.'

Ros can't believe I've agreed. I'm a bit surprised too. I could have ruined their evening by making Joe bring Kelvin back to mine, formerly ours. Still, I've never been inside their house and now's my chance.

Who'd say no to that?

Vicky texts me detailed directions for how to get to their place. She even includes a Google Map link. I can hardly tell her I've stared into her bedroom from the top deck of the number 2 bus more times than I care to admit. (I must, must, must stop doing that.) Maybe this visit will get it out of my system, seeing her sofas, sniffing her soap.

Joe's car is not parked in the driveway. Still running late, then. Typical. Back in the day, you were just 'late'. Mobile phones have given people permission to add 'running' to make it sound like they're in demand, rather than inconsiderate.

I ring the doorbell and wait. I know what Vicky looks like. God knows, I check out her Facebook page most days, to see where she's been, whether she's tried out that new hairdresser a pal recommended or reactivated her gym membership. Ever since Joe dumped me, I've managed to avoid meeting her in the actual flesh.

My walk with Ros has empowered me and today I reckon I can do it. If I meet her, maybe I can finally stop hating her. Then again, why should I? She ruined my life. She stole my husband. She stole my life. Of course I hate her.

She's shorter than I expected and, yes, it's a good haircut but I won't tell *her* that. Chopped into the neck, subtle highlights, one of those feathery fringes that, on me, would highlight my flat-screen forehead. She's dressed nicely too: tight-fit jeans, silk blouse with ruffles round the shoulders, fluffy polka-dot slippers. I sense her giving me the once-over too and wish I wasn't wearing Joe's old T-shirt, not that she knows it was his. It makes me feel vulnerable, unprepared, weak.

'Thanks ever so much, Gemma. I really appreciate this.'

She ushers me into the kitchen, which is bigger than I expected. 'I'll put the kettle on. Or can I do you a Nespresso?'

Then I notice the blood. On the worktop. On a big wodge of kitchen paper and a tea towel. On the cuff of her blouse. She sees that I've seen and goes pale. She reveals a badly cut finger, gushing blood. She sits with a lucky thump on a bar stool and gives an embarrassed little laugh.

'I shouldn't be allowed near tin cans. Honestly, look at the mess I've made.' She wobbles a bit, like she's going to faint. 'I just did it. Two minutes before you rang the doorbell. On a tin of tuna for Loopy, our cat. Sunday treat. I'm not very good with blood.'

And now she does faint, or at least swoon, and I have to catch her.

'Towel?' I ask when, two seconds later, her eyelids flutter open. 'Plasters?'

She waves at a cupboard above the sink and there's a very snazzy first-aid kit. Mine's an old biscuit tin with some perished Band-Aids. I must restock my biscuit tin. What if Kelvin cut himself badly? What kind of mother am I?

She doesn't direct me to any towels so I make do with the one hanging from a row of hooks by the sink which spell out L.O.V.E. I *hate* cutesy stuff like that.

I stem the blood with the towel and give her a glass of water. She apologizes. Again. 'I'm fine with Amelie if she grazes her knee or once when she fell off a swing and bit her lip. She's napping now, thank God. So much blood when she did that. Fell off the swing. Well, you have to, don't you? Be the grown-up. They rely on you. It's because I was by myself when I did it that I went a bit woozy. Thank you, Gemma. I really appreciate it. Let me make you a cup of tea.'

I have to push her forcibly back down onto the bar stool. 'I'll do the tea. Hot and sweet, whether you take sugar or not. You just sit still and keep that towel pressed down.'

I'm still not comfortable taking care of Vicky but I remind myself that it's my job so it's instinctive – plus, searching for mugs, I get to look inside her kitchen cupboards. It's actually quite satisfying to see that mine are way more spotless than hers. I know for a fact that she's got a new cleaner – she was asking for recommendations on Facebook a few months back – but she's being robbed by whoever she hired, if you ask me.

You could eat out of my cupboards, and my oven gets the full treatment at least four times a year. I may not have ceramic hobs and a state-of-the-art icemaker on the front of my fridge but I know what clean looks like.

We sip our tea from flowery mugs. Forced to make conversation because Joe and Kelvin are still not back, we struggle to find stuff to talk about. We cover the weather in under four minutes, then I ask a few stilted questions about Amelie. Then we pretty much dribble to a halt. When, at long last, Joe texts Vicky with his ETA (fifteen minutes), she texts back that I'm here but doesn't mention that she cut her finger.

'I don't want him to worry. He's always telling me what a klutz I am, stubbing my toe on the bed, treading mud into the den. An accident waiting to happen, according to him.' She does her little laugh, as if he's paid her a huge compliment.

That sounds like Joe. He was always telling me how forgetful I was or that I could never leave a slab of Dairy Milk unfinished. And so it became a self-fulfilling prophecy until I realized what he was doing. It's how he is. I see that now.

'Have you had a nice weekend?' Vicky asks after an awkward pause.

'Really nice, yeah. A mate of mine was doing a show in Kemptown last night so a bunch of us went along to support him. And this afternoon I walked to Rottingdean from the marina. With another mate. So, yeah, really nice. You?'

Vicky peeks below the bloodied towel. It's stopped gushing. 'There we go. Just a scratch. Oh, you know, the usual. We love having Kelvin. Amelie adores him. Ooh, I know, would you like to see his room? Then you can be sure he's got everything he needs when he's here.'

I really would. So I clean Vicky's finger, stick on a Peppa Pig plaster and she leads me upstairs. Even before we reach the landing, I'm sick with envy. Wide, sun-filled hall, stripped and stained wooden banister, stripy stair carpet, stained-glass window halfway up.

This should have been my house. It would have been if we'd moved out here after Kelvin was born. But, oh no, Joe didn't think it was for us. Too suburban, too snobby. It's like a punch in the stomach. Even Kelvin gets to live this life every weekend. It's just me who's missed out. I want to cry but I can't let that happen.

His room is big, bright and modern. View across the back garden to the Downs; one of those beds with a pull-out mattress underneath, if he has Mohit over. It's Ikea's greatest hits, from the bookshelves to the bean bag to the blinds. But it doesn't have anything of Kelvin himself: the Albion posters above his bed; the Anglepoise lamp that's lost its spring and keeps drooping down; the scuffed skirting board that I plan to sand and paint next weekend . . . the blue-and-white junk-shop chair I lovingly restored.

I smile to myself. I win. This may be where Kelvin sleeps two nights a week but it's so obviously not his home. I bloody win.

Vicky and I are lounging on matching corner sofas when Joe and Kelvin finally appear. Amelie is running around the carpet after Loopy, the cat whose tuna treat caused Vicky's bloodshed an hour ago. I can't deny, Amelie is very cute: pudgy knees, ringlety brown curls, a cheeky grin that could star in a Corn Flakes commercial. She's inherited Joe's big, expressive eyes. She's his little girl all right.

We've talked baby illness: Kelvin's mumps, Amelie's psoriasis. We've agreed that *Dirty Dancing* is the best film ever, bar none, and who wouldn't want to throw themselves at Patrick Swayze. We've even compared notes on bras and why can't some clever person come up with wires that don't dig in and straps that don't slide down.

'Tell me about it,' Vicky's saying as we hear a key in the door. 'I was a 34DD at 14. You try dragging those puppies around all day when you're not much more than a child and boys keep staring at you.'

I hear Kelvin's recognizable, scuffy footsteps and Joe's non-speaking loudness. A moment later, they come in, still buzzing from their day out.

'Mum! I climbed a wall. The instructor said I was a natural, didn't he, Dad?'

'Haywards Heath today, Kilimanjaro tomorrow. You smashed it, bud.'

Joe scoops up Amelie, who chuckles with delight. I remember when Kelvin was her age. He loved being swung around by his dad, even when it scared me.

Vicky takes Amelie off him. 'Right, shower, change and out we go. Will and Mary are expecting us at six. I've ironed your grey check shirt and your new jeans are on the chair. Well, go on, Joe. Just because *you're* running late, doesn't mean we have to.'

He doesn't 'go on', though. 'What have you two been chinwagging about? Did my ears burn?'

'Don't flatter yourself,' I tell him. 'Not when we could talk about Patrick Swayze.'

Joe frowns, like he doesn't believe us. Then he gives Kelvin

a big goodbye hug and heads upstairs. 'Same time next week, Kilimanjaro Man.'

Kelvin allows himself a proud smile. He impressed his dad. Result. 'We'd better get going, Mum. I've still got to do my homework.'

Vicky smiles too, pleased we've bonded. 'Thanks, Gemma.' She waggles her Peppa Pigged finger. 'Don't be a stranger.'

Chapter Thirteen

Ned

Grow a pair, Gemma said after our altercation in the pub. Not the first time I've received such helpful advice. Tanya had her own variation on this, whenever she thought I wasn't sharing responsibility for some problem or other: a neighbour who kept parking across our drive; an electrician who 'accidentally' overcharged us.

'Act your age, Ned,' she'd say, as if I was some recalcitrant child who wouldn't eat his greens. Or 'Why do you always leave stuff to me?' Or just a weary, eye-rolling sigh when I hadn't – yet – done something I'd promised to do.

In retrospect, I suppose she had a point. It was Tanya who gave such a ticking-off to the neighbour that he took to parking in the next street. And she threatened the electrician with the Small Claims Court until he coughed up what he owed us. I had and still have 'a pair' but Tanya's were always so much more effective than mine.

My aim from now on is not to sit back and let stuff happen to me, wash over me, like I have no part in it. I will be proactive, assertive and effective. Hasn't my job promotion proved that people like Karen have faith in me?

Karen.

I've certainly gone up in Andy's estimation as a result of my fling but, from a zero rating, that isn't hard. And I see now that I let her 'wash over me' that night when I went back to hers. I'd like to think I could have extricated myself if I *really* hadn't wanted to sleep with her, even though I felt cornered and didn't want to offend.

Actually it was pretty amazing. A woman like *her* making a play for *me*. Instead of feeling awkward, I should hold my head high. Instead of avoiding her, I should seek her out. I should be cool and breezy. As if I'm a player, not a bystander. I also accept that if I'd been more confident when I got chatting to Nancy after Andy dragged me to that club, she might not have done a runner. I liked her.

Andy tells me ad nauseum that, as a single man at my sexual peak, I should be out there making hay. Or 'way-hey-hey!' as he puts it. Robert Browning, eat your heart out.

'What's your problem with Karen?' he asks over lunch in our usual cafe. 'She's fit as a butcher's cat, in case you hadn't noticed.'

'I don't have a problem.'

'That's my boy. Fill your boots, Nedward.' Andy dips a chip into his ketchup and chews thoughtfully. 'Okay, I'm surmising that you and Tanya weren't at it like rabbits in the months leading up to your, let's be kind and call it a "break-up". Am I right or am I right?'

'We had a very regular sex life, actually. That's why I didn't see it coming.'

He nods respectfully. I still have the power to surprise him.

'She's water under the bridge now, bud. She'll be at it like rabbits with this new fella. Ergo, it's your turn to get some in. With Karen or with that fit waitress over there in the sexy apron or with whomsoever you choose. You're a good-looking fella. Bloody get on with it.'

Andy's right. I'm young(ish), free and single. This is my time. With Karen, with the waitress, with whomsoever. Master of my own destiny. Man about town. You try and stop me.

So, when Karen calls me into her office for a catch-up, I am proactive, assertive and 100 per cent effective. 'I'm just getting the figures double-checked by Dharmesh,' I tell her in a low-octave macho voice I hardly recognize. 'Now that Welby-Daniels is done and dusted, do you fancy trying out that Persian restaurant on Church Road sometime to celebrate? I've heard great things.'

She actually blushes because she wasn't expecting the next move to come from me. This is going really well. Right now, right this minute, I am invincible.

'That sounds great, Ned,' Karen replies. 'How about tomorrow?'

I'd been mulling over another stab at the SPAN support group, but they'll hardly miss me. And, if I'm honest, I can document these positive changes in my life far more successfully if I don't have to write them up on a flipping flip chart in a room above a pub every Wednesday.

Shame I won't see Gemma, though. The first time I met her, I thought she was a cow, but after our heart-to-heart last week, I see it's just a front. She acts tough on the outside because she doesn't want to get hurt. I can identify with that.

Before work the next day, I give the flat a bit of a tidy; bleach down the loo; chuck out some black bananas; clean sheets on the bed. It's not my favourite duvet cover: one of the ones Tanya palmed off on me when I was moving out.

It's a bit girly – a leafy number in browns and greens – but I can subdue the lighting. Anyway, Karen won't be here to scrutinize my bed linen. Not if I can help it!

I'm a player, not a bystander, I'm a player, not a bystander.

I'm actually pretty damn proud of the way I'm playing my date with Karen. In the restaurant, I take our coats and pass them assertively to the waiter, despite having to dash after mine a moment later to retrieve my hanky.

And, because I studied the menu online this afternoon when I should have been signing off on Welby-Daniels, I can act au fait with what's on offer. I steer us away from the kuku sabzi, a lurid green omelette, and tell Karen that, if she likes chicken, she can't go wrong with barg-e-morgh.

I sound so convincing that she says she'll have what I'm having and we both laugh about the scene in *When Harry Met Sally*, even though it's about orgasms and slightly close to home, if all goes according to plan.

'This is nice, Ned,' she says, topping up our wine glasses. 'I wondered if you were fearing the wrath of HR.'

'How so?'

'Staff relationships. Not that this *is* one, is it? We've hardly set up home together. But, you know, they laid into poor old Barry Richards and that tall woman, Ellie Something, from Accounts. They copped off at the spring conference and carried on for nearly a year. When HR found out, because he's management, they made him choose and he chose his job.'

I'd forgotten about Barry Richards. He couldn't dump Ellie Something quickly enough; I don't like the woman – too brusque – but she didn't deserve the elbow. And after five years climbing the corporate ladder, Barry slid down a snake and lost his company car. What price happiness?

'They weren't serious, though, were they?' I suggest. 'Just a work fling that got . . . flung.'

'Work flings do get flung in most cases,' Karen agrees. 'Mind you, I met *my* ex through my job. That was back in the day, when it was no big deal. God knows, we were all at it.'

Karen's probably ten years older than me. Eight if I'm generous. So that could have been twenty years ago, before social media, when nobody gave a monkey's who slept with whom, so long as you cleared your in-tray and left a tidy desk for the cleaner.

'How's your chicken?' I ask, knowing it's delicious.

She has her mouth full but gives a satisfied look which, if I'm not mistaken, is loaded with promise for later. I suddenly hope I flushed properly before I left for work. Sometimes it takes two goes.

When Karen pops outside for a ciggie, I have a little think to myself: might I kibosh my promotion by continuing this whatever-it-is – this fling – with her? Keeping it secret is quite a turn-on but I can't afford to lose my job. The rent on my flat takes a big chunk out of my earnings and I might not find somewhere else with a suitable spare room for Dora.

Am I over-thinking this? Andy would just go for it and sod the consequences. That's Andy all over. I've always been circumspect by nature. I need to find a middle ground: cautious but not paranoid, spontaneous but not reckless.

Over syrupy-strong Persian coffees and a shared slab of baklava, we talk family stuff, as we did on our previous 'date'. I tweak the facts to adapt to my new, positive attitude.

'Yeah,' I say, after a slurp of the vicious coffee. 'Better to cut your losses and call it a day if your relationship's past its sell-by date. More grown-up all round and, that way, nobody gets hurt.'

'Everybody gets hurt, Ned. How can they not? But I take your point. I love my life without Patrick. And you? How are you doing without your ex?'

'Tanya. Yeah, great. Couldn't be happier. Moving on is all about, well, moving on, isn't it.'

Karen clinks my coffee cup. 'I'll drink to that.'

I'm not the best at reading the signs, especially from women, but I'm pretty certain I'll be lucky tonight. This couldn't have gone any better and I instigated it. Me!

'I want you to do something for me, Ned.' She actually grips my hand when she says this.

'Yes. Sure. Happy to. What do you have in mind?'

'Are you free for lunch on Sunday?'

'Lunch? Ah, okay. I was thinking breakfast or brunch if we hooked up at the weekend. But Dora stays over Friday to Sunday. You could too, obviously, but um, no, that might be awkward. She likes being the focus, bless her. Comes from being an only child and the trauma of me and Tanya parting company. No, on second thoughts, we can't do breakfast, can we? Or brunch. Not without a bit of forward planning. Sorry, Karen.'

She sighs. I'm assuming it's disappointment. If we do start this fling thing proper, we'll need to work something out regarding Dora's visits. Maybe I can have her on a Tuesday/Wednesday until she and Karen get to know each other. Yeah, that could work.

'Forget breakfast, will you, Ned? I'm just talking lunch,' Karen says, slightly impatiently. 'It's Hattie's birthday. My daughter. She's 20. We're going out for a meal to celebrate. Me; Hattie, obviously; my ex Patrick and his latest girlfriend. And, well, you too if you'd like to join us.'

Not at all what I was expecting. Bloody hell, Karen wants

me to meet her daughter and her ex. Is this going too fast? In inviting her out, have I sent the wrong signals?

She must see the worry written across my forehead. She gives my hand a friendly pat. 'I can't give Patrick the satisfaction of coming alone, like I did last time. He's always flaunting some new floozy. He can't help himself. I need to show him I have a hinterland too, that he's not the only one with a younger partner. Let's call it my "fuck you!" moment. So I need you to be my date, Ned. I'd really appreciate it.'

'I'm your floozy?'

She hoots at the very idea. 'I like that. My secret floozy. Is that a "yes", then?'

My mind runs through the logistics. I'd need to return Dora to Tanya on Sunday morning and, if I'm honest, this really isn't what I had in mind. What the hell, why not?

Karen is pleased. She even kisses me. Nothing passionate but there's plenty of time for that. My mattress awaits. She slugs back her coffee and pulls her phone from her bag.

'And now I must call an Uber to whisk me home. I've got that Welby-Daniels meeting in London Bridge at 8.30 tomorrow morning and I haven't read your revised report yet.'

'Oh.'

I sound pathetic. I *am* pathetic. A loser, not a player.

After Karen departs, I hang back in the restaurant to down the last half-glass of wine from the bottle. The waiter brings me a brandy on the house so I down that too. How did I get tonight so monumentally and humiliatingly wrong? And then my phone beeps. It's a text from Karen.

'Sorry Ned. Bad night for Netflix-n-Chill. Let's *fling* proper again VERY soon. HR need never know.' It's followed by three red kissy-lips emojis. I stopped using emojis after I accidentally sent Tanya's mum a smiley face in a party hat. She'd never liked me anyway and her gallstones op went through without complications, so there was really nothing to be so touchy about.

I pick up Dora late afternoon on Friday and have a stab at being civil to Tanya. This Oman thing has really jolted me, ever since Dora spilled the beans – not just because I might lose my daughter but also because I'm still convinced I wouldn't have found out until they were on the plane. And that's bang out of order. It really is.

Tanya's obviously feeling bad about keeping it from me so she's super-friendly and chatty while I wait in the hall: what are our plans for the weekend? Isn't this warm weather a treat after all that rain? Can I use a couple of tickets to a kids' book event thing at the Dome on Saturday? Julian got them from a friend and wants me to have them.

'Yes, it's great,' I say coolly. 'And only a 4 per cent chance of light rain until Tuesday, according to BBC Weather.'

'Julian's Dome tickets? Can you use them?'

'Tell him thanks but we're sorted for Saturday.' I don't say what. I don't *know* what. I'll think of something.

Dora is all set, overnight bag packed and two chocolate rice cakes in case she gets peckish. As if I don't know how to feed her. And then she needs to do a last-minute poo and stomps upstairs. This could take twenty minutes minimum.

Tanya beckons me into the kitchen and, bloody hell, it's grand. If I didn't already know they use this room for preparing meals, I'd think I was on the Paris Metro: crazed cream tiles; big metal advertising signs for Michelin; Cinzano and Savon de la Tulipe; glass globe light fittings and a brass rail around the island unit. I half expect Julian to rock up in a beret and striped T-shirt, back from his onion-selling round.

'Nice,' I say, grudgingly. 'You finally got your Aga.'

'I'm not very adept. Julian's the cook around here.'

I wander over to the French windows – they could hardly have been any other nationality in this kitchen – and peer into the garden. It's so huge I can't even see the far boundary. Tanya is a pig in shit. Everything she ever wanted that she never had with me: veg patch; Adirondack chairs; top-of-the-range barbecue. For a man with no hair, Julian has done very well for himself. I'm no slaphead, though, so I win *that* round, *mate*.

'What about Oman?' I say, with my back to her for extra drama. 'Has Julian made his decision yet?'

Tanya doesn't answer. So I continue, 'I hate this. I don't want Dora to go and I won't let you take her. She's my daughter too and it was inexcusable of you to keep me out of the loop. Cruel, selfish, sad and utterly inexcusable.'

She comes over, stands beside me and gazes out onto the immaculate lawn, with raised beds beyond. 'You're right, Ned. I see that now. It's just I didn't want to put a curse on Julian winning the hotel contract, so I kept it to myself. I'm still glad I didn't plaster it all over social media but I should have told you. I'm really, really sorry, okay?'

She's apologized. Well, that's something, I suppose. But she's only sorry for not telling me. She still doesn't see that I should have been consulted from the off. To be fair – and I'm really trying to be – Tanya must feel torn: wanting to be with Julian but knowing that Dora needs *me* in her life. Because whatever her faults, she's never – explicitly at least – criticized my parenting. She knows I'm a good dad. I *am* a good dad and I can't be without my daughter. Does

113

she comprehend that I won't let it happen? While I silently process her apology, I admire their olive tree. It's a monster. I would love an olive tree like that. 'So *has* he decided?'

Tanya shrugs. 'We're still talking about it.'

My heart sinks. I was hoping she'd say they'd decided against it. If that was the case, wouldn't she have told me? 'And you want to go there, live there? It doesn't sound very "you", Tan.'

I see her reflected nod in the glass. 'I know what you mean. I like my life here.'

'Who wouldn't? Starting with that bloody Aga.'

'Not here-*here*. It's just a poncy cooker, when all's said and done. I mean here in Brighton. I like adventure, being spontaneous, taking the road less travelled. But Oman. It's a bigger step than I had planned.'

'Hang on, so you're *not* going?'

'I didn't say that, Ned.' She sighs. She's torn. Maybe I'm getting somewhere. 'I can't let Julian down but I honestly don't know what to do.'

I so want to put my arms around her, to tell her that if she comes back to me, she can nip this dilemma in the bud. We've yet to get a decent offer on our house. We could simply move back and delete this past year, as if it never happened. We could even run to an Aga. Plus, of course, Dora would be happy: Mummy and Daddy, back together. Isn't that what every child of divorced parents yearns for? A few years from now, she'll barely remember this nano-blip in her childhood.

But I don't do that and I don't say that and, anyway, the moment is broken by Dora bellowing down the stairs that she's done her poo and can we have Tesco trifle with ice cream for pudding tonight?

As we leave, I tell Tanya I'll be returning Dora late morning tomorrow because I've got 'plans'. I don't give her the chance to ask what my plans are. It's none of her business. Me keeping stuff from her is hardly in the same league as 'Omangate'.

Dora, Andy and I are crammed into the open carriage of a narrow-gauge vintage train, chuffing round a former South Downs chalk quarry. The driver has just told us that Sir Roger Moore came here nearly forty years ago to film a scene for *A View to a Kill*. Dora has no idea what any of that means and I'm not a Bond fan. Andy is super-impressed. We've come to Amberley Working Museum.

I was all for taking her to Drusilla's Park – again! – but Andy came up trumps. He'd texted on Saturday morning to wish me a good weekend. Bored probably. I told him I'd run out of things to do with Dora and he suggested this place. He visited years ago and loved it; we should give it a go.

I'd got Dora washed, dressed and ready for a 10 a.m. departure. She was well up for our outing, not a bit grumpy, so I let her have Coco Pops mixed with Frosties, knowing she'd get bored after four soggy spoonfuls.

My phone buzzed – another text from Andy. 'If yr doing Amberley, happy to join U. Need to be out of town 2day.'

Seriously? Andy's never seemed like a kiddie person to me and Dora can take against grown-ups big time if they patronize or talk over her. I respect that. I had a think about how to say 'no' and came up with: 'Great idea, bud. Maybe next time.'

Five seconds later the doorbell rang. Andy, of course. 'If it's such a great idea, bud, why wait? I could murder a coffee before we go. And, see, I got cinnamon buns from the Bakehouse and they're still hot. Get in!'

Andy turns out to be 100 per cent right; Amberley is amazing and, as long as Dora can run around, press a few buttons to illuminate dusty displays and have chips for lunch, we're in solid win-win territory. The train is creaky and smelly but that's as it should be. We wave at other visitors as we trundle past, practically at walking pace, and they wave back.

Dad was a train buff and was always taking us to some restored railway or other, ostensibly as a day out for me and Joanna, even though he was the one who got the most out of it. Mum would smile indulgently at his unbridled excitement.

Dad died fourteen years ago, Mum and I don't get on and Joanna lives in Sydney. I must not let Tanya and Dora become distant from me, literally or emotionally. I wallow briefly in a moment of chest-aching sadness . . .

'Jenny Agutter.'

I snap-to. 'Sorry?'

Andy lowers his voice. 'Jenny Agutter in *The Railway Children*. Sexy or what. And the other one, you know, who played her little sister. I read somewhere that she was 20 but acting 11. Those two popped up in some very lively dreams when I was a lad, let me tell you.'

'Why do you always have to lower the tone?'

'What tone? There is no tone. We're on a frigging train and it's lunchtime o'clock. Stop being such a . . . dad, Nedward.'

Dora has been doggedly chewing her way through a bag of Haribo, a gift from Andy. She looks up and does one of her best gurgly giggles. I love her giggles.

'Nedward! He called you Nedward, Daddy.'

'Yeah. For some reason, he thinks it's funny.'

'Nedward, Nedward, Nedward! It *is* funny.'

Andy has bonded with Dora over my infantile nickname. Terrific.

'Looky here,' he says, in an unconvincing cowboy accent. 'If we dismount at the next stop, we can find us some tasty victuals over yonder.'

Dora laughs at everything he says. She doesn't understand a word of it but she knows it's funny. Andy couldn't be more chuffed. I'm seeing him in a totally different light. His default setting is all bluster and bollocks but this version of him is actually very likeable. I'm touched that my daughter has brought it out in him.

After fish fingers and chips, followed by ice cream, we wander around the museum's vast collection of old farm implements, televisions and washing machines. Dora finds it incomprehensible that Andy and I remember some of these clunky old household gadgets from our childhoods, and can't get the hang of a black Bakelite telephone, where you turn a dial to make a call. 'How does it take photos?'

On the drive home, she snoozes, snuggled up in the picnic blanket I keep on the back seat for just such eventualities.

'So why did you have to be out of Hove today?' I finally remember to ask Andy.

'Oh, you know.'

'You've pissed off your latest girlfriend and you need to keep your head down?'

'Why do you always think the worst of me?' Andy looks genuinely aggrieved.

'It isn't that then?'

'I won't lie, it's along those lines. It's Debi. You know. In Sales. With the red hair and the big specs, looks a bit like

117

Zoe Ball? We've been seeing each other for a couple of weeks. And a) it's not working for me and b) it turns out she lives in the next frigging street. I practically need a fake beard and an Afro wig just to pop into the Anchor.'

'Aha, a work fling. Don't tell HR.'

'Why would I do that? I'm guessing you haven't told them about you and Karen.'

'There is no "me and Karen".' Best keep Andy in the dark about our date.

'Barry Richards and Ellie Something,' he suddenly remembers. 'Those shags cost him dear, poor sod. Plus I thought she had way better taste. Good call, Ned.'

'What is?'

'I can tell Debi we mustn't see each other because it's against company policy. Yeah, that should nip it in the bud. Must be on your mind. After your horizontal "conference call" with Karen. Wasn't that just a one-night stand? Not a permanent blot on your CV. Never fear, Nedward. Your secret's safe with me.'

Andy follows Dora's lead and dozes for the last twenty minutes of the drive. Good. The less we talk, the better I'm able to keep my relationship with Karen under wraps. She called me her secret floozy. I'm not sure where she and I are heading but I'm only in it for the short haul.

It's not that I still believe my destiny lies with Tanya, although obviously if she were up for a reconciliation, I'd be keen. I just can't see Karen and me being anything serious. I imagine introducing her to Dora. I try to but I can't; a sure sign that there's no future in it.

I'd like to think I've become less of a doormat since Tanya and I split up. Was I assertive enough yesterday, when we talked about Oman? Does she truly understand that me losing Dora is not down to Julian? He can take the job or he can reject it. I honestly don't care. Whatever he decides, it should not be allowed to affect my child's future. He and Tanya have barely been together five minutes, for God's sake.

I should have been more forceful. I should have lost my rag, made it 100 per cent clear that the thought of losing Dora terrifies me.

I try not to give in to it because if I do, I'll sink. So it's easier to pretend it's not happening. Which it still might not, of course. I must cling on tight to that thought and hope for the best.

I pull up outside Andy's and nudge him awake. 'Thanks for coming, Andy. You were right about Amberley. And you were quite the hit with Dora.'

He yawns and stretches. 'She's a delight. She really is. Okay, you screwed up your marriage but you still get to hang out with her. You are one lucky bastard, Ned.'

Next morning, I ring Tanya and Julian's doorbell three hours earlier than usual. Dora's more than happy to get home before lunch because she's got a birthday party at 2 p.m. which I might also have had to attend. You get a good class of party entertainer round this part of town. Top grub too. And yet I occasionally feel 'othered' by the other parents for being Tanya's cast-off. Maybe I'm just paranoid.

Tanya opens the door and I catch a glimpse of Julian in the kitchen beyond, wearing a butcher's apron and tussling with a beef joint the size of a small terrier. He gives me a jolly wave, then gets back to whatever it is he's doing.

'Nice time, puffin?' Tanya asks Dora, who, I'm pleased to

say, *doesn't* dash straight upstairs without so much as a 'bye, Dad'.

'Andy came too. We went to a museum with old things and on a train. And Andy calls Daddy "Nedward".' Then she runs upstairs.

Tanya pulls a face. 'Andy came too? Seriously? You're still friends with him?'

'He's a good guy. He just likes to pretend he isn't. Dora thought he was great.'

She frowns. I don't think I'm in for a ticking-off, though. Far from it.

'Oman,' she says quietly. 'We're not going.'

My turn to say, 'Seriously?'

'I'm so sorry, Ned. It was unforgivable of me to keep you in the dark. I can't possibly take Dora away from you.'

'I'd have put up a bloody good fight.'

'You won't need to. Dora's home is here in Brighton with her friends, all the things that are familiar to her. And with her dad down the road, obviously. It wouldn't be fair on you or her to mess with that.'

I feel my chin quiver but I manage to control it. I am elated. I'm not going to lose my daughter. I'd feared that I hadn't made my feelings clear, that I should have stood my ground, stamped my foot, staked my claim. Still, I must have done enough to make Tanya think – I mean, *really* think – about what she was doing. Could she contemplate tearing my daughter from my arms, because that's what it felt like? No, she couldn't.

I can't quite process it, truth be told; it's been all-engulfing, ever since Dora let it slip, and the relief is *huge*. I give Tanya a little hug and she hugs back. A weight has been lifted from my shoulders and the dark cloud above my head has dispersed. 'That's great news. Thanks, Tan. We can work through everything if we just talk, if we don't keep secrets. Really. Thank you.'

We have an unspoken moment. Because we have a history. That will never change.

'*You* look very smart,' she says and sniffs my neck. 'That's Armani aftershave, if I'm not mistaken.'

I do look smart. I treated myself to a new linen jacket and some jeans from M&S. I hope I've cut all the labels off. Plus the flowery shirt Tanya bought me that I'm finally coming round to.

'Yeah, thanks for having Dora back early. I'm off for Sunday lunch at the Ivy with a friend and her family.'

'Ooh! A girlfriend friend?'

Bloody right and I'm her secret floozy.

'Kind of.'

Tanya looks impressed. Maybe she's pleased that I'm moving on. Maybe there's a teensy stab of jealousy behind her magnanimous smile. It suited her to find a new partner and leave me single. Now, I'm moving on too and she can remember what she's missing.

I've walked past the Ivy loads of times since it opened in the heart of the Lanes, not far from a couple of my favourite cafes. I don't have an inferiority complex about where I can and can't go but the Ivy never registered on my radar as somewhere for me. I'm just not attracted to famous-name labels, whether it's trainers, Y-fronts, designer lager or go-to restaurants. But now I'm 'going-to' the Ivy and I'm open to persuasion.

I'm shown in by a 12-year-old maître d' and there they all are, waiting for me in plush green seats around a round table. Karen looks hot in a wrap-over silky number that displays a fabulous cleavage. Across from her is Patrick. I expected a Pierce Brosnan looky-likey, all greying temples and a handshake that could crack walnuts. He turns out to be tubby and hairy with a close-shaven beard to hide a double chin.

He has an attractive young woman each side of him. One will be Hattie, the birthday girl. The other will be his latest floozy. What's disconcerting is that they both look like younger versions of Karen, who avoids any embarrassment by swiftly doing the introductions. The one on Patrick's left is the daughter, Hattie. Come to think of it, she looks like a student, even though she's dressed for a special occasion. The other one is Lucy, which nearly rhymes with 'floozy' and I have to stop myself from emitting a bark of laughter.

I know why Hattie looks like Karen; they're mother and daughter. But for Patrick to hook up with a woman twenty years his junior, who just so happens to resemble his ex, well, that's pretty bloody shoddy, if you ask me. I give Karen's hand a reassuring squeeze when I sit down and she squeezes back. I'm so on this.

'Lovely to have you along to celebrate, Ned,' Patrick says in a chap-to-chap tone.

'Lovely to be here. Thanks for inviting me. Happy birthday, Hattie.'

Just before leaving home to drop Dora off, I suddenly thought, 'Shit, no birthday present.' Fortunately, I had a jar of fancy honey, given to me by Tanya's mother for Christmas, so I wrapped it in some brown paper and tied it with string. It actually looked quite good. Very Brighton. The birthday card was one I'd forgotten to send to Joanna a couple of years ago: a wispy watercolour of the South Downs.

Hattie is happy with my offerings, humble though they are. 'Thanks, Ned. Manuka. My favourite.'

'Is it? I don't know much about art. I bought it for the colours.'

Lucy has been silent until now but this prompts a loud guffaw. 'Manuka honey, Ravilious print. Oh Ned, that's priceless.'

Karen and Hattie glare at her. Clearly no love lost between them; mother and daughter versus floozy. Lucy reminds me of the girls at school who found it so hilarious when I asked them out. I decide to dislike her too, out of loyalty.

I was hoping for a full Monty roast with all the trimmings. I eat them so rarely: Sunday lunches with Dora usually involve pizza or burgers out or beans on toast at mine. I'm not sure who's picking up the tab so I wait to see what everyone else is ordering. Steak for Patrick and Karen, avocado Benedict for Hattie, quinoa and watermelon salad for Lucy.

Tanya used to say she had time to read *War and Peace* while I made my menu choice. I won't hold anyone up today so I swiftly opt for shepherd's pie. Not too expensive or alien (avocado Benedict? *Why?*) and you don't need a special knife to eat it.

There's a fair bit of family chit-chat about Hattie's studies and her student accommodation and Patrick's gift to her: a new laptop. Karen makes Hattie show me the silver bracelet she's given her.

'Laptops are for dissertations. Jewellery is for life,' she says, arching an eyebrow at her ex. I remember her telling me that he used to knock her about. I will be civil to him but I won't bond. Andy's a total twat with women but he'd never get physical or abusive. Give me an Andy any day.

'So,' Lucy says, leaning forward like the baddie barrister in a courtroom drama, 'how did you and Karen meet?'

'Work,' Karen replies. 'Not very exciting, I'm afraid. Not like you two. Go on, Lucy. Tell Ned how you and Patrick hooked up.'

'It's no biggie, is it, Patrick?'

Patrick is ordering champagne for a toast. 'Oh, I don't know, Lulu.'

Hattie winces at the nickname and studies the brushwork on my Manuka birthday card.

Lucy gives a melodramatic sigh but she's clearly keen to relate the story. 'I was seeing Patrick's neighbour. That Sixties block of flats near Embassy Court? They were – are – both on the fifth floor. It wasn't like Gareth and I had a major row or anything. I just got chatting to Patrick in the lift a few times and he drove me to Lewes once when my car wouldn't start and, well, we just kind of clicked.'

'Did you click in his sportscar?' Karen asks. 'Those seats aren't very accommodating.'

Hattie looks down. She's either desperately uncomfortable or mouthing 'Go, Mum!' to the remains of her asparagus starter. I'm with Hattie. This is awkward and compelling in equal measure. I'm a minor character in a tense family drama and it's not even on the telly.

We plough on with the meal but you could cut the atmosphere with a fish knife. Nobody takes an obvious pop at anyone; it's all bubbling away under the surface.

'Ooh, you're eating spinach,' Karen says to Patrick with a pursed smile. 'You used to say it was like the slime at the bottom of a fish tank.'

Lucy puts a proprietorial arm round him. 'We love spinach, don't we? We're a very veggie household.'

'So why are you eating a "twenty-one-day Himalayan salt wall dry-aged grass-fed UK rib-eye steak"?' Hattie asks, quoting from the menu.

Patrick can't actually answer until he's masticated a massive chunk of it. 'Special treat. To celebrate your birthday.'

'You could have celebrated with something plant-based, Dad. As your gift to me.'

Patrick rolls his eyes. 'I got you a laptop. The very one you asked for. You didn't mention any plant-based presents on your wish list, my sweet.'

Hattie harrumphs and pushes a slice of avocado around on her plate.

Things calm down again. Then, ten minutes later, as we're all debating whether or not we have room for pudding . . .

'Ooh, crème brûlée,' Patrick says excitedly. 'Do you still make that, Karen? It used to be one of your signature dishes.'

'I stopped making it after the time you and I were having a row and I got burnt on the arm with boiling sugar. Do you remember that, Patrick, or has it slipped your memory?'

Silence. Like a collective slap in the face and we're each processing the shock.

'Spoil the party, why don't you?' Patrick replies. 'Ruin your daughter's special day. You'll share a pud with me, won't you, Lulu? And let me guess what you're having, Hattie. Strawberry sundae with extra chocolate sauce? You know you want to.'

Hattie shakes her head, too distressed to speak. Maybe I can cool things down. I barely know these people, not even Karen, if I'm honest. Maybe I can lighten the mood, change the subject, remind everyone that we're here to enjoy ourselves.

So off I go. 'I once ate the whole cheese board. I thought

it was all for me. I didn't realize you only take a bit, not every last scrap, including all the crackers and the grapes and those nasty little fruit that look like tomatoes.'

'Sharon,' says Karen.

'Persimmon,' says Lucy.

'Fuck this,' says Hattie, pushing her chair back, grabbing her cardigan and stomping off. In her haste to make an exit that silences the restaurant, she forgets my honey. I decide to keep quiet about it.

Patrick picks up the tab for all five of us. I make a stab at paying Karen's and my share of the meal. I even offer to go through the bill and tot up what we owe. But Patrick's gleaming gold Amex card trumps my Coop debit card, not looking its best since it went through the soiled cottons cycle. Anyway, this meal wasn't my idea so I'm not going to argue.

Sex with Karen is out of the question now. We're both shell-shocked by the birthday meal from hell and Karen's worried about Hattie.

'She's staying with me, going back to Norwich tomorrow.'

'That's good. Does she have her own key?'

'Don't be ridiculous, Ned. Of course she does. She won't be waiting for me on the doorstep.'

'That's all right then.'

Karen shakes her head. 'She might not go back to my place. God knows, her father's driven her to drink in the past. And worse. I need to be sure she's okay.'

I understand. I'm a dad so I do, even though Dora's a fair bit younger, obviously. 'I'll come with you. Does Hattie have a favourite pub or bar?'

'No.'

'Maybe she'll buy a bottle of vodka at your local offie. Do you think that's likely?'

'I mean, "No, Ned!" No, I don't want you to come with me. By myself, I can make things better. If you come, it'll just make things . . . Thanks but I'll be fine. See you tomorrow at work. Bye.'

I'm all set to walk home but a 49 bus pulls up alongside me at Churchill Square. I sit on the top deck and reflect on the day. Tanya and Dora aren't going to Oman. I get to keep my daughter. She's staying here. Just a couple of miles from me. As for the rest of today – well, Karen has a complicated family life and do I want to get mixed up in it? Not really. Unless we keep the secret floozy thing purely physical. I could go for that.

Yes. I did okay today. I grew a pair. Or, at the very least, I dusted down the ones I already have. I did okay. Okay is progress.

Chapter Fourteen

Gemma

I bumped into Carole outside the newsagent's yesterday. She asked how I was and I said, 'Fine, thanks.' And I realized, as I headed home, that I really, really am. Yes, I'd just bought two family-size slabs of Cadbury's Wholenut to get me through the weekend but, as I figure it, I'm living like a nun and I need something to replace the Sunday sex I used to have with Joe.

If we hadn't been so good together, I might not have let myself down last month. That really was one of the more stupid, self-destructive things I've done in a long time and it won't happen again. Especially now I've met Vicky. I can't say she's someone I'd connect with if we met at the school gates or through friends. But I quite like her, despite myself.

It still makes me smile that he was so freaked out to find us chinwagging in his living room, like a pair of old schoolfriends. I could see the cogs turning slowly in his head; he isn't the sharpest knife in the drawer. 'Oh, Christ, what have they talked about? What's Gemma said? Why isn't Vicky throwing things at me?'

Men are shit, when all's said and done. They really are. It would never occur to him that we girls have an unwritten code of conduct. We're sisterly, sensible and fair. (Unless we're shagging someone else's man behind their back, of course.) What would I gain by dobbing him in? Apart from enjoying the fear on his Tom-Hardy lookalike face. Apart from giving him one small slice of the grief he gave me and Kelvin. Apart from showing Vicky that it's not very sisterly to screw someone else's husband.

So, yes, apart from all that . . . I took the moral high ground that afternoon and saved his neck. If I *am* going to tell her, I'll choose my moment. The longer I keep schtum, the longer he squirms. I have the power and he doesn't. Who's the loser now, Joseph Anthony O'Hara?

A part of me would love to confess the 'shagging Joe' thing to Ros but I daren't in case she judges me. I don't think she would but, even so, I can't risk it. Ever since Hayley shafted me by not telling me about him and Vicky, I haven't had a best friend. I thought I could manage without. I thought I didn't deserve one. I was very down on myself in those early months after he sodded off. I see that now.

And, okay, I don't pretend I'm remotely Ros's best friend. I bet she has shedloads of them. I don't even know what she makes of me. I just like having someone to tell (nearly) everything to and have a laugh with, and I don't want to wreck that by confessing all. Plus she'll ask lots of questions (I know I would) and I honestly don't have the answers.

I admire Ros. She's had to get on with life without her soulmate. Her loss is 500 per cent greater than mine. She could have crumpled into a heap, stayed in bed, stopped flossing her teeth or changing her socks after David died. She didn't, because of Gabriel. She's funny, smart and kind. And now she's got her own business, baking cakes for cafes and weddings. She's my friend and she's amazing.

Ros makes me go to SPAN. It plants a flag in the middle of the week, it's my night out, my time to be me. That said, Meryl still dominates every discussion and group exercise with never-ending tales of her ex and how his new relationship has messed with her head; I'm still not sure if he was discovering his gayness while he was still with her or after they broke up. Sometimes, when she takes up the whole session with her woes and doesn't give anyone else a chance to speak, I find it hard to find my tolerant side. If I even have one.

Ros and I have taken to going out for a pizza straight from SPAN. There's an up-market place (it's Hove, after all) with distressed Formica tables and bare brickwork near my bus stop so we debrief there over a couple of thin-crust Margheritas. It's the best bit of the evening. Maybe we only go to SPAN so that we can bitch about everyone afterwards. Why not? They're probably bitching about us.

'Have you noticed how Robin moons over Meryl?' Ros asks, after we've ordered. 'I don't mean he bares his bum. I think he secretly luurves her.'

'Even though she doesn't shut up? Ever.'

'They'd make the ideal couple. Like Jack Sprat and his wife, but with talking instead of bacon. Was it bacon?'

'Poor old Meryl,' I say with a sympathetic sigh. 'Gail goes on about acceptance and new horizons and drawing a line, and Meryl just doesn't get it. There's a point where you have to turn a page and forget about your ex.'

'And you're there, are you, Gemma?'

'Not entirely, no. But I'm way better than I was last year.'

'Well, that's good. I'm pleased. Joe screwed your past but you can't let him screw your future.'

'I know, okay! I *do* know that, Ros.' I shouldn't snap at her. What she's saying is for my own good. 'Sorry.'

130

Our pizzas arrive and for a minute or two, we're silently slicing, chomping and chewing. If I was on Death Row, my last meal would have to include stringy melted cheese.

This is a good moment to change the subject. 'How's Sweetcakes doing? Have you got many clients?'

'I have, as it happens. A new cafe in Kemptown and a gastropub on Ditchling Road. Plus two birthday cakes and a macaron tower for a friend's wedding. She's getting mates' rates but I figure it's good exposure if I give her lots of business cards.'

'Wow, that's awesome.' We chink Peronis.

Ros nods, pink-cheeked. 'It's so great to show David's parents that I can do this. Their seed money was really welcome but I don't want to feel beholden. I need to prove I can make this work without them.'

We get back to eating. Our time is precious before I collect Kelvin from Mohit's and Ros has to dash home to pay the babysitter. I eat every scrap of pizza on my plate; Ros asks for the last third of hers to be doggy-bagged for Gabe. It figures: she's supermodel thin and I'm a wobbly dollop.

'They didn't come back then,' she says, while we wait for the bill.

'Who didn't?'

'Ed and Andy.'

'Ned.'

She grins. 'Ah yes, Ned. The one you had a secret drink with.'

'Oh please. When I'm ready to be out there again, I can do better than him. Andy was all over *you* like a rash. Is that why you brought them up?'

'Oh please. When I'm ready to be out there again, I can do better than him.'

She so can. She so will. As for me, I have two family slabs of Cadbury's Wholenut in the back of the cutlery drawer, which means I'm happy-as for the foreseeable.

It's a shame that Ned and Andy *weren't* there tonight. I definitely saw Andy trying his luck with Ros. And Ned seemed so keen to get his life back on track as a single dad. He's gone up in my estimation since we had that drink. He's a good man and I shouldn't be hard on him simply because he wears his heart on his sleeve.

So, yes, I'm keeping on keeping on and there are only a couple of days a month when I don't want to get out of bed. Days when I need to avoid Janine in case I lose my rag and then my job. I won't stay at the care home forever. I just need some stability for the next couple of years.

There are only two things yanking my chain right now, neither of them major. (Niggly things are never major but that doesn't stop them getting to you because you keep thinking: Come on, you silly cow, you ought to be able to sort that.)

Niggly thing number one is Kelvin's new wardrobe. I got back from Joe and Vicky's feeling smug that his weekend bedroom may be slick and styled but it lacks the personal touches that make his *proper* room his home. That lasted all of eight hours. The next morning, waking him up for school, I caught sight of his crappy old wardrobe and cringed.

Joe and I bought it twenty years ago, when we first set up home together and it was ancient then. It's one of those cramped affairs, from the time of small coat hangers. That was fine when Kelvin was little and his clothes were little. Now he's nearly as tall as me, with too many clothes; anything I iron comes out creased and crushed. Kel has a massive fitted wardrobe at his dad's; he should have a proper one here. He never complains, bless him, but he deserves better.

I do an online search to see what's available and what will fit his room. It turns into a project one Saturday afternoon when I visit four big furniture superstores to compare and contrast. I finally settle on an oak-effect one from B&Q. It isn't the cheapest but he's my boy and I don't spoil him nearly enough.

The flatpack box is swiftly delivered and takes up residence in the living room, leaning against a corner wall. After a couple of days, I'm tempted to set it on four bricks, cover it with a cloth and use it as a coffee table.

Kelvin thinks I'm hilarious. 'How hard can it be to put a wardrobe together?'

'Very hard if the instructions are in Swedish or Chinese and there's a widget missing or there's a piece left over after you've finished. When you put your first bit of flatpack together, you'll see, smart arse.'

I must be going on about it at work a fair bit because Felipe offers to come round and assemble it. I can't let him. I should be able to do this without help, especially from a man. It's not rocket science; it's a wardrobe.

Finally, and I hate myself for it, I call a number from the local freebie directory and book an appointment with a guy who calls himself 'Flatpack Fred, King of the Allen Key'. That's another £50 to fork out, on top of the cost of the wardrobe, because I'm too feeble to do it myself. Pathetic.

Niggly thing number two is Vicky. She's started calling and texting, and has even invited me to be her Facebook friend. My life's so dull that I don't post anything on my timeline, from one month to the next, whereas hers is full of coffee mornings and dopey memes and endless photos of Amelie. Why would I reveal to her that she's living her best life, while I'm muddling through?

I answer the first text where she thanks me for coming to her rescue when she cut her finger. 'Happy to help, take care.' Brisk, verging on rude. That should shut down any further contact.

But, oh no, she seems to think we should meet up for a coffee some time. I don't dislike the woman. But seriously, no. Leave me alone.

Joe doesn't like it either. He leaves a long message on my phone one day telling me why I can't be mates with Vicky: Wouldn't be right. Can't happen, Gemzy. Nip it in the bud asap, eh. For both our sakes.

Well, if that doesn't tempt me to pal up with her big time, I don't know what does. I should be better than that. It would be wrong to make friends with Vicky just to piss Joe off. It would be so wrong. I ignore two more texts and hope she gets the message.

The following Saturday morning, when Joe comes round to pick up Kelvin for the weekend, it isn't just him on the doorstep. He's brought Vicky and Amelie too. Oh great, another chance to taunt me with his picture-perfect happy family.

While Kelvin hastily scrabbles his stuff together – we go through this ritual every week – I try to find my friendly face. 'Grumpy' won't cut it when Vicky's beaming at me like we're mates from way back. She waggles her hand at me.

'See! There's still a tiny scar but it's all healed nicely now, thanks to Florence Nightingale here. You rocked up at just the right moment, Gemma.'

'That's good,' I smile back but with arms crossed to keep things distant.

'We're off to Joe's folks. Nice day for a drive, if the weather holds. Isn't it, Joe?'

'Yeah,' he grunts, staring at me until I break eye contact.

'His dad's not been well. Seeing Amelie really perks him up, doesn't it, Joe? And Kelvin obviously.'

'Yeah.'

Kelvin bellows down the stairs. 'Did you wash my grey hoodie?'

I bellow up the stairs. 'Third drawer down. Where it's meant to be. Try there.'

Vicky does one of those 'kids, eh!' laughs. 'I bet he learned that from *this* one. Joe'll say, "We're out of cheese" and I'll say, "Middle shelf of fridge, two massive packs of it." Sometimes you can't see for looking, can you, love?'

This is like torture. I send vibes to Kelvin to gather his things asap and get Joe and Vicky off my doorstep. I don't want Kelvin gone but someone needs to yank us out of our loop of fake friendliness.

Vicky suddenly nods to herself, as if a lightbulb's been turned on. 'I've been texting you for days, Gemma, but I've not heard back. Is your phone working?'

'Perfectly. I just didn't fancy speaking to you, Vicky.' Well, obviously I don't say that out loud but I like how it sounds in my head.

'It has been a bit iffy lately. I think I need a new battery. Sorry about that.'

She looks relieved. She must have thought I was snubbing her. As if.

'No worries. I was just wondering if you'd like to come to dinner at ours next Friday. We've got a new dining table that expands to eight so I said to Joe, we should christen it with a nice meal. Are you free, Gemma?'

Joe glares at me. No, you're not; no, you're not; no, you're fucking not.

I give Vicky my broadest smile. 'Oh, that sounds great, Vicky. I'd love to come. How about I bring Kel over for the weekend at the same time? Save you coming here to collect him, Joe.'

I catch my reflection in the hall mirror doing a fist pump after they leave. Then I regret my moment of madness. It was worth it, to see Joe's face, but now I have to go there and watch them playing happy families in their beautiful house (with the grubby kitchen cupboards) and make small talk with Vicky. Mind you, Joe will hate it too, scared I'll let something slip, so it's not all bad . . .

I have a busy Saturday planned: clean every window I can reach, inside and out; make a mahoosive batch of chilli for the freezer; do my nails – fingers *and* toes. Tick, tick, tick. All done by half eleven. Why slob out on the sofa, feeling mopey, when you can do stuff that lifts your spirits? I love clean windows and manicured nails; simple pleasures because I'm easily pleased. Or just simple.

Flatpack Fred is due at half two. He rings the doorbell five minutes early. Just as well I'm ready. I've even got digestives. I'm expecting one of those patronizing old gits who makes you feel stupid for not attempting it yourself. I usually want to say to them: Oh, and how good would you be working in a high-dependency care home where most of your clients are seriously ill, have dementia, or both? Fancy a job swap some time?

Only he isn't Fred, he's 'Desperate Danno' Robertson, one of Joe's old mates from a lifetime and a half ago. Dan, who I nearly went out with before Joe swept me off my feet. I wonder if I'd have had him and his Allen key round if I'd known.

I'd forgotten his wide, dimply smile. His dark brown hair

is now grey but it suits him. He looks as lean and wiry as he always was.

'I was right,' he grins. 'I thought it might be you but I didn't like to ask, in case it wasn't.'

'Who's Flatpack Fred, then? Is this a wind-up?'

'Me. I am. Well, technically my uncle is but he retired last year so I took over the business and the name because it was easier to keep it. He'd just had all these polo shirts printed.' He opens his jacket to show me and, yes, he's *definitely* as wiry – and muscly – as he always was.

I show him what needs doing. 'It'll be great to have the wardrobe assembled while Kelvin's away. He doesn't think I can do it.'

'Obviously you can't or why would I be here?'

I bristle. I'm about to be patronized. He sees my frown and quickly backtracks. 'What I mean is, I'm sure you can do it but four hands are better than two.'

We could begin with a cuppa and have a catch-up on the last – what is it? – fifteen years. But I want to get this sorted now so we skip the niceties and get started. I've emptied the contents of Kel's old wardrobe onto the bed; we just need to get it downstairs. Dan takes the weight and I guide from above, making sure we don't scratch the banister or smash the lampshade.

'What are you going to do with it?' he asks, once we've got it in the hall.

'Put it in the garden with a note on it. This street's heaving with students so someone's bound to take it.'

'I'll have it, if that's okay with you. I do a bit of furniture restoring for a mate in Hastings who sells it on. With some TLC and elbow grease, I could easily have this looking the business.'

'Be my guest.'

'Flatpack Dan' is really impressive. He must have done jobs like this a million times. He unpacks everything on the living-room floor and takes it up in stages. I offer to hold bits up while he screws them together but he sends me away.

'Splash of milk, two sugars and not too strong please.'

I decide he's earned more than digestives and slice us both a wedge of M&S lemon drizzle. We sit on the back step to soak up the last rays of afternoon sun.

'I heard you and Joe had split up,' he says. 'That's a shame.'

'You make it sound like it was mutual. That we drifted apart, wanted to go our separate ways. All huggy and cosy and nice.'

'It wasn't like that, then?'

'He was seeing someone else. I kicked him out.'

'Yeah, I heard that too. Just wasn't sure if it was true.'

'Ever the loyal friend. Never assume your old mate's the guilty party. It must be down to the wife. All her fault.'

Dan looks shocked. 'Did I say that, Gemma? No, I didn't. I'm trying not to take sides with either of you.'

'That's very fair. But now you know who got shat on and who was the shitter.'

'Yeah.'

'And?'

'And if I saw him in the street or in a pub or whatever, I'd be hard pushed not to thump him. Couldn't he see what he was throwing away? The man's a fool.'

We sit in silence, sipping our tea, and I turn over Dan's words in my head. He said he wouldn't take sides but he has. Mine. I want to hug him for seeing it from my point of view. Too many times, I feel people blaming me, even if they never say it out loud.

'Me and Nicola called it a day a couple of years ago. You never met her, did you? We'd tried for years to have children but it didn't happen and it drove a wedge between us. I was all for fostering but she wouldn't consider it. I get it. I do. I'm not a woman – obviously – but I can see that it isn't the same as being pregnant with your own kid. Anyway, we pulled the plug and, in our case, it *was* mutual and we're glad we did.'

'Oh, that's sad.'

Dan stands up, hands me his empty mug and wipes garden dust off his bum. 'Yeah, well. It is what it is and we are where we are. Both of us. Now . . . let's get that wardrobe finished. Lovely cake, by the way. I usually get a couple of stale digestives.'

After Dan has gone, I tidy up and hang Kelvin's clothes in the new wardrobe. Another Saturday job done. Tick. Another reason to be cheerful.

Then I lie on the bed for a bit and admire Dan's handi-work. I *am* cheerful, and not just because of the wardrobe. I think about Dan. He didn't treat me like an idiot and he listened. He wouldn't charge me either. I didn't like that. I always pay my way. As he saw it, I'd have got mates' rates anyway for being an old friend, plus he went home with Kel's wardrobe. So win-win all round.

Dan was at school with Joe and they used to hang around together at weekends. So when me, Hayley and a couple of other girls started hanging around where they hung around, it was fairly obvious the hormones would kick in and some of us would hook up. Hayley started the ball rolling with Derren O'Malley and for a while I fancied Mark Rawsthorne from afar.

Then one boiling-hot summer day when we were all at the beach by the pier, I got chatting to Dan and really liked him. I could tell the feeling was mutual. We even talked about how much we loved *Men in Black* and fancied seeing the sequel together some time. Not quite a date but heading that way.

And then Joe and I slow-danced at a party and that was that. I have to admit, I barely gave Dan a second thought from then on because Joe was everything. I didn't think I needed anyone else or would want anyone else ever again. God, I was stupid.

Kelvin comes home from his weekend with Joe and Vicky and doesn't even notice that the flatpack box is missing from the living room. But I hear a 'wow' when he goes upstairs.

'Thanks, Mum,' he shouts. 'You did it then?'

'Oh, ye of little faith. I said I would, didn't I?'

My boy's not a great one for *thank-you*s but I do get the occasional hug, when he's in the mood, and I get one an hour later, when he comes down for his tea. He's had the full Sunday roast with Joe and Vicky but he never refuses omelette, chips and peas from his mum. He's my boy.

Ros is waiting for me in the Anchor with two large glasses of house red. We'll sit through SPAN, then head off for our Wednesday-night pizzas. I've been thinking about Dan since Saturday. Should I tell her about him? Sometimes it's good to have a second opinion when you're working through knotty thoughts and feelings. He's a good guy, a nice guy. They're thin on the ground. And I'm 90 per cent sure he still fancies me.

'Ring him up. Ask him out. What are you waiting for?' Ros's second opinion is instant.

'Don't be ridiculous. I hardly know him.'

'You do. You've got history. *And* he fancies you. Okay, I wasn't there but from what you've told me, I know he does, Gemma. And *you* know that too.'

'What if my version's a fantasy? What if I'm bigging it up for my own vanity?'

Ros nearly spits out her wine. 'In all the time I've known you, you have never, ever bigged anything up. You're the least vain person I've ever met. You're always doing yourself down, writing yourself off. Don't pull that face, madam, you know you do.'

I won't argue with her. Why bother?

'So are you going to call Flatpack Dan, get him to show you his toolkit?'

'I could tell him my screwing's a bit rusty and can he help?'

Ros has a deafening, infectious laugh and we both get slightly hysterical. This is exactly why I love my Wednesdays.

'Bloody hell, we could hear you two down the street. What's so funny then?' It's Ned's mate, Andy. He pulls up a chair and joins us, waving to Ned who's at the bar. 'Two large reds over here, bud.'

'We're talking flatpack wardrobes actually,' Ros replies, winking at me.

Andy shrugs. He has no idea what's amused us. He's just pleased it isn't him.

'Here we are again, then,' he says, passing round the drinks as if *he* paid for them. 'How's the SPAN clan been managing without us?'

'We've been in bits,' I tell him. 'I had a little cry, didn't I, Ros? Then we thought, sod it, they'd want us to come back.'

We chink glasses like old friends. To be honest, it *is* good to see them. The SPAN hard core – Gail, Robin, Meryl and Loretta – are fine but it helps to have fresh blood and I promise myself that this time, I won't tear chunks out of Ned, as if he's official spokesman for every divorced dad.

'How've you been, Gemma?' Ned asks. 'Still keeping us blokes in check?'

'Someone has to.' I know he's teasing and I don't mind. I kind of like it, actually.

'Got that, Andy? We're on our best behaviour tonight or else.'

'Does Andy *do* "best behaviour"?' I ask Ned.

'He's been a terrific friend this past year. When Tanya and I split up, I got all the CDs, she got all the friends. Andy's been a loyal pal, even if I only take half of what he says with a pinch of salt.'

'I *am* loyal,' Andy agrees, giving Ros a meaningful look. 'I'd make someone an amazing boyfriend.'

'I believe Meryl's looking to find love again. You could start there.' Ros does another of her loud laughs. But Andy isn't laughing.

We've almost forgotten why we're here. Then Gail appears, carrying her faithful flip chart. She waves and comes over.

'Hi all, looks like it's going to be a full house tonight. Marvellous, marvellous.' She beams at Ned and Andy. 'So pleased to see you chaps back too. Don't rush, you've still got five minutes while I set up. Back by popular demand, we're doing the trust game tonight. And Meryl rang to say she's hoping to update us on her current situation. See you shortly, then.'

She struggles up the stairs with her flip chart and we let her.

When she's out of earshot, I let rip. 'Not the trust game

again. It's pointless and embarrassing. It didn't teach us anything last time. Except to avoid it like the plague.'

Ros nods. 'It was fairly grim. Meryl in hyper-drive. Robin in shut-down. Loretta in the ladies'. Gemma in full sarky mode.'

'That doesn't sound like Gemma,' Ned says, smiling sweetly. 'Anyway, what's so bad about it? I'd find a session about trust really helpful right now, actually.'

Andy isn't convinced. 'Not for me, bud, but don't let me stop you.'

Ros and I exchange looks. I know what she's thinking. How about we skip SPAN and go straight to pizza. I nod. We gather our things.

'Ned, can you tell Gail that Ros's babysitter's just rung? She's throwing up and feeling faint. Which means Ros has to go straight home and she's a bit anxious. Aren't you, Ros?'

'I'm beside myself,' Ros replies, straight-faced.

'So I'm going with her for moral support. And to clean up the vomit.'

'And I'm giving you both a lift in my Audi RS7,' Andy chips in.

Ros's impressed. 'You've got an Audi?' Then she twigs. 'Yeah right.'

Ned is torn. Either he stays and finds out why Gail's trust game is so awful. Or he does a runner with us. Ros, Andy and I walk out of the Anchor, leaving him to decide.

A couple of hours later, the four of us have worked our way through two garlic breads, one dough balls, four pizzas, two tricolore salads, two tiramisus and two bottles of Valpolicella. Every twenty minutes or so, Ned says he feels bad about bunking off SPAN and we tell him to shut up and get over it.

'Gail, though,' he says, on his third attempt to guilt-trip us. 'She puts a lot into SPAN, doesn't she? I'd hate her to think we don't appreciate her.'

I promised myself I wouldn't lay into Ned tonight but really, he's too soft for his own good. 'Gail's fine. Hide of an elephant. Nothing fazes the woman. Not even Meryl. You didn't *have* to come with us, Ned.'

'Yeah, give it a rest, bud,' adds Andy. 'You need to be more spontaneous.'

'I can be.'

'Only if you plan it well in advance.'

Ros pours the last dregs of wine into our glasses. 'You're not missing anything, honestly, Ned. It's just some dopey American exercise Gail found on the Internet. Anyway, it's wasted on me. I trusted David and David trusted me. 110 per cent. Although maybe he had one last secret up his sleeve, dying on me like that without any warning.'

She does this sometimes, Ros. Not on purpose. Not for effect or sympathy. Every so often she reminds me – us – that she hasn't chosen to be our kind of single. We 'only' got dumped, whereas half of Ros's life was stolen from her and I don't know how she copes with that, day in day out.

Andy strokes her arm and she lets him. 'I can't even imagine what you're going through, Ros. My mum died fifteen years ago and I was a mess. But it's hardly the same thing. I know that.'

I've been assuming that Andy's a gold-plated chancer. Maybe he's a genuinely nice guy after all and my bullshit radar needs servicing.

Ros looks affected too. 'Thanks, Andy. I know I'm not the world's only widow and yes, I'm doing okay, all things considered. Even so, it does always feel, I don't know, unique to me. In my head anyway. Except when I dream. Then I always have David with me.'

No one knows how to break the moment, or even if we should. Fortunately the waiter comes over and Andy orders four grappas, without asking. I'm so relieved I'm on a late shift tomorrow; I haven't drunk this much in years.

'Guess what,' I tell them. 'I'm invited to a dinner party at Joe and Vicky's on Friday. No way was I going until I picked up that he really doesn't want me there. So I accepted. How should I play it?'

'Ice cool, obviously,' reckons Andy, 'and if it's a plus-one, bring along the best-looking guy you know.'

Ros claps her hands. 'Dan! Invite Dan.'

'He and Joe used to be mates,' I reply. 'It could come to blows.'

'Even better,' says Andy.

'Not going to happen.'

'I'm happy to be your new boyfriend,' Andy suggests. 'If that helps.'

'Oh, God, I wish I hadn't told you all now.'

Ned has been quiet through all this. 'I had to do that a couple of weeks ago. Show up as someone's new boyfriend. One of the most uncomfortable situations I've ever been in.'

Andy looks genuinely surprised. 'You never told me. Who was it?' There's a split second and then he says, 'Bloody hell. Was it Karen?'

'Hard to believe, Andy, but I don't tell you everything.' Ned looks pleased with himself. 'Anyway, I bet I know why you weren't told to bring someone, Gemma. Who wants to guess why?'

Ros gets it first. 'You're being set up. They've got some single guy lined up for you. To get you out of their hair.'

It hadn't even occurred to me. 'Oh great.'

'After David died, people did that all the time,' says Ros. 'Not straight away. They gave me a calendar year to get over him, then . . . bam. "Meet my brother, meet my ex, meet my dad." I was scared to go anywhere in case some apparently random guy was there too, who just so happened to know all about me.'

Over grappas, we split the bill, even though Andy pretends he was about to slam down the plastic. He *is* a gold-plated chancer, however hard he tries to hide it.

Ros calls a cab and goes outside to wait for it. Andy offers to keep her company. He *definitely* fancies her. Ned and I watch him grab his jacket and dash out after her and we can't help smiling.

'She is so out of his league,' I say. 'Plus David sounds like a tough act to follow.'

'Yeah, what Ros is going through has been a bit of a wake-up call actually. I need to count my blessings, be positive, look to the future.'

He looks so genuinely happy that it takes me by surprise. He's really cute when he smiles.

'Optimism suits you, Ned. Where did that come from?'

'Guess what? Dora's not going to Oman. I told Tanya how I felt and I honestly think she listened, took my feelings on board. I couldn't be happier. Well, I *could*, but, like I say, I'm working on it.' He smiles again, a big ear-to-ear grin that makes me grin back, even though I'm not sure why.

Then I find out what else he's so pleased about. 'I've got a date on Saturday.'

'With Karen? Who *is* Karen, anyway?'

'My boss. You know. The one you laid into me about at SPAN. God, no, not her. Her name's Nancy. We met recently

146

and then I accidentally bumped into her in the shop where she works. I had no idea she works there. Total surprise for both of us. And, well, I asked her out. I haven't been on a date-date in years.'

'Apart from Karen?'

'Karen doesn't count. I know that sounds bad but she doesn't. Nancy's a different thing altogether. I won't lie, Gemma, I'm petrified.'

I'm keen to learn more but it's nearly ten o'clock and I have to pick Kelvin up from Mohit's. I scribble my mobile number on a napkin. ' Why don't we WhatsApp each other? Before, during and after *my* dinner party and *your* date. What do you say?'

'Great. Yes. Great. That would be really – yes.'

On Friday night, I don't get myself in a state, trying to decide what to wear. I don't pull everything out of the wardrobe and force Kelvin to give his opinion. I don't tell myself my bum looks big in this and my cleavage looks crepey in that. I don't even resort to scuzzy T-shirt and tracky bottoms, just to show Joe and Vicky that I haven't made an effort.

I go straight to the dress I've had in mind ever since Vicky invited me. I bought it in the Zara sale about a year ago but I've never worn it: dark grey, short sleeves, fitted just-above-the-knee-length skirt to show off my half-decent legs. Black tights, black shoes and a silver rope necklace Joe bought me when Kelvin was born. Let's see if he remembers it . . .

I keep the make-up simple, apart from red lippy. I go the extra mile and blow-dry my hair, though. My reflection approves. I scrub up well. Maybe I always did.

Kelvin passes my bedroom, then scoots back to look at

me looking at me. 'Nice, Mum. You look really pretty and nice. You hoping to pull or something?'

I grab him, hug him tight and force him to stare at us both in the full-length mirror. 'I've already got a man in my life. We're doing fine, aren't we, matey?'

'Yeah. Mostly. Are you like, happy? I can't always tell.'

'Yeah. Mostly.' I kiss the top of his head. Soon I'll have to stand on tiptoes to do that.

Kelvin is staying with Joe and Vicky for the weekend, as per usual, so Joe offers to pick us both up. I say no thanks, we'll grab a cab. The last thing I need is him bending my ear all the way there about what I can/can't say . . . from telling Vicky I don't eat red onion to announcing how quickly I came on my wipe-clean worktop a few weeks back. The bus is good enough and I can save the cab fare for the return journey, minus Kelvin.

'Who else will be there?' he asks as we change from the 49 to the 22 at Elm Grove.

'I don't know. Vicky's new table expands to eight.'

'Won't it be weird, Mum? Being there with them? With her.'

'Yes. It will. I've got butterflies.'

'Don't go. I'll say you weren't feeling well. Like you've got a really bad dose of the shits.'

I laugh out loud and the woman next to me in the queue gives me a look.

'The shits. Nice one, Kelvin. Let's do that then . . . *not*.'

Kelvin laughs too, pleased with his oh-so-subtle sense of humour. 'Seriously, Mum. Go home.'

'Seriously Kelvin. No way.'

Since my last visit, when I had to tend to Vicky's cut finger, the front doorstep now has two miniature bay trees, trimmed into matching pom-poms. The house number is new too: etched into smoked glass and sort of suspended against the porch wall. I bet Vicky has a stack of *Interiors* magazines in the guest loo. I wish Ros was here so I could bitch to her. I'll have to save it up for Wednesday.

Vicky flings the door open and hugs me like a long-lost pal. Kelvin looks at me and grins. Then he gets the same treatment. I daren't catch his eye in case we start giggling. Actually, it's very sweet. Vicky really wants this to work, for us all to draw a line and move on. I do too, I suppose. I can't keep hating her, especially now that I've met her. Maybe it will help me *really* get over Joe. I honestly feel I'm ready for that . . . at last.

Vicky looks every inch the hostess in a flowery number with matching purple suede stilettoes. She'll have swapped the gravy-splatted, yolk-stained apron she's been cooking in for a spotless white one, with 'MistressChef' embroidered on the front pocket.

'Come in, come in. Oh, this is great. I can't tell you how pleased I am to have you here, Gemma. And Kelvin, although he's *always* here at weekends, isn't he?' She looks anxious, like she's digging herself a hole. But she can't stop now. 'And we love that too, obviously. Having you here every weekend. Course we do. Just ask Amelie.'

We're shown into the open-plan living room. I don't like mess and clutter but this is in another league of tidiness: it looks more like a health centre waiting room than somewhere where real people watch TV, read, have a kip . . . All glass and chrome and cream and beige, apart from some lime green fake fur cushions.

Joe has his back to me as he serves drinks. Vicky must have styled him too because these aren't the kind of clothes he'd have worn when we were together: a shirt so busy it could give you a migraine and super-tight skinny cream jeans that, from a distance, look like he's forgotten to put his trousers on. You need to be whip-thin to carry off trousers like that. Joe isn't. Not any more.

He spins round and that's when I see the other guests – oh, Jesus Christ: Hayley and Lee. Why didn't that occur to me? Vicky must be pinching herself at how clever she's been, reuniting best friends from back in the day. Maybe there's still time to say I've had diarrhoea all day and don't want to embarrass myself on her upholstery.

Credit where credit's due. Hayley doesn't expect a massive, tit-crushing hug, like Vicky's. She won't have forgotten the mouthful I gave her at Sainsbury's and is probably worried I might throw a vase at her. But I'm a grown-up and I'm civilized. I can do this. I'll be dignified and funny and I'll take the piss in such a cute way they'll hardly notice.

'You look great, Gem,' Hayley says, hoisting her curves to her feet. She has the same suede stilettos as Vicky but hers are bright turquoise. As good a place to start as any.

'Ooh, look. You and Vicky have got matchy-matchy shoes,' I say admiringly. 'Did you go shopping together?'

'I bought them in four different colours,' Vicky explains. 'Hayley asked if I minded her getting them too. So I'm like, imitation's the best form of flattery. You go, girl.'

'I've only got three pairs,' adds Hayley. 'Purple, turquoise and nude. We're always texting each other to make sure we're not wearing the same colour when we meet up, aren't we, Vic?'

What's going on here? Hayley's always been prone to putting her foot in it, but is she deliberately flaunting her friendship with Vicky or is she *genuinely* this unaware? I opt for 'unaware'. So they're best friends now. So what?

Through all this, Joe watches me. His face says: This shirt was not my idea, okay. His face also says: You look hot, Gemzy. I know what he's thinking. I will always know what he's thinking.

He suddenly remembers his hostly duties: 'What can I get you? Wine, Pimm's, Martini, Aperol spritz, builder's tea with ice and a slice?'

'Pimm's, please. I got really drunk on that once, do you remember?'

Joe laughs. 'Oh God, yes. Someone's wedding do at that pub in Shoreham.'

'Claire and Keith.'

There's a silence you could cut with one of Vicky's best knives. We have a history, me and Joe. Am I just meant to ignore that?

Vicky puts together a plate of party food for Kelvin so he can head upstairs for a session of Minecraft with Mohit. Good. If I behave badly, he won't have to see it.

I'm just thinking, Right, this is all of us then: Hayley and Lee, Vicky and Joe plus saddo single me. Then the doorbell rings. It could be yet another cutesy couple, of course, but what if Ned and Ros were right? What if I'm about to be paired off with another saddo single?

Yes, here he is: Vicky's cousin, Chris. At first glance, he's okay-looking. Nothing to swoon over but I don't expect Idris Elba's free tonight anyway. Slightly over-gelled hair, nice eyes, those invisible frameless specs, low-key un-nerdy clothes. And he knows how to arrive late without looking awkward or apologetic.

He hugs Vicky, shakes hands with Joe and gives a wave

to Hayley and Lee, like he's met them before. 'So, by process of elimination, you're Gemma, right?'

'Guilty as charged.' Why did I say that? Not clever, not funny.

He likes the look of my Pimm's and asks for one too. Then he scoops up a handful of peanuts and chucks them in his mouth in one go. I don't want to give Vicky the satisfaction but I think I'm going to like Chris.

Dinner is dedicated to all the recipe books in Vicky's kitchen: starter by Nigella, flatbreads by Paul Hollywood, main course by Hugh Whatsitty-Whatsit, pudding by Jamie.

Jamie's her favourite. 'He's so . . . normal, isn't he? No airs and graces. He just loves good food.'

'I think he's a twat,' says Joe.

'Oh, don't be rotten. He's lovely,' says Hayley.

Lee shrugs. He has no opinion. Not on Jamie, not on anything, really, for the whole night. I'd forgotten how boring he is. Hayley may as well have brought a table lamp as her plus-one.

Chris has been placed opposite me at Vicky's swanky new dining table, presumably so that we can fall in love across the rocket salad. 'Any thoughts on Jamie, Gemma?' he asks, with a twinkle.

'He's better than Gordon Ramsay.'

Vicky must have been cooking since dawn. Everything is delicious. Perfect veg, moist chicken and all the sauces are gooey and tasty. She even knows how to do that skid-mark thing across the plate.

'Right, so *this* is a fondant potato,' I say, trying not to speak with my mouth full. 'I see it on *MasterChef* all the time but I couldn't work out what the fuss was about. It's lovely, Vicky.'

Hayley agrees and helps herself to Lee's, spearing it straight off his plate. 'He's training for a 10k. I'm doing him a favour. You're so right, Gemma. Fondant potatoes and chocolate fondant. How did we ever manage without them?'

'You're a bit *too* fond of the fondants, Hayley,' Joe says, pleased with himself.

Vicky shoots him a look, as if they had the talk earlier about him not making any personal remarks.

Hayley reddens. 'Why, is there chocolate fondant for afters?'

'Peach clafoutis or pina colada fruit salad. Sorry, hunny.'

I don't eat out in posh restaurants much, if ever. I'm more your pub roast with all the trimmings kind of a girl. Joe and I never saw the point, not if we could have a Chinese take-away and curl up in front of the telly. Even so, I know this is top quality. Maybe the best meal I've ever had. No wonder Joe's tummy is straining against the buttons of his lairy shirt.

'This is brilliant, Vicky. Every single mouthful. I am so impressed.' And I mean it. I'm not being ironic or sarcastic. It really is.

It's Vicky's turn to blush. 'Aw, thanks, Gemma. That means a lot. We're all so pleased to have you here. To let bygones be bygones and for everyone to get on again. Isn't that right, Joe?'

'Yeah.'

Hayley has pushed away half of Lee's fondant potato, put off by Joe's jibe. 'It means a lot to me too. Gem and I go back such a long way. That has to count for something?'

I smile and raise a glass. I don't say: You're never going to be my best friend again. So don't think this means anything, because it doesn't . . . hunny.

I could be wrong but I get the feeling Chris has picked

up on the vibe between me and Hayley. He looks at us both, then raises a glass too.

'To friends –' he pauses for effect – 'especially Chandler and Phoebe.' I'm *definitely* going to like him.

The puddings are beyond amazing. Vicky could cook for me any day. Is this what swung it for her, while she was shagging Joe on the sly? My very best lasagne, with an inch of Cheddar on top, was never going to smash *that* contest.

Joe and Lee are talking football, Vicky and Hayley have gone upstairs to check on Amelie and Scarlett. (And probably to compare notes on how tonight's going.) That just leaves me and Chris.

'You're doing really well,' he says, voice lowered.

I'm a bit taken aback. Is he a mind reader?

'Vicky's told me all about, well, what happened. Between the three of you.'

'Your cousin stole my husband.'

'My mum and Vicky's mum are sisters so we all knew she'd met someone . . . Joe. We didn't know until he moved in with her that he was—'

'—a shit?'

'Married. We really didn't know. Mum said that Auntie Lou said that Vicky had met Mr Right and of course, we were all pleased for her.'

'Aw, sweet.'

'So you coming here tonight, being nice, is a major thing and you're doing brilliantly.'

I want to cry. I only met Chris a couple of hours ago, but he can see how hard this ordeal has been for me. I don't think it's even occurred to anyone else.

'I did hate Vicky for a long time,' I tell him. 'Part of me still does, even though I can tell she's a nice woman. She must have known Joe was married. Really it's Joe who's, who's—'

'—a shit?'

'A total shit. He hurt me and Kelvin more than he'll ever know. But I can't carry this anger around forever or I'll drown in it.'

Joe and Lee return to the table with cognac and glasses. Chris pats my hand reassuringly. Joe clocks this and glares. Honestly, who gives a flying fondant what he thinks? I'm warming to Chris by the minute.

I pop to the downstairs loo and, yes, there's a stack of *Interiors* magazines next to the pyramid of loo roll. I nearly WhatsApp Ned to tell him he was right – I *was* set up – but that can wait. I'll do it when I get home.

I leave the loo and suddenly Joe's there. 'I'm sorry, Gemzy. Swear to God I am. I couldn't stop her.'

'Stop her what? Sneaking off with you?'

'This. This whole fucking evening. Hayley, Lee. Not my idea at all. And certainly not pairing you off with Chris.'

'Yeah, well. I'm here, aren't I? I'm being the perfect ex. Polite, friendly, complimenting the perfect *new* wife on her fondant potatoes. Must be weird for *you* though.'

He nods, as if he's carrying the weight of the world on his shoulders. 'It is.'

'Your new wife is a great cook. Your new wife knows how to fold a napkin into a swan and walk in stilettos. While your old wife served you spaghetti hoops on toast and made you laugh till your face hurt. And I never, ever would have put you in such a hilarious pair of trousers. Still, we are where we are. And now, if you could stop blocking the way, I'd best get back to the fun.'

*

Just before leaving, I pop upstairs to say goodnight to Kelvin. I expect to find him still waging Minecraft war with Mohit but he's taken himself to bed. I can even smell the toothpaste on his breath when I give him a night-night kiss. I am a good mother. Official.

Chris offers me a lift and I accept. Out of the corner of my eye, I see Vicky give Hayley a thumbs-up. Job done. Just as she tidies her home to make sure everything's neat and sorted and where it should be, she's tidied up two lives. She's set up her cousin with her hubby's ex. She's as good as bought the wedding hat.

We make the ten-minute drive from Woodingdean to Bevendean. Not nearly enough time to firm up that we're made for each other. I do like Chris. He's my kind of guy. Same sense of humour, same sarky comebacks, same approach to the two-pudding dilemma: 'Can I have a bit of both, please?'

'Vicky knows you're gay, right?' I ask him as we accelerate past the university at Falmer.

'Kind of,' Chris replies, without blinking. 'I told her I was bi so she thinks I'm just waiting for the right woman – aka, you.'

'Oh dear. I'm not, though, am I?' It's not actually a question.

I can't see his face because he's driving but I can hear a big smile in his reply. 'You could be, I suppose. If I didn't have a boyfriend in Cardiff called Faizal. My family don't know about him because it's all fairly new.'

'Vicky thinks we clicked. When will you tell her?'

'Bless her, she's a great believer in positive thinking. "Chris isn't really gay. Chris and Gemma will click. Joe isn't a fuckwit." He *is* a fuckwit, isn't he?'

For a split second, I nearly defend Joe because he's so hard-wired into my emotions. 'I honestly think he could be a good bloke because he used to be. But he doesn't try hard enough. What's in it for him?'

Chris turns off the Lewes Road, into Bevendean, a few rungs down the social ladder from leafy Woodingdean. I direct him to my house and he pulls up outside.

'Yeah, well, he'd just better not hurt Vicky,' he says, turning off the engine. 'She's a good person. So are you. And they've made a nice life for themselves. They've got Amelie. I'm a godparent, actually. He'd be an idiot to throw all that away.'

'He had a nice life with me and Kelvin. He's got form.'

'So, what shall we tell Vicky? About us?'

It's tempting to lie but I honestly can't be arsed. 'You could tell her about Faizal. That might be a start.'

Chris nods. 'I didn't want to put a curse on it by blabbing too early. But you're absolutely right. I'll tell my family. What can they do? Fuck all. It was lovely meeting you, Gemma. Hey, I've got a mate at work, great guy. He collects *Star Wars* memorabilia and only eats corned beef. You'd really like him.'

'Ha ha.' I plant a kiss on his cheek. 'Lovely meeting you too, Chris. Enjoy Cardiff.'

Chapter Fifteen

Ned

I nearly rang Karen on Sunday night, after lunch at the Ivy, to check if her daughter was okay. But I didn't. Was I being a wimp? Or was I giving her the time and space to sort out her family issues in her own way? Yes. Both. Probably.

In fact, I don't talk to her again until Tuesday morning. She's been in meetings, I've been in meetings, yadda-yadda. Work is super-busy at the minute and the Welby-Daniels thing is so close to being signed off by Karen's boss and then by *his* boss that everything else is back-burnered.

We meet in the kitchen. I've gone to retrieve a pastry from the fridge to have with my morning cuppa. She's making herself what looks like a mug of boiling water.

'Oh hey, hi Karen. How are you?'

'Relieved. Grant's happy, Courtney's ecstatic. Thanks for pushing Welby-Daniels through so efficiently, Ned. It was hugely reassuring to have you on the project.'

'Happy to get stuck in. I used to think I hated working under pressure; actually, I thrive on it.' Total bollocks – I *do* hate pressure – but it's how we talk at work. Positivity at all times. Talk it up, don't talk it down. Bullshit is best.

'That's good, Ned. We've got a busy few months ahead. Ooh, that cake looks nice.'

'Want some? I can cut it in half.'

'Don't even tempt me. After that huge lunch on Sunday, I'm keeping off carbs till the weekend.' She pats her stomach as if it's fat. It isn't remotely. Tanya was just the same. Why do women *do* that?

Karen's brought up Sunday so I reckon I can too. 'Is Hattie okay? When your dad's girlfriend's not much older than you, that must be extra stressful. For Hattie. And for you too, obviously. I'll give it a few years before I start dating any contemporaries of Dora. Twenty at least.'

Karen looks uncomfortable. I'm not sure she realizes I'm joking, trying to make light of what must be a difficult situation for her.

She picks up her mug of water and heads for the door. 'I'd really rather keep personal stuff out of the office environment, Ned, if that's okay.'

I feel as though I'm 10 and have been rebuked by the headmistress. 'Oh. Sure, yes. Couldn't agree more, Karen.'

'Good. Have you had a chance to touch base with Denise yet? Now that Welby-Daniels is done and dusted – or as good as – we really need to build bridges with Ashford. Can I leave that with you?'

'Top of my list. After I've eaten my cake.'

She glides away, leaving in her wake a waft of the perfume I got to know up close and personal when I went back to hers that time. She still scares me. So cool, so in control. I really admire her. And I haven't given up on the idea of being her secret floozy, if I get another go at it. It was fun getting back on the sex horse and I'm dead keen on another gallop.

*

159

Brighton is having one of its unseasonably sunny February days; the sky is like a blue sheet and a couple of cafes have tables out on pavements, even though there's still quite a nip in the air.

Andy and I decide against pasty and chips in our usual place and, instead, buy two meal deals from Boots to eat on the seafront. Lunch hours in our office tend to last twenty minutes max, if at all, but I'm Andy's line manager now, so he can take as long as I do.

We perch on a wall and stare out to the Rampion wind farm, churning away on the horizon. I bloody love this city. I thought I couldn't without Tanya and Dora, but it's won me round. If I create my own memories here, new memories that don't hark back to life with Tanya, I can properly embrace Brighton – and Hove – as my home. Right now and from now on. I feel strangely exhilarated and not just because I'm really enjoying my tuna sandwich, stuffed with salt and vinegar crisps.

'So have you ended it with Debi in Sales?' I ask between bites. 'I hope you did it nicely.'

Andy looks aggrieved. 'I don't know why people think I'm such a bastard. Debi isn't for me, okay, but I'm not going to hurt her feelings just for the sake of it. Give me *some* credit, mate.'

'I thought you might be ghosting her. You only came to Amberley with me and Dora to avoid her. And that's a horrible thing to do to someone. Anyone.'

'I had a great time with you and the little 'un, as it happens. Anyway, how can I ghost someone I see at work every day? So yeah, we went for a drink and, at your suggestion, I subtly reminded her that office relationships are majorly frowned upon at QGT. She's just been shortlisted for Gareth's job and she's dead keen to get it so she thought *she* was pulling the plug, not me. See! I can be sensitive and thoughtful, oh ye of little faith.'

'Good.'

'Are you still schtupping the Ice Maiden?'

He's really irked that Karen's resistant to *his* charms. I'd actually appreciate his take on the Sunday lunch from hell, but I decide to keep it to myself for the time being. 'And you're the first person I'd tell if I was? Yeah, right.'

'I'll take that as a no, then.'

I finish my sandwich. 'That was delicious. Well, if Debi's off the scene now and you're looking to pastures new, there's always Ros.'

'Ros?'

'Ros. From SPAN. The single parents' support group. The blonde widow. Ros. Don't tell me you've forgotten her already.'

'I'd forgotten her name, that's all. I have been thinking about her, actually. She ticks several boxes: sexy, feisty, in need of some serious loving after her tragic loss. Lovely Ros. Oh yes. She could very easily be The One.'

'The *next* one, you mean.'

He does his aggrieved face again, then knocks back the last of his Pepsi. 'How about we do SPAN again? Let's go to another meeting. Tomorrow? What do you say?'

'Maybe.'

It would be nice to catch up with Gemma. Yes, she's too bitter and hard-done-by for her own good, but we made our peace last time and I'm not one to bear grudges. (Except against Julian, the world's most talented architect.)

'Nice one, Nedward. That's in the diary then: Wednesday, 7 p.m., SPAN. I'll convince the lovely Ros that her prince has come. Ooh, that reminds me. I know someone who reckons you could be *her* prince.'

'I told you. Me and Karen are none of your business. Nice try, though.'

'Aha, so there *is* still something going on between you two. Bloody thought so. Although the person to whom I am referring is not, in actual fact, the aforesaid Karen.'

I sigh. Sometimes Andy can be very annoying.

'Your recent intimate liaison with the Ice Queen has recharged your batteries, right?'

'Just spit it out, will you? We need to be back at our desks in five minutes.'

'Let's walk and talk.'

So we return to the office and Andy explains in his wordy way who's interested in me.

Nancy.

Nancy, who I got chatting to at that club a few weeks ago. Apparently she's mentioned me more than once to her friend Nick, who told Andy. Nancy, who did a runner when I wouldn't stop talking about my failed marriage. Nancy, who is much better girlfriend material than Karen.

That Nancy.

'Want her phone number?' Andy asks. 'Or you could "friend" her on Facebook? Or I could ask Nick to set you up with her?'

'No, no, no. I mean, none of the above, thank you very much.' I'm flattered that she's asked about me but Andy's a bit too hands-on for my liking.

We travel up to the fifth floor with three other people. Someone gets out, someone else gets in. Several times.

As the doors close on floor three, Andy stage-whispers a suggestion. 'She works in a shop on Sydney Street. Pottery and wind chimes and nonsense like that. Nancy. No reason why you can't swing by and accidentally bump into her, ask her out. What have you got to lose?'

'Thanks, Andy. Tell me later.'

'Later might be too late. Do it asap. Trust me, Nedward, you're pushing at an open door with that one.'

The Nancy news puts quite a spring in my step and, because the late afternoon sun is still out, I decide to walk home, rather than catch the bus. Western Road is always busy and buzzy; I like the Middle Eastern cafes and the shop window full of waving lucky cats. I should get one for Dora; she adores cheap, shiny tat, much to Tanya's disgust.

As I walk, I scroll back to my conversation with Nancy outside the club that night. I know I gave her *far* too much information about my break-up with Tanya, when I really should have been asking her about her. What a twat. Actually, it's been years since I chatted anyone up so it's no surprise I've lost the knack, if I ever even had it.

Maybe I didn't *completely* scare her off after all. I can't have been that bad or she wouldn't have mentioned me to her friend, Nick. Or . . . maybe Andy got the wrong end of the stick and she was just telling Nick what a loser I am. That also seems plausible: I did mention Tanya a *lot*.

I know I have nothing of any nutritional value in my fridge. I could pick up battered sausage and chips on Portland Road but I don't really fancy it. Nor am I in the mood to cook because I know I'll end up with a third night of pasta and pesto.

A good excuse to visit Taj supermarket: aisle after aisle of food from every country, plus weird veg, chewy bread and those sticky Indian sweets that attach themselves to your fillings and won't let go. I will buy myself something wholesome, healthy and interesting from the heat-up-at-home counter. Because I'm worth it.

That's when he sees me. Julian. Bollocks! I'm waiting for a fat slab of moussaka to be tipped into a plastic-lidded box when he creeps up and slaps me on the back like we're old pals.

'Thought it was you, Ned. Great to see you. Moussaka, eh? Looks nearly as good as mine.'

Bollocks. Bollocks. Bollocks.

'Julian. Hi. Yeah, no, I'm too knackered to make it myself tonight.'

Tanya will have told him I'm a talentless cook who couldn't even heat up tomato soup without pebble-dashing the microwave. I never needed to cook because Tanya loved doing it every night when she got home from work and who was I to stop her? (She threw that back in my face when we were breaking up, which I thought was pretty unreasonable actually. If she didn't always feel like doing it, she only had to say.)

Julian shows me the contents of his wire basket. 'I'm stocking up on harissa, sumac, za'atar, pul biber and kofte spice.'

I'm none the wiser but I nod approvingly. What a tosser. 'Nice one. I love . . . sumac.'

He puts his basket down and looks me in the eye. I'm a few inches taller than him so he has to stretch.

'Did Tanya tell you I've been wanting to get in touch?'

'No. Why?'

'About Oman. The whole nine yards. Have you got time for a quick drink?'

If he studies the contents of my wire basket, he'll see that the only appointment I have tonight is with a breeze block of moussaka and some over-priced salted caramel chocolate. And some kettle chips. And a mango.

Ten minutes later he's buying us two pints of bitter and a bowl of wasabi nuts in a trendy pub round the corner from Taj. He acts as if this is what mates do. He acts as if we're mates. I'm sorry, Julian, but wasabi nuts are for enemies, not mates, mate.

'I wanted to thank you for being so understanding while the whole Oman thing was going on. Cheers for that, Ned.' He clinks my glass. I have just been passively clinked. I do not reciprocate.

'Was I? I don't remember being understanding.'

'Fair point. It would have been a major bloody deal for all of us. I know how much it means to you and Dora, spending time together every weekend.'

How much it means? She's my daughter, you dipstick. 'I wasn't happy at all, actually, Julian. I'd definitely have dug my heels in if it had gone ahead. Tanya told you that, I'm sure.'

He nods. He knows. The incontrovertible fact is that I am Dora's dad, whatever he says or does.

'Still, it didn't come to that, did it? Okay, I was pleased and flattered to make it to the final three. But some things are just not meant to be, right?'

'The final three?'

'I suppose my heart wasn't in it. Ultimately. And they knew it, the people making the final decision. Close but no cigar. If I'm totally honest, it would have been a nightmare gig. I hear through the grapevine that the poor bugger who got the job is already being run ragged and she hasn't even relocated to Muscat yet. "We don't like the atrium, we want

165

a bigger atrium. We need more marble, less parking, more parking, less marble."'

'So let me get this right, Julian. They turned you down? You didn't turn *them* down?'

'Yep. And you know what, Ned? I'm relieved. I've got a great job right here in Brighton. Fantastic clients, the best partners. I've loved Tanya and Dora moving in to my house and bringing it alive. We're settled here. You're Dora's dad and you're here too. I'm no believer in fate but, on this occasion, thank you, karma.'

'How's Tanya about it?'

'Disappointed to miss out on an adventure, an experience we'd never forget. Still, I think she's starting to see that it's for the best. It *is* for the best.'

I finish my beer and make my excuses. My stomach turns over with anger as I stomp home. I've been played. Tanya played me. She lied. To keep me sweet? To make it look like she was the good guy and couldn't bear to keep me and Dora thousands of miles apart?

The moussaka sticks in my throat when I eat it. Revenge may be a dish best served cold, but moussaka bloody isn't.

Maybe that's why I decide to act on the Nancy thing. I need to be proactive. I need to put aside my anger with Tanya and move on. Would I *really* have objected if the Oman gig had come off? Or would I have reverted to default doormat mode? I will not let things happen to me again; I will be the one to *make* things happen.

The Nancy thing would also help me to put the Karen thing into perspective. Shagging your boss is a quick thrill, not a long-term route out of a rut. Karen isn't the problem – she's an amazing woman – but the set-up is. It has an inbuilt shelf life and that's not for me. I want to be an out-there boyfriend, not a secret floozy. I want to do ordinary things with an extraordinary woman. I don't want to be used as a weapon to distress a daughter or stick it to an ex. I don't have the temperament for confrontation.

I'm fairly sure I know the shop where Nancy works. I could easily nip there in my lunch hour. I tell Andy I'm skipping lunch to buy a new kettle.

'You really live life on the edge, Nedward.' He chuckles. 'Next thing, you'll be after one of those bean-bag trays so you can eat in front of the telly.'

(I don't tell him I've already got one, bought for me one Christmas by my mum. It's a really clever design, actually, especially if you're eating something sloppy like chilli.) I let him sneer. Better that than be coached all morning on how to hook Nancy. Like he's the expert.

The shop is called Kitten Kaboodle, on Sydney Street. I think I even went in there a couple of years ago, in search of a birthday present for Tanya. Brighton has no end of cutesy little places, full of over-priced bits of nonsense: candle-sticks made out of old cutlery; cutlery made out of old candlesticks.

Before I enter, I make up a story in my head: who I'm buying for, what I'm looking for, how much I'm willing to spend. (I can never lie unless I've rehearsed it first.) Once I've got my story straight, I amble in, like it's a spur-of-the-moment thing. And there she is. Nancy. Showing someone a display of knitted scarves that look to be made out of old pot scourers. She sees me so I act as if I haven't seen her.

'I'll leave you to have a think,' she's saying. 'I've got the green one and, honestly, it's always getting compliments.'

Now she's backing away from the customer and heading over. 'Ned? It is Ned, isn't it?'

I spin around, give a confused frown, then turn it into my best smile. I give good smile. I know I do. 'Oh, hi. Wow, is this your shop?'

'I wish. My friend Sasha owns it. I bet you don't remember my name.'

'I bet I do. It's Emma . . . Anna . . . no, it's Lucy.'

Her face falls. It really does. She is desperately willing me to remember who she is. 'I'm being an arse. Of course I remember you. And your name.'

'Go on then.'

'Nancy. And you live in Seven Dials and you're a native Brightonian.'

She gives my arm a playful thump. 'Oh, you. Are you looking for anything in particular?'

A proper girlfriend, I want to say. 'I'm after a birthday present for my mother. She likes anything flowery.'

The other customer is harrumphing by the scarves. Nancy gives me a 'wait there' nod and returns to her. I study some coasters made out of tyres and a lampshade made out of fuse wire. I may as well buy something for Mum, even though her birthday was months ago. I plump for a set of white porcelain tea-light holders that look like tulips. That'll do nicely. Not too pricey either.

'Spooky,' Nancy says, when she returns. 'I was just about to show you the tulip lights.'

'Wow, seriously? Were you?'

'Gotcha. The biter bit.'

I have no idea what she's talking about.

'You teased *me*, Ned. About not remembering my name. And now I'm teasing *you*. About the tulip – oh, never mind.'

I'm suddenly scared of screwing this up. I give her arm a playful thump. 'Oh, you.'

Our chit-chat is interrupted by an angry door slam. Scarf woman has exited in a huff. Shocked, Nancy and I look at each other, then burst out laughing.

'Oops,' I say. 'I think I just lost you a sale.'

'Those scarves are over-priced and itchy. Like wearing a Brillo pad round your neck. She's better off in M&S.'

'So shop assistants are lying when they tell me they've got this sweater or that shirt and they're always getting complimented on it?'

Nancy grins. It's a cheeky grin. I like it. 'I can't speak for other shop assistants but yeah, I've been known to bullshit. Those tea-light holders, though. They're really sweet. Your mum will be thrilled. If I take the price tag off, I can gift-wrap them now.'

'God, you're good.'

'Sometimes I can be really bad too.' Another grin but this one's unbelievably flirty. I am definitely *in* here.

While we have the place to ourselves, we make more small talk: this shop, this street, my lunch hour, my mum's love of flowers.

'I'm really sorry, Ned,' Nancy says suddenly, 'for rushing off like that. Outside the nightclub. I kicked myself as soon as I'd done it.'

'No worries.'

'*Yes* worries. It was shitty and shoddy. No excuse but I'd just broken up with my boyfriend, after four years together. You talking about your ex got to me. You could have been reading my mind, speaking my words, although I think you mentioned a daughter. Harry and I didn't – don't – have kids, thank God.'

'Dora. She's 8.' I resist the urge to show Nancy a fat file of photos on my phone. 'It was a shame you disappearing like that. Ten more minutes and I might have asked you out.'

'Well, we've been talking for at least twenty so you can ask me out twice now.'

'Okay, here goes. Fancy meeting up for a bite to eat some time?'

'Yes. Definitely. I really would.'

'Is Saturday too soon?'

'Saturday's perfect.'

I haven't forgotten that Dora's with me for the weekend, as per usual. I'll figure something out. Tanya can't stop me having a date, a life, maybe even a future.

I'll figure something out.

When I get back to my desk, Andy asks if I got my kettle? I'm amazed at my quick thinking.

'They didn't have the one I was after. I've ordered it.'

'A kettle is a kettle is a kettle. That's classic Nedward.'

I don't mind him taking the piss. I risk a quick smile to myself. I have a date on Saturday. With someone who fancies the pants off me. But, if mutual removal of pants is what Nancy has in mind, how will I 'perform', knowing Dora's in the next room and might report back to her mum?

Then I remember. Dora's best friend Bethany's mother, Verity, is always inviting her for a weekend sleepover. I've declined until now because my time with my best girl is precious and I love our Saturday evenings together: I love being the one to make her tea and tuck her in and be her dad. I text Verity to ask if Dora could possibly stay over this Saturday night and I get a practically instant 'yes!'

That's sorted, then. If all goes well, Nancy can sleep over

at mine. I'd really love to have her. More than once. If all goes well.

At six o'clock, Andy is at my desk, tapping his watch and cocking his head towards the lifts. I ignore him. He hates being ignored. Plus I'm trying to finish a bridge-building email to Denise in Ashford.

'SPAN,' he says, once I've pressed 'Send'. 'Well, come on, bud. Those single-parent mums won't chat *themselves* up.'

'Ros, you mean? You haven't got a hope in hell.'

'Like you'd know. Suddenly you're the expert on all matters ladeez related.'

I nearly say, 'Actually Andy, I've got two on the go right now.' Obviously I don't, though.

He's dead keen on Ros and, I won't lie, it would be good to see Gemma again. Plus I have a few issues to talk through with the other single parents: dating and confidence and, top of the list, trust issues with your ex. So, yeah, why not?

I feel bad. I do. Especially as Gail saw us all carousing in the Anchor bar and said 'Welcome back' to me and Andy. She doesn't need to put her heart and soul into SPAN but she does because she's a good person. And we're so obviously not, for doing a runner.

Andy, Ros and Gemma act as if they've just bunked off school. I'm the only one with a guilty conscience. I let it go. I don't wish to be tonight's designated whinger and, actually, this is fun. An unplanned Italian meal out with nice people.

Andy's on his best behaviour, Ros isn't falling for any nonsense from him and Gemma only takes the occasional pop at me. I've really warmed to her actually. She's funny, feisty and fearless; if anyone deserves some happiness, it's her. It turns serious in the blink of an eye when Ros brings up the difference between her and us. Breaking up with Tanya does sometimes feel like a kind of bereavement, but nobody died. I mustn't ever forget how lucky I am, compared to Ros. Even thick-skinned Andy gets it and that's a personal best for him.

As it turns out, we have a really enjoyable evening. I like these two. Andy's all over Ros like a rash and even offers to wait with her for a taxi.

'She is *so* out of his league,' Gemma reckons.

She's right. Andy isn't ideal boyfriend material at the best of times, and certainly not after the passing of the perfect husband.

I tell Gemma about my date on Saturday. She looks impressed. 'No need to be petrified, Ned. If she's as great as you say, you'll be fine. Just remember, she's probably petrified too.'

'By me? What's to be scared of?'

'Exactly. Nothing at all.' But she's obviously picked up on my anxiety, because then she adds, 'Look, why don't we swap numbers so that we can WhatsApp each other and compare notes: my dinner party, your date?'

'That would be great, Gemma. Seriously?'

'No, I'm just suggesting it to mess with your head, Ned. Of course, seriously. Why else would I say it?'

'Fair enough.'

I'm actually quite touched. Underneath her tough-guy act, Gemma's got a good heart, even if she tries to hide it most of the time.

And with that, she's off to pick up her son and head home to wherever it is she lives.

*

Much of the time, I don't know what to do with Dora on a Saturday. Either that or I compile a list of fun outings the length of Sussex and she turns her nose up at every one of them. Okay, we don't always have to be busy seeing things, doing things, but I don't want her to return to her mum's saying all we did was watch junk telly and eat junk food.

Today is different. Tanya told me yesterday that Dora would love a new party dress and she didn't suppose I'd be up for (aka capable of) choosing one with her. So that's what we'll do: shop for the dress, lunch somewhere nice, maybe a movie in the afternoon, then I'll take her to Verity's for her sleepover, and get ready for my hot date.

I might also buy myself a new shirt from somewhere a bit more edgy than M&S, to show Nancy I've made the effort. Brighton's full of high-end, trendy clothes shops, some too intimidating even to enter. I'm no good at knowing what suits me. That was always Tanya's job.

We're just doing our final wees before catching the bus into Brighton when my phone rings. I don't recognize the number. Oh God, it'd better not be bloody Julian, wanting to be best buds again.

It's Gemma. 'Sorry, I never rang you when I got home. You must have been wondering how it went.'

'Oh, hi. No. Yes. How what went? Ah, I know. The dinner party.'

'You'd forgotten all about it, hadn't you?'

'Kind of. Dora's here. I'm in dad mode.'

'Sorry. I didn't mean to disturb you. I'll let you get on.'

'No, no, you're not disturbing me. Your boy's at his dad's, isn't he?'

'I dropped him off last night. You were right, Ned. I was 100 per cent set up.'

'I knew it. Listen, have you got plans for today?'

She pauses to think about it. 'Let me see . . . sod-all this morning, followed by sod-all this afternoon. And bugger-all with a cherry on top tomorrow.'

'Do you fancy lunch with me and Dora? Or is sod-all too urgent?'

She laughs. I made Gemma laugh. 'Yeah, okay. See you at one at the Clock Tower.'

By 12.45, Dora has had two tantrums, ten minutes of self-pitying sobbing and a good hour of full-on, high-energy sulk. Now I know why Tanya wanted *me* to buy the dress. This is a test she knows I will fail. Just as Dora loves all things tacky and cheap, she will also zero-in on the nastiest, shiniest, pink-iest dress.

Anything *I* find on the rails is 'boring, Daddy' or 'not nice colour, Daddy' or 'I hate it, I hate it'. I kind of hoped I'd come across a frock that ticked both sets of boxes: shiny but tasteful, raspberry pink rather than bubble-gum pink. Not going to happen.

Gemma finds us perched on the wall by the Clock Tower, barely talking to each other.

'Hiya,' she says, in that super-friendly voice you use when you're trying to engage with a child. 'You're Dora. Like the explorer. I'm Gemma, like the . . . um, like the tremor.'

Dora forgets her sulk. 'What's a tremor?'

'It means "shaky",' I explain, not knowing where the hell we're going with this.

Gemma isn't put off. '"Shaky" as in "shaking hands". Pleased to meet you, Dora.'

She makes a big thing out of shaking Dora's hand and gets a gurgly giggle out of her. Which is more than I've managed all morning.

Dora's hungry so we go for lunch in a nearby cafe in the Arcade. I find them deep in conversation when I get back from the loo.

'But pink's my best colour,' Dora explains, as if to a fool.

'Mine too. I love pink cupcakes and pink fluffy slippers and pink lipstick but I prefer other colours for dresses. Red or blue or purple. That way, I don't look like all the other girls.'

Dora nods earnestly. 'My best friend Bethany loves pink. And Clara and Gracie.'

'All the more reason to be different, to stand out from the crowd.'

Over Dora's head, I give Gemma a double thumbs-up. This is brilliant.

'But it's your call, Bub,' I say, trying a bit of reverse psychology. 'If you want to look exactly the same as Bethany and Clara and Gracie, that's cool too.'

Dora has a little think. 'I can look at other colours. Then I'll choose the one I like best.'

'Good idea,' agrees Gemma. 'Now, who fancies a pink ham sandwich and a pink strawberry smoothie?'

I was actually up for a falafel wrap and a latte but daren't muddy the waters.

'So, Gemma. The dinner party at your ex's. Spill.'

She gives a brave little smile. I hope she wasn't humiliated by him or belittled by his new partner. She doesn't deserve that.

'It was all right, I suppose. Better than I'd expected. Amazing food. I looked pretty great, which helped. And yes, Ned, I know I'm a scruff-bag today but I can pull out the stops when I need to.'

'You don't look like a scruff-bag.' As I say it, I realize it's true: Gemma's actually really attractive, when she's not scowling or glowering.

'I did look great. I know I did. Joe was staring at me all evening. Vicky looked good too but a bit, I don't know, suburban.'

'Who did they set you up with?'

'Chris. He was really nice. Funny, good table manners, clean fingernails.'

'Bullseye.'

'Gay.'

Dora looks up from her Charlie and Lola book. 'Gracie's mum's gay. So's her other mum.'

'Gay?' I say. 'What was the point in that? Were they hoping you'd "turn" him?'

'He's Vicky's cousin. She thinks he's bi and just needs to meet the right woman. Me!'

I can tell Dora's about to ask what 'bi' is but fortunately our smoothies arrive and she's instantly distracted.

'So the set-up was a major fail.' I don't mean to laugh but I can't help it. Gemma laughs too.

'Yeah, well. I went, didn't I? I got a chance to see Joe and Vicky doing the whole host-and-hostess thing. I even caught up with my oldest friend, Hayley. We lost touch after the break-up.'

'There you go. You got something out of it.'

'God, no. She's too thick to be a proper bitch, just an accidental one. I'm much happier with Ros as my friend. We'd never have met if Joe hadn't dumped me. Or you two.'

'Me and Dora?'

'Okay, you three. Dora, Andy and you.'

Our sandwiches arrive. Dora eats everything, including the cucumber garnish. I suspect she wants to impress Gemma.

She even manages two scoops of pink ice cream while we idle over cappuccinos.

'Tell me about tonight, then,' Gemma asks, zipping her mouth to reassure me she'll be cryptic in Dora's presence.

'Dora's going for a sleepover with Bethany, aren't you, Bub? And I'm going out for a meal with my new friend, Nancy.'

'Are you looking forward to it?'

'Kind of. It's good to be out there again, whatever happens.'

'Where are you going? How will you act? What will you wear?'

'1) Marrocco's on Kingsway. 2) Like someone with confidence, ideally. 3) I thought I might buy a new shirt.'

She glugs back the last of her coffee. '1) Never heard of it. 2) Just don't be a dweeb. And 3) Let's find you the perfect shirt. And that dress for Dora. Well, come on.'

She drags us to TK Maxx and in about twenty minutes we're queuing to pay. I seem to be buying two shirts, both with designer labels, both half price. Dora is utterly in awe of the dress she chose, with Gemma's help, which is not shiny, not tacky and definitely not pink. It's dark turquoise velvet with long sleeves and a little white collar. She looks like a proper princess in it, not a Disney iteration. Best of all, she doesn't hate me anymore. Tanya will be gobsmacked.

There isn't enough time for a movie now and Gemma needs to be off. She said she had sod-all to do this weekend; I get the feeling she doesn't want to outstay her welcome. Shame. Like Andy before her, she's been quite the hit with Dora.

Just before she runs for her bus, she reminds me of our deal. 'Text if you need moral support tonight with Nancy. I can't tell you which fork to use with fish but I know how we women think and what we want from a date. Ring me, Ned, okay?'

I've never really had a female friend before, but – and this surprises me, after our rocky start – I really like Gemma. That bitter exterior hides a kind, sensitive soul with a wicked sense of humour. I'm actually pretty pleased that we stuck with it, after such a bad start, and got to know each other.

Marrocco's is filling up; I'm glad I booked a table. I'm fifteen minutes early, of course, which gives me time to decide if my new shirt should be tucked in or hung loose. I prefer tucked in, as a rule, but this one is fashionably short and keeps popping out anyway.

Gemma said I suit stripes so that's the one I'm wearing. The label says: Luigi Fontanelli. No idea who he is but it has to be a step up from my usual chain-store brands. The other shirt I bought is designed by someone French, Pierre Someone? It looked a bit old-fashioned but Gemma convinced me it's 'on trend'. I might take it back next week: this one will do just fine and I really don't need two 'going out' shirts. Unless Nancy and I have a second date, of course.

While I wait, I send Gemma a quick text: 'Wearing striped shirt. Untucked. Should I pay for meal or go Dutch? Not sure what's done these days. Help!'

Nancy is five minutes early, which I take as a good sign. She looks as if she's made an effort but not gone overboard. She's wearing a striped dress that could be a close cousin of my shirt. Is this a sign?

'Spooky,' she says. 'I nearly wore jungle-print trousers. If I had, maybe you'd have gone for something jungle-printy too.'

I laugh, even though I'd rather rock up stark-bollock naked than wear anything even remotely 'jungle-printy'.

I decide to throw caution to the wind and assume I'll pick up the bill for us both. I'm on a pretty decent salary these days, especially with the promotion, while Nancy's just a shop assistant.

I scan the menu. 'Ooh, spaghetti with seafood. Delicious. Actually, I should have asked: is this place okay for you? Do you have any dietary requirements? So many people do these days. My ex, Tanya, couldn't eat anything that was – Oh, bloody hell, I've started already.'

'What couldn't she eat?'

'No, really. Not important.'

'Harry was a fussy eater. He hated garlic and all veg, except sweetcorn and baked beans. Nothing leafy, *ever*. I think he must have been spooked by a caterpillar in some salad when he was a kid and he never got over it. What couldn't yours eat?'

'Aubergines, blue cheese and fudge. Not in the same dish, obviously. She'd say they didn't agree with her. There aren't many who'd dare to disagree with Tanya. But that's it. No more talk of exes. What do you fancy?'

We order quickly: olives, calamari to share, two spaghetti vongole and a bottle of Pinot Grigio. So far, so good. Nancy is amazing at eye contact. I try extra hard to return it, not something I'm comfortable with, but I don't want to look shifty.

'This is really nice, Ned,' she says, smiling straight at me. 'I've often thought about you, wondered how you were getting on.'

'You know what, I'm doing okay, all things considered. I'm loving my weekends with Dora. I'm looking to the future, rather than wallowing in the past. And I've just been promoted. By Karen. She's my boss. We get on really well, actually. At work, I mean. Nothing more than that.'

Note to self: stop rambling, you fool. Retain an air of mystery.

'She must love being with *you* too.'

'Karen? Only in a work setting, obviously. She's my boss.'

'I meant Dora. Hey, who's she with now? Did you get a babysitter?'

'Sleepover with her best friend, Bethany. Was that a thing when you were little? I hardly ever stayed the night at friends', back in the day. Or maybe it *was* a thing but I wasn't invited.'

She pats my hand. 'Oh, don't, Ned. You'll make me cry. I guess it's more popular now. Sleeping over's another thing altogether when you're a grown-up, isn't it?'

'Do you feel like a grown-up? I don't.'

'Sometimes. I'm nearly 30. It's bound to kick in soon.'

There are six rings of calamari so it's easy to share them out, three each. Nancy eats with gusto, which I find unfeasibly sexy. Then she mops the oily, lemony juices from the plate with a chunk of bread. That's quite the turn-on too.

It's going well. I honestly think it's going very well indeed. When Nancy pops to the loo, I ring Gemma. She hasn't replied to my query about splitting the bill. Plus I want to tell her that I'm having a great time.

'That's good. Have you said she looks nice yet?'

'Oh God, no. I should have done that when she arrived. Is it too late now? Will it look like an afterthought?'

'Just say it when the moment feels right. She'll have spent hours in front of her mirror, deciding what to wear.'

'And is it okay to pick up the tab? I can afford it. But I don't want to make her uncomfortable, like she's beholden to me.'

'Fucking hell, Ned. You sound like a character from Jane Austen. "Beholden" means "up for a shag", does it?'

'Course not. Well, only if she wants to. Dora's at Verity's, after all.'

Thank God I look up because Nancy's coming back from the loo. I hang up and shove my phone in my pocket. She gives me a quizzical smile as she sits down.

'Verity,' I gabble. 'Dora's friend Bethany's mum. Verity. Just checking-in with me.'

'Is there a problem? Is Dora okay?'

'She's fine. Can I top up your wine? I'll order another bottle to go with the spaghetti.'

Why did I lie? Why didn't I just say it was a friend asking if I'm having a nice evening? I could even have come clean and said: 'Listen, Nancy. I'm out of practice at this dating lark so I'm getting tips from a friend about bill-splitting. Thank you for your patience.'

The phone business does slightly break the moment. I was doing so well and now I feel rattled. Nancy's anxious too because she knows I was lying.

We're just getting our nerve back, with talk of bad holidays (me: Dubrovnik, her: Florida), loathed school subjects (me: German, her: Maths), celebrities we've met (me: Alan Titchmarsh, her: someone from *Game of Thrones*) when my phone buzzes in my pocket. Another text. It'll be Gemma with her expert opinion on going Dutch.

Nancy does another of her quizzical smiles. 'Shouldn't you get that?'

'Not urgent. I know Dora's fine so let's ignore it.'

More wine. More chat, now a little laboured. How old were we when we ate our first prawn, our first avocado? I tell Nancy about the time I put a fag end in my mouth at a party, thinking it was a peanut. No, I couldn't spit it out. Yes, I ate it. We're nearly back in the happy zone

181

again and, I'd like to think, Nancy is finding my ineptitude endearing.

Another text.

'Just answer it, will you?' Nancy snaps. 'It's like a car alarm going off every five minutes.'

It's Gemma. 'Deffo pick up tab. Forget about "beholden".'

'OK,' I text back. Now just go away.

Nancy has put down her cutlery and wiped her mouth, as if she's done eating, even though her plate is still heaving with vongole.

'I know where we're going with this,' she says, emotionlessly.

I don't. So I say, 'Oh?'

'I went on a blind date last month. It was a non-starter from the get-go. I'd planned for that, just in case. I got Melanie, my flatmate, to text me to say I had to rush home because she was locked out and I was the only one with a spare key. So what's *your* excuse for pulling the plug on tonight?'

'There isn't one.'

'I'd so like to believe you, Ned. But I'm very vulnerable at the moment and you're not making it easy.'

Time to come clean. 'It's my friend, Gemma. We both had dates this weekend. Well, hers was a dinner party at her ex's. Last night. And we said we'd ring or text each other if we needed to. I didn't. Need to. But she did anyway. Ring, I mean. That's not an excuse, Nancy. It's the truth.'

She doesn't believe me. 'You and Gemma said you'd ring each other if you needed to. Yeah, whatever. Look, I've got the beginnings of a migraine so I think I'll just head home. Finish my spaghetti, will you? Bye then.'

She pulls two £20 notes from her purse and flings them

on the table. Then she's gone. I don't finish her spaghetti. I don't even finish mine. I tell the waiter that my guest wasn't feeling well and then he thinks I'm saying that the food upset her and it all gets a bit sticky.

When I get home, I ring Gemma.

'Hey, Ned,' she says. 'Hang on, while I get my cup of tea, then you can tell me all about it. Is Nancy there? Have you gone back to yours – or hers – for Netflix and chill?'

'She went home. She said she had a migraine. Your non-stop texting spooked her.'

'Seriously? How?'

'She thought I'd got you to call me with some made-up excuse so I could abort the date.'

The line goes quiet and then I swear I hear Gemma trying to muffle her laughter.

'It isn't fucking funny, okay.'

'Sleep on it. It *will* be, tomorrow. Oh, I'm sorry, Ned. If she's such a sensitive little flower, you're best off without her. So, neither of us scored this weekend then. Not even close. Oh well, see you at SPAN? Night-night, matey.'

I'm still hungry so I eat cold tinned spaghetti on toast in front of the telly, using the bean-bag tray Mum gave me. Not the best evening, if I'm honest. Pretty disastrous, actually. And yes, I'd laugh along with Gemma, if it happened to someone else.

But it didn't.

Chapter Sixteen

Gemma

Judy has lost an earring. One of her favourites. She has a velvet musical jewellery box and it's stuffed to the hinges with necklaces, bangles, brooches and earrings. Every time I admire a pair, she'll say: 'Thank you, darling, they're my favourites.' They all have a story to tell and, since she moved into Willowdene and accepted that she'll die here, her earrings are a link to the life she led before she got poorly.

And what a life! If I get to do, in my three score years and ten, what Judy did in just 1965 or 2008, I'll know I've lived. If I can believe her – and why shouldn't I? – Judy has been a dancer, a wife, a travel rep, another wife, a widow, a civil servant, a dominatrix and a lollipop lady. I think she did those last two at the same time, before her cancer set in. She may even have had clients who paid extra for a seeing-to in the lollipop costume. She'd tell all if I asked. Every pervy detail. I love Judy.

This morning we've been in search of the missing earring. We've pulled her bed away from the wall – with her in it. We've taken everything out of her bedside table, de-cushioned her armchair and scrabbled around in the bottom of her wardrobe. When I say 'we', I mean 'me' . . . with Judy bellowing orders, like I'm her own personal maid.

'Did you look in every shoe box, Gemma? And my handbags. Try the snakeskin one. I found $180 in there once. God knows where it came from.'

I sigh. I haven't the heart to remind her she hasn't used a handbag since she got here and, although she owns some amazing shoes, she only ever wears slippers.

'Show me it again,' I ask, to give myself a breather. 'The earring you've still got.'

'For God's sake, darling. Vivien next-door's got a better memory than you and *she* thinks she's married to Boris Becker.'

She holds it up. It's a lairy, multicoloured rhinestone clip-on. It's very ugly. It's very Judy. 'Got that, have you, ka-ka-for-brains?'

I pretend to look shocked.

'And now *you* say, "Find it yourself, you old bag, if you're going to insult me."'

'Or I could just flounce out in tears.'

'You wouldn't dare. It's your job to indulge me.'

I flop in the chair by her bed. 'Let's stop looking. That way, it's bound to turn up.'

'Unless someone stole it.'

'Good point. I'll keep an eye out for any one-eared residents.'

She searches through her jewellery box. 'I'll just have to wear these, then. They're my favourites. What do you think?'

Diamanté pineapples. Felipe would love them.

'Perfect. It's gammon with pineapple for lunch so you're very on trend.'

She giggles and I can see the 18-year-old strawberry-blonde

bombshell who broke hearts when she did summer seasons in Cromer.

I'm about to get up – Janine's on the warpath – when my phone jumps in my pocket. I stay seated and take the call.

'Hey, hi, Gemma. It's Dan. How's the wardrobe?'

Dan . . . Dan . . .? Oh yes, Flatpack Dan, King of the Allen key.

'Hi, Dan, what is this? Customer feedback?'

'Kind of. I ought to do it more often. So is it still standing? The wardrobe, I mean?'

'It is. It opens and closes and it doesn't even wobble.'

Judy looks up from her earrings. I give her a 'none of your business' frown, which intrigues her all the more.

'Great. I wouldn't want to be known for wobbling wardrobes.'

There's a pause. Neither of us speaks. Is that all he wanted to know?

'Is that all you wanted to know? Only I'm at work right now.'

'Don't mind me, darling,' Judy bellows from her bed. 'Just pretend I'm not here.'

'Who's that?' Dan asks, slightly spooked.

'No one. Talk later, okay? Got to go. Bye.'

I know I won't be able to leave without telling Judy more.

'Dan. I knew him twenty years ago. He put together a wardrobe for Kelvin's room and wanted to know if it was still standing.'

'You fancy him something rotten or else why would you have gone all red?'

'That's where you're wrong, clever clogs. It's *him* who fancies *me*.'

'Doesn't explain your flushed cheeks, darling. He's phoned

about the wardrobe but really, he's dying to ask you out. Am I right or am I right?'

'Are you nosy or are you nosy?'

'I *am* right. I know I am. Go. Meet him for a drink. Bask in his admiration. It's the best feeling in the world, being wanted. There might even be some hanky-panky in it, which would take the clench out of those shoulders. If you *don't* go out with him, I'll tell Janine you stole my earring.'

Sausage casserole for tea. I tore the recipe out of a magazine in the doctor's waiting room when I was pregnant and now it's my stand-by, never-fails, signature dish. Comforting and filling. With a big splodge of buttery mash on the side. I dish up two platefuls and bring them through so that Kelvin and I can eat off our laps in front of *The Simpsons*. My kind of evening. Just me and him and ice cream for afters.

But the TV is muted and Kel's chatting away on *my* phone. Probably Joe. He always rings when we're eating.

'Here she is,' says Kelvin, beaming at me. 'My mum who paid you to put my wardrobe together and then pretended *she'd* done it. Would you like to speak to her?'

He holds out the phone. He's loving this. I've been caught out and it's a fair cop. He takes his dinner, unmutes *The Simpsons* and settles on the sofa.

'Hi, Dan,' I say, walking him into the kitchen. 'Thanks a bunch for dobbing me in.'

'How was I to know you'd taken the credit? It's pretty funny, actually.'

'Yeah, well. I like Kelvin to think I can do everything. Supermum, that's me.'

'Nobody can do everything. You should cut yourself some slack.'

He's right. I'm being lectured by a man I barely know, who I haven't seen in years, and he's picked up on my insecurities, the bastard.

'I've pissed you off, haven't I?' he says sheepishly.

'Kind of. Kelvin will love this.'

'He sounds like a nice kid. You've done a good job, Supermum.'

'He is. And I have, no thanks to Joe. Have you really only rung to check on my wardrobe?'

'Yes.'

'And you ring *every* customer? Twice? You should email a standard feedback form. Much less hassle on your part.'

He gives a weary sigh. 'Bloody hell, Gemma, do you give everyone a hard time like this? Or have I done something to deserve it?'

'Sorry. I'm pulling your leg. I'll stop now. The wardrobe's a huge success and Kelvin loves it. Maybe a bit less, now that he knows you made it, not me.'

'That's good. Another satisfied customer. But after all the grief you've given me, I'm wondering if I should just quit while I'm ahead.'

'Quit what?'

'Saying it was great to see you after all these years. Telling you what an arse Joe is, but you know that already.'

'Oh, I do.'

'Good.'

'Anything else? Only my sausage casserole's getting cold.'

'I've started so I'll finish. Do you fancy meeting for a drink sometime?'

I know I should say yes. I want to say yes.

'Yes.'

I catch a reflection of myself in the door of the microwave.

I'm smiling. Dan's really keen. Someone other than Joe wants to spend time with me.

'Good. That's – no, I mean, that's very good.' He sounds surprised. 'Are you free on Thursday?'

Am I free? Am I free? Apart from SPAN and Ros on a Wednesday, my kitchen calendar is blank until Christmas.

'Let's see, Thursday . . . Thursday. Yes, I can do Thursday.'

'Nice one. How about we meet in the Mesmerist on Prince Albert Street at half seven?' He sounds relieved. I shouldn't have given him such a grilling.

I have a date. Judy would be proud of me.

Kelvin's practically licked the pattern off his plate by the time I zap some heat back into my casserole and rejoin him on the sofa.

'Remember when I made you a pot stand,' he says, 'and you really liked how I'd painted it. Only Mohit had done it and I didn't tell you and then you found out and you were really annoyed with me because I should have told you.'

'Yes?'

'*That.*' He grins. 'Can I have my ice cream now or do I have to wait for you?'

Probably out of guilt, I let Kelvin watch half an hour of *Top Gear* before bedtime while I rerun my conversation with Dan. I knew he'd call. I may be out of the dating loop, I may not be as gorgeous and amazing as Ros, but someone out there fancies me. And it's a proper person, not my ex.

I can't expect Mohit's mum to look after Kelvin two nights running, though. And I won't give up Wednesday with Ros. These days, I can take or leave SPAN but I love hanging out with her. I know I'll have a couple of hours of grown-up talk, a glass or three of wine and a laugh. It's actually medicinal. It lifts my spirits. I *will not* miss it.

And I won't ask Joe and Vicky to have Kel on the Thursday because I just bloody won't.

I need someone to babysit my boy and my support circle is non-existent. I should have thought of this before I said yes to Dan. It's times like this I miss my mum and dad more than ever. Mum died before I met Joe. Dad at least got to be a grandad for the first two years of Kel's life.

Then I have a brilliant idea. If I offer to babysit Dora for Ned next time *he's* got a hot date, maybe he can come here on Thursday and keep Kelvin company. I'm pretty sure they'd get on and it would be good for Kel to see that not all dads are macho, self-absorbed, bullying bastards.

I phone him with my proposition and he says yes, which is a relief. He doesn't see any hot dates on the horizon after his disaster with Nancy. I'd forgotten about her. Poor old Ned. He's even more out of practice than me.

I know I'll be nervous on Thursday, keeping cool and in control, not screwing up like Ned did. I can wear what I wore to Vicky and Joe's because it gave me cleavage *and* confidence. My dating suit of armour.

Plus Dan majorly fancies me so I'll let him do all the heavy lifting.

I can't remember who suggests it first, me or Ros. Maybe we say it at the same time: 'Let's not bother with SPAN and just go for a pizza, like we did last week.' I get so much more sense and support from her than I do from Gail's gang of losers and I'd like to think she does from me too, even if it means missing the latest episode in Meryl's soap-opera saga with her ex.

So we steer clear of the Anchor and meet at the restaurant we went to last week with Ned and Andy.

The waiter recognizes us and gives us 'our usual table'. He also brings two glasses of Cava on the house. It has to be because Ros is so gorgeous. I bet this happens to her wherever she goes. I'm not jealous, not if I get a free drink out of it.

'Are the gentlemen joining you?' the waiter asks and we have to think for a minute. We don't know any gentlemen. Ah, he means Ned and Andy.

'Not tonight,' I tell him. I'm a bit disappointed not to see Ned. Only because I wanted to find out more about his disastrous date. We order quickly so we can launch straight into catch-up mode.

Ros chinks my glass. 'Guess what? Sweetcakes has a new customer. A hundred gold-frosted cupcakes, to launch an ad agency. Friend of a friend so I mustn't screw up. A hundred!'

'Wow, well done, you.'

'I just need to juggle my time more effectively. I can bake a batch a day and freeze them. *And* I pushed the boat out and bought a new chest freezer. They do say "speculate to accumulate"; my old one kept icing up. If I get a few more regular jobs, it'll be time to expand the kitchen. Turn it into a proper business space. New oven, walk-in larder, island unit, the lot.'

'That's brilliant, Ros. You so deserve Sweetcakes to take off.'

'I do. For me, for Gabe. Even for David, in a weird way. Is that too weird?'

'Not at all.'

'It'll mean I have no social life, apart from our Wednesday nights. I can't annoy any of my regular gigs by sidelining them.' She looks anxious as she chomps on a bread stick. My turn to be supportive.

'I can't bake to save my life, Ros. But as long as you keep an eye on me, I can be a spare pair of hands if you're up against it. Or I can look after Gabe. You know I'm always kicking my heels at the weekend.'

'Depends how crap you are. Thanks, Gem. I might take you up on that. At least this job gives me a genuine excuse to knock back Andy. That guy is so persistent. He's always sending me texts, memes, messages, funny GIFs. Look.'

She scrolls through WhatsApp and it's all Andy, post after post after post.

'Is he wooing you or stalking you?'

'He's harmless. Just mystified that I don't want to go out with him.'

'Why not? Go on a date. Meet him for a drink. Bask in his admiration. It's the best feeling in the world, being wanted.' I'm parroting Judy, whose advice I seem to have taken.

'Seriously? Andy? He'll think I'm interested and, honestly, Gem, I couldn't be more not. Ooh, here come the arancini.'

I nearly keep quiet about Dan. I don't know why. But if I don't share my news with Ros, who can I tell: Kelvin? Judy? . . . Joe?

I choose a roundabout route. 'If you *do* go ahead with your kitchen. You know, making it bigger, better for your business. If you do go ahead, I can recommend a guy. Flatpack Fred but his name's Dan. He did Kelvin's wardrobe and he's a really nice guy and he tidied up after himself and he used to be a mate of Joe's and . . . he asked me out.'

Ros stops eating. Her eyes widen. Her jaw drops.

'What?' I snap defensively. 'D'you think he did it for a laugh? Or Joe put him up to it? God, what if Joe put him up to it? I can't go. I'll tell him I'm ill.'

I wait for a reply. Our arancini go cold. Ros looks sad. Ah, so she *does* think I'm being set up. Bloody great.

'Oh, Gemma. He really has fucked with your head, hasn't he, that ex of yours?'

Not just my head, I nearly reply. Ros must never know. 'Meaning?'

'Meaning you're your own worst enemy. What if Dan's asked you out because he fancies you? Has that even occurred to you?'

'It has. A bit. The Joe thing trumped it. That he was getting his own back at me, for not . . . for not . . . for not respecting him any more. For seeing him for the selfish sod he is. That must really get to him.'

'Good. I'm glad.' Ros tops up my glass. 'Forget about Joe and concentrate on Dan. He fancies you. Do you fancy him?'

'Yeah, maybe. He did a great job on Kelvin's wardrobe.'

Ros hoots with laughter. 'He's good with his hands. Well, that's a start. When are you seeing him?'

'Tomorrow. Just for a drink. Not a meal or anything. I asked Ned to sit in with Kelvin for the evening. You don't think that's a mad idea, do you?'

'Ned's one of the good guys. *And* pretty damn cute too. Now if it was *him* sending me flirty messages every five minutes, I might be tempted. He just needs some of Andy's chutzpah. Ned's definitely the cute one, right?'

I shrug and bite into my second arancini. To be honest, I hadn't really noticed.

Thursday night and I'm all set. I'm still not sure if Dan's the man for me, but does it matter? It's a night out and I'm owed so many since the divorce. I put on the dress I wore to Joe and Vicky's, then take it off again. Too dressy, too keen. My best jeans and a dark red M&S shirt will do just fine. I put on low-key make-up and create a few curls with my ancient tongs. Yes. Good.

Kel knows who I'm meeting and is surprisingly cool about it. 'You look nice, Mum. Why isn't Wardrobe Guy coming here?'

'He lives in Portslade so we're meeting in town. You'd look nice too if you'd only put a comb through your hair.'

'Why? I'm not going anywhere.'

'What will Ned think?'

He shrugs. Not even worth answering. Kelvin reckons he's old enough not to need a babysitter so I take care never to call it that. Ned's coming over to 'keep him company'. Kelvin's sensible for his age but he's still a kid. Sometimes I don't want him to grow up because he'll go off to uni and I'll be all alone and he won't need me any more. And then I hate myself for being so needy and weedy and pathetic.

Ned texted earlier to ask about parking. And was there anything he should bring, to entertain Kelvin?

'Park on drive. Something about steam trains. He's doing a project.'

Ned replied with three giant thumbs-ups. I hope he isn't *too* enthusiastic. Kel doesn't do enthusiasm; he inherited that from Joe.

At 7.10 on the dot, I see a Kia covered in seagull crap pull up outside the bay window. Ned is here. I have six minutes to do the introductions and show him where to find tea bags before running for my 7.24 bus. No chance to ask for the gory details about his date with Nancy then!

Kelvin *has* put a comb through his hair, as instructed. Ned hasn't. Kelvin gives me a knowing 'duh-uh' look but I think he's pleased to see that Ned will be a pushover.

'Kelvin. Hi,' Ned says, with a cheery smile. 'Your mum tells me you're doing a steam-train project.'

'Yeah?' Kelvin replies suspiciously.

'I love steam trains. Have you been on the Bluebell Railway? Or the train at Amberley? I took Dora there a few weeks ago. My little girl. They filmed one of the James Bonds at Amberley. Can't remember which one now. In a chalk pit. I'm not a big Bond fan myself. I prefer futuristic stuff and sci-fi. Have you seen *Avatar*? That has to be in my top five of films of all time . . .'

I leave them to it, before I can worry about what Kel will make of Ned. Just because I think Ned's a really nice guy doesn't mean he's going to be a hit with my son.

Dan is squeezed into a space at the busy pub bar, checking his watch. I'm only ten minutes late – bloody buses – but it's enough to worry him that I've stood him up. That gives me a bit of a boost, a sense of power. I should be late more often.

His face, though, when he sees me. It isn't just relief. It lights up. It really does. Did Joe's face ever light up? It must have done. In the beginning . . .

'Here you are then,' he says with a happy smile.

'Here I am.'

'Right. A drink. Let me get you a drink. Can I get you a drink? What would you like?'

He's all of a fluster. I'm loving it. 'White wine please. I'd find us a table but it's chocka in here.'

'White wine. Right. It is. Chocka, I mean. I nearly got us bar stools twenty minutes ago but that bloke beat me to it.'

Dan's been waiting twenty minutes. No wonder he's flustered.

'Actually, I have a plan,' he says.

'Dan, Dan, he's the man with a plan.'

He laughs. He's starting to relax. 'Let's give up on drinks here. I did some work for a bar round the corner a few months back and Jonah, the owner, said the cocktails are on him whenever I'm passing. Only I've never passed until now. What do you say?'

Fifteen minutes later, we're sitting in a cosy Fifties-style booth in a proper hipster hangout, working our way through an iced jug of mojitos. Dan looks dead pleased with himself for bringing us here. He's even more chuffed when Jonah delivers a platter of chicken wings, some fierce guacamole and a stack of nachos. All of it on the house.

'Do you see much of the old crowd?' he asks, topping up my tumbler.

'Hardly. Do you?'

'Claire and Keith a few times a year. That fizzled out when me and Nicola split up. I suppose I didn't care enough to keep the friendship going.'

'I caught up with Hayley recently. Remember Hayley?'

'Not exactly the sharpest knife in the drawer, was she? Oh God, are you still best mates?'

'She knew Joe was screwing around but she kept schtum. She could have sided with me when I found out. But she didn't. And then just to rub salt in the wound, she buddied up with Vicky. So, no. Hayley and I are history. Her loss. I saw her at Joe and Vicky's. Can you believe it – Vicky invited me round to theirs for dinner?'

'That's good, isn't it? You've all drawn a line and moved on. And I don't have to thump Joe next time I see him . . .'

'Be my guest. Vicky wants us to be mates. Me and her. Plus she was keen to set me up with her cousin, Chris. That's why I was invited.'

'Ah.' Dan frowns. Is he wondering if he's got a rival? 'And was it a match, you and the cousin?'

'We really got on, actually. I liked him from the off.'

'Clever old Vicky.'

I could come clean and tell Dan that Chris has found his Mr Right in Cardiff and I'm still a free agent. I don't. Let him think I'm swatting away admirers like flies. Chris would approve, I'm sure.

'How was it, seeing Vicky and Joe in their own place? Did it help you to move on?'

Good question. I like that Dan can see it from my point of view.

'It was fine. Vicky's a nice woman and Joe's . . . Joe. No change there. It was all a bit, I don't know, "suburban" for me, which is funny because a few years ago, I'd have loved a house like theirs, a life like theirs.'

Dan abandons his half-gnawed chicken wing. 'Back when we were kids, I never thought I'd have grey hair, wear slippers, actually *like* slippers. I thought we were all charmed, special, forever young. And I thought you and Joe were the golden couple out of all of us.'

'More than Claire and Keith?'

'Way more. You two were so great together. You matched each other: looks, confidence, drinking capacity, the lot.'

'I had hollow legs back then. I've only had two mojitos and I'm already feeling drunk. Are you?'

'A bit.'

'We reckoned we were special too, me and Joe. We were a bit smug, probably, thinking we'd cracked it so young and we'd never be single again. Well, Joe hasn't ever been single because he moved straight on to Vicky. But I bloody am.'

'Join the club. I never actually thought me and Nic were

set for life. Nothing's a cert, is it? But I didn't think I'd be dating again in my nearly-forties.'

'Are you dating now, then?'

'I'd like to think this is a date. Am I wrong?'

'You're not. But are you, you know, "out there"?'

He has a little chuckle, like there's a long answer and a short answer. 'I signed up to a dating app a couple of months ago because that's what you do, right, when you're ready to be "out there" again. I got bombarded by women. Not in a flattering way. Single men under 80 who look semi-okay are really in demand.'

'Why did you ask *me* out, then?'

'Because I fancied you when I was 17 and I had very good taste. Then and now.'

We smile at each other. I knew it. Then and now.

'Good answer,' I tell him eventually. 'If we finish this jug, do we get another freebie?'

Dan waves it in the air and Jonah gives a nod from the bar. Result!

He settles in his seat, pleased with how it's all going. 'I'll tell you about my last date, shall I? And why I'm so pleased I ran into you.'

'Go on then.'

'Jodi. Artist. Bright red hair. Mid-thirties. Drop-dead gorgeous in her photo, like a Sixties film star. So many of the women who've been in touch scared me because they were so keen. Jodi was laidback, funny, well worth meeting.'

'But? There's a "but", isn't there.'

'Everything was great about her except – you're going to hate me for this but just hear me out. Everything was great . . . apart from her boobs.'

Despite the alcohol, I'm lost for words.

'Fake. *So* fake. They looked like two grapefruit. And she had one of those dresses with a low, scoopy front, so all you could see was boobs, acres and acres of them.'

'I thought you lot liked big boobs.'

'Me lot? Which lot's that? Put it this way, I like *real* boobs, proper boobs, soft boobs. The thing is, I couldn't take my eyes off them, but not for the right reasons. And she thought I was keen but I really, really wasn't.'

He's laughing as he tells me this and pretty soon I've joined in, until I think white rum is going to come shooting out of my nose.

'Why do women do that?' he asks, when we've both recovered. 'And puffed-up lips and those eyebrows that look like caterpillars?'

'I don't do that,' I say.

'You really don't and it's brilliant.'

'So how did you leave it with Jodi?'

'I told her I'd bumped into an old friend and I needed to find out how she felt about me. It's not bullshit either because I have, haven't I?'

'Looks like it.'

We kiss. We actually kiss in the bar and we don't even notice when Jonah brings over a fresh jug of mojitos.

I don't know if it's flattery or drink or just the sheer novelty of being kissed, and being reminded of the 'me' I used to be . . . but I feel fantastic.

Then I remember I've been out over three hours and it's a school night and Ned's still with Kelvin and what if they hate each other and I need to separate them?

I turn into Cinderella, grabbing my bag and telling Dan I have to go home. We walk to North Street, where I'm more likely to find a cab. We kiss again. Now I feel old, silly and self-conscious.

'Are you sure I can't come with you?' Dan asks. 'Just to make sure you get home okay. You are a bit smashed.'

'No,' I say. 'No, I'm fine. I need to send the babysitter home. Well, it's a friend really, not a – it's a friend. And make sure Kelvin isn't playing Minecraft under his duvet because I'm not there to pull the plug. I need to get home, Dan. Sorry.'

The cab comes so quickly that there's no time for a final kiss. I fling myself into the back seat and bark 'Bevendean' at the driver. I suddenly feel sick.

I need to get home right now, and not just to check on Ned and Kelvin.

Chapter Seventeen

Ned

Some bright spark from the Basingstoke office sends me additional subsections to the Welby-Daniels report. Nearly a month late and it reads like it was written by a toddler on a Go-To-Work-With-Mummy day. Of course, it's muggins here who has to consolidate it into the finished document, updating a reference here, inserting an addendum there. Bloody inconsiderate and highly unprofessional. Having said that, it's hardly challenging work and if I play my cards right, I should be able to spin it out all week.

I know Andy wants to debrief about his weekend. Has he made any headway with Ros? He is so out of his league with her. Anyone can see that. Anyone but Andy. Mind you, when he goes for something, he invariably gets it. I find his success rate inexplicable but then I've never been a very good reader of the female psyche. Tanya can confirm that and frequently did.

So I plug in earphones, as if I'm transcribing something important, and every time Andy's head bobs up over the partition for a chat, I bat him away with a harried, dismissive wave.

I'm just relieved I didn't tell him in advance about my

date with Nancy. I'd have got the full Andy lecture on 'What the Laydeez Like', from favourite aperitif to most responsive G-spot. Who wouldn't want a lecture from Hove's answer to the Walrus of Love? Worse still, if he knew I'd been out with Nancy, he'd want to know how it went, did I try that eye-contact-plus-earnest-nod thing and was she insatiable in the sack?

It's bad enough that Gemma laughed at my disastrous date, even though she was actually the reason it went tits up. Okay, I shouldn't have been so shifty every time my phone beeped but I didn't want it to look like I had someone on hand, phone-a-friend style, to talk me through the evening. I can blame Gemma for not being very sympathetic to how it went but I only have myself to blame for being such an idiot. Old Ned is harder to shed than I thought.

I take a break from Welby-Daniels – these amendments are infuriating – and do a google search of 'female psyche'. There must be a book out there that I can leave on the cistern and dip into when I'm on the lav. Nothing heavy or psychological. Nothing written by a bitter woman (probably admired by Tanya!), which is likely to drain away what little confidence I'm clinging on to. Just a simple guide to making emotional headway every day. Letting the good outcomes outweigh the bad choices.

And here it is. It's called *This is Now: New Moves for the New You* and apparently Oprah loves it, *Grazia* serialized it and a Little Mix member has made it her bible. Best of all, it's geared towards women. How can that not be an invaluable aid to a dopey man like me?

I nip out at lunchtime and find *This is Now* splashed across Waterstones' front window. It must be the one to read if it's getting such full-on coverage. I buy a copy without even opening it. (I shall ignore my tendency to buy how-to books, then shove them on a shelf where they will gather dust and have to work by osmosis.)

I do read the blurb on the back and I'm inspired. I *will* become 'my own best support system'. I *will* 'create strategies that source a sense of self'. I bloody will.

Back at the office, with a Subway melt, some Haribo fried eggs and a banana smoothie to stave off any afternoon rumblings, I think about getting back to the Welby-Daniels amendments but put off the moment with a quick scroll though my messages.

It's mostly boring: alerts from my bank; a new film I might like on Netflix; a nudge from Gail at SPAN hoping to see me again on Wednesday, when they'll be discussing how to get through birthdays and bank holidays as a single parent. I think not.

. . . and a WhatsApp message from Tanya. 'We're having a little party on Sunday. Hope you can come. Do bring a plus-one. Your friend from the Ivy? 2 p.m. onwards. Dress code: wear something bright.'

I reread it a couple of times, looking for any snarky subtext or little digs. This is my conclusion:

- 'We're' is a gentle reminder that she and Julian are a 'we'. I hadn't forgotten.
- 'Sunday . . . 2 p.m. onwards'. Well, I return Dora every Sunday afternoon so I'd be a special brand of plank to drop my daughter off and *not* pop in for a Pimm's and some griddled sweetcorn.
- 'Your friend from the Ivy?' Ha! My Sunday lunch date with Karen must really have needled Tanya. No idea why.

I can't invite Karen. It doesn't feel right. And I blew it with Nancy. She'd have been the perfect date for this. I suppose, at a pinch, I could ask Gemma. She scrubs up well and I'd value her take on the Tanya/Julian set-up. Shame about Nancy though.

- 'Wear something bright.' Is that a Tanya or a Julian instruction? Will guests be turned away if they rock up in beige? How tempted am I to go as a Goth?
- And finally . . . does she *really* want me to come or is she just flagging up how settled she is in her new life with Julian? 'Look at my lovely home, look at my lovely friends. See how well it's worked out for one of us. And it ain't you!'

I do a quick RSVP. 'Thanks. We'd love to.' Just that. (There's a chapter in my book called 'Less is More'. And it's true: less really is more. New Ned is fighting back.)

The next day, I have a noon meeting with Karen. She's long ago moved on from Welby-Daniels but will need to know that it's all in hand and she needn't concern herself with it.

I nip to the loo at 11.55 to have a quick wee – she still makes me super-nervous – and to check I don't have toothpaste in my hair. All good. When I poke my head around her office door, she's putting on her jacket.

'That building site across the road is so noisy. Let's get out for an hour and have a working lunch.'

I was intending to repeat yesterday's excellent Subway/Haribo/smoothie combo, or pasty and chips with Andy, but Karen's my boss and isn't someone you can easily say no to. Very much like Tanya, in that regard.

We choose a Chinese place round the corner that does a set lunch for £8.95. To be precise, Karen chooses. I'm not good with noodles and tofu. I hate chopsticks but don't like the patronizing look you get from waiters if you ask for a spoon. It's also her idea that we each have a Tsingtao beer which is guaranteed to have me snoring at my desk by three. Again, I don't desist because I'm nervous.

Why has she brought me here? What does she want from me? Will Welby-Daniels come back to haunt me if I don't get these late revisions up to spec? Above all, it's imperative that I prep with deep breaths in order to protect my emotional epidermis (Chapter 5, *This is Now*).

'All good your end?' she asks, crunching on a prawn cracker that I know for a fact has never seen the sea in its life; I read an article.

'Work-wise, you mean? Oh yes, everything's ticking over nicely as it happens. I've put Andy in charge of the Tunbridge Wells project. It's a bit unwieldy, in terms of capacity and infrastructure, but I figure he needs a chance to show us what he can do. Plus there's zero collateral damage if he comes up short. Which he won't, if I keep an eye on him.'

Listen to me. Can I talk the talk or what?

'Don't overload him, Ned. Andy can be way too cocky for his own good. That's why *you* got promoted and *he* didn't.'

'Absolutely. I'll check in with him on a daily basis, catch any glitches.'

'Yes, do. Actually, I meant is all good with you, life-wise? Part of my role as line manager is to make sure my staff are okay. We're both divorced so I know that can take a while to recover from.'

'True.'

'Now that you've seen my ex in all his glory, well, you'll know that it's not been a bed of roses for *me*.'

'How's your daughter, by the way?' I may have forgotten her name but my concern's genuine.

'Doing her best. That's all I can ask. Hattie knows I'm there for her, if she needs me. I have no wish to molly-coddle her.'

I try to pick up a spring roll with chopsticks and watch it land with a splash of sweet and sour sauce on Karen's plate. With any luck, she'll think I did that on purpose.

'I'm fine,' I tell Karen, rewinding to her question. 'I'm doing really well, all things considered.'

'That's good. You know you can always come to me if you need to offload.'

My instinct says 'no way' but I give an appreciative nod to show willing.

'You can come to me even if you *don't* need to offload, Ned. I think we've established that we fit well together, away from a workplace setting.'

I'm not sure what Karen's getting at, so I concentrate on spearing a slippery slice of beef. Actually, I have a very good idea what she's getting at and it's making me feel slightly uncomfortable.

'What do you think?' she asks, letting her food go cold. 'Shall we pick up where we left off?'

'Office relationships, though, Karen. Remember Barry Richards and Ellie Something? It didn't do either of them any favours when they were found out. I'd hate our careers to go into freefall because of what we do out of office hours.'

'Agreed, relationships can ruin careers, if they're serious. Barry Richards and Ellie Something were both married, weren't they? And it went on for years, with everyone knowing about it. Not a good look for either of them. Relationships can be secret but they needn't be serious. They don't even have to be proper relationships.'

This is not good. I decide silence is my best response. I chew on some beef; it's remarkably tough so I can't reply anyway.

'All I'm saying, Ned, is that a purely physical, mutually beneficial arrangement need go no further than your mattress or mine. We're both single, sensible, sexual people. Who can it hurt? No one.'

I don't want to turn her down. That would be ungentlemanly. Plus I have a terrible fear that she'd exact revenge, like transferring me to the mad house that's our Southampton office. Bodies are buried there. Opioid habits have started there. Careers have ended there. Doesn't Ellie Something work in their finance department?

My head says: no. My dick says: think about it. Old Ned would accept her kind invitation because he felt cornered and he needed validation via sex. New Ned must stand firm, albeit not literally.

'I've got a girlfriend,' I say, in a slightly high-pitched voice.

'Ooh, this is new. Tell all.'

I've started so I have to see this through, but I need to do it in a way that will cause Karen the least discomfort. 'Nancy. Her name's Nancy. We met a while back, then reconnected recently. Early days but it's going well. Nancy. Yes.'

I'm impressed with her composure. She doesn't seem too fussed that I've turned down her kind offer. Maybe she thinks I can be Nancy's boyfriend *and* her fuck buddy.

'I'm pleased for you, Ned. That's great news. All I will say is: take it slowly. The first relationship after a messy divorce is invariably not The One. I know that to my cost.'

'It seems to be working for my ex.'

'So far. Seriously. Protect your heart. It will break more easily the second time around.'

I promise Karen I will. Nancy deserves that much at least. For a mad moment, I even think she *is* my girlfriend but I've screwed up that option twice now.

I do silently thank her for saving me today, though.

Andy has commanded me to meet him in the Anchor at 8 p.m. Which means, if I'm lucky, he'll amble in at half past. I wouldn't normally jump to his tune but I have nothing else planned for a quiet Tuesday night, apart from corned beef with spicy rice and a leisurely scroll through Netflix.

Karen's proposal did stir the old loins and I'd be lying if I didn't fantasize about us naked on top of her desk, with pages from the Welby-Daniels report stuck to our clammy arse cheeks. I'm only human.

My instinct was instant: to say no, even if I had to tell a whopper in the process. And not just because Karen's my boss. Beneath that scary carapace is a sensitive soul and nobody likes to be rejected. But mostly because she's my boss. I don't thrive on risk taking or thrill seeking. Quite the contrary. It may make me predictable, boring even, but there are worse crimes. My emotional epidermis will thank me.

I'm at the Anchor on the dot of eight. I've brought *This is Now* to read while I await Andy. It's a bit cringey in places but, if I only pick up ten good tips from it, it will be worth the £12.99. Chapter 2: 'Mistakes Make us Human, Regrets Help us Learn'. So far, so cheesy.

My phone rings. It's Gemma. We haven't been in touch since she laughed at my disastrous date with Nancy. I'm minded to bear a grudge but, honestly, what's the point? It's done with. Mistakes make us human.

'How are you?' I ask.

'Yeah, good. Pretty good actually. Guess what, I've got a date.'

'Hey, well done, Gemma. That's great. Good for you.'

'Are you patronizing me?'

'Course not. I didn't mean it to sound like that. Who's the lucky guy? Is it a guy?'

'It's a guy. I'm not turning lesbian just yet. It's Dan. I told you about him. We knew each other years ago and, well, he asked me out.'

'My advice: avoid all texts from "helpful" friends.'

She laughs. I let her. 'It's just I need someone to keep Kelvin company. Not a babysitter because he's not a baby, but I don't like leaving him alone either. And I don't really have anyone else to ask . . . So I wondered, could you maybe do it, Ned, if I promise to babysit Dora next time *you've* got a date?'

I'd be a complete bastard if I said no. So I say yes. I nearly ask her if she wants to come to Tanya and Julian's party with me on Sunday but I'll wait till the weekend. Who doesn't love a last-minute invitation?

Fifteen minutes elapse and still no Andy. This is unusual, even by *his* standards. I'm about to buy another pint when in walks, of all people . . . Nancy. This can't be her local. Didn't she say she lived in Seven Dials? She isn't meeting someone because she heads straight over to me, as if she knew I'd be here. What's going on?

'Hi, Ned,' she says, with a relaxed smile. 'What can I get you?'

While she's fetching our drinks, I try to think this through. Has Andy set me up? He's not coming but Nancy is? I wouldn't put it past him.

She returns with two lagers and a packet of dry-roasteds

which she rips open with her teeth and splays on the table for sharing. I let her explain herself.

'I'm sorry, Ned. Have I discombobulated you?'

I love her for using that word. It's one of my favourites. It always gets a chuckle out of Dora. 'Yes. I am a bit. Not to mention discomfited.'

She takes a glug of lager, then begins. 'You probably don't know this but your mate Andy is mates with my mate Nick. Brighton's a village, right. And Hove, actually. Everyone knows everyone., don't they? Anyway, I happened to be out with Nick last week and we bumped into Andy and he asked about you and me. I said we'd gone on a date, but I didn't think you were that keen and that you'd got someone to call you to give you an out but Andy said . . .' She tails off.

'Andy said?' I prompt.

She blushes , which only endears her to me even more.

To put her out of her misery, I hazard a guess. 'Andy said I'm not clever enough to come up with a stunt like that? And then he said I'm gagging for it or something equally charming?'

She nods and breaks into a very endearing, warm smile. 'Pretty much, yes. Anyway, he persuaded me to give it – you – another go. So he set up tonight. I only wanted your number, but Andy insisted. And I went along with it because I wanted to see you. To say sorry for running off like that. As soon as I was out of Marrocco's, I said to myself, "You total flake, Nancy Carmel Parkin. What have you done?"'

'You *didn't* have a migraine?'

'I had a hissy fit, more like. Breaking up with Harry really knocked my confidence. For a while I lost all sense of self. My feelings felt so raw, exposed.'

'You'd worn down your emotional epidermis.'

'Oh God, yes. Exactly that. And rather than believe you, I decided you were playing games with me. So I did a runner.'

'I really wasn't playing games.' I know Andy's already told her this, but she needs to hear it from me. My version. The truth, even though it makes me look like an arse. 'I had an over-eager friend at the other end of my phone who decided I needed her help. I haven't been on a proper date for, it must be, fifteen years. She kept texting and I didn't stop her. I should have stopped her. I'm really sorry, Nancy. And I'm really pleased you're up for another crack at it. Us, I mean.'

We're both vulnerable. We're both nervous. We make a silent pact; let's be vulnerable and nervous together. Two emotional epidermi are better than one. We agree to meet up again . . . but not at Marrocco's.

I do a quick mental audit of my weekend plans. Dora will be with me but maybe Gemma can babysit on the Saturday night so that I can see Nancy. I didn't think I'd be taking her up on her quid pro quo childcare idea so quickly. Or perhaps Nancy can be my plus-one at Tanya and Julian's Sunday party. Suddenly the jigsaw pieces of my messy life are fitting together. I suggest either or both to Nancy, but it's not to be.

'I'm so sorry, Ned. I've promised to visit my folks at the weekend. They moved to West Wittering when Dad took early retirement. What time's the party?'

'2 p.m. onwards.'

'I could make it by four, if I leave straight after lunch. What if I join you later?'

That might work. Tanya will assume I'm Billy No-Mates and there's no plus-one. Then, two hours in, I suddenly present Nancy. That might work very well.

'Fantastic, Nancy. Let's try for that. There's a dress code, by the way.'

She looks worried.

'You're requested to wear something bright. Would that be okay?'

'Absolutely. I love bright colours. I'm a walking rainbow.'

Later, when I'm brushing my teeth, I rerun our encounter, from the moment she entered the pub. Every bit of it makes me smile.

Nancy is a walking rainbow. She really is.

Andy's at an awayday on Wednesday and Thursday so I don't have to hear him crowing about how he got me and Nancy back together. I'm impressed as well as grateful – I really didn't think he had it in him to set up something like that *and* to keep it a secret. I don't care what Tanya says, Andy is a good man and a proper mate.

Even so, I can do without him implying that I'm too stupid to sort out my life my own way. I'd like to think that if Nancy and I had *genuinely* bumped into each other, we'd have drawn a line and tried again. We're not idiot pawns on Andy's chess board, whatever he likes to think.

I sneak out of work early on Thursday. Welby-Daniels continues to do my head in and I want to get home in good time to pick up the car for my babysitting session with Gemma's son. She said he's doing a project on steam trains so I've saved some good YouTube links and pulled a couple of books off my shelves. I was quite the train buff at his age.

I really don't know Bevendean: there are still huge swathes of Brighton that I've never explored. I stay in my cosy comfort zone and rarely venture anywhere I can't walk home from. I need to do something about that; widen my horizons, shift my perspective, boldly go.

Gemma's street is all Sixties houses, probably ex-council,

not that I'm casting aspersions. One or two have rusted wheel-less caravans in the drive, some look like student houses with Indian bedspreads at the window and crates of empties by the front door. I should know. I lived in one.

Number 49 has a scarily manicured lawn, a massive pot of red geraniums by the red front door and a convenient off-road space for my car.

I can see that Gemma's anxious to get away to her date so I don't burden her with daft questions about bedtimes and house rules. Kelvin thumps downstairs, we're swiftly introduced and she dashes out. I don't get a chance to tell her how good she looks. She really does. I wasn't expecting that.

She has just the right kind of curvy figure to suit tight jeans and that hint of cleavage will definitely distract her date. She should make an effort more often. I won't tell her that, in case she bites my head off.

'Have you eaten?' I ask Kelvin.

'Yeah, no. Biscuits. Mum's left us a pizza and coleslaw.'

I pull a face. 'My mum used to make coleslaw. It was like the bits you find down the plughole when you've finished washing up.'

He's not sure what to make of me. 'She didn't make it. Lidl did. And the pizza. There's yoghurts for afters.'

'You don't fancy fish and chips, do you?'

Kelvin looks at me like I'm mad. Who doesn't fancy fish and chips?

'Great. I could murder a cod supper, with a side of mushy peas. Okay with you?'

Kelvin reckons the nearest chippie is five minutes away so I suggest we walk there together; ostensibly to make sure I order what he wants. Plus it seems like a good idea to break the ice on neutral territory.

'We didn't go to Rocksy's Fish Bar for a long time,' he tells me as we head towards the shopping parade I drove past on the way here.

'Rude service? Cold chips?'

'Mum went right off it. Couldn't stand the place. So we had to go to the one on the Avenue, which is further away. Then suddenly she's like, we can go to Rocksy's again. She can be a bit funny sometimes. You know. Unpredictable.'

'Yeah, well. Aren't we all?'

'My dad isn't. He never shifts on anything.'

'What about you?'

'A bit of both probably.'

Rocksy's is a proper old-skool chippie. No pretensions, no sepia prints of old trawlers or wall charts of brill, barbel and flounder. The vinegar is non-brewed condiment and the salt is shaken from a catering-size container.

Kelvin sticks with small cod and chips which, he warns me, is massive. I have the same. While we wait, I try to get him to open up.

'So. This project. Have you started it yet?'

'Not really. Mrs Berg said we could choose from steam trains, early aeroplanes or vintage cars.'

'And you chose trains. Good call, bud. I'd have done the same.'

'Not really. I said I wasn't fussed and they're all boring so she gave me trains as punishment. Don't tell Mum.'

'Right, Kelvin, that means my challenge is to make you "fussed" about steam trains. Have you ever been on one?'

'I don't know. Maybe.'

'Next school break, I'll take you and your mum on the Bluebell Line. That's a promise.'

He shrugs. He is *so* not fussed.

214

When we get back to the house, Kelvin finds plates and cutlery. But I convince him that fish and chips are best eaten with fingers, out of the polystyrene tray, sitting on the back step. He eats silently and doggedly and we finish at the same time.

He grins. It worked. I'm getting there.

'Steam trains,' I say, when we've tidied our chip wrappings. 'What do you know about them?'

He shrugs.

'When do you have to hand your project in?'

'Friday. Not tomorrow, the next one.'

'In that case, we can't wait until the school holidays. You need to get your dad and, and – I don't know her name . . .'

'Vicky.'

'You need to get your dad and Vicky to take you on the Bluebell Line *this* weekend. You'll learn so much, doing it for real. And then your project will practically write itself.'

Kelvin shakes his head. 'We're going to the Amex. We go to all the home games. Dad tells everyone he's Albion's number one fan. Or sometimes we go to Auntie Marie's, Vicky's sister, in Fishersgate, because they think I like hanging out with Brandon because we're the same age. Only I don't but nobody asks me.'

'Sunday, then.'

'We don't do anything on Sundays. Not really. Kick a football. Eat lunch. Vicky takes all morning making it. Then Dad drops me back home and Mum makes me do my homework. The end.'

'Weekends can be a bit predictable.'

He kicks a stone, watches it land in the flowerbed. 'They didn't used to be, when Mum and Dad were together. We did all sorts: day trips, zoos, London. One time we drove to

Dover because Dad wanted to buy a van off someone. But it was a rust bucket so we went to Dover Castle instead. It was awesome.'

'Weekends are tough when families break up. I'm a single parent too, did your mum say?'

Kelvin isn't interested in me. 'They're not "single", though, are they? Dad and Vicky. They're like a proper family. They've got Amelie. They think they've got me too. And Mum's all by herself and she gets really sad.'

I nod. I have a massive lump in my throat and I can't speak. I'm sad for both of us, Gemma and me. And Kelvin too, obviously. He isn't managing this at all well. I wonder if it gets to Dora too. Somehow I doubt it. She's tough as old boots while Kelvin seems to be quite a sensitive little chap, like I was at his age. (Who am I kidding? Like I still am . . .)

I haul myself up off the step. 'How about we watch some YouTube films about steam trains, to give you an idea of how to start your project? And those yoghurts won't eat themselves.'

Kelvin doesn't get up. 'Mum's always telling me to be kind and to make peace, whenever me and Mohit have a bust-up. He's my friend from school. Even if *he* started it and I'm like, I didn't do anything. She says: "Better to be friends than enemies." You know what I want? I want Mum and Dad to be kind to each other, to be together again. Vicky's okay. But she isn't my mum and *they* aren't my family. Mum and Dad are my family.'

He looks so hurt and hunched, sitting there on the back step trying to make sense of it all. I want to give him a hug but he'd hate it and I'd lose any ground I've made.

'You can't go back to how things used to be,' I tell him

gently. 'Stuff happens for a reason. I'd like to be a family again with my ex and my little girl. My "Vicky" is called Julian and he seems like a decent bloke. Still, we are where we are, you and me, and we have to look forwards, not backwards. Does that make any kind of sense?'

'Not really,' he says, getting to his feet. 'They're strawberry yoghurts. My least favourite. But I know where Mum hides her secret stash of chocolate. We could eat that while we check out your trains.'

We watch a few of the videos I pre-searched at work, some in scratchy black-and-white, and there are moments when Kelvin actually engages. He can't believe that the locomotives power the pistons that pull the train with steam from boiling water. And that some poor bugger has to shovel in coal, non-stop, to heat the water to create the steam. It *is* pretty amazing when you break it down like that. I loved the simplicity of it when I was a kid and I want Kelvin to love it too. I think he nearly does.

Then he shows me how Minecraft works and steam trains are soon forgotten. My turn to be engaged and amazed. We eat all the chocolate.

Kelvin's been in bed a good half-hour when Gemma tips in through the front door. I have no chance to ask her if she had a good time because she hurtles straight upstairs to the bathroom.

I don't know her well enough to ask if she's okay. Does she need me to hold her hair out of her face while she's sick, which I did more than once for Tanya when we first met. I turn off the telly, wash up my mug and put a note in her chocolate drawer, saying 'Sorry. The yoghurts are all yours'.

Gemma emerges ten minutes later, looking pale. Her stilettoes have been replaced by slippers and she's removed her make-up.

'Nice evening?' I ask.

She nods. 'Too many mojitos.'

'Do you think you'll see him again?'

'Probably. Yeah, why not? We had fun.'

'Fun is good.'

She smiles to herself. 'How was the boy? Did you get grumpy Kelvin or chatty Kelvin?'

'Chatty definitely. He's a great kid, Gemma. Really good company. *We* had fun too.'

'Phew, that's a relief. Thank you for helping me out, Ned.'

'I meant to say earlier, you look really lovely. I bet Dan's jaw dropped when he saw you. Don't frown like that – you do.' Well, she does and she needs to hear it.

She actually blushes. For a second or two, it's awkward. Have I overstepped the mark, misjudged the moment? I wish I'd kept it to myself, if it's going to make her uncomfortable.

'Yeah, I scrub up well when I put the effort in. That was Joe's idea of a compliment.'

'Ah, that would explain why you're not very good at accepting one.'

She nods and gives me a shy smile. I realize I'd better go before I stick my size 9s in it again.

Just when you think the jigsaw of your life is starting to click neatly together, the metaphorical cat knocks it off the coffee table. On Friday night, with Dora tucked in bed at mine, I'm quietly anticipating presenting Nancy to Tanya and Julian at the garden party on Sunday.

On Saturday morning, not so much. Nancy texts me from

the train, en route to her folks; she can't leave straight after lunch because a cousin is popping over at three and she's expected to stay, pass around the biscuits, do the dutiful daughter routine. 'But let's get together soon. I'd really like that.'

Gemma it is, then. Unless she has plans with Dan, I can't imagine her having a heaving social calendar. I need to make the invitation sound spontaneous, rather than an after-thought. Even though it is.

'Seriously?' she says. 'You want me to meet your ex?'

'Tanya said to bring someone and I thought of you.'

'Does this mean *you* have to meet Joe?'

'I'd be up for that.'

She says she'll think about it and call me back. A couple of hours later, Dora and I are at Hove Lagoon, slurping on ice creams from the Big Beach Café. I'm trying Dora's favourite flavour and it really does taste of bubble gum. (It's foul.)

My phone rings. It's Gemma. 'Yeah, why not. But I'll need to fetch Kelvin from his Dad's at six.'

I arrange to pick her up at the St Peter's Church bus stop at 2.30 so that we can all arrive at Tanya's together. To fulfil the dress code instructions, I've unearthed an ancient yellow T-shirt, complete with 'Pulp' logo, from the back of my wardrobe. It's bright all right. I wear it with some lime green jeans I bought on a whim but forgot to return. Dora is still in everyday Boden, planning to change into her party outfit when she gets there. She will, no doubt, want to make a grand entrance. She will look adorable and everyone will be obliged to say so.

'What colour will Gemma be wearing?' Dora asks as we drive past the Royal Pavilion.

Shit, shit, shit. I forgot to tell Gemma about bright colours. I was so relieved I'd found my plus-one that it totally slipped my mind. Maybe she'll be in that red top she wore on her date with Dan. She looked great in that. Her cleavage flashes through my mind. I've always had a thing about cleavages.

'I don't know what she'll be wearing, Bub. We'll find out in a minute, won't we?'

Gemma's waiting at the stop, as planned, and only two cars and a bus hoot when I pull over to the kerb to pick her up. She's in a navy dress. Not even remotely bright. I can't decide whether to warn her or let it go. How many people bother with dress codes anyway? I'll keep it to myself for now. Probably best.

'Why aren't you wearing something bright?' Dora asks as we drive up Dyke Road.

'Why aren't *you*?' Gemma replies, quick as a flash.

'I will do. Mummy's got my red dress ironed.'

'Ah, not pink then. Good choice, Dora.' Then to me. '*Should* I be wearing something bright?'

'Sort of. Just some daft idea of Tanya's.'

'Which you didn't tell me about. Oh, great. Look at me. She'll think I'm stupid, stroppy or boring. Probably all three. Why the f— why didn't you tell me, Ned?'

'I forgot. Tanya's a control freak so it'll be good for her to realize that she can't oversee everything.'

'Especially the twat in navy.'

Dora giggles in the back seat. She loves it when grown-ups say naughty words.

I have to admit, this is not a good start. Gemma is uncomfortable and angry and it's all my fault.

It soon changes when we're shown through Julian's ludicrously large kitchen and out into the garden. It's one of those March days that thinks it's June. There are already twenty or so guests chit-chatting and they're all wearing red, white and blue.

Tanya swans over in red dungarees, with a blue-and-white stripy sailor's T-shirt underneath. Julian presents a tray of Prosecco cocktails; he's in navy chinos, baggy white linen shirt and a red belt. Everyone's in red, white and blue, even Gemma. Everyone but me.

'What happened to "wear something bright"?' I ask, too wound up even to do the introductions.

'I changed my mind. I let everyone know, ooh, at least a week ago. I'm sure I sent you a message. Maybe I didn't. Sorry about that.'

She turns to give Gemma the once-over. 'Hi, I'm Tanya. I love your dress. Is it Toast?'

Gemma double-checks what she's wearing. 'No, it's cotton.' She smiles, to make sure we all know she's joking. 'It's nearly ten years old. I think I got it from Peacocks. Hi, I'm Gemma.'

Tanya encourages us to mingle and takes Dora upstairs for her costume change. Julian's still with us, holding out a tray of little salmony-pancakey things. I'd forgotten all about Julian. Easily done.

'Sorry about the clothes thing, mate,' he says with a conspiratorial grin. 'You know what she's like. On Wednesday, she nearly changed it to Hawaiian shirts. I said: "No, Tan, it's too late. You'll only annoy everyone."'

Gemma clinks my glass. 'This way, she's only annoyed one person. Happy days.'

It's a good party. It'd be churlish to pretend otherwise. I catch up with Nick and Nev who've moved to Hastings; with Matt and Jane who dropped me like a cold spud when

221

Tanya and I broke up; with Bethany's dad and Gracie's two mums. I spend at least twenty minutes talking to a friend of Julian's about his seafood allergy and how it nearly killed him on the Algarve. Nobody remarks on my ridiculously conspicuous T-shirt and luminous jeans, probably out of embarrassment. I am the elephant in the garden.

The one person I barely talk to is Gemma. She's really fitting in with Tanya and Julian's friends and it isn't just because she's correctly colour-coded. At one point, when I'd desperately love a break from Seafood Allergy Guy, I see her doing silly dances on the patio with Dora and Bethany. As I demolish a massive dollop of Eton mess, I spot her deep in conversation with Tanya and an ex-neighbour. As I hack myself a slice of pear tarte Tatin – Julian makes the most amazing puddings – I hear a loud hoot of laughter and see Gemma, Nev and Nick doubled up in hysterics. Someone is being, quite literally, the life and soul of the party and I think it might be her.

'She's great,' Tanya says, sitting beside me on a rattan divan. 'I'm really pleased for you, Ned.'

'Gemma, you mean?'

'Of course, Gemma. I'd never have had her down as your type. Maybe you've changed.'

'We all change, Tanya. Mistakes make us human, regrets help us learn.'

'Bloody hell. That doesn't sound like the Eeyore Ned I used to know. You really *have* turned a corner. Well done, Gemma.'

I remain silent. Less is more.

'How did you meet?'

Tanya won't be satisfied until she hears the full story. I really don't want to tell her about SPAN because she doesn't deserve the satisfaction of knowing I needed a support group after our split. She'll feel vindicated and/or sorry for me. I don't need that.

'Friend of a friend,' I say cryptically. 'You know how it is.'

'Is she the one you went to the Ivy with?'

'No, that was someone else.'

Tanya looks impressed. 'Look at you. Quite the man about town. Go, Ned.'

It's weird. Tanya suddenly thinks I'm a player so she curtails the condescension and natters away like we never stopped being nice to each other. I've gone up in her estimation. Mind you, I started in the basement so I couldn't have gone down any lower. Or is it relief that she doesn't have to feel sorry for me anymore?

Because Tanya thinks she's up to speed on my love life, *I'm* more relaxed than I expected. But really, she has no idea who I'm seeing or how I'm doing. I feel full of optimism about Nancy. That's a secret I'll be keeping very much to myself for a while yet.

In fact, I'm feeling bullish enough to bring up something that's been needling me for a while. 'Julian told me he didn't get the Oman job.'

'Yes? And?'

'But you told me it was *your* decision not to go. Why lie?'

She looks sheepish. 'I wasn't lying. I really didn't want to go. Lucky for me, he got knocked back. I'm sorry, Ned. I should have been honest with you. My bad.'

I decide to be magnanimous. They're not going to Oman and I haven't lost my daughter. Tanya knows that I know she was economical with the truth and, in my book, that's a result.

'Apology accepted. Any news on the house sale?'

'Two offers. Both fell through. Now it's gone quiet. Would you be okay if I let it for a year?'

'Absolutely.'

It's a wonderful family home with so many good memories. All those Christmases; all those birthdays; all those wet Sunday afternoons, with the three of us snuggled up indoors. It's where I was happiest. Maybe I could buy Tanya out and move back, when the time is right. Mind you, I'd hate to live there on my own.

If it all works out with Nancy, maybe I won't have to.

At half five, Gemma has to collect Kelvin from his dad's so we leave together, giving a rushed mwah-mwah to Tanya and Julian and major daddy hugs to Dora. At the front door, Julian does a matey thumbs-up: Gemma's passed the test with *him* too. Seriously! As if I need his approval on any aspect of my life!

I hear myself saying 'wanker' under my breath as we get in the car.

Gemma hears me. 'He seemed okay to me.'

'I'm allowed to be unobjective, aren't I? Just like you are about Vicky.'

'Fair enough.'

'Did you pick up on how desperate Tanya was to know how we met? We definitely fooled her into thinking we're an item. Thanks for coming, Gemma. You really got me out of a hole.'

'What hole?'

Best not tell her she was in reserve when Nancy dropped out.

'What hole, Ned?'

'Nothing. Bad choice of words. Sorry.'

'Did you invite me at the last minute to sub for someone else?'

'Kind of. But it wasn't for definite. Her coming. Nancy, I mean.'

'Go on. I'm all ears.'

My bluffing skills aren't up to this. If I lie, I'll tie myself in knots. 'You know how our date went tits up, me and Nancy, and she left me at the restaurant? Course you do. You thought it was funny. Well, we met up again and I kind of invited her to the party. Only she couldn't come after all and, well, I was really, really pleased when you could come instead. You were such a hit with everyone. Bloody hell, Gemma, you were amazing.'

I mean it. I'm not even bullshitting.

'So you didn't tell me there was a dress code *and* you didn't tell me I was second best. Is that you being nasty or just plain stupid?'

'Stupid. 110 per cent. Me all over.'

She doesn't speak again until I need directions to Joe's. I wait in the car while she goes to the house to collect Kelvin. Even if I readjust my rear-view mirror, I can't quite see Joe at the door, just a big, bulky shape in jogging bottoms.

A moment later, Kelvin bounces into the back seat. He seems pleased to see me.

'Hey, Ned. Loving the T-shirt.' He giggles. He's being sarky. I like it.

We talk steam trains all the way to Bevendean. Gemma gazes out of the window, not remotely interested and still angry with me. I can't blame her.

I pull up outside their house. Kelvin gives a wave and heads indoors. Time to do his homework. Gemma holds back.

'Thanks for inviting me, Ned. I enjoyed it. Next time, don't play games, okay? Not with *me*, anyway.'

I really wasn't playing games, I want to say. I was just being an idiot. Instead, I shout, 'Sorry, bye, thanks,' to her retreating back. I feel bad. I'm an A-grade arsehole.

Too late to tell her how dazzling she was and how everyone loved her – and how grateful I was that she came. Instead I let slip that she was a stand-in for Nancy, which she didn't need to know. Less really is more. Never mind, I'm sure she'll think it through tomorrow and stop being so cross.

At least *she* wasn't the one in the luminous jeans.

Chapter Eighteen

Gemma

I act all cool when Ros yanks me through her hall, into her kitchen. I try really hard not to look envious of her beautiful home. This how I want *mine* to be. This is who I want to be. This.

Over the last couple of months, I've had the chance to compare my modest little house with two I really ought to envy. But I don't. There was a time I would have killed for a place like Joe and Vicky's in Woodingdean. Not any more, thank you very much. It's sterile and beige and bland. No warmth. No personality, despite the dayglo cushions.

I wasn't too taken with Tanya and Julian's home either, at the smug end of Dyke Road. Too pleased with itself, too many musty old carpets and overstuffed settees, too many arty-farty ornaments and naff-on-purpose knick-knacks. 'Dust-catchers', my mum would have called them.

Ros's house though . . . it's like a clever blend of both places: modern Ikea chairs around a junk-shop table; basic metal shelving heaving with hundreds of books, stacked every which way. Nothing about the place looks over-done or showy; it's about making a home, rather than making an impression. It's stylish in a not-trying-to-be kind of way. A bit like Ros. I wish I had her taste. I don't know how to find cool stuff. I'm too high street, too Argos.

The kitchen is a bombsite – if bombs were made of flour, icing sugar and edible glitter. That's why I'm here.

We were all set for a Wednesday catch-up in our usual Italian. I'd even decided that I was going to try the goat's cheese and artichoke pizza, because I should get out of my Margherita comfort zone.

And then Ros rang in a flap. 'I need to finish these sodding cupcakes for a 5.30 a.m. pick-up. Can you help, Gem? Actually, that's not a request. Please, please help.'

Ros knows I can't bake cakes. Why bother when you can buy a better one readymade? But I did say I'd help if ever she was up against it. Four hands are better than two, even if 50 per cent of them are mine.

She sits me at the table, the only clear surface in the kitchen, and gives me a quick lesson in what I'm here for.

'Right, I pipe a cupcake. I put it on this tray. This tray here. Are you listening, Gemma?'

'I love your tiles. They're so "you". Did they come with the house?'

'David found them in a reclamation yard. They're Arts and Crafts, I think. They don't cover the whole splashback so he patched them with some others from a junk shop. See, these ones have peacocks and these ones have doves. Sod the sodding tiles. Just listen, will you?'

'I can't help it. Your kitchen's so lovely.'

'It's too small and too badly laid out for this baking malarkey. It is what it is, though. Did you hear what I said about the cupcakes?'

'You ice them and put them here. What do I do?'

Ros looks heavenward. She doesn't have time for this.

'You stick this edible "Jackdaw Project" label on the top. Don't press hard or your thumb'll go through and I'll cry. Then you put it carefully in this box here. Each box takes forty cakes. Don't overcrowd them or I'll cry even more. Then, when the box is full, I fling edible glitter over them all. Do I need to make you repeat that?'

'*No!*' Does she think I'm thick or something?

'I'm sorry, Gemma,' she says, patting my arm with floury fingers. 'I'm just a bit wound up. The first batch didn't rise. God knows why. I'll donate them to Gabe's class tomorrow. They'll be thrilled.'

I give my hands a thorough scrub in her downstairs loo – another person with a downstairs loo – and get started on the cupcake production line. I'm so gentle – too gentle – with the first few labels that they don't stick. Then I get the hang of it; firm enough to stay put, without mooshing up the beautiful swirly rosette of gold-frosted butter cream. I don't know who the 'Jackdaw Project' is but they must like cake.

'Imagine starting up a new ad agency right now,' Ros says, as she expertly squirts butter cream across a row of cakes. 'Brave or what?'

'No braver than starting up a baking business.'

'Brave or stupid. Ask me again this time next year.'

I know Ros is stressed, but she's the type who thrives on it. She's loving the adrenalin rush of cranking out this order, even if she has to rope in a klutz like me.

When we're done and all the cupcakes are packed and stacked on a hall table, Ros creates a quick supper for us from whatever's in her fridge. I've never eaten quinoa salad before or wedges of cold roast butternut squash or raw shredded Brussels sprouts, dressed with anchovies, almonds and lemon juice. In fact, I'd gag if I saw that on a menu. At first, I eat out of politeness but I can't lie, it's really, really delicious. Even the sprouts and anchovies. I hate anchovies. And sprouts.

Time to tell Ros about my two dates. She's all ears, obviously.

'Why didn't Nancy come to the party?'

'Otherwise engaged, I suppose. So I was second best, runner-up. Ned decided I don't have a life and I'd be free at short notice. Bloody cheek, right?'

'But you *were* free at short notice. I don't get it, Gem. Why are you so down on Ned? Okay, he should have told you why he was asking you so last-minute, and he could have mentioned the dress code. But cut the guy some slack. And you had a great time, didn't you?'

'I don't like being used, taken for granted. It was quite funny, though, because his ex and her new bloke thought we were an item. So I went along with it and they really liked me. He wasn't expecting that. I reckon they'll be disappointed when they find out we're not together. Then it's Nancy's turn to feel second best.'

Ros considers me for a moment, then narrows her eyes. She's about to say something more, but changes her mind. 'Never mind all that. Tell me about Dan.'

I put down my fork and have a little think. 'Yeah. It was good. He was nice. He's ready to be in a relationship again.'

'Well, that's a start. And you? Are *you* ready?'

'That's the problem. I'm not as ready as him. If anything, he's a bit *too* keen.'

Ros laughs. 'Oh no, what a nightmare. How could he? Next thing, he'll be wanting to see you again, the bastard.'

It does sound ridiculous when I say it out loud.

'Is it the sex? Are you nervous about that, Gem? Perfectly understandable. You and me have been living like nuns for so long, our lady bits have probably sealed over.'

I can't tell her about me sleeping with Joe. She'd be so angry. No, not angry. She'd be disappointed in me for being so weak and pathetic. She has a dim view of Joe, which is one of the things I love about her. We may not have known each other for very long, but Ros is on my side, no matter what. Not like bloody Hayley.

'No, not the sex. I suppose I'm scared by how much he likes me. I'm bound to be a let-down.'

Ros actually gets out of her chair, comes round the table and gives me a hug. I wasn't expecting that.

'You are a wonderful woman, Gemma. That shit of a husband made you think you weren't but you are. I can see it, Dan can see it. Ned too, I shouldn't wonder. You truly deserve to be happy.'

'So do you.'

'We're not talking about me. Please see Dan again. Go at your own pace. You don't need to throw yourself into his arms but don't push him away either. *You* call the shots.'

I nod. She's right. Joe's turned me into this sad excuse of a woman. I can exorcise that by seeing Dan. Joe'd be so furious. 'Okay then, Mrs Pot-calling-kettle-black,' I say as Ros pulls a dish of leftover rice pudding from the fridge, all crusty and brown on top, just how I like it. 'I'll see Dan again and *you* go for a drink with Andy.'

Ros groans. 'Why? If I was looking to replace David – which I'm not – it wouldn't be someone remotely like Andy.'

'He might be different when it's just the two of you and he's not showing off. If it's not to be, at least you gave the poor guy a chance.'

231

We take a spoon each and dig into the cold pudding.

'Will you, Ros?'

'Will *you*, Gemma?'

We nod. We eat. We will.

Dan and I have plans for Sunday. He needs to deliver a restored Sixties sideboard to his mate in Hastings who flogs them on for him and do I fancy coming along for the ride? I say yes and not just because Ros told me to.

1)   I like Hastings.
2)   I like day trips.
3)   I like Dan.

Why should I feel uneasy that he's so keen? I should be flattered, I should be grateful, I should just go for it. My confidence is slowly returning, boosted by Ros, by my performance at Tanya's party and, most importantly, by Dan himself.

Ned hasn't been in touch, not even to say sorry for letting slip that I was Nancy's understudy. So what? His loss. Saturday dads come in every shape and size; are he and Joe all that different? Users and losers, takers and fakers. Sod the pair of them.

Before my day out with Dan, I have a lunch date. Felipe's doing my Friday shift so that I can take Vicky up on an out-of-the-blue invitation. We're meeting at a new restaurant in Kemptown at 1 p.m. I'm having lunch with the woman who stole my husband and she's picking up the tab. I hadn't seen *that* coming.

She rang as I was on the bus, going home from Ros's, with five reject cupcakes in an ice-cream tub for Kelvin. I didn't expect the call. Why would I?

She got straight to the point: did I fancy lunch on Friday, her treat? In the spirit of openness and because I couldn't come up with a quick lie, I said yes. If I'm honest, I suppose a bit of me likes the idea of unnerving Joe: his old wife and his new wife meeting as mates. Let him be unnerved and confused. He deserves much worse.

Vicky is already there waiting when I arrive. Her hair is blow-dried to perfection and her dress looks pricey. I've put on the navy one I wore to the party. It did the job then and it gives me confidence. Plus I've got good legs, way better than hers. And that won't change, whoever scrambles Joe's eggs or washes his boxers.

Vicky leaps up, arms open for a hug. She looks pleased to see me. I don't get it. I wouldn't if I were her. 'So glad you could come, Gemma. Look at the old lush here. I've already started on the Prosecco.'

We sip and scan the menu. Liver and crab for Vicky, salmon and lamb for me.

'Don't be stingy,' she says, breaking open a bread roll. 'This isn't costing me a single penny.'

'Joe's treating us? That doesn't sound like him.'

'True. He can be over-cautious with money. No, I won lunch for two in a raffle. Three courses plus wine, cheese and chocolates. I've never won a raffle in my life.'

'And you asked *me*?'

'Joe thought I'd drag Hayley along. We often do brunch or grab a salad after our HIIT workout. But we're off for a spa weekend in a fortnight, for her fortieth, and a little of Hayley goes a long way. So I thought of you. We're friends now, aren't we?'

'How does Joe feel about that?'

'He's super-fine with it. He's not one to say how he feels,

unless the Seagulls score a hat trick. Well, you know that. Deep down, he's fine with it. I'm sure he is.'

I'm super-sure he isn't. What if I blab to Vicky about The Shag on the worktop? What if I crack and tell her every sleazy detail? I won't . . . yet. But I've got it up my sleeve, just in case.

'You were quite the hit at our dinner party,' she says as we knock off the Prosecco and start on the Soave. 'I know Hayley was pleased to see you.'

'Was she? She must know we'll never be friends again. I've moved on. I've got new friends now.'

I don't mean to sound so bitter. Hayley didn't screw Joe. This woman opposite me, slicing through her pink calves' liver, she's the one I should be bitter about. And yet here I am, eating out with her. Does that make me a hypocrite? Probably. There's no such thing as a free lunch; maybe I'll pay for it with rage-induced heartburn when I get home.

'I really liked Chris,' I tell her. 'How cool to have him for a cousin.'

Vicky goes pale. She pushes the last bit of liver aside. Is she going to be sick?

'Oh, Gemma. I could tell as soon as he arrived that you'd get on. And when he gave you a lift home, I had a little smile to myself. Joe told me not to be silly but I honestly thought I'd hit the bullseye. You looked so good together.'

I know what's coming but I pretend I don't. More fun that way. 'I should give him a call some time,' I say with an optimistic smile.

Vicky gulps. She's going to spit this out, however painful. 'He's gay, Gemma. We thought he liked boys *and* girls. You know, bisexual. Well, he certainly used to. He had a girlfriend all through uni. Not any more, though. He's got a boyfriend and it's serious.'

I can play this two ways. I can tell her I knew from the moment I met him. Or I can act shocked. I opt for shocked. Totally lost for words. Speechless.

'I know,' Vicky says, to break the silence. 'It wasn't what anyone was expecting. He says he's really happy and he can't wait for us to meet this new chap of his and, well, that's wonderful. I thought I was doing a good thing. Trust me to make a hash of it.'

'It was a nice thought, Vicky. But you needn't worry about me. I met someone too. His name's Dan, he's really nice and that's all you're getting for now. No one else's business until we're ready to go public.'

'I'm pleased for you, Gemma. Really. This has been so – so horrible, such a strain on all of us. If you and Dan are as happy as me and Joe, that would make my day.'

Wouldn't it. Then you can stop feeling guilty for your starring role in ripping my family apart. You could have walked away from a married man with a child but you didn't.

And now I'm seriously starting to regret being here, sitting opposite the woman who stole my husband, even if he was more than happy to be stolen. I should have just said: Sorry, Vicky, we'll never be friends so let's not even try. I didn't, so now I'm here and I'm expected to play nice, share cute memes on Facebook, meet Vicky and, who knows, maybe even Hayley for brunch every couple of weeks, like we've been best mates since forever.

I'm seconds away from saying all that. I really am. I may need another glass of wine first. And it's not something you can spit out while a waiter's spooning gravy over your lamb shank.

So I hold off. Not the time. Not the place. Not the moment. That will come. Sooner or later.

It comes sooner than I thought. I nip to the ladies' before our desserts arrive and Vicky emerges from the cubicle beside mine a couple of minutes after me.

'Ooh look, honey and satsuma handwash,' I say, taking a big squirt. 'I should have that on my ice cream.'

Suddenly she gives me a massive hug, the sort you give when you haven't seen someone for six months. I hug back, rather than leave my arms dangling limp by my sides. Then she lets go and I see she's crying.

'Thank you, thank you, Gemma. You don't know what it means to me, you forgiving me like this. Joe didn't think you would but I was like, she's a good woman. She's ready to draw a line and move on.'

'You reckon?'

She nods, dabbing at a streak of mascara with her pinky. 'You're here, aren't you. That means the world. Seriously, Gemma, it does.'

I fetch her a couple of squares of loo roll, to lull her into a false sense of security. Then I let rip.

'This isn't me forgiving you, Vicky. This is me being polite, accepting your invitation to lunch because you owe me big time. I won't lie: three courses plus wine, cheese and choc-olates does not mean I forgive you. Not by a long way. You and Joe broke my heart. And Kelvin's, bless him. You think I can "draw a line and move on" because this restaurant does nice handwash?'

I've shocked Vicky out of her tears. Now she gulps like a winded carp. 'Of course not.'

'Tell me then. Go on. Your chance to explain yourself. Why did you steal my husband?'

She looks down at her ridiculous nude stilettoes. I want to ask her how she can even walk in them but we're not here for that.

'Well, tell me.'

'I didn't know he was married. Swear to God I didn't. When he told me, it was too late. I was in too deep. So many times I wanted to walk away but I couldn't. I was scared. What if I made him choose and he chose you? Then you found out and you kicked him out and I was pregnant with Amelie. And, well, here we are.'

Here we are. In the ladies' of an up-itself restaurant, finally having the conversation we never had. I don't want to forgive Vicky and I won't. Still, I can't hate her. She looks so pathetic in her daft shoes that scrunch up her toes and blister her heels, judging by the Band-Aids.

And then it occurs to me . . . if I hadn't found Vicky's sunglasses in Joe's glove compartment, he might have 'chosen' me and we'd still be together. Muggins here would have been none the wiser. Would that have been better than *this*?

No. Really, really . . . no.

I give Vicky a hug. Tomorrow I'll hate *myself* for doing it but I can't hate her.

I'm relieved that Joe picks Kelvin up straight from school on Friday afternoon so I don't have to face him. He'd only want to hear my version of lunch with Vicky. Which would be awkward because I don't know what *her* version is. I'm guessing she said it went really well and doesn't mention any tears in the toilet.

One day on and I still don't hate her. Joe having a bit on the side maybe wasn't the nicest way to learn that I'd married a bastard. I could still be living with him, in blissful ignorance, if I hadn't found out about Vicky. I have to be grateful for that.

Did she really think, if forced, he'd have chosen me over

her? She could be right. Joe doesn't like complications. Staying with me would have been simpler than starting over with Vicky. Except I didn't give him the choice. As soon as I knew the truth, I wanted him gone. Plus of course, she was pregnant. How would that have worked? Would Joe have abandoned Vicky *and* Amelie? I hate the way my marriage ended but it's not Amelie's fault; she needs a dad just as much as Kelvin does.

Kelvin blamed me for sending his dad packing. He was too young to understand why I had to do it. Should I have forgiven Joe, turned the page and pretended it never happened, for Kelvin's sake?

No.

I did the right thing, even if it broke my boy's heart. And mine. These past couple of years haven't been easy but I like who I'm turning into. I'm losing the bitterness and weariness and cup-half-emptiness. I'm not saying my cup's half full. Not yet. But at least I *have* a cup and it's got some cold tea in it. That's good enough for me. For now.

I like having this Saturday to myself: no plans, no errands, no chores. I'm easier on myself on *that* front too. These days I'll leave dirty dishes in the sink when I go out and not stress about them. The laundry can wait too. I'm less obsessed with filling every second so that I don't have time to be hard on myself. Is that because I'm less hard on myself? It feels good.

I have a big breakfast. Big for me, anyway. Two fried eggs, tinned tomatoes, two slabs of toast and a warmed-up sausage from last night's tea. I leave the pan and plate on the worktop, which for me is quite an achievement.

Maybe I'm easy on myself today because I have my Hastings adventure with Dan tomorrow. He's picking me up at nine and the weather forecast says sunny. I'm spending the day with a man who has fancied me half his lifetime. It makes me smile. I like how it feels. I'm aiming to make it last all day.

By mid-morning, I'm having a coffee in a cafe off London Road. I walked here from home. I should do that more often, rather than jump on a bus. I even buy *The Times* and work my way through the main section.

My phone jumps. A text from Kelvin. 'Vicky said to tell you I got an A for that project about steam trains. Vicky says you should be ever so pleased because she and dad is. xoxoxo Kelvin.'

I *am* pleased. *Ever so.* I don't even mind that Vicky heard it first. Kelvin struggles at school. He thinks he's stupid – who knows where he got that from? – and he holds back in case he gets things wrong. Mrs Berg told me at Parents' Day that he needs to work on his confidence. Well, this can't hurt.

I'm in such a good mood that I decide it's time to let go of being angry with Ned. Okay, he didn't tell me what I was supposed to wear to that party. And yes, I wasn't Nancy. But I had a good time and I didn't embarrass myself. What's to be angry about? Like Elsa, I should just let it go.

I ring his number. He'll be so thrilled to know he got Kelvin interested in steam trains. *I* couldn't have managed that and Joe definitely couldn't. I'm about to hang up when he answers, breathless and distracted.

'Yes? Hello?'

'Ned? It's Gemma. Are you okay? You sound like you're having a heart attack.'

'Me? No. I'm fine. How are you?'

'Have I called at a bad time?'

'No. Well, a bit. No, not really.'

'I'll keep it quick. I just wanted to let you know that Kelvin got an "A" for his steam-train project. So thank you for helping. It'll really boost his confidence.'

'Did he? Wow, that's great. Tell him well done from me. Look, sorry, Gemma. I am a bit, you know, tied up right now. Can I ring back later?'

I can hear someone calling him in the background. Nancy?

I thought he'd be pleased to hear about Kelvin, but he's obviously got more important things on his mind 'No need, Ned. That's all I wanted to say. Have a good weekend. Bye.'

Nancy. She must have stayed over. So they're definitely a thing. I'm happy for him. I am. Ned has Nancy and I have Dan and he's mad about me.

It might have been nice to have had a proper chat. We haven't talked since the garden party. Okay, I was angry that he only invited me because Nancy was busy. I'm over that now. It's not worth staying in a strop about.

We're both getting our lives back. We're both moving on.

I'm genuinely pleased for him. Seriously.

Go, Ned!

Chapter Nineteen

Ned

Nancy has a Picturehouse membership card. She sees a new film every week. She doesn't read the previews so she doesn't always know what she's in for. She likes the surprise element. She doesn't mind foreign films either. What a great attitude, to be so open. To go with the flow. In a good way.

I drift. I know I do. I get swept along by a passing current because I don't have the motivation to hold on to a rock. I thought drifting made me flexible and spontaneous but it drove Tanya potty. 'Going with the flow' isn't a good thing if you let it excuse you from taking responsibility for your life. Obvious, when you think about it.

Nancy does a Park Run every Saturday and is learning conversational French every Thursday because she enjoyed it at school and she'd love to banter with a Parisian waiter when ordering a Pernod and everybody should have a second language.

Nancy makes her own bread. She did a one-day workshop because Harry's parents gave her a bread machine one Christmas but she always felt it was cheating. Why bother making a loaf if you can't do all that kneading and pummelling? It's *so* therapeutic.

241

Apparently, the workshop guy said well-kneaded bread dough should have the feel of an earlobe. She loves that. I'm no perve but I do like the silky softness of a room-temperature lobe. I can't visualize Nancy's. Small, I imagine. Delicate. Neat and tucked in, rather than loose and tufty like mine.

I'm seeing Nancy – and her earlobes – tonight. Her diary is so packed that we've had to wait until now to meet. I pretended to have a busy social life too but, apart from SPAN on Wednesdays, my only dates are with Netflix and the microwave. And if Nancy and I are a probable possibility, I see no need to return to SPAN. I've turned a page.

We've arranged to meet at the Heart and Hand for a quick drink before the film starts. It will be good to see her again in the flesh, after a week of WhatsApping. I only hope I'm not an anti-climax.

When Tanya and I first hooked up, we were on the phone to each other 24/7. 'You hang up first . . . No, you hang up first.' Social media was yet to become 'a thing'. We'd settle down on our respective sofas for long, flirty phone calls that occasionally got quite explicit, even though sexting had yet to be invented.

It's weird, though; I know so much about Nancy and yet we've barely spent more than a couple of hours together. The bread-making . . . the Park Run . . . her mum's dicky heart and obsession with *Les Misérables*. I even know her parents' names: Doug and Lorraine. They have a dachshund called Skip. They're retired teachers and her mum's damson jam goes perfectly with Nancy's hand-pummelled bloomer.

We meet at the pub, as planned. Nancy's hair is grabbed by one of those plastic bulldog clips on top of her head. It's messy and unkempt, with loose strands trailing around the nape of her neck; it's unbelievably sexy. Her ears are small, shell-like, pierced with delicate coral studs. Is it so wrong to want to kiss one of those ears? How soon do I get to do that?

'Here we are then,' she says giving my arm an affectionate pat, as if I'm Skip the dachshund. 'Third time lucky, eh?'

'Third time? Is it? Let's see, we first met at the club on the seafront. Then in your shop, but that wasn't a date. Then the date.'

'Which I ruined by flouncing out like some Pound Shop prima donna.'

'The Pound Shop Prima Donnas. I've got their second album.'

Nancy hoots with laughter. I flush with pleasure.

'Then you came to the pub to find me,' I continue, determined to bring us up to date. 'Then this. Tonight. Now.'

She gives me such a big smile, as if all those false starts were there for a reason. I smile back and chink her pint with my pint.

This. Tonight. Now . . . Us.

'The film's Icelandic. How are you with Icelandic films?' She genuinely expects an intelligent answer.

'I didn't realize they *made* films. I don't know anything about Iceland. Apart from Björk. And Eyjafjallajökull.'

Nancy's head tips to one side, like a quizzical sparrow. It's actually very sweet.

'Eyjafjallajökull,' I say again, relishing my excellent pronunciation. 'The volcano. It ruined a holiday for me and Tanya. 2010. Oh God, that didn't take long. Me bringing up my ex.'

'I told you all about Harry and the bread machine. We each have a history. It's allowed.'

'Harry and the Bread Machine. I've got *their* album too.'

Who's this witty guy prompting peals of laughter from

the delightfully engaging woman with the endearing lobes? Have I always been this funny? Tanya must have thought so once but, in our later years, she'd give a weary, eye-roll response whenever I trotted out some pun or a made an amusing observation.

An Icelandic film, though. A new experience. It feels adventurous, edgy, uncharted. 'I am so up for this, Nancy. I've got a good feeling about it.'

I'm referring to the film, obviously. But we both pick up on the subtext. We've had a couple of false starts. Maybe they were part of the journey, to get us to tonight. We're both *so* up for this.

There's still time for a second round of drinks. I don't want to be in the gents' during the film but I've made myself nervous with the significance of our evening; I need Dutch courage. This date is a big deal. I fetch us two halves of lager and some crisps.

Twenty minutes later, we realize we've missed the start of the film because we've been too busy talking. I'm all for seeing it anyway. It's Icelandic. How much sense is it likely to make, with or without a beginning?

Nancy thinks not. 'I love the ads, the trailers, the opening credits. Let's see it another time. Do you mind, Ned?'

Do I mind? Hardly. Nancy thinks I'm funny. If that's not a result, I don't know what is.

'I'm starving,' she says, emptying the crisp packet into her mouth. 'How about some chips to share?'

'Or a portion each? Hey, maybe I should have brought you *here* on our first date. This is going so much better than Marrocco's.'

'I know, right. We can always go back to Marrocco's for our . . . our fifth date.'

'Definitely.'

We're a bit giddy and it isn't the alcohol. I'm finding Nancy such great company. Funny, self-deprecating, clever. I can only hope she thinks I am too. I like listening to her, even when I'm not actually listening to her.

'So it has to be a good thing, right? Couch to 5k, then graduate to Park Run every Saturday morning along the seafront. I hated running at school. I'd do anything to get out of it. And now look at me. I'm gutted if I don't improve my time, week on week. You should try it, Ned. You've got the physique for it.'

'Absolutely. Couldn't agree more. Physique for what?'

'Running. You're all wiry and muscular.'

'Trust me, I'm not.'

'I'd need to see under that shirt some time to find out for sure.'

'Any time.'

But, we both decide, not tonight.

'I'm right, aren't I?' she says, making serious eye contact. 'It took us forever to get to . . . this. We shouldn't ruin it by rushing it.'

'I suppose so.'

'Plus it's a school night and I can't spring you on my flatmate without advanced warning. House rules. Oh God, am I being presumptuous? I am, aren't I?'

'No, you're right. If we're going to be something . . . be something *together*, I mean, then we can wait. It adds to the excitement. It's like five sleeps to Christmas, then four, then three.'

Nancy loves that I've compared her to Christmas. It's not bullshit. I mean it.

'We can still have a massive snog, though.'

'It would be churlish not to.'

We kiss in the pub, we kiss in the street outside Wahaca, we kiss at the bus stop. I feel like a 14-year-old, except I never snogged like this when I was 14. Then she gives me one final kiss and is gone, on the number 7 to Seven Dials.

I wave her off. I didn't get to kiss her earlobes but I will.

The next day, I instigate an unnecessary meeting in Worthing, telling Karen I need to say hi to the new team. She often swans off early on a Friday afternoon to get her hair done so our complicity is tacit.

I drive along the coast road, with a Springsteen playlist as my soundtrack, and give the Worthing folk thirty minutes of my time because they're expecting me. My real destination is Dunelm in Shoreham. And it can't possibly wait.

When I got home from my night out with Nancy, I made myself a cup of tea, threw myself on the sofa and watched a bit of *Newsnight*. It was then that I glanced around my flat and realized for the first time that I live in a shithole. A shithole of my own making. How can I invite Nancy here? What will she think of me?

The crappy sofa, the tilting bookshelves, the ketchup stain on the rug, the dust bunnies procreating in every corner. At some point, I stopped seeing the bachelor habits I'd got into, but I see them now. I even write 'mess' in the dust on the coffee table, as if I need reminding.

It wasn't a particularly nice flat when I moved in but I wasn't fussy, after splitting up with Tanya and spending a month on Andy's sofa bed.

I was dug down so deep in my trench of self-pity that I didn't care how I furnished the place. I got a load of random recycled stuff from Emmaus and felt a little better, knowing my dosh was supporting a homeless charity. The sofa was sitting outside someone's house with a 'take me' sign taped to its arm. So I took it and, with Andy's help, we got it indoors, without scraping off too much paintwork.

The sofa would do. Everything 'would do'. I didn't require better. Only Dora's room got special treatment and even that's hardly a palace. I can never compete with Tanya and Julian.

I can't suddenly magic my flat into a high-end des res. The bedroom needs painting and the bathroom is grim. But I can buy new stuff: rugs, cushions, a couple of arty framed prints, a lampshade for the living room, new towels and bedding for Nancy's first sleepover.

Maybe I'm tempting fate and we're doomed never to get beyond a snog at the bus stop. I hope not. I hope Nancy will fill an important space in my life and I don't want to blow it because of a manky bath mat.

I hurtle round Dunelm with a big trolley and chuck in anything that takes my fancy. I don't have a clear plan and I'm rubbish with colour schemes but I figure that if I stick to greens and blues everywhere, I can't go wrong. Nancy said it herself: she's 'a walking rainbow'. She won't feel at home in a bland setting.

It's Wednesday and Andy has suggested a drink tonight, but not at the Anchor as we don't want to be guilt-tripped into attending the SPAN meeting. I'm pleased that the support group is there for people like Meryl and Robin, who clearly need it. It isn't for me and I'm hoping it never will be, ever again. Nancy could very well be my first-class ticket out of singleness. Yes, I've got an adorable daughter and, yes, my promotion at work has given my ego a huge boost. But I haven't felt fulfilled or content since Tanya and I split up. Having Nancy in my life would give me purpose again.

I've spent the last hour scattering cushions, unfurling rugs and hanging prints. The flat still looks a bit glitter-on-a-turd but it's the best I can do and the bathroom's hugely improved with new towels, tufty mat and two ylang-ylang candles on the cistern. My phone rings. Mum's had a fall? Andy's blown me out? Nancy thinks I'm a prat and doesn't wish to take our relationship any further?

'It's me.' Tanya always does this, arrogantly assuming the whole world knows who she is.

'Tanya?'

'Yes, it's "Tanya". Don't be an arse.'

'I can't be long. I'm just off out.'

She expels her usual weary sigh. 'You *do* know you can take a mobile phone with you when you leave the house? The clue's in the name. Who are you meeting? One of your lady friends? I like Gemma, by the way. Has she got used to you talking in your sleep?'

'I'm meeting Andy.'

'Ah, the man who thinks punctuality is for losers. In that case, Ned, I think you can spare me a minute of your time.'

I sit on the sofa, chucking a couple of the new cushions on the floor. 'Go on then. What can I do for you? Is Dora okay?'

'She's fine. I just wanted to make sure you've remembered about the weekend.'

'Absolutely. I do have a calendar, you know.' I can't possibly tell her I'd forgotten – until two seconds ago – that Dora, Tanya and Julian are off to Wales early on Saturday to spend Easter week with his brother and family. I really should write things down.

I'll miss Dora, of course, but actually the timing couldn't be better. Me and Nancy need two days of 'just us', without Dora screaming from her bedroom that her socks hurt or there's a spider.

'You have a great holiday, Tanya. Say hi to Julian and give Dora a big daddy hug from me. Bye then.'

I practically dance my way to the pub. For a whole weekend, I am to be horny Ned, not keeper of the Koala & Friends backpack, wiper of the dripping nose, audience to the repetitive dance routine.

Andy is already there, at a quiet table away from the TV *and* he's got my pint in. Something's wrong. I'm not sure what, and I can't put my finger on it. Then, as he launches into his usual: 'Hey fella, how's it hanging?' I think perhaps I'm mistaken.

'It's hanging very well, thank you for asking.'

'And I'm pretty sure I know why, you sneaky bugger . . . Nancy. Nick told me. Nice one, Nedward. Have you "sealed the deal" yet?'

'You honestly think I'd tell you? Mate, you really need to tone it down sometimes.'

'Too late. The wind changed so I'm stuck like this.'

And yet, and yet . . . this is not the Andy I know and love. Something's missing: a sparkle in his eyes, a swagger in his shoulders. I won't push. I won't probe. It's for *him* to tell *me*, if anything's wrong.

'So,' I say, cool as you like. 'All good with you?'

He stares into the froth of his pint. 'Couldn't be better. Pig in shit, me.'

'Oh, for fuck's sake, tell me what's happened. Has Karen given you another bollocking? You probably deserved it.'

He knocks back a large gulp of beer and seems to crumple

in on himself. 'Guess what, Ned, I'm a dad. I found out last week. I have a 23-year-old son called Aaron. I've often wondered if I might have a kid but I didn't know how to find out. Or I didn't *want* to find out.'

I'm shocked, so I try to be funny which I realize, too late, is crass and insensitive. 'Ah, so you're a single parent after all. Maybe you should be at SPAN tonight.'

He glares at me. I deserve it. Men are crap at important conversations. I need to do this better. 'Tell me, Andy. It might help to get it off your chest.'

'Gillian. My first girlfriend. We were quite serious for a while. My mum thought we'd get married. That was the last thing Gill had in mind. Even after she fell pregnant, she said we were too young to be shackled to each other. So she had an abortion. Well, she *said* she did but now I know different. Maybe she had cold feet. Or she wanted the kid but she thought I didn't.'

'Did you?'

'No. Not then. Christ, no. I was nineteen. I wasn't ready for any of that. But it could have been good for me. Who knows how my life might have gone if we'd stayed together, brought him up together? The kid.'

'Aaron. How did you find out?'

He pulls a folded envelope from his pocket but has second thoughts about letting me read it and puts it away again. 'He'd done some detective work a few years back and found me. There are shedloads of Andrew Muirs but only one Andrew Christopher Winston Muir. Always said I was a one-off, didn't I? Anyway, he waited until his proper dad – his stepdad – had died and then he waited some more, until it felt like the right time to make contact and did I want to meet him?'

'And?'

'I do and I don't. I'm curious. How could I not be? But what's in it for him? An afternoon with *me*. I can't inflict that on the poor lad, after all this time.'

This isn't an Andy I've seen before. He's never been self-critical or hard on himself. I always suspected there was a vulnerable soul underneath the bluster. I didn't realize it was so close to the surface.

'What will you do? How will you respond? Aaron deserves an answer.'

He knocks back the last of his beer and hands the empty glass to me. 'I'm going to make like an ostrich and stick my head in the sand. We've managed without each other this long. Another week, another month, isn't going to hurt. A year, even.'

Andy's my friend. He needs to hear an alternative point of view. 'Or you see him soon as. To make up for lost time. Isn't that worth considering?'

He nods for a moment, deep in thought. 'There. Done. I've considered it. I'll stick with Plan A, if it's all the same to you, not that it is, is it? Hey, I could murder a Jack Daniels, no water, no ice. Have one yourself, Nedward. Your treat.'

My efforts to spruce up the flat are premature. It's Friday night and I am invited for supper at Nancy's. Her flatmate, Melanie, is away for the weekend. The planets have aligned and, if all goes according to plan, we will shortly 'seal the deal'.

Andy's confession about being a dad has been on my mind. I want to tell him to write back to Aaron, or at least to acknowledge receipt of his letter. Even at 23 – God knows, even at 37 – we still feel like children when we're rejected or ignored. But Andy has the hide of a rhino and won't be persuaded to do anything he doesn't want to do. I'll leave him to think through the pros and cons: better to be a dad or to be alone?

I know the answer from *my* perspective. The split with Tanya was horrendous. I felt like a failure. Totally without purpose. Despite that, I have a real role and it's for life. I'm Dora's dad, even when she's at her most precocious.

Yes, there's the knowledge that my genes won't fizzle out when I die. But it's so much more than that. This little being is part of me and depends on me. No matter what happens, I'll always be Dora's dad and she'll always be my girl, even when she's got little beings of her own.

Aaron had a stepfather, who took on the role after Andy excused himself. Has it harmed him, not having his biological dad around? Probably not. Actually, it's Andy I feel sorry for. He was too young to take on the responsibility of parenthood, but he will have missed out on so much. For his sake as much as Aaron's, I hope he decides to contact his son. The quality of both their lives would be improved by making that father–son connection asap.

On a whim, I've taken the day off. I wonder whether to contact Gemma, see if she's had an early shift at the care home and fancies lunch. I talk myself out of it. I've got an inkling I annoyed her the last time we met. Not telling her there was a dress code for Tanya's party was hardly the crime of the century. As it was, she fitted right in, whereas I looked like Timmy Mallett.

I should have told her I invited her at the last minute because Nancy couldn't make it. That way, she wouldn't have over-reacted when she found out. She had a great time and everyone liked her, especially Tanya and Julian – so why the hissy fit afterwards?

I'll give her a ring in a day or two. I need to know how she is. I like her company, her attitude, her laugh. I like her in my life. I'll definitely give her a ring. Soon.

For now, I shall enjoy my own company, make the most of my amazing city, having Friday free to be me. Bring it on.

I make myself crumpets and baked beans for breakfast, always a treat when I was little, and take them back to bed. After I've polished them off, licking the plate to get all the sauce off – something I can't do in Dora's presence – I allow myself ten minutes of extra shut-eye. Who's to stop me? Nobody, that's who.

I wake up three hours later but I don't care. I still have an afternoon to enjoy before going to Nancy's. What now? Inspired by her positivity, I decide on a run: down to the sea, eastward along the front as far as Fatboy's cafe, then back home via Wish Park. How hard can that be?

I find a kind of a kit: creased shorts, my 2012 Olympics T-shirt and some trainers I've barely run for the bus in. I set my phone to count my steps and plug my ears into an inspiring runners' soundtrack. Mo Farah, watch your back.

As it happens, my socks keep slipping down into my trainer heels, creating two nasty blisters, and I only get as far as the seafront before calling it a day and limping home. Better socks next time. I am bloodied – literally – but unbowed.

Two Netflix movies and a second round of crumpets and beans later, I'm thinking about what to take to Nancy's – wine? toothbrush? condoms? – when she WhatsApps me.

'Grrr! Flatmate has stomach bug & not going away for

weekend after all. Can I come to you? Will bring food & cook at yours. Hope ok? xxx N.'

Before thinking it through, I reply. 'No probs. No need to lug food here. I'll do dinner. See you half 7ish. xxx N.'

Right. I could send out for pizzas or a Chinese, I could make my signature spag bol, but I remember Tanya once saying that every man who can't cook makes spag bol. Mac 'n' cheese, then. That's just pasta with a beige sauce, instead of a red one.

I sprint to Sainsbury's and return with everything I need: mac, cheese sauce, salad, garlic bread, wine, olives, trifle. (Who doesn't like trifle? Especially with extra squirty cream and chocolate mousse on the side.)

The flat, though. It may have ylang-bloody-ylang candles on the cistern but it's a tip: breakfast and lunch pans 'soaking' in the sink and my running gear in a sweaty pool on the living-room floor, where I climbed out of it.

In the space of an hour, I manage to do more cleaning and tidying than I've done in the last six months. I can't let crap accumulate any more, if Nancy's going to become a regular visitor. Maybe I'll get a cleaner. I'd be supporting a one-person business, enhancing the hygiene of my environment and I'd never have to scrub the arse end of a loo again.

When she rings the doorbell, wine is cooling in the bucket I used to mop the floor; olives are in a saucer, hand-painted by Dora, and the mac 'n' cheese is browning in the oven. I've even washed the big ugly cut-glass fruit bowl that stores house keys, spare buttons and the key to bleed the radiators, to serve the salad in. I'm wearing my other TK Maxx shirt – the Pierre St Pierre one – and some clean jeans. I am pretty bloody pleased with myself.

Nancy really is a walking rainbow. It's as if she auto-installs a Technicolor app to my flat just by coming through the door. Her hair is now maroony-purple and she's wearing huge linen dungarees, the colour of Colman's English mustard. Her sandals match her hair and her toenails are metallic blue, reminding me of my grandad's Cortina. I'd have been so proud if she'd been able to come to Tanya and Julian's party dressed like this: two Timmy Malletts against the world.

She thrusts a silver-foil parcel into my hands. 'I made cheese straws and I wasn't going to leave them for Melanie. You haven't made cheese straws too, have you?'

I shake my head like a fool. I'm dumbstruck by her delightfulness.

She bounces onto the sofa and looks around. 'Ooh, this is very . . .'

'Gloomy? Grubby? Blokey?'

'That wasn't what I was going to say. Although, yes, "blokey" fits the bill. But you *are* "a bloke", aren't you? I was hardly expecting potpourri and doilies.'

'Potpourri and the Doilies? Is that another band name?'

'It sounds more like a tea shop to me,' she says with a grin, enjoying our running joke. 'Hey, let's open one in the Cotswolds. I'll do the cheese straws. What will you do?'

'Eat them.' I'm already halfway through my second and they're delicious. Delicate, slightly sharp, extremely moreish. Very much like the woman who made them.

The wine's been breathing for an hour and is already a glass down because I slugged one back after my shower, for Dutch courage. I'd love to make a toast but I don't want to look like a fool. Keep it low key, Ned. We're merely two single people, meeting for macaroni.

Instead, Nancy leans forward, pops an olive in her mouth and chinks my glass. 'We made it. This far. And I, for one, am very pleased. Here's to . . . to supper, Pinot Noir and good times.'

Of course, we don't do any eating. Not until past midnight. After our first hasty thrash on the sofa, we adjourn to the bedroom where the new duvet cover still has tramline creases from the packaging. I hope I've taken all the pins out. No, that's shirts, you twat.

I need to keep calm. This isn't a quick tumble with my boss. This is Nancy. Nancy could be my future. I need to keep calm. But the significance of all this makes me hesitant and fumbly as we stroke and explore each other. I tell myself I can do this better. Tanya never complained, did she? Not in the early days anyway. Her voice suddenly pops up in my head: 'For Christ's sake, Ned. Just get on with it, will you? I'm getting pins and needles.'

Fortunately, Nancy takes charge. The first thing she says is: 'Can I smell burning?'

Shit! My mac 'n' cheese. I hurtle to the kitchen stark-bollock naked, taking extra care when I open the oven. It's this side of charcoal. If I scrape off the burnt bits, the rest will be edible.

I stumble back to bed, pleased that I've salvaged supper. After that, the sex is excellent, really very, very good indeed. I pat myself metaphorically on the back. I have not come up short or disappointed Nancy. We fitted together just right and we know it.

We stay in bed, propped up by my stupid scatter cushions, to eat cold mac 'n' cheese. Is it because of the sex or is this the best meal I've ever made? Nancy fetches us seconds so she must think so too. We've worked up quite an appetite.

I watch her padding back with our plates. She has small breasts, small hips, reddy-gold pubic hair and a Maori-style tattoo circling her left thigh. She is, quite literally, perfect. We sit cross-legged and eat. 'Cross-legged' could be awkward and exposing when you're naked with someone for the first time. And yet, I feel totally at home and at peace.

'This is good,' she says, with her mouth full.

'The sauce could be cheesier.'

She gives me a playful nudge. 'This. Us. *This* is good.'

'It really is.'

We don't have room for the trifle so that's breakfast sorted. I give Nancy my Pulp T-shirt to sleep in and she looks so sexy in it. Her snores are snuffly, like a snoozing hedgehog. I breathe in rhythm with her. Her ins and outs are slower, deeper than my mine.

How long I have been breathing too fast? From stress? Anxiety? Nancy will calm me down. We can breathe in tune. It feels good.

I wake up to the smell of toast toasting and something frying. And no Nancy.

'Ham and eggs okay with you?' she asks, standing at the stove in my moth-eaten at-home cardigan.

'I don't have any ham. Should I get some?'

She waggles a tin at me. I must have bought it when I moved in. 'You do the second batch of toast and I'll make coffee.'

Second only to last night's supper, Nancy's breakfast is so perfect that we don't need the trifle after all. Just as she's given my tattiest cardigan a new lease of life, she's explored the contents of my kitchen and concocted a breakfast I could have cooked for myself any time, but never did.

The breakfast gives us a second wind and we go back to bed. Dora will be here again next weekend so I have to make the most of my time with Nancy. If anything, the sex is even better than last night. Now we know each other's bodies and what we like. Plus we're in no hurry and the pace is leisurely until we're ready. We come together. I don't think she's faking it for my sake. It feels so real. And then the fucking phone rings.

'Let it go to voicemail,' Nancy mumbles, her hair in sweaty question marks across her forehead.

'Okay. No. What if something's happened to Dora?'

I find my phone on the sofa and answer just before it goes to message. It's Gemma. Has she called at a bad time, she asks, assuming not. Well, yes, actually. But I can't say that. She's not to know Nancy's in my bed, in my life.

'Kelvin got an "A" for his steam-train project,' she tells me, the reason for this call. 'So thank you for helping. It'll really boost his confidence.'

That *is* good news actually. He's a terrific kid.

'Wow, that's great. Tell him well done from me. Look, sorry, Gemma. I am a bit, you know, tied up right now. Can I ring back later?'

It doesn't help that Nancy's calling from the bedroom. 'Oi, Ned. We're not done here.'

Before I can explain that I have company, Gemma wishes me a nice weekend and hangs up. I'm relieved that she's not angry with me any more about the party invite. Her call was a kind of olive branch. I wish I'd asked her more about Kelvin and his project, but the timing was awkward although, actually, I don't see why it should be. We're both grown-ups. We're both sexual beings with wants/ needs.

And right now, I want/need Nancy. I run back into the bedroom, tackle flapping, and throw myself on to the bed. She gives a gratifying giggle and we pick up where we left off.

Chapter Twenty

Gemma

My new garden bench is drying after its second coat of rich pine wood stain, so Dan and I sit on the back step for coffee and a cheese sandwich. I've loved perching here – to read, daydream have a natter, have a cuppa – ever since Joe and I bought the house eight years ago. Yes, it's a pain if someone wants to get past and okay, it isn't as comfy as a proper seat. To be honest, I've never minded.

So I can hardly tell Dan I don't need the knackered old bench he found in a salvage yard in Shoreham and has been doing up for the last two weekends: sanding it down, choosing and applying the wood stain, even making a 'coffee table' out of an old railway sleeper to go with it.

'Gift horse, mouth,' I tell myself. A month from now, you'll wonder how you ever managed without a proper garden bench, you ungrateful cow. Besides, I don't want to put Dan off. It's the thought that counts and he's the most thoughtful man I've ever met.

'If you could only have a cheese and Branston or sausage and Branston sandwich for the rest of your life, which one would you choose?' Dan often does this: Kit-Kat or Aero; *Line of Duty* or *Luther*; shower or bath?

'Both. But I'd prefer piccalilli.'

'I'd have cheese. Because that would mean there's cheese in the world and you could also have it on toast or pasta or a baked spud. Sausages aren't so versatile.'

'You're daft, Dan Robertson.'

'You're not the first to tell me.' He kisses the top of my head, shoves the last bit of sandwich into his mouth and hauls himself up to stain the bench legs.

I go indoors to start on dinner. To any passing stranger, we must look like an old-school, traditional couple; man make bench, woman roast cow. Maybe that's because we were already so set in our ways when we got together.

Having said that, Dan does a mean lamb curry with all the trimmings and, last weekend, I forced him *not* to help me when I put some up shelves on the landing. Yes, they were wonky and, okay, he had to redo them but I was making a point.

These past few weeks have been brilliant. My life has changed – my weekends in particular. Kelvin goes to Joe's on a Friday afternoon and Dan rocks up an hour later. Or I go to his place in Portslade, practically the entire route of the 49 bus, if he doesn't swing by to collect me. We even had six whole days together when Joe and Vicky took Amelie and Kel to Center Parcs in Sherwood Forest for the Easter holidays.

Our trip to Hastings was the clincher. In fact, he didn't really have to take the sideboard to his mate's; he just wanted an excuse for a day out with me. It couldn't have been nicer: good weather; chips on the front; a wander round the little indie shops where I bought a sundress, and a ride to the top of the town on the funicular railway. Kelvin would have loved that.

We kissed a bit too. Actually we kissed a lot. I don't wish to sound big-headed but it was obvious that being with me meant so much to Dan. He'd stroke my arm for no reason or smile at me while I was eating an ice cream.

'Why didn't we do this when we were kids?' he asked, as we sat on the grass at the top of the hill.

'You know why. Me and Joe had got together and you hooked up with – who was it, Emma Maitland?'

'That lasted all of five minutes. I didn't want to be with Emma, I wanted to be with you.'

'Good things come to those who wait.'

We couldn't take it any further that day, even though we were desperate to, because I had to get back to Brighton to pick up Kelvin. We got it together the next weekend, though. I came over for his legendary lamb curry and stayed for scrambled eggs. He was lovely in bed. Not cocky and urgent like Joe; gentle and kind and thoughtful. I've only known sex with Joe; time to try other ice-cream flavours.

Actually, if I'm honest, a combo of Dan and Joe would be ideal; cocky *and* thoughtful, urgent *and* kind. But it's early days and we're only just getting the hang of each other. We were both with previous partners for years. Now we're older, wiser, and we know what we like in bed.

The bench is Dan's latest project. Before that, he fixed my broken banister and, after his first night at mine and not having anywhere to put his watch and phone, he brought round two Fifties bedside tables that he'd lovingly restored. He really has an eye for that stuff.

'I don't have anything to give you,' I told him, after he'd lugged them upstairs and placed them each side of my bed.

'You do, Gemma. You so do.'

We didn't even take each other's clothes off that time. We

were in too much of a hurry. I know that it isn't sex I'm giving him. He's a good-looking guy, he can get that anywhere. I'm giving him 'us', after all these years. He has what he's always wanted and it's a bit scary. What if he finds out that I wasn't worth the wait? What if I'm not good enough to be his girlfriend?

The disappointment would be too much for both of us to bear.

Sunday should be the day of rest. The bench is finished, the beef's in the oven, the veg is prepped. Dan tempts me back to bed and it's good but it isn't great. God knows, there were times with Joe when he'd come like a tornado, while I lay back and thought of *Strictly*. Women need different buttons to be pressed. We've pressed them ourselves often enough. We know what lights the spark.

After nearly a month with Dan, I thought *he* did too. Not this time, though. I find myself wondering if leeks and carrots will be enough or should I do some frozen peas too? I've got this gorgeous man on top of me, and all I can think about are vegetables.

Actually I'm cool with it. I won't say anything. I don't want to undermine Dan when he adores me so much. 'Gift horse, mouth,' I tell myself again. Don't be negative or nitpicky. Just enjoy being loved.

Instead, I pick a fight while we're washing up.

'The gravy *was* lumpy,' I say, drying up some forks. 'Nice of you to pretend it wasn't, but it was.'

'The gravy was great. Mind you, mine's like wallpaper paste, so what do I know?'

'Exactly. Listen, I don't mind. Lumpy gravy's not a disaster. Nobody died. And the roasties were perfect.'

263

'They were.'

'But I'm not Mary Berry. I'm not Nigella-bloody-Lawson. I won't have you putting me on some kind of gravy pedestal.' I actually *say* that, for fuck's sake.

And, because it's funny, he laughs. Who wouldn't? I sound ridiculous.

He stacks the last pan on the drainer and dries his hands on his jeans. Then he takes the wet roasting tin from me, puts it down and wraps his arms around me.

'Gemma O'Hara, I would never, ever put you on a gravy – or any other kind of – pedestal. Cross my heart and hope to die.'

I should laugh and hug him back. I should quietly accept that I sound like an idiot. But no, I have to dig myself deeper into the massive great hole I've made myself.

'Don't patronize me. Just don't, Dan.'

I huff off into the garden and sit with a hard-done-by thump on the bench which, thank God, isn't still wet from wood stain. Dan's done nothing wrong but I feel hemmed in, suffocated. Will this work, me and him? I don't know.

He gives me five minutes, then comes out with some tea. 'See, I made it in your favourite mug,' he points out. 'Then I spat in it.'

I laugh so loud it scares next-door's cat. Dan laughs too, pleased his throwaway line has got me down from my gravy pedestal.

'It was a *bit* lumpy,' he says, putting his arm round me. 'I should have agreed with you. And then got a mouthful for being over-critical.'

'I need to get used to this whole relationship thing again. Cut me some slack, eh?'

'As much as you like.'

We sit for a while. He strokes my hand and twiddles with my fingers. I like my bench. I like Dan. Gift horse. Mouth.

'Right,' I say, standing up purposefully. 'Time to collect Kelvin. Your chance to meet my boy. Are you ready for that?'

He nods. I haven't kept Dan and Kelvin apart on purpose, it's just the way my co-parenting schedule works. I want them to meet. If Kelvin gets on with Dan half as well as he got on with Ned, we should be laughing.

I wonder how Ned and Nancy's relationship is developing. Has he put *her* on a gravy pedestal? Is she The One? Ned may not be very worldly but he's not stupid. He won't settle, just to stop being single.

Is that what *I'm* doing? Is Dan my route out of singledom and a shield against any further advances from Joe? Have I 'settled'?

'Come on then,' Dan says. 'Kelvin time.'

Dan wonders if he should wait in the car. He hasn't seen Joe in years and that's been fine with him. And fine with me, ever since Dan and I got together. Today, I feel different. Today I decide they need to meet again, to get it out of the way so it doesn't turn into a 'thing'.

Anyway, it really isn't a 'thing'. They used to be mates, back in the day, but they lost touch. Joe's my ex. Dan's my boyfriend. No big deal.

'Come to the door with me,' I tell him. 'I'm sure Joe would like to say hi.'

'Are you?'

'It might be a bit sticky at first. But *he's* moved on, hasn't he? With Vicky. And now I've moved on too. With you. We can do this, Dan.'

'O-kay.' He doesn't sound convinced.

As it happens, Joe's in the drive, vacuuming his car seats. He's never cared about crud on his shoes, but car seats must be spotless.

'Hi, Joe. You missed a bit,' I say with a smile. It's a silly in-joke between us. I can't even remember how it started. Probably not the best moment to give it an airing.

He bobs up and turns off the vacuum cleaner. He's composing his face into a 'greeting-my-ex' expression but it shifts into a frown when he clocks Dan.

'Bloody hell, is it? Desperate Danno? It only bloody is.'

Dan isn't fazed. 'You haven't changed a bit. Apart from the hair. You were a martyr to your mullet back then, as I recall.'

Joe pats his tum. 'Yeah, well, there's a few extra pounds I could do without. What brings you round here, bud?'

'Me,' I chip in, breaking into the bromantic reunion. 'Or rather, Dan brought me. He wanted to say hi and he's dying to meet Kelvin.'

The cogs in Joe's head click and whirr. Finally the wires connect. I can't blame him for being slow on the uptake. Why would he expect my new fella to be his old friend?

'So you two have . . . hooked up? Wow, you kept pretty quiet about that, Gem.'

'You kept pretty quiet when you and Vicky "hooked up".'

It's getting tense, thanks to me, so Dan makes a quick gear change. 'Nice wheels, Joe. You must be doing well for yourself. Not like *my* old banger.'

'I am, as it happens. Yeah. Still in plumbing and central heating but I partnered up with a pal to build the business. We've got three engineers on the payroll so, yeah, it's all good. And we love living here. Me, Vicky and the little 'un. Yeah, it's all good.'

There's an awkward silence while Joe gives Dan a hard stare, despite the chatty banter. He's definitely unnerved by us but he daren't say so.

'We'd better get a wiggle on, Gemma.' Dan senses we're done here. 'I still need to fix that dodgy window for you.'

I nod and give him my most loved-up smile. 'So, Joe. Can I have my boy back?'

Joe goes indoors to fetch Kelvin. This has been great, everything I'd hoped for. He's definitely put out that I'm with Dan. Good.

'Okay?' I ask Dan.

'Couldn't be better,' he replies and kisses my forehead. 'I'd forgotten what a macho man he is.'

'What a macho man he *thinks* he is. It's all front. Especially the beer belly.'

Kelvin comes out, followed by Joe and Vicky, carrying a sleepy Amelie.

'Wow,' I gush. 'She's grown so much since I last saw her.'

Vicky beams. Joe frowns. Kelvin kicks a bit of gravel across the driveway.

'Nice to meet you, Kelvin.' Dan holds out a hand for shaking.

Kelvin's turn to be unnerved: Mum's new boyfriend. He hesitates, then gives Dan's hand a quick, self-conscious shake.

Finally, after a lot of foot shuffling and half-arsed chat, we're in Dan's car and heading home.

'Did you have a nice weekend?' I ask, even though I can tell without even looking that we've got grumpy Kelvin in the back.

'Yeah.'

'Done your homework?'

'Nearly.'

'Want some help?'

'*No!*'

Dan throws me a quick smile as we turn down Warren Road. We can do this.

Kelvin was in another of his grumps this morning, even when I reminded him that Wednesday is only two sleeps to Friday. Plus I've got the mother of all period pains, which means I need to be sure I think before I speak at work, to avoid making any sarky comments or letting rip with a big fat swear word. Felipe feeds me Maltesers whenever I pass him in the corridor and lunch is my favourite: fish pie. So far, so good. I intend to make it to 6 p.m. without biting anyone's head off.

My short fuse is lit late afternoon when Judy's son and daughter-in-law come to visit. Anyone can see that Willowdene is clean, comfortable and cosy, and the staff always go above-and-beyond because we love our residents. We're care workers, not prison warders or bouncers. The clue's in the name.

Judy's visitors have had a long drive down from Oxford, with roadworks on the M25, so I fetch them tea and biscuits without being asked, and encourage them into the day room so that Judy gets a change of scenery from her usual four walls. And I walk Keith to the crafts room so that Judy and Co. can have the sofa and armchair by the French windows. Above-and-beyond. It's not so hard, even for a prison warder like me.

'That cardigan isn't my mother's,' says Son, jabbing a finger at me. 'What have you done with the Wedgwood-blue cashmere one we bought her for her birthday?'

'I am here, you know,' Judy says, waving her hand in the air. 'I'm still the full shilling.'

'We know that, darling,' says Daughter-in-Law. 'You're looking really well today.'

'Happy to explain,' I say, with my best fake smile. 'Judy loves that cardigan but it can be too warm for her. Her room gets so much sun. So she gave me £20 and I got her that one in the Factory Shop, with a fiver to spare. It washes really well and it doesn't have buttons.'

'Buttons are bastards,' says Judy, 'so are zips. I never thought I'd take to elasticated waists but here I am. Shoot me now.'

I laugh. It's one of her catchphrases. Son and Daughter-in-Law frown in horror. If they only saw her as often as I do, if they'd ever wiped her bum or given her a little hug when she's defeated by her Corn Flakes, they'd know that this is Judy on a good day. This is full-on Judy, with her blue eyeshadow, pink lippy and zebra-print turban.

I leave them to it, even though Judy wants me to stay. *That* doesn't go down well with her visitors either. I must be drugging her or brainwashing her. Maybe I've got myself mentioned in her will and all they'll be left with is her jewellery box of plastic pearls and rhinestone tat. Why else would I like being around this inspiring woman?

I'm putting on my coat, ready to head off to Ros's, when Janine finds me. I can tell from her face that I'm about to get my wrist slapped. I will keep my snarky replies to myself, I will not lose my cool, even though my hormones are all set for aggro.

'Mrs Woodley-Palmer,' she says, with a meaningful stare.

'Mrs Palmer-Woodley, you mean? She had visitors today. I wish they'd come more often. She makes such an effort when they do.'

'Pity *you* couldn't, Gemma. Make an effort, I mean, and

try to keep your smart-alecky comments to yourself. Nobody cares what you think.'

I smile. I nearly bite my tongue into two equal sections.

'They were asking about her cashmere cardigan. Apparently it was from Selfridges.'

'I sold it for heroin' . . . is what I want to say. 'It's in her chest of drawers,' I reply. 'Folded in tissue paper, the way Judy likes it. I'd have fetched it for them if they didn't believe me. Shall I get it for you now, Janine, if *you* don't believe me either?'

'There's no need for that. Just be civil, if you could, Gemma. I shouldn't need to keep telling you. Anyway, Alan's picking me up in five minutes so *I* need to head off too.'

No apology. No humble pie. No chance. But I didn't lose my rag, so who's the grown-up around here?

'She sounds like a nightmare,' says Ros, as she checks a tray of random root veg roasting in the oven. 'You do like chorizo, don't you?'

'She is and I do.'

'And you could have been assistant manager instead of her? What happened?'

'I didn't apply for the job. I didn't think I was up to it. Joe agreed but I can't blame *him*. I talked myself out of it. You know, that voice on your shoulder telling you you're a waste of space. Or is that just me?'

'God, no. That's every woman, whether we admit it or not. We're too apologetic, too hard on ourselves. Even the toughest woman wakes up in the middle of the night and thinks she's crap.'

'In Janine's case, she's right.'

'Well done you for not losing your cool.' Ros chinks my glass.

I've brought some Argentinian Malbec from the offie. I know bugger-all about wine but this stuff's lovely.

Our weekly Wednesdays are at Ros's now. Kelvin's happy to eat at Mohit's and, this way, I still get my midweek night out. The last thing we want to do is spend it at SPAN. Sometimes I help Ros to get a cake order completed, as long as she doesn't expect me to bake anything.

Last week, I emptied a shoebox of till receipts onto the kitchen table and sorted them into date order. Ros's good at everything, except admin. Which is something I *can* do. I used to keep Joe's books, from when he first started out.

Ros wants me to look at her accounts, kept in a tatty hardback ledger, with Post-It notes peeking out of every page. Please can I make it more businesslike? If she registers for VAT, she needs to get her admin in order and it's better if *I* do that than burn a batch of pistachio macarons or put salt in the whipped cream. (Ros stopped me just in time.)

We eat at the kitchen table, surrounded by apricot flap-jacks, cooling on racks. Once again, I can't identify half of what's on my plate but it tastes amazing because Ros's stirred in a shedload of harissa.

'Well, come on,' she says wiping a finger round her plate to scoop up the last slick of garlicky sauce. 'Catch me up on your love life, Gemma. I'm living it vicariously.'

So I tell her how it's going with Dan . . . and how I pissed off Joe . . . and my new bench . . . and, yes, he knows what's what in bed . . . and I can't complain.

'That's never stopped you before.' Ros grins.

'I've had it with being a whinger and beating myself up about everything. I don't want to be that Gemma any more. I kept my cool with Judy's family and with Janine, didn't I? That's a personal best for me.'

'What's the problem, then?'

I shrug. What's she on about?

Ros tops up our glasses without asking. Then she launches straight in. 'You've been through the wringer with Joe. He sapped you of your confidence, your identity, your optimism. You said it yourself. You thought you were a waste of space. And now here you are with a wonderful new boyfriend who's good with a hammer and good in bed and has fancied you for decades, and all I'm hearing is . . . meh.'

'I've never said "meh" in my life.'

'You don't need to, Gemma. You just seem so . . . underwhelmed. Dan may not be the future but he's the perfect present. Enjoy. Celebrate. Gloat.'

'I gloated to Joe and he bloody hated it.'

Ros loads our plates into the dishwasher. She doesn't say a word. All I see is her back and it's grumpy. I'm an expert at detecting grumpy backs, living with Kelvin.

'What?' I say. 'Why aren't you pleased for me?'

'Because *you're* not pleased for you, you idiot. The only joy you've extracted from this new relationship is that it pisses off your ex. You deserve way more joy than that. You know you do.'

I wish I could argue with her, tell her she's got it all wrong and that Dan is my future. All I can come up with is: 'Gift horse. Mouth.'

She gives me a hug. 'Aw, love. Is that really how you see it?'

'Dan adores me. I know he does. I should just be grateful. But it's like he adores the idea of "us" because it's what he's wanted since we were kids. How can I live up to that? I'm bound to fail. Tomorrow, next week, next year. And then he'll run for the hills and I'll be alone again, only with a new set of scars.'

Ros regards me for a moment. 'That's a hangover from Joe, isn't it? Constantly thinking you're going to screw up. I reckon Dan knows exactly who he's in a relationship with, and he's *not* expecting perfection. It's *you* he wants. Warts and all. And, yes, you might fail, if failing means messing up every so often. He'll fail too. And that's okay. That's life. If you're serious about each other, moments like that will bring you closer together. I'm certain of it, Gem.'

I nod, and she gives me another look.

'What?' I try not to sound defensive, but don't quite manage it.

She sighs. 'I'm still not hearing that you want to be with him. And that's okay – of course it is, but you shouldn't use your fear of failure as an excuse. You really need to stop judging yourself so harshly because nobody else does.'

I'm not in the mood for this. 'That's enough character analysis for one night,' I tell her, with my best smile, to prove it's cool and I'm cool and can we change the subject now *please*?

'Okay, I'm done here.' She peels two flapjacks off the rack for our pudding. 'Hey, I wonder if Ned still goes to SPAN.'

'No need. He's got Nancy now. In fact, he reckons we should go for a drink next week, the four of us.'

He'd texted to suggest it, a few hours after I'd rung him. With Nancy there, he'd been far too distracted to enjoy my news about Kelvin's 'A' and I felt stupid and clumsy for barging in on their cosy weekend. I'm not wild about a double date but could hardly refuse without sounding snarky. Nice work, Gemma. Hoist by your own petard.

'So Ned gets to meet Dan and I get to meet Nancy. Apparently, she's got purple hair. Trust Ned to pick a woman with purple hair.'

'But you'll go along with an open mind. You won't take against her just because.'

'I told you. Whingeing Gemma is history. I'm sure I'll like Nancy and her purple hair and I'm sure Dan will approve of Ned.'

Ros laughs. 'Did you hear what you just said?'

'I mean, I'm sure Ned will approve of Dan. Same difference.'

'If you say so, madam. Hey, do you think this flapjack needs white chocolate drizzle on top? I've still got time to do it tomorrow morning.'

'Can't hurt.'

She nods. Good plan. 'I'm going out for a drink next week too. With Andy.'

'Wow, seriously?'

'It's just a drink. I need to give him a chance. What if there really is a decent, humble guy underneath all the bullshit?'

'Or just more bullshit? You want to know what I think?'

Ros nods. She really does.

'Andy may not be the future but he could be the perfect present.'

I still don't get how it happened. Maybe the planets collided or fate's having a laugh or karma pulled a fast one. Maybe I've travelled back in time and I'm still married to Joe and we're a proper happy family, just like we used to be.

We've gone out for the day: me, Kelvin . . . and Joe. There's no Vicky, no Amelie and definitely no Dan. Yes, they exist but they're not here to remind us of our 'real' lives, our 'normal' lives. It's just us three, pretending to play happy families.

Two hours ago, Dan drove off to help a mate with a house move. And I had no plans, apart from giving my armpits and legs an industrial waxing . . . maybe bleaching my moustache and sandblasting my flaky feet – all the things men don't notice but would if we didn't.

Then I got a text from Kelvin saying Vicky's on her spa weekend with Hayley, Amelie's at her nana's, he and Joe were going on a trip to the Bluebell Railway and did I want to come? My guess is that Joe's forgotten how to manage a day out with sole responsibility for his son, minus Vicky as back-up: googling the destination; remembering water and snacks; carrying the unwanted hoodie around all day 'just in case'. When Joe takes Kelvin to the Amex for a home game, he's in his comfort zone. That's his limit.

Before Dan came on the scene, I might have felt uneasy, spending the day with my ex. But look at us; we've moved on. Here's our chance to be proper co-parents, without any emotional baggage getting in the way. And if, every ten minutes or so, I can mention how happy Dan makes me, I'll be ahead on points.

Ros would warn me off a day out with Joe and she'd have a point. Is she also right about me using my fear of failure as an excuse? I *am* frightened of screwing up – thanks to Joe – but is that the real reason I'm scared to fall for Dan? I don't think so. He's lovely (gift horse, mouth, and all that) but . . . but what? Why must I over-think this? Why can't I just lighten up and enjoy the ride? I give myself a serious talking-to. I need to live in the here and now, and stop over-analysing everything. Be chilled and open to adventure, take it day by day and go with the flow. How hard is that, for pity's sake?

Kelvin's really looking forward to today's outing. Ned did

a brilliant job, sparking up his interest in old trains, and getting an 'A' for his school project was the cherry on the cake. He often asks when Ned's coming round again and I've had to explain that we won't be seeing much of him now because he's in *luurve*.

'Like you and Dan?'

'I don't *luurve* Dan. It's early days, pal.'

'But you will?'

'Sheesh, I don't know. What's with the interrogation?'

I'm wearing the dress I bought in Hastings with a denim jacket. I look really good and I can tell, as I walk down my front path to Joe's car, that he thinks so too. Good. You blew it big time, sunshine, and here's what you're missing.

He still drives like Lewis Hamilton on Pro-Plus so we screech into the Bluebell Railway car park in under half an hour. For the first time that day, I wish we were with Ned, not Joe. Ned would be super-keen to tell us everything he knows about steam engines and signals and disused lines like this one. And Kelvin would be like an excitable sponge, soaking it all up.

Joe knows bugger-all about steam trains and doesn't even pretend to. He takes the path of least resistance and gives Kelvin £20 to spend in the gift shop while we have a cup of tea and wait for our train to East Grinstead.

'What's all this about, then?' Joe asks. 'Why the sudden interest in old trains?'

'His school project. He got an "A". He must have told you.'

Joe's obviously forgotten but pretends he hasn't. 'Trains, though, Gemzy. Promise me we haven't spawned an anorak.'

'Our boy's found something that interests him so let's take the piss?'

'I wouldn't. You know that. Not to his face, anyway. Is Dan a trainspotter? Is that where he got it from?'

'Not Dan, no. I do have other friends.'

'And you and Dan? All going well, is it?'

'It is, actually. Really well.'

Joe gives Kelvin a wave as he emerges from the gift shop with £20 worth of souvenirs, tightly clutched in a carrier bag. 'You knew it would wind me up, didn't you? You and Desperate Danno hooking up.'

'It crossed my mind. But I figured you'd be cool about it, because of you and Vicky and how I was the last one to know. I think we make a pretty great couple actually.'

'He looks more like your granddad, with all that grey hair.'

'Trim as anything. No beer belly. Not an ounce of spare fat. Anywhere.'

Joe instinctively looks down at his tum. Bullseye.

Kelvin arrives and shows us what he's bought: a book about steam trains for him, a fridge magnet for me and a driver's badge . . . for Ned.

'Oi, mate,' Joe says in mock outrage. 'Where's *my* souvenir?'

'You're not interested, Dad. You know you're not.'

'I am!'

'You weren't interested enough to read my project.'

Banged to rights. Joe promises he will, and we get on the train. The smell of the steam and oil, the musty, dusty uphol-stery, the chug of the engine . . . it's definitely a new experience but I can't pretend it's something I need to do too often. I will, though, if it makes Kelvin happy. Maybe we'll invite Ned next time.

'And it's working out for you, Gemzy? You and Dan?'

Okay, I wanted Joe to be unnerved but not *this* much. 'Why wouldn't it? He's a great guy.'

'He fancied you when we were kids. I got there first.'

'You "got there". Nicely put, Joe.'

'You know what I mean. He didn't stand a chance.'

'That was then, this is now and what you think, how you feel, really don't matter. Just be happy that *I'm* happy, okay?'

We trundle through Horsted Keynes Station. Kelvin's glued to the window, taking in every last detail.

'You're right, Gemzy, and, if Dan gives you what you want, I'm pleased for you. But ever since that night in your kitchen, I can't stop thinking about you and me. What we were, what we *are* together.'

'Sex,' I say in a near whisper. 'That's all it was.'

'And it's better with Dan? Better than us? I'm not ready to believe that.'

Kingscote. Next stop East Grinstead, then back to Sheffield Park. Kelvin looks like he's died and gone to heaven.

'Dan wouldn't hurt me, ever. That's what makes it better. 100 per cent.'

I need to stand my ground and make a case for Dan. But deep down I'm terrified that Joe's right. I've tried to delete the moment I let my guard down, and I've not told a soul what happened. And yet, however hard I press 'delete' in my head, it won't shift.

Joe's with Vicky now and I'm with Dan. And yet we fit together, Joe and me, whether I like it or not, whether I fight it or not. How can I change that? What if I don't want to? Then what?

When he drives us home and comes in for a cuppa, when he sits with Kelvin at the kitchen table and looks through his train project with him and occasionally catches my eye and smiles, he knows and I know that this – whatever 'this' is – isn't going away. And I'll never have it with Dan, however hard I try.

Because he's not Joe? If that's the reason, I'm doomed to

being alone. Or do I give in, start seeing Joe again and do to Vicky what she did to me? Being with Dan has reminded me how good it feels to be loved. Being with Joe would be a disaster because I can never trust him again, even if the sex is as good as it ever was.

It's doing my head in, thinking about it, and then, as he's leaving and we're chatting in the hall, he suddenly kisses me hard and I let him and give as good as I get, and we both know that we could so easily pick up where we left off.

In a heartbeat.

Chapter Twenty-One

Ned

I like running. If you'd told me a year ago that I'd look forward to getting up at 5.30, putting on proper kit and pounding the pavement for an hour or so . . . if you'd told me that I might even be quite good at it, I'd have said 'jog on'.

As a kid, I hated running and I was at a school famous for it, with two alumni making it to Team GB and one nearly winning a bronze medal at Rio. If boys had periods, I'd have used that as an excuse to get out of every games lesson. When I did try my best, I was teased mercilessly by 'Ron' Jovey, our bully of a sports teacher. Today he'd be 'outed' as a sadist.

Nancy knows all this and yet she's very nearly convinced me that I cut quite the dash when we run along Hove seafront together. She loves my legs. She reckons, with calves as shapely as mine, I could be a drag queen. (She's great with compliments, even slightly left-field ones like that.)

Nancy reckons she's more in tune with her body when she runs than when she walks. She's like the Duracell bunny. Just wind her up and let her go. She's tiny and taut and sinewy and sexy. We generally run together on Tuesday mornings, sometimes Thursdays too, from my flat. Then we shower, grab some breakfast, occasionally fit in a quick shag, and go to work.

Our schedules are strangely symbiotic. I have Dora from Friday p.m. to Sunday p.m. And Nancy goes to her folks in West Wittering most weekends. Her mum's in poor health and her dad finds it hard to cope alone through the week so she does the laundry, gets the car washed, fills the freezer with stews and soups. I'm so in awe of this brilliant woman who has graciously become my girlfriend. She's thoughtful, caring, funny, wise and a ruddy delight under the duvet. I count my blessings.

I've yet to meet her folks. There's no hurry for that. But we are off to Amsterdam on Friday for a long weekend. Her oldest friend, Olivia, lives there and Nancy wants us to meet. That feels like a good sign to me.

We got the Dora–Nancy meeting out of the way early on. I didn't want it to be a big deal for either of them. Tanya owed me a weeknight out with my girl so we took her to her favourite ice-cream parlour on Western Road.

'Can't we find somewhere less clichéd, Ned?' Nancy asked, after I'd made all the arrangements. 'Single dad, new girl-friend, only daughter, caramel sundae?'

'Dora can be in a foul mood but she calms down as soon as she walks into that place. Every time. I think it's the additives. Trust me, Nan, I know what I'm doing.'

I was right; Dora was chatty and charming and loved Nancy's Hey Duggee T-shirt. Nancy was relaxed and daft and loved Dora's sparkly baseball boots. They tried each other's ice creams and had hysterics when I dropped a half-melted scoop of rum & raisin on to the floor. We kept the date intentionally short – just over an hour – so that

Dora wouldn't have time to turn stroppy, and it was a total success.

I've been feeling a bit awkward about how I left things with Gemma. Was it obvious that Nancy and I were having sex when she rang to tell me about Kelvin's school project? Was I rude/smug/hyper-ventilating when I answered? Did I make her uncomfortable?

I'm fairly sure she's still seeing her new chap. Dan, is it? When I think back to how we met, in that support group for single parents, it occurs to me that Gemma and I should celebrate our return to coupledom. Why don't we get together, see who we've hooked up with and how we're doing?

I text her to suggest a drink – me, her, Nancy, Dan – and she texts back 'Great idea.'

We're on.

On the walk to the pub, Nancy runs through a quick recap of who we're meeting and why.

'Right, so Gemma *isn't* an old friend. You met her at a speed-dating thing in a pub. I didn't think people speed-dated any more, you quaint old dinosaur.'

'It wasn't speed-dating. It was SPAN, a support group for single parents. She gave me a bollocking and we sort of hit it off.'

'And now *she's* met someone too. Another happy ever after. We'd better not drink too much, Ned. We're running to the West Pier and back tomorrow morning. I might even let you beat me.'

'On our run or are you being kinky?'

'Oh, ha-dee-ha.'

Gemma and Dan have nabbed a table by the window. It isn't a pub I know but it seems okay . . . for Brighton. I'm far more au fait with the hostelries of Hove. We do all the hellos and handshakes and who-sits-where while Dan gets a round in.

He must be a positive presence in Gemma's life because she looks really well: her hair's shorter, shinier and her clothes are less apologetic. Dan's got that George Clooney vibe: 'Yep, I've got grey hair but I'm still one sexy dude.' He is. *And* he can assemble a Billy bookshelf without having bits left over. She's fallen on her feet all right.

Nancy is looking unfeasibly sexy in clown-legged jeans and a funny-shaped sweater. I don't know how she makes this stuff work but she does.

'So,' she says, after breaking the foam on her pint. 'How did you two meet? Who made the first move?'

Gemma and Dan look at each other. Who wants to answer?

Dan jumps in. 'We first met back in the Middle Ages when we were 16.'

'I was 17. You were nearly 20. Same age as Joe, remember.'

'We met as kids. How's that, Gem? We nearly had a date. I was working up to it. And then Joe swept her off her feet and I had to wait another twenty years to try again.'

'Aw, that's lovely.' Nancy sighs. 'I'd be horrified if any of the guys I knew back in the day looked me up. *We* were a bit stop-start too, weren't we, Ned? But not with a twenty-year hiatus.'

Gemma knows how Nancy and I met, and even helped me choose what to wear for that first disastrous date at Marrocco's. I decide Dan doesn't need every detail.

'We met at a club a few months back,' I explain. 'Then we lost touch, then I bumped into Nancy in the shop where she works and . . . the rest is history. So, to us and to starting over.'

We clink and drink. It's a bit awkward after that. What else do we have in common, apart from the newbie couples thing? I know I suggested this get-together but now I'm wondering what the point was.

'Where do you work, Nancy?' Gemma asks. I didn't have *her* down as the one to disengage the pause button.

'Kitten Kaboodle. Do you know it? With the deckchair awning and the beach hut made of old newspaper in the window. For all your pointless-bits-of-nonsense needs.'

Dan smiles. 'My ex loved that shop. If you gave out loyalty cards, she'd be ahead on points. I've still got the set of coasters made out of old Penguin covers.'

'Ah yes, big sellers, them.'

'D'you like working there?' Gemma persists. Why is *she* asking all the questions? To avoid being interrogated herself?

'I do. It was just a stop-gap but I'm still there, three years on. How about you?'

Gemma pulls a frowny face. 'I work in a care home. It was just a stop-gap too but I'm still there, five years on. Maybe not for much longer, though.'

Is this a change of direction for Gemma, prompted by her new relationship? 'Have you got a new job?' I say. 'We should celebrate with some Prosecco.'

'Drown my sorrows, more like. I don't get on with my boss. Mostly because she's a cow. I reckon she's about to sack me.'

Dan looks surprised. 'You can't sack someone for no good reason.'

'Oh, she'll come up with something,' Gemma replies bitterly. 'Like I'm not professional enough. I wouldn't put it past her to say I've stolen stuff from the residents. Or that I called her "a jumped-up, jobsworth, lazy, arrogant chancer" in front of all the staff.'

Nancy is horrified and impressed in equal measure. 'Gemma! You didn't?'

'Not yet. I'm choosing my moment.'

Dan gives her hand a squeeze. 'Don't do anything until you've got your ducks in a row, love.'

This doesn't go down at all well. 'What ducks? What row?'

'I just meant best get another job lined up before you say anything you might regret. Jobs don't grow on trees.'

'First ducks, now trees. What is this? Nature corner? Thanks, Dan. Really helpful advice. I'll bear that in mind.'

I'm with Dan on this. I don't know how much maintenance Gemma gets from Joe or what her monthly mortgage is, but this is not the time to stomp out of regular employment, just to prove a point.

I choose my words with care, knowing Gemma has a temper and won't want to feel got at, especially as this night out was *my* idea. 'Dan's lucky, being self-employed, answering to no one but himself. The rest of us are beholden to the whims of our employers, whether we like it or not.'

'So we have to do as we're told? Never question anything? Never stand our ground? Bollocks to that.'

Nancy gives me a supportive smile, as if to say 'Nice try, Ned.'

I'm not done here. Maybe, if I make this a wider discussion and take the spotlight off Gemma, we can convince her not to act in haste.

'Okay,' I say. 'Here's a for-instance. I'm in a bind at work at the moment too. I got promoted recently, Dan, so I need to prove I deserve it, that I'm middle management material.'

Dan nods. 'What exactly is it you do? I asked Gem but she didn't seem to know.'

'I'm Senior Logistics Analyst, South-East Region with

QGT. We're a nationwide logistics, facilities, resources, auditing and professional services network. You've probably seen our logo on the side of trucks. Three cream cogs against a teal-blue background.'

His eyes glaze over slightly, so I carry on with my for-instance. 'Okay. Anyway, one of the branches in my cohort has cocked up with a major project they were down to do. Wrong format, wrong deadline, unproven methodology, the whole nine yards. Now, I know where the problem lies and how to fix it pronto before the cock-up goes public. So, do I quietly get it sorted? Or tell my boss what's happened, preferably in writing, so that if the shit hits the fan, it'll be their fan and not mine?'

'You nailed it just now, Ned,' says Dan. I'm starting to like this guy. 'I'm Flatpack Fred. No employees, no boss. I don't have dilemmas like this because I'm only answerable to myself, thank God.'

'You know what *I* think,' Nancy chips in, because she's heard this saga countless times. 'Sort out the problem quietly. Keep the cock-up to yourself. Discreetly but firmly get the Crawley office to fix it under your watchful eye and let the results be proof that your boss was right to promote you.'

She's right. Why make waves? Why antagonize the people you'll need onside for the next project, next week, next year?

Gemma isn't having it. 'Seriously? And if Crawley can't fix it, you do realize *you'll* be the baddie because it happened on your watch. Goodbye middle management, hello daytime television. I say: tell your boss asap. Read Crawley the riot act through a loudhailer and make it clear that, if it goes tits up, they'll be in the dole queue before you are.'

And there we have it: Nancy, the peacemaker, Gemma, the hothead. Not that I'm surprised – it's very much her modus operandi. She didn't try to save her marriage after she found out her husband was screwing around. She kicked him out, all guns blazing. As a consequence, she's taken years to get her life back and, if you ask me, she's still an emotional mess. She thinks confrontation is the only solution, as I learned to my cost when we first met. No wonder she doesn't have many friends. And even though *I* know what a softy she is underneath, she keeps it very well hidden.

I wish I could get a handle on this tendency of hers to self-sabotage. It isn't healthy. It won't move her forward. It's almost as if she's addicted to disappointment. Is that down to her ex or has she always been so pessimistic? It makes me sad. Gemma has so much to offer, so much love to give. But she has to love *herself* first.

Nancy and I debrief in bed, with mugs of tea and cheese on toast.

'Why didn't you want to go for a curry with Gemma and Dan?' I ask between mouthfuls. Nancy's normally up for eating out. Not like her to come home hungry.

'Oh, I don't know, Ned. We'd done what we went out for. It's like when you introduced me to Dora; just a quick howdy to break the ice. I didn't need to spend the whole night with those two.'

'True.' I polish off the last toast triangle, wishing I'd smeared more Marmite under the molten Cheddar. Nancy calls it a crime against humanity. 'And?'

'And what?' She sounds sleepy.

'And what did you think of them?'

She thumps her pillow to puff up the feathers. 'Nice. Fine. Perfectly pleasant. What do you want me to say?'

I sense that Nancy didn't take to Gemma, which is a shame

because, despite our ups and downs, Gemma is a friend now and I'd hate to lose her. 'I wasn't sure what to expect from Dan. Yeah, he seems like a decent guy. Gemma deserves happiness after everything she went through with her ex.'

Nancy mutters something into her pillow that I don't quite catch.

'Sorry, I missed that.'

'I said, "You only know her side of the story." From what I can see, she's not backward in coming forward. In some ways, I admire that: it must be hard to be in a relationship with someone who's so bloody confrontational the whole time, so ready to assume the world's against her.'

Nancy's spot-on but I'm staying loyal to Gemma. 'That's a bit unfair.'

'Ah, but is it? If you're constantly on the attack, you don't have to make an effort. You don't have to compromise or see it from the other person's point of view. Gemma certainly isn't blessed with self-doubt.'

'Are you kidding? She's riddled with it. All that front is a . . . a front. Underneath her bolshie exterior, there's a frightened little girl, terrified to come out.'

'Yeah. Whatever. I need to sleep.'

'Honestly, Nan. Gemma's a pussy cat, once you get past the bluster.'

'I'll take your word for it. Can we give the run a miss tomorrow and do sexy fun instead? I'm too knackered now.'

She's asleep in seconds. I lie there for a while, thinking about Gemma. Is she really a softy underneath or do I like to tell myself she is, to justify our friendship? Is Dan the right guy? I liked him and I liked them together but, if I'm honest, I'm yet to be convinced.

As far as my situation at work is concerned, the last thing

I intend to do is follow Gemma's advice and go in, all guns blazing. If Nancy is indeed my future, I mustn't do anything to affect my career progression. Slow and steady wins hands down.

I'm just putting together a strategy to fix the Crawley cock-up when Karen calls me into her office. Is she a mind reader or what? I've had a two-hour video call with Becky and Graham and they know they have to go the extra mile in order to salvage the situation, if they want to keep the head office heavy squad out of the equation. I've told them I'll do all I can to get everything back on track but I need to know they're with me. They say they are. We can but hope.

'All good, Ned?' Karen asks, half looking up from her tablet screen. 'Well, sit down. You're making the place untidy.'

I sit in a slouchy way, rather than bolt upright and guilty. I need to give the impression that everything's under control. We've got a few things to catch up on so I plan to bury Crawley in a litany of other stuff and stick to generalities, rather than specifics.

'Everything's ticking over nicely, Karen: Welby-Daniels; the East Anglian expansion; the Crawley project; the Loadstar saga.'

'Matt Jackman?'

'I'm seeing him next week for a review of where we are. That should keep him sweet till the end of the financial year.'

Karen snaps her tablet shut and finally looks up. 'I'm impressed, Ned. I really am. A couple of the guys on the interview panel thought you were too cautious, too circum-spect. Priya wanted to give the job to Andy, for God's sake. I had the casting vote and I'm pleased to say you haven't let me down.'

She reads my red face as embarrassment, rather than guilt. I *have* to sort out the Crawley project asap or it won't be just me who looks stupid.

'I was a bit daunted at first, Karen, but I knew you had faith in me when I maybe didn't. Not totally. I'm like the duck, paddling like fury under the surface. I'm getting there and that's the main thing.'

'Thanks for being so honest, Ned. Andy would have bullshitted away any problems. You've always played a straight bat and I admire that. So . . . how are things generally? How's your love life?'

Oh God, she isn't suggesting another session of no-strings nooky? I'm scared I'll agree to it, just to keep her off the Crawley scent.

'Good. Yeah. Pretty good, actually.'

'What's her name?'

'Nancy. Early days, obviously, but we're both happy. Looking to the future. We're off to Amsterdam for the weekend. Mini-break kind of thing. Nancy's idea because her best friend lives there.'

Karen nods and smiles. Then nods a bit more and smiles again. 'And now you're meant to ask me about *my* love life.'

'It's none of my business.'

'I think it is, Ned. We have a history.'

I gulp a golf ball down my throat. I hope she didn't hear it.

'Don't panic.' She smiles benignly. 'Our history is just that. History. As it happens, I've met someone too. Randall. Via a dating app. I'm not sure we're looking to the future, like you and Nancy, but we're certainly making the most of right now.'

I'm pleased for Karen. I really am. She's a stunning woman.

Totally out of my league, obviously. It was never a league I wanted to be in. It sounds like she's found someone who suits her. I should just be grateful that she shagged me when no one else would. We got each other through a dry patch.

She looks at her watch. 'Sorry, 3 p.m. conference call with the new guy at Loadstar. Anyway, I'm glad it's going well. On every front. Any glitches work-wise, you know you can come to me. That's what I'm here for, Ned. Okay?'

'Okay. Cheers, Karen.'

Back at my desk, I rerun that bit about glitches. Does she know about Crawley? I doubt it. I only just know myself and I had to wheedle it out of them. Was it a test to see if I'd 'fess up? Could very well be. Am I being paranoid? Totally. Which is all the motivation I need to sort it pronto, before she's any the wiser.

Andy's head appears over the partition. 'Hey, Ned. Fancy a pint and a pie tonight?'

'Yeah, why not. Nice one, bud.'

'Amsterdam? You jammy wotsit. Want to squeeze me into your suitcase?'

Andy is overdoing the enthusiasm. Any minute now, he'll ask if I'll be frequenting the city's famous coffee shops, nudge-nudge.

'I went there for a mate's stag do a few years ago. Bloody amazing place. Red-light district, chips with mayonnaise long before it caught on here . . . all those coffee shops selling weed. Promise you'll spark up a fat one and think of me, pal.'

It's easier to agree than remind Andy I don't handle dope very well. (Tanya can vouch for that, after a party where I took my trousers off to dance.)

'So it's going gangbusters, then? You and Nancy.'

'I've never understood "gangbusters". It means "good", right?'

'Ah, Nedward, you never let me down.'

We're in the Anchor, I've treated us to two Jack Daniels, two pints and two steak-and-ale pies with chips and buttered cabbage.

'Nancy and me are going "gangbusters" with knobs on,' I tell him. 'So if I haven't thanked you properly, I'm thanking you now for getting us together. I'd still be a sad sack at SPAN, if it wasn't for you.'

'And now *I'm* the sad sack. Who'd a thunk it?'

'You? Never.'

He stares into his pint and sighs. I'm hoping the pie and chips will snap him out of it.

'I'm not doing too well right now, as it happens,' he eventually mutters.

'Can I help? I'd like to. You've helped *me* so much. I owe you. Is it your long-lost son? Did you meet? Was it a disaster and now you wish you hadn't?'

'Aaron *is* on the agenda. But no, thanks all the same. It isn't Aaron.'

'Go on then, mate. In your own time.'

'It's Ros. I can't stop thinking about her. She's in my head 24/7. Clean thoughts too. Nothing pervy. Maybe one or two. I've never met a woman like her. I've never felt like this, not since Aaron's mum.'

'So ask her out. Tell her how you feel.'

'We met for a drink and, guess what, she doesn't want to know. She likes me "as a friend". Fat lot of use that is. It's right up there with "it's not you, it's me". Do women think we're stupid or what? I know in many ways we are. Stupid,

I mean. We still hurt. We still know when we've been kicked in the knackers.'

'Rewind. What happened? Are you sure that's what she meant? Easy to misconstrue.'

Our pies arrive. We take a minute to thwack HP sauce onto our plates and for Andy to tip half a ton of salt over his cabbage. Men are all about priorities.

'I was so chuffed when she agreed to go out with me,' he says, putting his fork down and picking at the pastry with his fingers. 'I thought I'd have to plead and plead and then get knocked back. So we went to a pub near her, up in Muesli Mountain where she lives.'

'Muesli Mountain? That's an actual place?'

'Aka Hanover. All lumpy jumpers, wind chimes and veg boxes. D'you mind, mate? I'm pouring my heart out here.'

'Sorry.'

We carry on eating. Why compound Andy's misery by letting our pies go cold?

'So we meet and she's as drop-dead lovely as ever. More maybe because absence makes the heart grow fonder. And we talk about this and that. Her late husband. Her cake business. Her son. I nearly tell her about Aaron but my gut instinct says not to make myself vulnerable, just in case this doesn't end well.'

'And it doesn't. That's a real shame.'

'Will you let me finish? Anyway, I haven't even said my bit about how I want to know her better and she must be ready to move on since the loss of her hubby. But she gets in there first, doesn't she? She holds my hand in both of hers and she looks me in the eyes and I really think I might have worn her down. And then she says: "I like you, Andy, but as a friend."'

'Did you tell her you want more than that?'

'I may be stupid but I'm not a sadist. I mean, masochist. Are you going to finish those chips?'

'All yours.' I slap my tummy. 'Nancy's got me doing 10k runs round Hove. Can you believe it?'

'That's it? That's you being sympathetic?'

'I *am* sympathetic. Honestly, mate. I got the bum's rush from Tanya and that was after fifteen years together. I've done rejection and I've got the scars to prove it. Be honest, you hardly know Ros. You'll get over this. You'll be beating them off with sticks.'

'Will I, though? I kind of felt Ros was my last-chance saloon. I don't want to be one of those 50-year-old losers with a comb-over and a Thai bride, who only married me so she can feed her family in Bangkok.'

I need to pull him out of this slough of despond. I try another tack. 'There's someone out there, just for you. I know it. Look at me and Nancy. If I can do it, you certainly can. You're a great guy.'

'I'm not, I'm a shit. I've had another letter from Aaron and what have I done about it? Bugger-all.'

'Yet. You've done bugger-all about it *yet*. Write back to him. You don't have to meet until you're ready. He's your son, Andy.'

'I don't want him to be disappointed.'

'And he won't be disappointed if you ghost him? For fuck's sake. This is the right thing. *Do* the right thing.'

'Yeah, maybe. Yeah, I know it is. Can you believe what she said? "I like you . . . as a friend." Talk about damned with failed praise.'

'Faint, not fail – How about another JD, bud?'

If you'd told me six months, a year ago, that I'd be Andy's

agony uncle, that *I'd* be in a long-term relationship and *he'd* be in an emotional mess, I'd have laughed bitterly and asked what you were on. And yet here we are. I feel for the poor guy. I really do. Bullshit and bluster can only get you so far. I hope he can work through all this and be as happy as I am with Nancy.

We *are* happy. We *are* sorted. Nancy's 110 per cent sure she is. Me, just occasionally, not so much. Up in the nineties, I reckon. I'm getting there . . .

We're here. In Amsterdam. Nancy organized everything: the flights, the hotel, the minicab to Gatwick at the crack of dawn. Tanya was just the same, wouldn't let me near any travel arrangements, but that was because she's a control freak (and because of the Crete Fiasco, when she was pregnant with Dora and I got my months muddled).

Our hotel is very chic; an old bank, I think, acquired by one of the international chains and done up very stylishly. We're both tired from our early start but that doesn't stop us shagging, fully clothed on our enormous bed, as soon as we get inside our room.

Tanya would spend her first half-hour in a hotel room opening and closing cupboards in search of the safe and the spare pillows; resetting the air conditioning; trying out the telly; sniffing the shower gel; arranging her bits and bobs on the bedside table and ironing everything that got crushed en route, despite her immaculate packing.

Nancy's my kind of holiday companion. She travels light, she doesn't plan to watch any TV and the sex is *heel goed*, with more to come. I couldn't be happier. I really couldn't.

We're meeting her friend, Olivia, tomorrow. She's married to a postman and they have a 2-year-old daughter. Today we'll get our bearings and see where we are in relation to all the famous stuff: the Rijksmuseum, Anne Frank's House, the tram stops and cheese shops.

So we walk and we walk and we walk; along quaint old canals, over picture-perfect bridges, past the flower market that's on the cover of my guidebook. We end up in a coffee shop that doesn't sell spliffs but does sell cheese toasties and beer. Everyone here is a tourist and I feel a bit cheated but I do get to try out *Alstublieft* and *Dank U* on the waiter.

'Put that bloody book away, will you, Ned?' Nancy says in a stage whisper. 'Everyone speaks English in Amsterdam.'

'I like to make the effort. Hey, apple cake is *appelgebak*. And cream is, wait for it, *slagroom*.'

She glares at me.

I put the book away. 'You went to school with Olivia, right?'

'We were friends from day one. We drifted apart in our teens. She was a girly swot and I was a bad influence. Our mums put us in touch again after uni and we were best mates all through our twenties.'

'Until she came here.'

'She's still my best mate. I just don't see her so often. I was matron of honour at the wedding. She met Jeroen on holiday in Goa. He's great. You'll love him. Livvy too, and Maia.'

'That's the dog?'

'That's the baby. The dog's called Frenkie after some soccer player. Any other questions?'

'Just the one. Can we screw in the shower when we get back to the hotel? To make up for not doing it on the plane?'

'Shut up.' She gives my arm a playful punch. I'll take that as a yes.

*

We screw in the shower before *and* after supper, knowing the second time that the non-slip rubber bath mat is vital underfoot. Cracking your head open on foreign tiles, in full coitus, is not something you want to include in your travel insurance claim.

My guidebook lists a typically Dutch restaurant which just so happens to be opposite our hotel, so, rather than wander aimlessly around Amsterdam in search of the perfect restaurant, then resort to McDonald's, we go there for supper.

Holidays with Tanya always involved a boiling-hot route march to some far-flung taverna or brasserie recommended by a friend, which invariably turned out to be under new management or a breeding ground for bacillus or a hangout for pickpockets – and, on one particularly memorable occasion, all three.

This restaurant is wood-panelled and welcoming; the food is stodgy, rather than chic. I love that Nancy isn't fazed by a plate of boiled-to-buggery root veg with a fat slab of bacon on top. We've worked up quite an appetite.

'Did you bring Harry here?' I ask, as we think about puddings.

'This restaurant or Amsterdam?'

'Either. Both.'

'Amsterdam. Once. I'd never have dragged him inside a place like this. Very much your pizza-and-burger man, Harry. He liked Dutch frites though.'

'Did he get to meet Olivia and, and . . . tell me how to say his name again.'

'Jeroen, pronounced Yuh-roon. Harry kept calling him Urine. We came over before Maia was born, so that he and Jeroen could see Celtic play Ajax. Which gave me and Olivia

297

time to hang out together. She didn't think much of Harry and she was right.'

'Ah, so this is like a job interview? I have to win over Olivia. And Urine?'

'Don't you *dare*, Ned. Yeah, pretty much. No pressure, though.'

'That's a relief. Do you fancy some *appelgebak* with *slagroom*?'

'Let's have one portion and two forks. I want them to like you and you them. Weren't you just the same about me meeting Gemma?'

'I've barely known Gemma six months. It's not the same at all.'

'So me thinking she's a bit of a cow isn't a problem, then?'

'She isn't. Not when you get to know her.'

Nancy gives a loaded sigh, but before I can press her, the *appelgebak* arrives and it's *lekker*.

Back at the hotel, the second session of sex in the shower is even better than the first – and not just because of the bath mat. I want to take the massive mattress home with me; best I've ever slept on. So far, everything about this trip has been perfect. And I haven't even met Olivia and Jeroen yet.

Nancy is out like a light within thirty seconds. I can't sleep. I love watching her snuffle and grunt, but it doesn't nudge me into nodding off. I make a cup of tea and pull a chair over to the window. For the first time in my life, I'm in a hotel room with a decent view, rather than a row of bins and the occasional staff member stubbing out a ciggie.

It's half one and the canal is quiet, with a skyline of twinkly lights and a regular stream of cyclists whizzing past. I see a party in a house across the water, which spills out on to the pavement. The guests are smartly turned out; they look like bankers and hedge-fund owners. I always thought Amsterdam was full of dopeheads and squatters; the city I've seen so far is well-heeled and high end.

I finally have a breathing space to take stock of why we're here. Nancy wants me to meet her oldest friend. To show Olivia how happy she is? To get her approval? I can't deny that she's the best thing that's happened to me since Dora was born, and it's hugely validating to know that we're on the same page about each other. We've only been together for just over a month but this feels right.

I want this weekend to go well, so I mustn't blow it by being Old Ned. I must be New Ned, who wears on-trend shirts and doesn't mind making an arse of himself speaking bad Dutch . . . New Ned, who has hot sex in hotel showers. I daren't let Old Ned out, not even for a second. Poor old Andy fears he'll end up marrying a Thai bride, just to avoid being alone at 50. If I don't hang on tight to New Ned – and Nancy – I might not even be that lucky.

Olivia and Jeroen live on the top floor of a narrow canal house in the Jordaan, a hip little neighbourhood of small streets with big names . . . Tweedelindendwaarstraat, Eersteboomdwarstraat. I'm in good shape from all those morning runs but it's still quite a climb up to their landing and the timed light clicks off before we get there.

The door is on the latch and we're greeted by Maia and Frenkie, a yappy mongrel with a cropped tail and black markings over one eye, like a canine pirate. Maia is wearing pyjama trousers, one leg up one leg down, a tutu, a T-shirt and an adult-size baseball cap. Sideways. She must get style tips from Nancy.

We enter to the smell of strong coffee and warm croissants. Nancy runs straight into the kitchen and gives Olivia
the biggest hug. Jeroen steps forward nervously and shakes
my hand with a finger-crushing grip. He is beefy and blond.
He knows *he* has to approve of me too. Then he scoops
up Maia, sniffs her bum, pulls a face and carries her to
the bathroom.

It takes all of twenty minutes to get to the unspoken
reason for our visit.

'Harry wasn't right for you,' Olivia declares as she froths
milk for our coffees. 'You knew that deep down, didn't you,
hun?'

Nancy bristles ever so slightly. 'Hindsight's a wonderful
thing, Livvy. If you knew now what you knew then, you
wouldn't have studied zoology or got alcohol poisoning at
my twenty-first or had that tattoo.'

'Everything's a lesson. Even the stuff you regret later. Don't
you think, Ned?' Olivia hands me a scalding glass beaker of
coffee. (Don't they *do* handles in Holland?)

'All depends on the tattoo,' I reply, channelling New Ned's
keen sense of humour and cheeky twinkle. 'So do I get to
fill in a questionnaire? Why I'm the ideal candidate to be
Nancy's boyfriend?'

Jeroen returns with a newly Pampered Maia. 'Please ignore
my wife. She takes her friendship with Nancy very seriously.
It's not personal, Ned.'

We sit around a big table sipping coffee and smearing
croissants with strawberry jam. I had a massive buffet breakfast at the hotel, as you are contractually obliged to do, but
these are impossible to resist.

'I'll say it now to get it out of the way, okay,' Olivia
announces. 'Then I won't mention it again. Harry was a

charmer, no doubt about it, but he hurt my friend. And that hurt me. My friend's enemy is my enemy.'

'Isn't it "my enemy's enemy is my friend"?' I ask, Old-Ned style.

'Not in this case. I won't let it happen again.'

Nancy has had enough of being talked about as if she's not here. 'Livvy, stop. That was then, this is now. I can take care of myself.'

We go to the Saturday Lindengracht market, all five of us, plus Frenkie. This isn't a touristy treat for our benefit. This is where Olivia and Jeroen do their shopping: every kind of herring, cheese, bread, meat and veg. Olivia is buying the ingredients for supper tonight: what do we fancy? Nancy and I shrug, overwhelmed by the choice. 'Surprise us,' Nancy suggests.

Despite the buffet breakfast and croissants, we 'must' have *appelgebak* at a nearby cafe. This is a Jordaan tradition, so who are we to refuse? Maia, ever her own person, eschews the moist slabs of apple and pastry in favour of a plateful of little meatballs and eats every last one. Dora would have had the cake. Dora is a conformist. Maia is a rebel. Good for her.

Our Saturday unfolds organically and that's just fine with me. Us. Jeroen reckons Nancy and Olivia need some 'girly' time so do I fancy joining him and his brother for a cycle ride to Amsterdam Forest and back? No, I flipping don't. I've never been a confident cyclist and, in a city like this, I could get slagroomed under a tram. I tell him thanks but actually I'm super-keen to see Rembrandt's *Night Watch*. That does the trick.

Jeroen saddles up and cycles off; Nancy, Olivia, Maia and Frenkie set out for an afternoon of clothes-shopping, more coffee and talking about me . . . and I mooch. I head for the Rijksmuseum, just so I have a destination. But I really can't be arsed to queue for an hour with coachloads of pushy tourists to see the star attraction, *Night Watch*. It's just a painting of a bunch of people.

Instead I walk some more: up one canal and down another, until I'm back in the heart of the city. I stop for a beer when the fancy takes me and stay put in the final cafe for a couple of hours, shooting the breeze with a local character called Jaapie, who wants to tell me about Amsterdam in the Seventies, when he was a roadie, then a squatter, then a junkie, then a living statue of Elvis. Great guy.

I manage to find my way back to Olivia and Jeroen's. With a few beers under my belt, the stairs are even steeper. Nancy has been tasked with bathing Maia and putting her to bed so I chat to Olivia as she prepares supper. It would be rude to refuse the ice-cold Amstel she offers me.

'How are you at salad?' she asks.

'Eating it or making it?'

'Both.'

'Yeah. Good. Yeah. I can do that.'

She hands me a knife, assesses my sobriety, then takes it away. 'On second thoughts, why don't you wash the lettuce? Are you just drunk or stoned as well?'

'Drunk. A bit. Mellow. Happy. This lettuce is pretty.'

'So, Ned. Do you think you're the man for Nancy?'

I nod. A New-Ned nod, not an Old-Ned nod, which I hope will reassure her.

'Good. Nancy doesn't deserve to be dicked around, to have her heart broken again. Seriously. If you hurt her, I'll come after you with this.'

She picks up the knife, almost in slo-mo, then swaps it for a benign wooden spoon. Even so, I get the message.

'I'm not like that, Olivia. I've never been a heartbreaker. Not in my nature.'

'Not on purpose anyway.'

'I won't dick her around. Swear to God.'

She gives me a 'hmm' look and returns to scrubbing spuds. The jury is out.

The meal is amazing: olives and artichoke hearts from the market, followed by calves' liver with teensy fried potatoes and salad from the market, then peaches and gorgonzola . . . also from the market. I drink too much wine in an effort to keep Old Ned at bay. I think it works.

Jeroen laughs at my jokes (I manage not to call him Urine), Nancy beams at me and occasionally squeezes my hand. Olivia softens. Surely she can see that I'm not another Harry.

I am New Ned, the nice guy who, because he's rat-arsed, may break a beer glass but would never break a heart.

We walk back to the hotel to clear my head, rather than grab a cab, and it works . . . kind of. Last night, Nancy was the one craving sleep. This time it's me. Even *Germany's Got Talent*, minus subtitles, will not keep me awake.

'You liked them, didn't you, Ned?'

'Really nice. Can you turn that down a bit?'

'Jeroen's great. Wicked sense of humour. To be so funny in a second language, that's quite a skill.'

'Absolutely.'

'It's hard enough being funny in English, right? You were funny tonight and not just when you fell over Maia's scooter.'

'Was I? Good.' I yawn expansively.

Nancy's quiet for a minute or two. She even turns off the TV and bedside light. At flipping last. Bedtime.

She's still wide awake. 'Isn't Maia the cutest thing? So quirky and, I don't know . . . independent.'

'Mmm-huh.'

'You won Olivia round. Not at first. She's like a mother hen, always worrying about me. I know she gave you a bit of a grilling but only because she wants me to be happy. She wants *us* to be happy. We're happy, aren't we, Ned?'

'Very, very. We really are. Night-night then.'

I wake a couple of hours later and can't get back to sleep. 'We *are* happy, aren't we, Ned?' Nancy's words bounce around my brain. Why did she ask? What did she mean? When will we know?

Of course we're happy. Completely . . . And yet . . . I can't quite relax into it, lie back and let it wash over me. Am I experiencing doubt, or surprise that I'm no longer single? I can't quite put my finger on what's niggling me. Does Nancy feel it too, or why else would she ask the question?

Our flight home is at 3 p.m. so we have the morning to soak up one more Amsterdam experience. I'm all for more sexy time, cocooned in our hotel room, but Nancy points out that we can do that at home.

We don't fancy culture and anyway, the queues to see the *Night Watch* are bound to be even more bonkers on a Sunday. I enjoyed yesterday's bar crawl and would love Nancy to meet Jaapie, the addled local. I can't see her agreeing to that either.

So we do a *Rondvaart*, as my invaluable guide book calls it: a seventy-five-minute cruise around the city's inner circle of canals, taking in a hundred highlights. How can that not be the ideal way to see all the bits we've missed?

'It's so touristy,' Nancy reckons, wrinkling her nose.

'Hello, we're tourists. Just because *you've* been to Amsterdam before—'

'—three, no, four times. This is my fifth.'

'Just because you've seen it all, doesn't mean I should miss out. Go on, Nan. A hundred highlights. We'd never see them on foot, even if we stayed another week.'

She harrumphs and acquiesces.

We're photographed as we embark by a bored woman in one of those velvet horned hats. I suspect we're both scowling, so that's a few euros saved when they try to flog us the snap. Tanya was a sucker for the uncommissioned tourist photo. Every so often, she'd come across her collection in the back of a drawer and relive the moment; her beaming like a surprised film star and me, a fuzzy blur or obscured by someone's elbow or squinting up at an approaching rain shower.

For all her ambivalence, Nancy is keen to grab the front seat of the canal boat and beats three elderly Japanese women to it. I'm appalled and impressed in equal measure. I wouldn't have dared.

We set off, with the humorous commentary of our onboard guide, Marijke. On our left Anne Frank's house, on our right some very grand houses that rich Amsterdammers used to live in. Marijke relates the tale of poor artisan workmen spitting chewed tobacco below the Italian marble floor as they laid it, knowing a nasty brown stain would take several decades to bleed through.

Nancy is horrified. 'Why would they do that?'

'To exact revenge for bad pay, bad conditions. Up the workers!'

We pass more grand residences and rickety houseboats, weighed down by tomato plants and, no doubt, a good crop of weed. One bright red boat has a life-size, waving Buddha. We wave back. We squeeze under tiny bridges, festooned with padlocked bikes. We're encouraged by Marijke to shout '*Hoera*', to produce an echo. It's touristy but we're tourists.

And then the crying starts, one row behind us. A young couple – French, I think, possibly Belgian – and a little boy wailing so hard it makes my ribs shudder.

He drowns out Marijke. He practically drowns out a jackhammer churning up chunks of cobbled pavement. I feel for the lad but even so, I *will* his maman and papa to make it stop.

Embarrassed, they scoot up their things and move to the back of the boat, where there are rows of empty seats.

'Thank God for that.' I waggle my fingers in my ears to recalibrate them.

'It's unbearable, isn't it?' says Nancy sympathetically.

'I know. And right behind us too.'

'I meant, seeing your child in such distress and not knowing what to do.'

'Oh, he's fine. He's bored or he needs a wee or he's just had a wee and needs something done about it.'

'I'd cry too if I was sitting around in wet Pampers.'

'The thing is, children – babies, toddlers – cry as though the world is ending for all sorts of reasons. But rarely because the world *is* actually ending. Dora kicked off at a wedding once, just as all the vows were being spoken. The church was really echoey – like that last *hoera* under the bridge – and the bride's mother gave us such a look. As if it was *our* fault.'

'What was wrong with her? Dora, not the bride's mother.'

'Teething. Or sheer bloody-mindedness. She can still turn on the waterworks when she wants attention. Don't look at me like that, Nan. It's true.'

'Maia isn't like that.'

'Course she is. They all are. We love our kids to bits but they're hard bloody work. We'd worry if they weren't.'

Nancy looks perturbed. If she was expecting some flowery speech from me about the joys of parenthood, she's had a rude awakening. I'm not sure why I've become so aerated but I don't want her clinging on to a fairy-tale fantasy, just because Maia didn't scream her lungs out in our presence yesterday.

'I get it,' she says eventually. 'I get where this is coming from.'

'I'm just telling it like it is. Prompted by little Pierre or Jean-Claude or whatever that kid's name is.'

'You don't want any more children and you're flagging it up now so I know where I stand.'

'Seriously? Is that where you reckon this is coming from?'

'Go on then. Don't waffle or avoid answering. Just tell me: do you want to be a father again?'

I can't respond instantly because I don't know. Nancy crosses her arms and gazes out on to the bobbing canal as we putter past the Amsterdam Opera House, which, according to Marijke, was opened in 1986 and is known as the Stopera, because the city's squatters objected to it. I bet Jaapie was one of them.

I have an answer. 'Not yet. I don't want to be a father again *yet*. It's too soon. We're too new. We need to give it time.'

'Because we're only just getting to know each other?'

'Exactly.'

'I agree. I do. And I don't want you to think I'm only with you because you're my route to motherhood. I couldn't bear that.'

I put my arm around her. 'We're doing great, you and me.

Here. Now. Let's just be spontaneous, take it day by day. See where we end up when we get there. Can we do that?'

She nods and kisses my cheek. 'But this isn't going away, Ned. Just so's you know.'

Chapter Twenty-Two

Gemma

I head off for work that day, not planning to be unemployed by the end of it. Who would, with bills to pay and a jet-set, luxury lifestyle to keep up? Do I regret it and wish I could turn the clock back? Hell, no. *Que será será*, and all that. There may even have been a spring in my step when I punched the code into the Willowdene keypad and let myself out for the very last time, with the heavy oak door slamming loud behind me.

Wasn't it Ned, when we all met up for that drink, who said I should bite my lip at work? Such lame advice and typical Ned. If he wants to keep his head down, never make waves, never say what he thinks, that's his choice. I'm a wave-maker. Always have been, always will be. When a wimp like Ned tells me not to do something, I'm programmed to do the opposite.

And now here I am, out of work because I couldn't stand by any longer, watching Janine being such a bitch. I bet, if HR had given Kelvin her job, he'd have made a better fist of it. She's a liability and I couldn't take orders – or shit – from her one minute longer. So sue me.

I'd just checked in on Judy because she was, is and always

309

will be my very favourite resident. She was bolt upright in bed but fast asleep, with her daywear turban nudged down over one drawn-in eyebrow. I knew she'd be distressed if she woke and found herself like that so I tiptoed in and tidied her up. While I was at it, I gathered up all the junk jewellery she'd spread across her lap before nodding off, probably in search of a lairy brooch or naff necklace.

I'd been angry with myself for fixating on Joe and 'that kiss', after our day out with Kelvin. That's my only excuse; I was spoiling for a fight, and I took it out on Janine. He'd started texting again, every couple of hours, stirring up my emotions, invading my brain. Was I okay? Could we meet? When? Where? He's always known how to get to me and, there he was, stirring it up all over again.

Which is why Janine got the brunt of my mixed-up emotions. All she'd said, when she saw me tidying Judy's jewellery, was: 'Stealing the valuables, Gemma?' And, yes, in the cold light of day, I can see it was a throwaway remark, a crap joke because they're the only kind Janine's capable of.

'How dare you accuse me of theft?' I replied, surprising us both.

At least one of us – me – was sensible enough to take our discussion into the corridor. The last thing I wanted to do was upset Judy.

Janine shrugged as if she didn't care what I thought. That's when I seriously lost it. If she'd only said: 'Just joking, Gemma' or 'Me and my big mouth' or 'Why am I such a bitch?' . . . well, obviously, I'd still have my job.

But she didn't, the blue touchpaper was well and truly lit and I didn't hold back. 'I can only imagine you're projecting, Janine. You help yourself to Donald's fruit basket or Janet's

Ferrero Rocher . . . maybe even the leather armchair that suddenly went missing from the lobby, so you think we're all as bad as you.'

I struck a chord. I'm sure I did because I know what she's like. I can't prove it about the chair but Felipe thinks so too and Janine went letterbox-red when I said it.

She whipped her mobile out of her pocket and pressed 'Record'. 'Say that again, Gemma. Call me a thief on record, right here, right now, and I'll have you marched off the premises so fast, your feet won't touch the ground.'

I smiled. It wasn't a nice smile. 'Don't worry, love. Your secret's safe with me.'

'I won't have you disrespecting me. Like you've done ever since I got promoted and you didn't.'

'Tell you what, why don't I disrespect you from the comfort of my own sofa? That way, we're both happy. Stuff your job, Janine. I quit.'

What was I thinking? Why couldn't I change the habit of a lifetime and swallow my words, swallow my pride? Now I've got no job and definitely no reference. I didn't even get to say goodbye to Judy and Felipe and Carmen in the kitchen and the two Jims who I like to call Ant and Dec, and Monica and Alf and all of them. I tell myself there's loads of agency work out there and an experienced care worker like me will be snapped up in a heartbeat. I hope I'm right.

Dan comes over for supper and I suppose I should tell him I've lost my job, although it's actually none of his business where I work or who I call a thief. He might even think it's funny. I might, too, when the dust settles. Or when I've got another job. Or when Janine gets down on her knees and begs me to come back. (Oh, and look, there's a flying porker, banking over the West Pier.)

'Ooh, . . . onion gravy,' Dan says, swooshing a forkful of mash through it and giving me a grin.

Kelvin's happy too: pork chops and mash with peas and sweetcorn is one of his favourite meals. Dan's too, by the look of it. I decide to keep my news to myself for now because I'm in no mood to defend my behaviour. It might be me who has to get down on both knees and do the begging.

I am my own worst enemy: official. Why can't I be cool-headed and canny like Ned's sainted Nancy? Why can't I engage my brain before doing something stupid?

I listen to Dan and Kelvin chatting away about why onion gravy goes so well with mash and whether English mustard is nicer than French (Dan reckons it is, Kelvin isn't fussed) and I see how good my life could be, if I could only act like a grown-up. Kissing my ex is not on. Nor is resenting Ned for his unquestioning happiness at hooking up with Nancy.

I was on the bus, coming home from work, still shaking with anger at my spat with Janine, when he texted. They'd had an amazing time in Amsterdam, their hotel was amazing and Nancy's friends are amazing. Plus, they'd had a chat about their future and it got a bit tense but they came through it and now everything's . . . amazing. I don't want to piss on his chips but life cannot possibly be that good 24/7, even with a new girlfriend. Typical Ned with his cup half full. Overflowing the rim, more like.

After Kelvin's gone upstairs, Dan and I flop on the sofa and watch a rubbish film on the Syfy channel. I'm keen to keep our conversation light: why does the cloned cop need to reach the people in the forest? Who is that replicant woman? Shall we finish off the Battenberg or save it for tomorrow?

I'm sitting in my favourite position, with my back against the arm rest. Without asking, Dan puts my feet in his lap and starts to massage them. I'm not sure he even knows he's doing it. I'm a sucker for a stroke of my hair, a squeeze of my shoulders, especially when they're tense and knotted, like they are right now. This is bliss. I let out a little sigh, my way of saying: don't stop. I even close my eyes, which is no loss to the stupid film which I can follow without watching.

'Nic never let me touch her feet,' Dan says, gently rubbing each grateful toe. 'She was so ticklish. Honestly, you'd have thought I was assaulting her, rather than helping her relax.'

'More fool her. You don't have a foot fetish, do you? Now's the time to tell me.'

'I've got a Gemma fetish. I missed you this weekend.'

'Yeah, me too. Did your mate's house move go okay?'

'Really well. He's moved to Durrington. Way more bang for your buck outside Brighton. Three bedrooms, huge garden, garage, garden room. Definitely food for thought.'

That spooks me. Is he saying *we* should think about moving? Him and me? Based on what? A relationship that's barely past its trial period? I don't reply.

'So what did you get up to on Saturday?' he asks a bit later, coming back from the kitchen with two mugs of tea and the last of the cake.

'This and that. Nothing much.' Now's the moment to tell him I went out for the day with Kelvin and Joe. The moment passes.

'"This and that?" Ooh, very mysterious. Are you working for MI5?'

'FBI actually.'

I feel torn. If I *don't* tell Dan about Joe, I'm turning it into a thing. If I *do* tell him, can I keep it low key, so-what, end-of? I've pretty much decided not to say anything, but can I keep it up? Of course not.

'Joe took Kelvin to the Bluebell Railway so Kel dragged me along too. Ned's turned my son into a train buff, God help us.'

'Was Vicky there too?'

'No, she was at a health farm with Hayley. Poor Vicky. Two whole days with her. Can you imagine? I'd rather have my kidneys out.'

But Dan isn't up for a bitch about Hayley. 'Why didn't you say? When I rang you? Why didn't you say where you were, who you were with?'

'God, I don't know, Dan. Maybe so's I wouldn't get the third degree, when it's even less of a big deal than it was at the time.'

'This is hardly the third degree, love. I know how you feel about Joe and how hurt you were about what he did to you. Why wouldn't I want to know that you two can be civil, for Kelvin's sake?'

'We *were* civil, as it happens. It was good for Kel to see us getting on.'

'Why keep it from me, then?'

He's right. Why lie? I'm suddenly on the defensive about a perfectly harmless day out with my boy and my ex. Okay, there was the kiss but I'm hardly going to 'fess up to that. It shouldn't have happened and it won't happen again. So it's nobody's business but mine. It's certainly not Dan's.

'Maybe I didn't tell you because I thought you'd be annoyed. And we'd end up being snarky with each other and then I'd wonder if I wanted you to stay tonight after all.'

'Do you want me to go?'

'Yes. No. I don't know. It's your call.'

'I'll stay then.'

'Good.'

'Good.'

'Anything else you haven't told me?'

Yes. The kiss. I kissed my ex and I liked it.

'Yes,' I say. 'There is one thing.'

'Go on.'

'I told Janine to stuff her job. I walked out. As of today, I am officially unemployed. There you go. Now you know.'

My time is suddenly my own. I need to find another job pronto, maybe even agency work, but for this week at least, I can earn some cash-in-hand helping Ros with two foodie markets, one in Worthing, the other in Bexhill. I'm so proud of her. She sells out faster than any of the other stalls – probably because her white chocolate Florentines and macadamia macarons are to die for – and she gives me a £30 bonus both times, on top of my earnings, as thanks for all my hard work. Any time, I tell her, and I mean it.

I weigh up my options. Do I really want to stay in the care sector? What else am I good at? *There's* a list that wouldn't take long to write. Right now, I'm okay with my mad walk-out, even though I still feel bad for abandoning Felipe and Judy.

Dan was cool, which I wasn't expecting. He wants me to be happy and, if working for Janine was making me miserable, he's glad it ended. I can do no wrong in his eyes, which is a bit scary because I 'do wrong' all the time. Like not telling Joe to keep his distance. I don't actively encourage him; I tell myself I can handle him. I even pretend all we're doing here, batting friendly texts back and forth, is getting on with each other for the sake of our son. Yeah, right.

Then, out of the blue, I get a text from Ned. He needs me asap. Can we meet for lunch on my next day off? He doesn't know that every day is 'off' right now so yes, why not? I suggest today because I've cleaned the house from top to bottom, I've done some admin for Ros, I've been for a walk and I'm terrified of getting hooked on daytime telly. Today's perfect.

Why does Ned need me? Is he having problems with Nancy and thinks I can help? Have they split up? It wouldn't surprise me. She seems quite high maintenance. The mean-spirited part of me would be quite glad if they *have* split up: I wish Ned only the best but I honestly can't see what he sees in her. What am I missing here?

Maybe it's Dora. What if Ned needs specific advice about his girl from another mother, something he can't ask Tanya without showing up his shortcomings? If that's what it is, I'm flattered. Plus I like being with Ned. There's no pressure because we're just friends, nothing more. We'll never be more than that, even if either of us wanted to take it any further. Which we don't, obviously. Anyway, he has Nancy now and I have Dan.

We meet at a cafe near his office. I'm looking forward to seeing him without our shiny new partners in tow. He's in a suit, which I wasn't expecting. He suits a suit. He looks really good.

'Yeah, I know. Mr Corporate or what?' He shoves his tie in his pocket and recommends the lasagne. 'Go on, my treat. They do a great tiramisu too.'

I've made a bit of an effort because it's not often I have a lunch date. The last time was with Vicky and that one got emotional as soon as I reminded her she'd nicked my husband. I'm wearing a swishy brown pleated skirt and a black shirt, both nearly new cast-offs from Ros. She wears swishy things with white trainers so I'm trying that too and I'm pretty pleased with how I look. Even though it's only for Ned's sake, who's just a friend, after all.

While we wait for our lasagne, he tells me why he needs me. It *is* about Nancy but it isn't about them having problems. Ah. Okay . . .

'Has Dan had a birthday since you've been together?' he asks, polishing his fork absentmindedly on a sleeve.

'No. Should he have done?'

'It's just, I was wondering how you played it? If he had had, I mean.'

'Ned, can you start again? And put that bloody fork down.'

He grins one of his goofy, little-boy grins. He may think he's matured emotionally since being dumped by Tanya, but he still acts like a kid and, actually, it's not as annoying as it used to be.

'Nancy turns 30 next week. So it's a big one and it should be marked as such. Don't you think?'

'I can't even remember my thirtieth. Can you remember yours?'

'Mum gave me cufflinks and I lost one within hours of putting them on. In a flowerbed. Who wears cufflinks anyway?'

'Actually, I think I turned 30 around the time Dad got his cancer diagnosis. So it didn't feel right to celebrate. Maybe I'll do something for my fortieth.'

'You should. Leave it to Dan.'

I let out a hollow laugh. 'If we're still together.'

Ned looks shocked. He really is an innocent, totally

trusting in 'happy ever after' for both of us. 'Seriously, Gemma? You don't think Dan's the one for you?'

'I don't know. Nobody knows. Is Nancy the one for you?'

There's a moment's pause. 'She could be. It feels right. Yeah, right now, it feels right.'

Our lasagnes arrive and we dig in. I've suddenly lost my appetite so I just moosh mine around on the plate. Now that I know why Ned needs me, we can cut to the chase.

'Okay,' I say in a businesslike tone. 'You want to buy a birthday present for Nancy but you don't know if it should be something daft and jokey or something practical that she really needs or something soppy and serious. You don't want to misjudge where you are in your relationship. Am I close?'

'Spot on. I think I know where I am, where *we* are. But it's a minefield, Gemma. What if I blow it by buying something too trivial or too loaded with meaning? She'll see me for the idiot I really am.'

'Is that so bad?' Does he really think Nancy doesn't get him yet? I certainly do. And he gets me. I don't know when that happened but he does and I like it. 'I mean, she'll have to see the real you at some point.'

He stops eating too. 'Oh, I think Nancy's got the measure of my idiot quotient by now and she hasn't run for the hills. Is jewellery too . . . loaded with meaning?'

'It doesn't have to be. Unless it's an engagement ring.'

He nods, deep in thought. 'How about a necklace? Something simple and silver. There's a nice jewellery shop on Portland Road.'

'There you go. Sorted.'

Ned looks relieved and returns to his lasagne. 'This is brilliant. Thanks, Gemma. Hey, if I'm in the shop and I can't decide, is it okay if I take photos and send them to you for a second opinion?'

Seriously? Do I have to? He takes my silence as a yes.

'Tanya was always miffed if I got her something boring for her birthday, and I was rubbish at "sexy" presents. Did Joe ever buy *you* sexy stuff? Actually that's none of my business.'

'You're right. It isn't.' I eat some garlic bread to shut down any more questions.

Joe *did* often buy me sexy stuff, as it happens. At the time, I was flattered. Now not so much. Our sex life was never dull, whether I was wearing a black lace waspie or a winceyette nightie with a cocoa stain down the front. I feel a shudder in my groin and pretend I'm cold. How can the bastard still have that effect on me?

As if on cue, my phone beeps. Another text from Joe. He's still thinking about me. He can't concentrate. He wants us to get together, '*be* together soon as, Gemzy'.

'Everything okay?' Ned asks, seeing my face.

'Just Kelvin to say he's going to Mohit's after school.'

'Say hi from me. He's a great kid, a real credit to you. Aren't you hungry? You've hardly eaten a thing.'

'I was. It's passed.'

Ned suggests we share a tiramisu. He and Nancy always share puddings, even when it's crumble and he wants custard and she wants cream. He goes off on some long story about apple tart in Amsterdam and the funny name for cream in Dutch and how they shared a slice and blah-blah-blah. I stop listening. Ned's getting boring. I care about him as my friend, but I don't care about him as Nancy's boyfriend. Why would I?

On the bus home, I feel deflated and restless and mixed

up, so I text Joe and say I've been thinking about him too. Because I have. At least with Joe, I know the territory. It may be rocky but it's familiar.

And, because I'm not a total cow, because I *do* have a conscience and don't want to hurt anyone who doesn't deserve it, I decide to pull the plug on me and Dan. I *wish* I could feel as certain about him as Ned does about Nancy but, no matter how hard I try, it's just not there.

I'm tempted to end it with him by voicemail because I'm too spineless to hear his reaction. But he doesn't deserve that. Instead, I get home, pour myself a large glass of the wine we didn't finish at the weekend, sit on the bench in the garden and dial his number. He takes it well. Actually, I don't give him time to reply, so that could be wishful thinking on my part. I say what I need to say and hang up. The end.

He'll be relieved in the long run. He can do way better than me.

Chapter Twenty-Three

Ned

Karen wants to see me at eleven for a quick catch-up on any Welby-Daniels fallout and the latest on Loadstar. I'm really flattered that they've put me in charge. It would have been out of the question a year ago. Back then, I was too busy wallowing in self-pity about my failure as a husband and human being. I couldn't have been trusted with the office stapler. Wooing and facilitating new clients was a job for the big boys, not an invisible, underwhelming idiot like me.

The promotion . . . Nancy . . . taking up running . . . new bed linen . . . All these things have put a spring in my step and a purpose in my outlook. Karen can see it and it reflects well on *her* too; she chose the right person. I have stepped up to the plate, grabbed the wheel with both hands, bitten the bullet and I'm ready to kick some corporate arse.

I really should be prepping our meeting but I've been sidetracked by a bit of online window-shopping for Nancy's thirtieth birthday present. I can't fuck it up by under- or over-playing our relationship. It was really helpful talking it through with Gemma last Friday. I'd have been nervous about going for a silver necklace, if she hadn't offered to help me choose. She's a true friend. I'm so pleased that she's met someone too. Dan's a lucky guy.

With two minutes to spare, I tap a few Loadstar bullet points into my tablet that Karen and I can run up the flag-pole. Best not be too prescriptive or inflexible at this stage in the process. And then the shiny head of Andy looms up over the partition. The sooner I get my own office the better.

'All good with you, my friend?'

'Absolutely, Andy. I'm busting for a slash before my eleven o'clock with Karen so can we bookmark till later?'

'Not a problem, bud. You enjoy your one-to-one with our glorious leader.'

His head bobs down, then reappears ten seconds later.

'Any chance of a sesh in the Anchor tonight? Or are you seeing Nancy?'

'Andy mate, can this wait?'

'Course it can. Not a problem. Splendido. See you there at half seven. The grub's on me, if you fancy. Well, off you trot. You don't want to be late.'

Karen is cool. Karen trusts my judgement. My hastily cobbled-together thoughts re Loadstar are just the ticket and she admires my bullet points. I am totally smashing it. However, there's still a potential shit-hits-fan scenario on the agenda and I need to keep my wits about me.

'I've heard things are bumpy in Crawley,' she says, right out of the blue . . . or is it?

'Bumpy?'

'Well, how would you describe it?'

'Becky and Graham have been a bit lackadaisical. I'm on the case.'

She takes off her glasses and rubs the bridge of her nose.

My French teacher, Mr Radley, used to do that, just before I was majorly bollocked. *En français, naturellement.*

'How are you handling it, Ned? Give 'em an inch and they'll walk all over you. Especially Becky. She's a bit too full of herself, if you ask me.'

I could bluster or change the subject but you can't kid a kidder; Karen would see straight through that. I'm being tested and I can't fail.

'I've given them till tomorrow to reset back to zero. If they don't, I'm tearing them a new one. Both of them. I'll bring head office in if I have to and they know that, especially Becky. I won't tolerate inferior work, poor judgement or buck passing. Not on my watch. Last-chance saloon with a cherry on top.'

There's a pause while Karen puts her glasses back on and blinks. Have I played this all wrong? Should I have followed Nancy's advice? Was the bit about tearing them a new one a graphic image too far?

'Wow, Ned. I wasn't expecting that. Go get 'em, Tiger. Use me as Nasty Cop, if you need reinforcements.'

'Thanks, Karen. Good to hear we're on the same page.'

I can't stop smiling as I amble back to my desk. She called me 'Tiger'. I polish off my saved finger of Kit-Kat in one mean mouthful, slug back the last of my forgotten cappuccino and get ready to sort Crawley, once and for all.

I am a tiger.

There's some broccoli quiche and salad in the fridge, made by Nancy, but if Andy's offering to buy me a burger, I'd be a fool to say no. Who knows when he might offer again? He's not so much cheap as thoughtless. And I'm a soft touch when the beers need buying. I always have been. I don't even mind.

Once again, he's there before me. He's wearing a smart check shirt and, if he had any hair, it would be combed down neatly, with a fresh parting. Andy doesn't ever pay his way or care what he wears. Something is very, very wrong.

'I won't order the burgers just yet,' he says, returning with pints and peanuts. 'I'm expecting someone.'

He sounds quiet and nervous. He looks small and tense.

I'm thinking a woman but he rarely makes an effort, even for them. Then I get it. 'Aaron? You're expecting Aaron?'

He nods and emits a strange gulping sound that he tries to disguise as a throat clearing.

'Wow, Andy. That's fantastic. I'm so pleased you made contact. Mate, I'm really proud of you. You won't want me around, like a spare wheel.'

'Just for the first half-hour, till I get my nerve.'

'What changed your mind? About seeing him?'

'Oh, just – God, I don't know, Ned. I kept thinking about that day in Amberley with you and Dora and what I'd missed out on because I didn't think I needed to be a dad.'

'And you do now?'

'Maybe. But you can't just turn it on, can you, twenty years late? Anyway, he already had a dad who taught him how to do up his laces and mend his bike and wear a condom.' Andy laughs at the irony. 'I'm just a fat bloke in a tight shirt.'

'What time's he due?'

'Half seven. He's coming from Burgess Hill. All these years and he's only lived ten miles away. Makes you wonder, doesn't it?'

I'm flattered that Andy wants me to meet Aaron. Even so, it isn't right. I shouldn't stay. 'I'll buy the next round and I'll get you a whisky chaser to calm your nerves. But I'm not staying. I'll even forgo my free burger. You don't want me here.'

He nods. 'Fair enough. He might think *you're* his dad because you're better-looking. Bugger off then, before he rocks up. It'll be okay, won't it? Course it will. See ya, Nedward.'

While I have sole custody of the TV remote, I'm watching *Interstellar*, one of my favourite films. Nancy hates sci-fi or anything with 'dystopian' in the blurb. I couldn't even persuade her to watch *Galaxy Quest*, which never fails to have me laughing like a drain. Her broccoli quiche is lovely but I don't go a bundle on the salad until I drown it in mayo. I couldn't do *that* if she was here either.

I'm tempted to ignore the two texts that bleep their arrival, just as we're getting to the best bit of the film.

Andy: 'Aaron is a great kid. Polite, smart, funny. Poor sod inherited my monobrow. Wants me to meet his mum. You know . . . Gillian. No rush. Best take it slow. He liked me!!!'

Nancy: 'French class spoiled by usual show-off. Row with Mel about loo roll. U r sooo lucky, living alone. Coming to yrs 2nite. Yr chance to say no xxx'

I get back to *Interstellar* and ten minutes later, I hear her key in the door. I love Nancy being here although, if I'm honest, I relish my 'me' time too. From the way she kicks off her shoes in the hall, I'm guessing she hasn't had a great day. I mute the telly, put the kettle on and open a new packet of Hobnobs.

'Bloody Mel. I know it's her flat so she's Head Girl but, guess what, she doesn't like the loo roll I buy! Who knew loo roll could be too narrow? It didn't help that I lost my temper, told her to stick it up her bum and then laughed because what else is she going to do with it?'

A hug is called for. The understanding hug of the thoughtful boyfriend. I've learned so much since Tanya. I know not to interrupt when Nancy's off on one; I scrub mugs properly, rather than a quick sluice under the tap; I even keep a box of Tampax in the basket under the sink.

Nancy flings herself on the sofa and polishes off the last of the salad, straight from the plastic tub. I return with two teas and hunker down beside her.

'We could do an early-morning run tomorrow,' she suggests, tucking her chin into my armpit, like an over-familiar kitten.

'Can't. Sorry. I need to be at my desk by half seven to prep for a conference call with Crawley.'

'Ah, Crawley. What have they done now? Used the wrong font? Called your MD a cockwomble?'

'He *is* a cockwomble. No, I'm all set to read them the riot act. They've taken the piss for long enough.'

'I thought you were going to cut them some slack, keep them onside.'

'They've run out of road, Nan. I won't be taken advantage of. No more Mr Nice Guy.'

'Ned, you're sounding like an arse.'

'I'm taking charge. I should have done it weeks ago.'

Nancy pulls herself up from prone. 'Ah, I get it. You're going to be a bastard because Gemma told you to.'

'Gemma wipes arses in a care home. I'm hardly going to take managerial advice from her.'

'And yet you listen to her, rather than me. You'll wave your willy around because your best mate said you should.'

I don't get it. Granted, Nancy was already in a mood when she got here but I thought I'd hugged that out of her. Suddenly she's spoiling for a fight and I don't know why.

Who cares who said what about Crawley? I don't need guidance from Nancy *or* Gemma. I am a tiger.

'Don't do your innocent face, Ned. You know what I'm talking about.'

'I really don't. Have a Hobnob. Find something you want to watch on the telly.' I hand her the remote.

'I wish I'd stayed at *my* place now,' she says, stomping off to the bedroom. 'What are you like, Ned? Gemma says jump, you ask how high. Fuck's sake.'

I'm guessing we won't be having sex tonight. I watch the rest of *Interstellar* but, really, it's just background noise . . .

Nancy and I have rarely argued since we got together. I suppose we're still in our honeymoon period. Okay, she can get a bit sharp with me sometimes but I've always been annoying. I know that. And there are times when she talks and talks and barely notices when I try to chip in. That's couples for you. You can't tick every box when you meet someone. Neither of you will be perfect. Who needs perfection anyway, especially after a period in the wilderness? And that's okay. You give and you take.

In this instance it's Gemma who Nancy's taken against and I get that, I really do. She's an acquired taste. She speaks as she finds. Plus there's no rule that says all women have to like each other. It's a shame, though. After a shaky start, Gemma's a big part of my life. I like her energy, her attitude, what she brings to our friendship. Our shared experience, as dumped single parents, has bonded us in a way that I don't have with Andy – or Nancy.

Maybe Gemma feels it too. I hope she does. Either that or she still thinks I'm an idiot.

Chapter Twenty-Four

Gemma

It does sound daft when I try to explain it to Ros. There are times, mostly at two in the morning, when I even ask *myself* what the fuck I'm doing. Why do I always have to press the ejector seat, just as I'm getting somewhere? You don't need to be Dear Deidre to know the answer to that. It's basic stuff. I'm a textbook self-saboteur.

There I was, assuming my future was sorted and secure with Joe. And then it wasn't. It didn't come gradually and it wasn't expected. Boom. One day you're a happy family, the next day you're weeping into your Cheerios and wondering what damage you can do with a Homebase veg peeler. In a matter of seconds, I lost control of my life. It was stolen from me. And, as a control freak – which I am; I *know* I am – that was the worst part.

I was suddenly in freefall, and no amount of scrubbing, hoovering or colour-coding my knicker drawer was going to bring back what I'd lost. So now *I'll* pull the plug, *I'll* do the dirty, *I'll* make the grand exit so that no one else can do it to me, ever again.

I thought Ros would understand because she's my friend and she knows how I tick. She also knows that I don't take kindly to unwanted advice or 'helpful' home truths. That doesn't stop her.

'Surely you can get your job back,' she says, over two large glasses of wine in her local. 'They know what a hard worker you are, Janine especially.'

I've been round to help Ros get an urgent order out. If I never look at another rainbow-layered sponge cake, it'll be too soon. She's made eight of them for a big civil partnership celebration in Regency Square. The icing is rainbow-striped too which, it turns out, I'm pretty good at. (Control-freakery has its advantages when you're in charge of the icing bag. I was always the best in my class at colouring-in and drawing straight lines.)

'Ros, I don't want my job back. It was only ever meant to be temporary. I was good at it and I loved some of the residents, Judy especially. Now I need to find out what else I'm good at.'

'Doing my books? Putting my paperwork in a ring-binder in date order?'

'Yeah. I'm not bad at that. I used to do Joe's books. His filing was even worse than yours.'

'Packing cupcakes without smudging the frosting? Washing endless baking tins? You were fearless just now with that rainbow icing.'

'*I* was surprised at that too. It's actually quite satisfying.'

Ros chinks my glass. 'Interview over, Ms O'Hara. You're hired. Can you start last week?'

I laugh. I knew Ros would cheer me up.

'I mean it, Gemma. I can't keep Sweetcakes going without another pair of hands. We both know baking's not your strong point but it *is* mine. You're brilliant at all the other stuff. Seriously. I'd have gone under without you. If you join the team, I can honestly say I've increased the workforce 100 per cent.'

I'm speechless. She isn't joking.

'I can't pay you much at the moment. Maybe you can juggle it with a bit of agency work? I really feel I've got something good here and I need you on board. Well, *say* something, you prannet.'

'Can I think about it?'

'If you must.'

'I've thought about it. Yes. That would be – I can't believe – Yes.'

'Right,' Ros says, giving me a hug. 'That's your job sorted. Now, about dumping Dan. Have you lost your mind?'

'I knew you'd say that. Just hear me out, will you.' I hope Ros gets how I feel. 'If Dan had sent me giddy with lust and dizzy from thinking about him 24/7, we'd still be together. On paper, he ticks every box, but in my heart, he doesn't. If he was The One, I'd know. I wouldn't have to think about it, Ros, I'd just know.'

I wonder if Nancy ticks all Ned's boxes. Bloody Nancy. And bloody Ned, for falling for her, with her big eyes and her wacky clothes and her oh-so annoying optimism.

Who *wouldn't* be captivated by all that? Just me, then.

On the way home, I pick up Kel from Mohit's. I want to tell him about my new job but I'll give Ros time to change her mind. *I* would, if I was her. I'm gobsmacked. I'd love to be a proper part of Sweetcakes, working alongside my fantastic friend. I didn't think I was anything other than a spare pair of hands. Mind you, I've always known I was good with accounts. Joe relied on me. I don't know who does his books now. Vicky, I hope.

Ros didn't get why I ended it with Dan. I probably didn't explain it properly. I just know that we don't have a future so it's better to pull the plug now, rather than let our relationship hit the buffers in a month, a year, whenever. She promised to respect my decision, even though she thinks I'm bonkers, and wondered if it would be okay if she approached him about updating her kitchen, now that Sweetcakes is taking off.

'Be my guest,' I told her. 'Me and Dan are grown-ups. We can be civil. He'll do a great job. You'd best have him over to measure up when I'm not around, if that's okay. Just to avoid any awkwardness.'

It's getting late, for a school night, so I send Kel off to bed sharpish, then make his packed lunch for tomorrow and empty the bins. Same old same old, except I am no longer unemployed. I am now 50 per cent of Sweetcakes. Well done, me.

When my phone rings, I'm relieved it isn't Joe. I mustn't encourage him. I'm better than that. It's Felipe.

'I am sorry to ring so late,' he says in his perfect English. I miss Felipe. Maybe he can ditch his job and work for Sweetcakes too.

'No worries. I've been meaning to call you for ages, hun. Guess what, I've—'

'I need to tell you something. I can't leave it until the morning.'

Now he's spooking me. Is he okay? Is Martin okay? Have they broken up?

'It's Mrs Palmer-Woodley . . . Judy. She died. I'm so sorry, Gemma. I know how much you liked her and she really missed you, after you left.'

For the second time tonight, I'm lost for words.

'It was peaceful. She was not in pain.'

'Thank you.' That's all I can say. 'Thank you for letting me know, Felipe.'

'I have something for you. From her. I want to pass it on to you before her family get here. She told me last week that, if she died, you must have her musical jewellery box.'

Typical Judy. She knew that heaving box of plastic tat made me laugh. Sometimes she'd wear all her necklaces, like a huge glittery snake, to surprise me when I brought her medication. Or she'd put on mismatched earrings because 'why the hell not?' I'm pretty sure her son will bin the lot if I don't accept. So yes, I'd love that.

When the phone rings again, it *is* Joe. And because I'm floored by the news about Judy – even though it was expected – I say okay, he can come round.

'That's rough, Gemzy,' he says as he makes me a cup of hot, sweet tea. 'She must have loved you. You're so good with old people. My gran loved you to bits.'

'Your gran was a sweetheart. Tough as old boots, just like Judy.'

We take our teas to the sofa. I don't want sex, even though I'm sure that's what he's here for. I just want my hand held, my hair stroked. Joe puts his arm round me and kisses the top of my head. This will do.

But will it? Can I accept his comfort without wanting more? Would it be so wrong to sleep with him again? He used to be mine, and we still have a history. That can't change. It wouldn't be scraps from the table. It would be me claiming back what's rightfully mine.

'You're still The One,' he whispers in my ear. 'I don't know what I was thinking. You'll always be The One.'

They're words. Comforting words to soothe me. Maybe

Joe is my One too. Is that possible? What if this is as tidy and complete as my life gets?

I don't stop him when he kisses me. I justify it to myself because I'm upset about Judy and I need it. It's mine. If Joe has any sense, he won't push. Not yet. He knows me well enough to gauge my state of mind. He knows I'm here if he wants me. And I *do* want him.

My head is so cluttered that I don't hear the living-room door open. It's Kelvin in his *Star Wars* PJs. All three of us look shocked. Joe and I spring apart. Kel tries to make sense of what he's seen: Mum and Dad kissing. That must mean something, right?

'Dad?'

'Hey, champ. Can't you sleep?'

'What's going on?'

I need to explain because it'll be me who lives with the fallout after Joe's gone home. 'I had some sad news about a friend of mine, love. She died. I was very upset so your dad was comforting me.'

'Who died? Do I know her?'

'Judy. No, you don't. Anyway, you're off home now, aren't you, Joe? Thanks for everything.'

Joe kisses my cheek, ruffles Kel's hair and makes a swift exit. 'See you then, Gemzy. Let me know if there's anything I can do. Vicky too, obviously. Laters, champ.'

I'm expecting grumpy Kelvin at the breakfast table, as per usual. Kel will never be a morning person. He isn't grumpy, though. He couldn't be happier. He knows what he saw last night and it's good news.

'You and Dad are getting back together.'

'No, love. We're not.'

'I saw you kissing. Don't say you weren't because you were. Why would you do that if you weren't getting back together?'

'I told you, Kel. Your dad was comforting me, that's all.'

He gives me a cynical sneer and ploughs on with his Cheerios.

'He was. Honestly, love. My favourite resident from the care home died and I was really upset. I still am. Such a lovely woman. You'd have liked her too. I should have introduced you.'

'You're always saying I should tell the truth and that lying is wrong. But you're doing it now. I know what I saw, Mum. It was a proper kiss, like you and Dad used to do when you thought I wasn't looking.'

'We go back a long way. We know each other so well. You shouldn't read anything into it, Kel.'

He pushes his cereal away, unfinished. He must be really upset to do that. 'I just thought – it just looked like—'

'Looked like what?'

'That you two loved each other, like you did before you split up. And we could be a family again. We could be happy again.'

'I *am* happy.'

He doesn't reply. He can see right through me.

'We're not getting back together, Kel. We'll never be like we used to be. We're older. We've changed. You, me *and* your dad.'

He looks so sad. I thought he'd adjusted to our set-up, our separate lives. Kids adjust all the time. They're way more resilient than grown-ups.

He grabs his blazer and leaves for school. No hug. Not even a 'bye, Mum'.

I watch him walk up the road. His head is down and he's scuffing his feet. I've let him down. Again . . .

He desperately wants us to be a family like before. Is he so wrong to think it's a possibility? *Is it* a possibility? Yes, I finished with Dan but does that mean I want Joe back in my life? I've made new friends. I've left my job (okay, that wasn't entirely planned) and got a better one. I'm happy. Mostly.

And yet, Joe still knows how to press my buttons. Maybe he always will.

I can't help wondering if Ned ever lusts after Tanya. Somehow, I don't think so. Plus, of course, he and Nancy are living the loved-up dream. How can I *not* be jealous at the thought of them together, both so sure *their* story will end with happy ever after? Why does their joy hurt so much?

Chapter Twenty-Five

Ned

I've just done my best morning run yet, and I didn't even have Nancy alongside to keep me on track. I tried a different route and it made all the difference: down to the sea, three circuits of Wish Park and back home for a shower and four toasted slices of Nancy's wholemeal, slathered in her mum's damson jam. No stopping to pretend to re-tie my trainers while I got my breath back. No stitch. No painful lungs or crampy calves. My 'Pounding Pavements' play list really helped and I was particularly bullish, thumping along the seafront to 'Eye of the Tiger', because, yes, I *am* a tiger.

The Crawley business is sorted, thanks to yours truly. Karen even mentioned me in dispatches to our MD, in order to speed up the long-promised move from open plan to an office of my own. She's really embarrassed that it's taken so long. And the Crawley crew are grateful that I called them out, apart from Becky, which was to be expected. Okay, it was initially a bit sticky but I sent each team member a personal thank-you for their speedy and professional response. Respect all round, I'd say.

Andy's in good form too. He even bought me a Danish

pastry and a latte from the cafe downstairs because he 'felt like it, okay'.

'You look good, mate,' I tell him, sticking my head over the partition.

He really does. He's wearing one of his usual shirts with the frayed collar, and his workspace, as ever, looks like it's been trashed by vandals. But there's something in his demeanour, the upright way he sits in his chair and stirs four sugars into his double espresso. He seems . . . energized.

'I'm a dad,' he says, beaming. 'I like saying it. I'm a dad and I've got a son. I don't have to change his nappies or help with his homework. I can meet him for a pint and a chinwag, maybe catch an Albions game or see some stand-up. It's great, Nedward. I am unfeasibly pleased with how it's all panned out.'

'Me too, bud. You deserve every bit of it. Aaron must be pleased too.'

'Not just Aaron. I got my nerve up and rang Gillian last night. We were on the phone for nearly two hours. I'm going to hers for Sunday lunch. I don't see us picking up where we left off but you never know.'

'So you're over Ros, then?'

'Ros was a passing fancy. I am 110 per cent over her.' He awakens his sleeping PC screen and shoos me away. 'Now, could you please sod off. Some of us have got work to do.'

For the last few days, Nancy's been saying she doesn't want to make a big deal of her birthday; thirty is just a number, right? I'm not to buy her anything extravagant. Better to keep my money saved for the (aka '*our*') future. She also doesn't want a big celebration so no surprise party or romantic gesture please. Small is beautiful, low key is okay.

Fine with me. All of it. But she can't refuse the necklace I've bought her. In the end, I didn't send Gemma a folder of photos from the jewellery shop for a second opinion. I really ought to be able to decide for myself what my girlfriend might wear. So I only sent her five and she responded speedily, saying the one that looked like silver macaroni was her favourite but 'Don't listen to me – I hardly know Nancy, do I?'

I've booked us a table tonight at Marrocco's, to make up for the meal she didn't finish on our first, nightmare date. And at the weekend, Dora and I are tootling over to West Wittering to drop in on her and her folks, for a special birthday tea. I'm bringing a bottle of single malt to ingratiate myself with her dad and Dora's making Nancy a card. It will, no doubt, be covered in glitter which will imbed itself into their Axminster for the next fifty years.

I text Nancy mid-afternoon to confirm that we're meeting at 7.30 at the restaurant.

She replies: 'I'm just as happy with a takeaway on the sofa, Ned. Birthdays aren't important. Even the big three-oh.'

I will brook no attempt to downplay my plans. 'Marrocco's it is, madam. See U there.'

I'm just thinking about an early departure from work, so that there's time to have a bath, put fresh linen on the bed and gift-wrap Nancy's necklace before heading for the restaurant. Then a phone call changes everything.

It's Gemma. Gemma never rings during the day. Her bitch of a boss, Janine, strictly forbids her staff to make or take personal calls. Gemma deserves better. I've no doubt she's brilliant at her job but she's too good for that place. I must tell her so, next time I see her.

'Ned, I don't know what to do. It's Kelvin. I don't know who to turn to.'

'Turn to why? What's he done?'

I can hear her breathing deeply to calm herself.

'What's happened, Gemma?'

'We had a row. Sort of. He was so angry with me this morning. He stomped off to school, then his form teacher rang and said Kel hadn't come in and was he okay? I haven't the faintest idea where he is, Ned. I'm worried sick.'

Kelvin doesn't seem like the kind of lad to skive off school and get into mischief. He's too sensible. Just like me at his age. But I don't want Gemma to panic any more than she already is.

'I'm sure he's fine. There's bound to be a perfectly good explanation.'

'Which I'd know, as his mother. If he was at the dentist or in bed with a temperature, I'd bloody know.'

'Maybe Joe's taken him out for the day. From what you've told me, I wouldn't put it past him.'

'I thought that too so I rang Vicky. Not to tell her Kel's gone missing, in case he *isn't* with Joe. Just some nonsense about a lost T-shirt. She'd have said if Kel was there or with his dad, wouldn't she?'

'And you don't want to ring Joe direct?'

'No, no. Absolutely not. This is his fault too. I won't go into details but it is. So I can't tell him what's happened. It'll just make things worse. What shall I do?'

I'm scared to state the bleeding obvious, knowing I'll have my head bitten off. But I'll risk it. 'You've phoned Kelvin, haven't you, Gemma? Of course you have. Lots of times, I shouldn't wonder.'

She doesn't bite my head off. 'Every ten minutes. He won't answer. The thing is, he broods, like his dad. Stomps off to sulk and goes silent and makes everyone else feel guilty. Well, it's worked and I do, okay? I feel bloody guilty. And I just want him home.'

I drive straight over. If we do a street-by-street search of Bevendean, we might come across him, hanging out on a corner with a bunch of the local wrong 'uns. Can't see it myself, though. Gemma watches me park in front of her bay window and comes out to meet me. She's calmed down but her face is pale and her arms are crossed. 'The little – when he rocks up, I won't know whether to hug him or give him hell. I'll hug him, obviously, the little . . .' She lets out a faint whimper, then locks it back inside. I get it: if it were Dora, I'd be a gibbering wreck. I suggest the street-by-street search; Gemma isn't convinced. 'Doesn't sound very Kelvin.'

'Call the police?'

'No. He's bound to come back when he gets hungry or scared. Oh God, what if he's too scared to come home because he knows he's in big trouble?'

'Gemma, do you think he'd answer his phone if *I* rang? I'm not trying to big myself up. It's just, I did get on with the lad.'

'He'll know you're with me, that I got you to call him.'

'Not necessarily. It's worth a try, isn't it?'

She nods. Kelvin's angry with *her*, not me.

He answers on the second ring, even though he doesn't recognize my number. 'Hello?'

I try to sound relaxed, cool, matey. 'Hey Kelvin, it's Ned. Remember? The steam-train nerd. Ned the nerd, right?' Gemma shoots me a glare. Get on with it, will you?

'Oh, yeah. Hi.'

'I've just been speaking to your mum and she's wondering where you are. She said something about fish and chips for tea. Have you had your tea yet?'

'No. I don't care. Tell her I don't bloody care.'

Gemma can see from my face that he's hung up. 'Well, that went well. Got any other brilliant ideas, Ned the nerd?'

I resist a Poirot-style smile. 'I do, as it happens. Kelvin's at Brighton Station. I could hear the departure announcements in the background. We can be there in fifteen minutes if I put my foot down. Well, are you coming or what?'

Brighton Station isn't big by London standards, but big enough when you're trying to find someone. Anyway, what if Kelvin's already boarded a train and is heading to Hastings, Luton or Littlehampton? Then there are all the cafes and shops and that bit at the back with the bike stands and taxi rank. Needle, meet haystack.

Gemma didn't say more than half a dozen words on the drive from Bevendean. She just looked down at her bitten fingernails, occasionally picking at a torn sliver of skin. I took my lead from her and kept quiet; not the time or place for small talk. When we got there, I dropped her off at the entrance, to start searching for Kelvin while I parked the car. I used the time to send Nancy a quick message, warning her that I might be a teensy bit late at the restaurant because Gemma was having crisis and I'd offered to help. She didn't reply. I'm guessing that means she's cool with it.

I see Gemma and Kelvin as soon as I hit the concourse, sitting next to each other on one of the benches by the piano. I'm not sure if I should approach or leave them to it. If Gemma's giving Kel hell, my presence might tone it down a bit. She has every reason to be angry with him, but not right now. On the other hand, if they're involved in some mother/son bonding, they don't need me barging in. Up close, I see that Kelvin is all clenched up, kicking the bench leg with his heel and giving off major vibes of non-cooperation. He's too small for his school blazer and he's been saddled all day with a backpack the size of Sussex.

Gemma shrugs 'I give up' at me because whatever she's said to Kelvin isn't registering. Or, at least, he won't show that it is.

'That's it then, is it? *You* skive off school and *I* get sent to Coventry?'

Kelvin stares up at the departures board, giving nothing away. Inside, he'll be relieved that his adventure's over and he can go home. But he mustn't drop his guard just yet or he'll be in danger of crying. I was that boy, back in the day. I know what he's thinking, how he's feeling. I really connect with this little lad.

'Right, you two,' I say, rubbing my hands together, then wishing I hadn't. 'I've parked badly so let's be having you.'

You could hear a pin drop on the rubbish-strewn floor of my Picanto. The silence is so loaded, so uncomfortable, that I have to play some very loud Springsteen to fill the space. Gemma said her bit at the station. Now she's staying silent to avoid exploding. Kelvin sits in the back, head at right angles to us so that he doesn't have to catch anyone's eye in the rear-view mirror. It's another fifteen-minute drive – Brighton Station to Bevendean – but it feels much longer.

Once home, Kelvin stomps up to his room and slams the door, bloodied but unbowed. Poor lad. He's painted himself into a corner. Sooner or later, he's going to have to come downstairs and exchange whole sentences with his mum, if only to ask for cheese on toast and a hot chocolate.

Gemma, meanwhile, is in the kitchen, aggressively getting supper ready. I want to hug her, tell her Kelvin's awash with hormones that make him cranky and horrible. I want to kiss her furrowed brow and reassure her that the pair of them will laugh about this, ten years from now.

'Macaroni and meatballs. There's enough for three, if you want to stay.' Her back's to me. Is she crying?

The mention of macaroni reminds me of Marrocco's. If I head off now, I should be bang on time, even if I have to arrive at the restaurant in my work clothes and no bath.

'I can't tonight. It's Nancy's birthday meal.'

She spins round, wiping a stray tear from her cheek with the flat of her hand. I can't help it. I hug her. That's what friends are for. She looks so sad, so forlorn. She lets me, for all of ten seconds, then she jumps back as if I've given her an electric shock.

'That's really not helping, Ned. But if you could talk to him. Find out where he's been and how I can make it better. Could you do that, please?'

I glance at my watch. I can spare a quick five minutes with the lad.

I knock on his door. No answer. I knock again. 'It's Ned. Can I come in, Kel?'

The door swings open and there he is, sitting at his desk watching a black-and-white YouTube clip of old trains on his laptop. I'll happily accept responsibility for that.

'Okay if I sit here?' I perch on his bed and look around his room. It's scrupulously tidy and organized. Who by? Kelvin or Gemma? For some reason, I get a lump in my throat. This room – this boy – has got to me and I don't know why.

'Is that why you were at the station?' I ask tentatively. 'To look at the trains?'

He turns on his chair to face me. He's ready to talk. 'First of all, I took the train to Seaford. Then I came back to

Brighton and went to Worthing. I only had a Seaford ticket but nobody stopped me, even in my stupid school uniform.'

'I did that once. When we lived in Pinner. As long as you don't have to go through the ticket barriers, you're fine. I went all over the Underground system and only one woman asked why I wasn't at school.'

'What did you say?'

'Dentist.'

Kelvin nods, quietly impressed.

'Why, though, mate? Why did you skive off like that? Your mum was so worried.'

'Serve her right. She's a liar, even though she says lying's wrong.'

I want to tell him that grown-ups lie all the time, but I'll save that for another time.

'She said Dad was kissing her to make her feel better because someone died. An old lady in the care home. But it wasn't that kind of kiss. I may be a kid but I'm not stupid.'

'Ah. Right. I can see that would be confusing.'

'And then, when I asked her if they were getting back together, because that's what it looked like, she said no. I want us to be a family again, Ned, like we used to be, before Vicky and Amelie came along. They're okay and everything but I want it to be me and Dad and Mum again. Just us. Like we used to be.'

Gemma is sitting on the sofa when I come downstairs. I can smell supper cooking, from the kitchen. My pasta always boils over when I'm away from it. Maybe Gemma has a trick to stop that.

'He told you, then,' she says, not looking at me.

'Train to Seaford, then a train to Worthing. Plus a couple

of hours mooching around at the station. He had a cream cheese bagel for lunch and an iced coffee. And a Mars bar.'

Gemma shakes her head. 'Why he disappeared. Did he tell you that?'

I sit down. I'm not looking forward to this. Either it's none of my business or it really, really is. 'You kissing Joe? You not being a family again, even though Kelvin wants you to be? That?'

'That.'

'He's confused, Gemma. It's tough on kids, what we've been through. You and Joe. Me and Tanya.'

'It's confusing for grown-ups too. I'm pretty bloody confused. Aren't you?'

'Sometimes.'

'I thought I'd got over Joe. I honestly thought Dan would help there. Draw a line. Move on. But how could he? That's why I dumped him.'

I am genuinely gobsmacked. 'You dumped Dan? Why, Gemma? He's a great bloke.' Even as I say the words, I feel a tiny jolt of satisfaction. I was never convinced that Dan was the one for her. She must have realized it too.

'Because I can't trust myself to be happy. Everyone goes in the end. My mum, my dad, Joe, Judy . . . you.'

'I haven't gone anywhere. See, I'm right here talking to you.'

'You've got Nancy and you're happy. I've got no one, apart from Kel. That's why Joe's my best option. With Joe at least I *feel* something, even if it isn't love.'

'He's with Vicky now.'

'So? I'd only be doing to her what she did to me.'

I'm sitting across from this wonderful woman who's seriously lost the plot. She needs to know that.

'No, Gemma. That's wrong. If you think like that, everyone will get hurt. Especially you.'

She waves me away and heads for the kitchen to check on dinner. 'You're sorted, Ned. You have someone. I won't be lectured by you. Thanks for today. I appreciate your help. Really. But aren't you meant to *be* somewhere?'

I need to tell her that I'm not remotely sorted and I'm not trying to lecture her and that this thing with Joe cannot happen. Still, she's right. I *do* have to be somewhere, and I'm already late . . .

. . . Although amazingly, only by twenty minutes in the end. I don't have Nancy's birthday present with me; I'll give it to her on Sunday, when Dora and I meet her parents. I even find a space close by the restaurant. The Gods of Parking have been kind to me all day.

I meet her in the doorway. She's leaving as I arrive. She's wearing a purple dress which matches her hair. She looks lovely.

'No,' she says when she sees me. 'I don't care, Ned. Just bloody no.'

'Kelvin went missing. Gemma didn't know who else to turn to.'

'No.'

I can explain, if she'll only listen. 'I didn't mean to stay so long but Kelvin opened up to me. I couldn't just walk away. The poor lad's in quite a state. So's Gemma.'

'Your "friend" Gemma is a walking disaster, from what I can see. Once a fuck-up, always a fuck-up. And that's fine because, God knows, we're all fuck-ups. But *I'm* your fuck-up, Ned. Not her. *I* should come first.'

'You do, Nancy. Honestly. I could see the evening running away with me. Then I remembered what you said: that you

346

didn't want a fuss and you didn't mind if we just had a takeaway on the sofa. Then I got here anyway, and only a bit late. So everything's good, right?'

'Wrong.' Nancy looks at me sadly. Almost pityingly. 'I've given you so many chances, Ned. From the day we met, when all you did was talk about Tanya. And do you know why? Because I thought you were dependable and decent and because I thought you wouldn't hurt me. Instead, it feels like you're sleepwalking through our relationship, going through the motions: a boyfriend should do this, a boyfriend should say that. We have fun, we're good together. We are, aren't we? But I don't think you *love* me.'

When I try to find the words to respond, she holds her hand up. 'I know what you're going to say and, yes, it *is* still early days, and that's fine. It is. But can you honestly see yourself with me a year from now? Five years from now? If the answer's no, then you need to tell me . . . because I won't be hurt again, Ned. I just won't.'

I want to say yes. Of course I do. But that would be the easy way out. I'd be lying and that isn't fair on Nancy. Or I could say what's in my head, which is that no one knows what the future holds, least of all me. How can anyone be sure of anything? I'm about to speak; but she stops me. Again.

'No, Ned. Don't say anything. You couldn't answer straight away and that's all I need to know. I don't want to see you again. It's over.'

After she's gone, I slump on a seafront bench. The sun's gone down and the wind farm is coated in a cloudy haze. I started today in full tiger mode. I don't feel quite so all-conquering now. I feel stupid and clumsy and insensitive. Mostly confused. I *thought* I was doing all the right things.

And even when there was occasionally something I couldn't quite put my finger on, I was sure we'd find a way through.

I tried. I really did. But maybe I tried *too* hard. I know you have to work at relationships, but, if they're meant to be, they should come easily, no effort required. I was always so worried about who I was – which Ned I was – when I was with Nancy, I never quite relaxed. I never quite trusted myself, or her, enough to be the real me. That can't be right, can it?

I never had to try hard with Gemma, to be someone I wasn't. When we first met, and she laid into me at SPAN, I dismissed her as 'not my type'. (To be fair, she isn't someone you instantly warm to. She prides herself on that.) Then I started to get the hang of her. It was gradual, subliminal, unintentional. I looked forward to seeing her, being with her.

When she told me she was seeing Joe again, it actually hurt. Like a stitch when you're running. It dawned on me with a dull thud that I didn't *want* to leave for Marrocco's and Nancy. I wanted to stay with Gemma and Kel. And not just because I was worried about them.

I tried to tell her that she was doing herself down, selling herself short. She didn't listen. She didn't care.

What if Gemma settles for some twisted, toxic version of a relationship with her ex, partly because she believes she's owed it – deceiving Vicky as *she* was deceived – and partly because she thinks it's all she deserves? Does she truly think this will make her feel better?

And if his parents are screwing on the quiet, for all the wrong reasons, how does Kelvin get his happy family back? It could seriously harm him.

Every aspect of this is wrong but she won't listen to me.

She thinks I'm a twat. I *am* a twat. For being so blinkered and dense, for not seeing what was staring me in the face.

Who was staring me in the face.

Gemma.

Chapter Twenty-Six

Gemma

Felipe drops off Judy's jewellery box. He's had to close it with two heavy-duty rubber bands because the hinges are knackered. I invite him in for a cuppa but he can't stop.

'Martin's driving me to a gig in Eastbourne. I'm doing my brand-new Ariana Grande routine. Come and see it some time, Gemma. I miss you.'

We hug each other tight for a full minute; he adored Judy too.

'I'll pick out some jewellery for you,' I promise him. Judy would love that her plastic pearls and Diamonique earrings continue to star in his drag act.

An empty weekend stares me in the face. Kelvin's at his dad's and glad to be away from me for a couple of days. We've found a way of living in the same house but we're a bit like lodgers, passing on the stairs. He still hasn't forgiven me for confusing and upsetting him. If Joe comes round again, we're going to have to be more careful.

Maybe I should have hitched a ride to Eastbourne with Felipe and Martin. Too late now. I'll probably start watching TV around four and only press 'Pause' to zap a mystery tub from the freezer: it's either chilli or stewed rhubarb. Who cares . . .?

I don't want to dump myself on Ros. She sees enough of me during the week, now that I'm on board with Sweetcakes. I'd hate it if she stopped being my pal or workmate or both. If Ros ended our friendship, I'd have no one. Not even Ned, who's ghosted me since I let slip about me and Joe. He saw how spineless and pathetic I am and he ran for the hills. Anyway, Ros is busy. She rang this morning to say she's got a date. 'Not with Andy. That was never going to happen. Let's catch up tomorrow.'

I check out Judy's jewellery. Some of it makes me laugh: the enormous ruby cluster earrings; the necklace that looks like a string of sprouts – Judy thought so too; the huge peacock brooch she'd pin to her dressing gown when she was entertaining.

I find a bright bead necklace for Dora; that's if I ever see her again. Then a pair of Fifties clip-on earrings that Ros would love. I'm just pushing a glittery plastic flower, set on a comb, into my hair when I notice a scrap of paper at the bottom of the box. It's folded in quarters and it's addressed to me.

'Darling Gemma . . . if you're reading this, I must have snuffed it and Felipe's given you my jewellery box. I hope all these ridiculous bits of nonsense bring you pleasure. You made my final years so much more bearable. Do have a happy life. Don't be so down on yourself. Don't be scared to act the giddy goat. And don't you dare give the pearl rope to Oxfam. When I had it valued in 2005, it was worth £500. Much more now, I expect. All love, Judy xxx'

I find the pearls and loop them twice round my neck. I hardly ever cry. It's just not who I am. Ned's seen me cry twice – once when we had that row at SPAN and again last week, after Kel did his disappearing act. Crying's weak and pointless. It gets you nowhere. It certainly got me nowhere when Joe sodded off with Vicky.

I cry now, though – for Judy because I wasn't with her at the end and because these pearls prove we meant something to each other, whether they're valuable or not. We cheered each other up on dark days. We'd laugh hysterically at one of Janine's bossy laminated 'notice to residents' or the flower arrangement in the lobby, decorated with Monica's slippers.

Whenever I felt gloomy or angry or lonely, Judy would cheer me up. She'd talk non-stop about her life: what this necklace represented . . . where that brooch came from . . . her lovers, her triumphs, her disasters. I was Judy's friend and now she's gone, and all her amazing stories with her.

'Do have a happy life. Don't be so down on yourself. Don't be scared to act the giddy goat.' I know I frustrated her with my downbeat attitude. Cups *are* half empty, in my experience; rugs *are* there to be pulled out; the light at the end of the tunnel is bound to be an oncoming train.

I need to change that, in tribute to Judy. I need to act the giddy goat and I deserve to be happy. Unless I've left it too late . . .

Sunday isn't much better. I stay in bed until ten and don't get dressed until noon. I've forgotten what to do with myself. I don't miss Dan – which says it all – but I miss his presence. When he was here, I could watch him stain my bench, fix my banister, fill my life. It's great that my kitchen table doesn't wobble any more but that's hardly the basis for a proper relationship.

I snooze on the sofa with Ross, Rachel and Joey burbling away in the background. Sleep is my way of pushing all the shit out of my head. I'm woken by my phone.

'Gem, it's Ros. Is this a good time?'

'Define "good time".' I sound snarky. That's not fair on Ros. 'Yeah, it is. Kel won't be back from Joe's until eight. I'm just, I suppose you'd call it chilling.'

'You want to know about my date, don't you? It wasn't really a date, just a drink and a chat. I really need to tell you about it.'

'I'm all ears.'

'If you're sure. You'll probably hate me. I'd hate me.'

'Okay, I hate you. Why?' There's a long pause. 'In your own time, Ros.'

'I went for a coffee with Dan. You recommended him. To update my kitchen. More work space, built-in larder, island unit, the whole nine yards. He came round when you weren't here, like you suggested. And, oh my God, you never said how fit he is. You must be mad, letting him go.'

'Probably. Go on.'

'He stayed for ages, taking measurements, showing me different worktop options. He really knows his stuff. I didn't want him to leave so I said could we meet again tomorrow – today – so we could go through some brochures together. We met at a cafe on St James's Street and I had my brochures and he had some preliminary drawings on his tablet. But we never talked kitchens.'

'You talked "me"?'

'Well, yes. Obviously. How could we not?'

'Does he hate me?'

Ros laughs. 'Hardly. He really cares about you but, how did he put it? "Some things aren't meant to be." He was really sweet, actually. I want to see him again, Gem, but not if you don't approve.'

I think this through. Who do I hurt by saying no? All

353

three of us, if Dan feels the same about Ros. I have to tell her it's okay, because Dan isn't mine to be needy and greedy about.

'He's all yours, Ros. Course he is.'

'Are you sure? I haven't fancied another man since David. I thought it might never happen. And okay, *this* might not happen. But I'll give it my best shot.'

'I'm sure I'm sure,' I tell her because, actually, I am. Ros is lovely and so is Dan, and they deserve to be lovely together. It isn't the happy ending I expected but it feels right.

And then the despair sets in, with a side order of self-pity. Judy wants me to be happy but how? Who with? When? I'm pleased for Ros and Dan; he really wasn't the one for me. So why can't I act like a grown-up and be pleased for Ned too? It can't *just* be because I think he can do better than Nancy. When Kelvin bunked off school that day and I was beside myself with worry, the first person I thought of was Ned. I didn't consider anyone else and certainly not Joe. I wanted Ned. Once Kel was back home, Ned hugged me and I felt safe. I felt a real connection between us.

There's no point picking at that now because he has Nancy. And I have no one.

My mood of despair isn't broken by the ring of the doorbell but at least I have something to distract me.

Has Dan come round to ask my permission to see Ros again?

It's Vicky. She's make-up free and dressed in workout gear and hoodie. I suddenly feel trapped and guilty. Has Joe told her about us kissing? Has Kelvin? I need to stay calm. I have nothing – *much* – to be ashamed of.

'Gemma, hi. Am I interrupting anything? Have you got a spare ten minutes?'

I can't come up with a lie in time. 'Yes, sure. Are you okay, Vicky?'

She bursts into tears and rushes past me into the house, settling on the sofa where she gives her nose a noisy blow. I let her recover while I put the kettle on.

'He's seeing someone,' she explains, in a shaky voice. 'Joe. He's got another woman. I know he has.'

'White, no sugar? Or I can do you a coffee, if you don't fancy tea.' I'm stalling, desperate to get my story straight.

'I don't want tea. I want your advice. God knows, I put you through this when I was seeing him behind *your* back. So I was like, Gemma knows the signs. She'll know what to do.'

I actually laugh at her brass neck. Can she even hear what she's saying?

'Seriously, Vicky? You're asking *me*?'

'I know, I know. I'm a hypocrite and you have every right to tell me to sod off.'

It's tempting. But I need to know what she knows. 'What makes you think Joe's seeing someone?'

'He's suddenly gone all shifty and secretive. Going into the back garden with his phone after supper. Snapping at me when I ask him who he's texting. I've smelled perfume on him too. Either he's seeing another woman or I've totally lost it.'

'Sorry, I can't help. I didn't pick up on any of that when he was seeing you. I must have been really unobservant . . . until I found your sunglasses.'

She nods and looks down. 'Yeah. The sunglasses.'

I think I'm in the clear. How *can* Vicky know that Joe and I fucked three months ago and might well have fucked again, if Kel hadn't walked in on us? She wouldn't be sitting on that very sofa, wiping her eyes, if she did.

'What do I do, Gemma?'

'I don't know. I'm sorry. I can't help.'

She gets it. She exits as fast as she entered. 'I shouldn't have come. What was I thinking? Asking your opinion. That's like – I'm so sorry, Gemma. I really am. For everything.'

There's a part of me – the vengeful, vindictive part – that's pleased. Now you know what it's like. See how *you* cope with the hurt and the rejection and the loneliness.

But another part of me feels grubby and guilty. If this is revenge, why can't I enjoy it? Ned warned me that everyone would get hurt. Ned, who doesn't pick up on signs or atmospheres, who can't read a woman or anticipate a situation. *That* Ned.

He saw this coming and he was right.

I've landed Sweetcakes an order – my very first – and I couldn't be more chuffed. A Facebook friend was looking for someone to make a fortieth birthday cake for her husband at the last minute. It isn't a big earner but Ros has got a gap in her schedule and knocks out a red velvet cake with cream cheese frosting, bright green pecan-brittle crumbs and sparklers.

En route to Hangleton to deliver the cake, I ignore Joe's texts. I don't have a free hand, for one thing, and daren't drop the box. I skim-read a couple of them on the bus home and, as usual, he wants to see me. He needs to talk to me. 'Call me asap, Gemzy. Please?'

Vengeful, vindictive Gemma is seriously tempted. If Vicky suspects that Joe's playing around, why not give her something else to be suspicious about? Have I had it with being passive and put-upon? Have I stopped caring who I hurt or how?

In the end, though, I don't answer – not because I'm *not* vengeful and vindictive, but because I don't want to hear what he has to say. Mind you, I'm not surprised when I get home and there he is on the doorstep. He has a holdall and I doubt if it contains Kel's football kit.

'I've left her, Gemzy. I've left Vicky. It's only ever been you. You know that.'

I don't want the neighbours gossiping, the ones who remember Joe from when he lived here. What the hell, I'll hear him out. I wave him through to the living room.

'Go on then, Joe. Tell me why it's only ever been me. Apart from Vicky, of course.'

I'm expecting bullshit and bravado but he surprises me. He starts crying. Joe, who'd get really uncomfortable if Kel threw a wobbler and would leave me to comfort him. Joe, who sat through *Toy Story* stony-faced. He makes big gulpy noises as he tries to rein in his tears. First Vicky, now Joe. I aim to stay dry-eyed.

'When you made me choose, I chose Vicky because she was pregnant—'

'—and because you thought I'd cope alone better than her. You did, Joe. As compliments go, it's right up there.'

'I felt cornered, what with a baby on the way. Not my finest hour, Gemzy. But I'll make it better. We can be a family again. You, me and Kelvin.'

Fuck him for bringing our boy into it. I've learned to live without Joe, but Kel hasn't. He wants things back to how they were, as if that can ever happen.

'Why would I trust you again, Joe? What's in it for me?'

He comes towards me, to show just what I'd get out of us being together. I hold up a hand, like a traffic cop, to stop him.

'No. Not the sex. I've made a life for myself without you. I've got friends now, and a job that makes me happy. *I'm* happy.'

'That's why I want us to try again. I'm totally in awe of you. Seriously. You always did kick ass but now, well, you're incredible.'

To the outside world, maybe. Inside my head, inside my heart, I'm still a waste of space.

'What if I move back with you and the boy for a week or two, couple of months maybe? See how we get on.'

'Reapplying for your old job on a trial basis?'

He laughs. I've always made him laugh. It isn't just sex that ties us together. 'If you and Kelvin think it's a goer, I'll stay. If not, we gave it our best shot.'

It *could* work, I suppose. I've changed this past year and I won't tolerate any shit. Joe knows that and he's up for it.

'I won't agree to *anything* without Kelvin's say-so,' I warn him.

'I guess that means I can't kip here for now, even on your sofa?'

'I'm sure your folks will put you up.'

Joe came here thinking I'd welcome him with open arms . . . and legs. I haven't slammed the door on him, but it's no shoo-in either.

'This is a big deal, Joe. Give me some time and space. Let's see how Kel feels.'

'Okay. But you're thinking about it?'

'I'm thinking about it.'

Over the next couple of days, I do nothing *but* think about it. I won't say anything to Kel, though, until I know my own mind. I even write a list of pros and cons.

Pro: Good sex.
Con: No sex.
Pro: We will be a family again.
Con: Joe will break my heart . . . again.
Pro: I'd feel secure.
Con: Until he cheats on me . . . again.
Pro: Ned has Nancy. He's happy, settled, spoken-for. Why
    should *I* be alone?
Con: Is Joe the one I want to be with?
 (Answer: No, he isn't. Just as Dan wasn't.)

As I see it, I have a depressingly short list of options:
1) I can lick my wounds and see who else is out there. There
   must be other good, grounded, honest men ready to fall
   for someone like me. There must be . . .
2) I can give up completely on future relationships. Kelvin
   will get used to it and it means I never have to shave my
   legs – or be hurt – again.
3) I can give Joe another chance. On my terms. One strike
   and he's out. We wouldn't be starting from scratch. We'd
   be picking up where we left off. I'm older, wiser, and I
   won't take any shit.
4) My final option isn't an option. It's too late. If I'm honest,
   it never *was* an option. That's why I wouldn't let myself
   believe in it. Out of my league and now, out of my life.

Now I see that Ros picked up on it from the off; always
asking what I thought of Ned, how I felt about Ned. If
she'd only come right out and told me straight, rather than
hinting at it, I might have made a move. (Yeah, right, Gemma
O'Hara. As if you've got the confidence to do something as
scary as *that*.)

What if I'd talked it through with Judy? She'd had a string of relationships and was full of self-belief. She'd have told me to go for it, to go for Ned. Why didn't I confide in her?

The mess I've made of my life is all down to me. I've let myself become *this*. Too proud, too pessimistic, too bloody-minded and too ready to believe that I'm not worth anyone's love. I've painted myself into this corner and now I'm stuck here. I'm safe here. I can't get hurt here. Who am I fooling? This really hurts.

When Vicky rings, optimism and pessimism have slugged it out and I'm coming round to Option 3 – giving Joe a second chance – if not for me then for Kel. I wonder how she's doing since Joe walked out on her. Does she know yet that he wants to try again with me? Has he even told her? Maybe he's playing his cards close to his chest until he's sure I'll take him back.

'How are things?' I ask, all innocent.

'I'm in bits,' she replies. 'And you?'

Oh God, she's worked it out. She's set a trap. 'I'm okay.'

'I found out, Gemma. I know who Joe's been with.'

'Ah. Right.'

'He's been cheating on me for nearly a year. I confronted him and he came clean so I kicked him out, just like you did. I don't want him here. I can't bear to look at him. I was like, "move in with your fancy woman, you utter shit". And, you'll love this, Gemma, he hasn't moved in with her because she said no.'

But I *haven't* rejected him. Not yet. Maybe not ever.

Vicky's in full flow. 'I should have known, from all the times he was off to Preston Park to "fix her boiler". Yeah, and the rest, pal.'

'Preston Park?'

'Her name's Naomi. I dump him, then Naomi dumps him. The lying bastard's kipping on his mum's sofa. And I'm like, serves him right, right?'

Vicky keeps talking but I'm not listening. I've heard enough. Vicky kicked Joe out because she found out about Naomi. And Naomi kicked Joe out because she didn't see him as a serious relationship. Now that he needs a roof over his head, I'm the only game in town. *Gemma's a soft touch. I know how to win her round. She'll take me in, the stupid cow.*

Never mind being a family again, with me and Kel. Never mind the chance to clean the slate, start afresh, make things right.

Joe doesn't really want to be with me. But no one else will have him. And no one else wants to be with me, especially not the man *I* want to be with.

Chapter Twenty-Seven

Ned

'Mum won't stop crying. I keep asking her what's wrong but she won't tell me.'

Kelvin sounds really distressed. I'm glad he's got my phone number and flattered that he thinks I can help.

'Has she hurt herself? Is she in pain?'

'I don't know. I don't think so. She's just sitting on the sofa crying and crying and it's not like normal crying. Do you want to hear? I'm in my room right now but I can hold my phone outside the door.'

'Have you tried talking to her? Or giving her a hug? Hey, she's got her secret stash of chocolate in the kitchen drawer. That might help.'

'No!' Kelvin is losing patience with me but I don't know what else to suggest.

The Welby-Daniels team has come to Brighton for dinner on us and a chat about new projects. I'm their point of contact and, although they get on with Karen, they prefer to deal with me. Our table at the Ivy is booked for 7 p.m. and it's ten past six now . . .

'I could come over, Kelvin? If you really, really want me to. It's just a bit busy right—'

'Yes. Please, Ned. I'm scared. Bye.'

As I hurtle through Brighton in a taxi, I text Karen with my apologies. I say it's a family crisis; and it is, kind of. Gemma's family. So's Kelvin. We've not spoken since the Brighton Station thing, when she said she and Joe were getting back together and I told her she'd get hurt. *Has* he hurt her? I don't do violence, because I don't come over as a threat to anyone, but I will thump him if he has.

I overpay the taxi driver in my haste to be of help. Kelvin lets me in and the poor chap looks so distressed that I have to give him an almighty hug. He can't speak without the floodgates opening so he takes me straight to Gemma and watches anxiously from the doorway. Her crying has subsided. She looks terrible. Her eyes are puffy and her face is ugly, angry, defeated.

'Oh, great,' she says. 'Have you come to gloat?'

'Kelvin rang me. He's worried about you. So am I.'

'I'm fine, I'm fine. Couldn't be happier, now that I know I'm all set for Option 2.'

'What's Option 2? I don't understand.'

'You don't, do you? That's you all over, Ned. Missing stuff, not getting stuff. But, God knows, it seems to be working for you. Happy ever after, eh.'

I shake my head. Why is she so angry with me?

She wipes her eyes on her sleeve, tidies her hair and sees Kel in the doorway. 'You okay, love?'

'Kind of. Do you want a hot chocolate?'

'That would be lovely. Make one for Ned too.'

Kelvin goes into the kitchen, relieved to be busy. I love that kid.

I sit on the sofa, making sure I don't crowd Gemma. 'So,

madam. What's all this about?' If I keep it light, she might open up.

'Go on, be smug. Gloat at the saddo from your ivory tower. You've found your life partner. You've gone up the ladder while I've been played by a snake.'

She laughs at her own joke but it's not a nice laugh. I can see why Kelvin's scared.

'Joe, you mean?'

'He nearly convinced me to give him another chance. And I was up for it because I had nothing, I have nothing, I have no one. I told myself it was for Kel's sake but the truth is, I don't want to be alone. Then I find out he only wanted to move back with me because it's better than dossing down under Brighton Pier.'

'Joe's a shit, Gemma. You should know that better than most.'

'I'd have settled, though. I see you with Nancy. Sharing puddings, weekends away, the perfect couple. You've come through all this, Ned. You won, I lost.'

'I'm not with Nancy. She ended it.'

Gemma's eyes widen.

'I was late for her birthday meal, after Kelvin went missing, and she dumped me.'

'Bloody hell, Ned. Why didn't you say?'

'No one knows. Not even Andy.'

'You should have told me, especially as it was all my fault. Don't shrug it off. It *is* my fault, because I forced you to help me find Kel, of course. I'm the reason you were late for Nancy.'

Oh. That. I shrug again. 'You really weren't, Gemma. Kelvin's a great kid. I wanted to help.'

'Let me have Nancy's number so I can call her and explain.'

'Why are you so keen to take the blame?'

'Habit?' she replies, with a sad smile. 'Okay then, if it wasn't my fault, why did Nancy dump you?'

I try the words out loud for the first time, to see if they make any kind of sense. 'She doesn't think I'm fully "there" for her. And she's got a point.'

I pause. Do I say it? Why the hell not? What have I got to lose? 'Nancy's 100 per cent right. I'm not fully there for her because I'm distracted. I can't stop thinking about someone else.'

Gemma frowns, trying to make sense of all this. 'Tanya?'

'Of course not Tanya. I keep thinking about *you*. For pity's sake, Gemma, why are you making this so difficult?'

I don't expect her to fling her arms around me and declare her undying love. Not yet, anyway. My words need to sink in. A smile would help. Anything to stop my pulse racing and my forehead breaking out in big beads of sweat. I need her to respond, to stop my words hanging in the air, all exposed and vulnerable.

She gives a bitter laugh. 'Here we go. Second best yet again. Nancy dumps you, so I'll do. Like the substitute in the supermarket delivery. You wanted Hovis, have some crispbread.'

'That isn't it at all. Just listen to me, will you? Nancy reckons we're all fuck-ups and she's right. We are. All of us. But she said *she* should be my fuck-up, not you. She isn't, though, Gemma. She really isn't. You're my fuck-up and I'm yours. And that's why we should be together.'

Gemma's expression is unreadable. Does she even understand what I'm saying? Is she silently accepting what must be the world's worst back-handed compliment? Am I getting through to her?

'No. No, Ned, I'm not having this. You're telling me you didn't know how you felt about me until your girlfriend dumped you.'

Fair enough, I could have pitched it better. 'Could we – you and I – could we have a future together?'

Gemma stands up, shakes her head, composes herself. 'Never mind Ned's hot chocolate, Kel,' she shouts in the direction of the kitchen. 'He's just going.'

Then, to me. 'This isn't good enough. I don't deserve this. I won't be second best. Ever again. You need to go now, Ned.'

She shows me the door and I'm too knocked back to bleat my objections.

I skid into the Ivy half an hour later and throw myself into the vacant chair, between Karen and Malcolm, Welby-Daniels' MD. I eat what's put in front of me, tasting nothing; even some lamb pebble-dashed with pomegranate seeds, which would normally make me dry-heave.

Malcolm calls me a 'star' and tells Karen to hang on to me before I'm headhunted by a rival. Karen tells Malcolm that my imminent bonus should act as a very acceptable golden handcuff.

I'm the hero of the hour and this should be a great evening but it isn't. How can it be when it means nothing? I have nothing.

To fill my empty evenings, I scroll through property websites on autopilot. I tell myself that if I see somewhere that ticks all the boxes, I should buy it. Financially, I'm flush, especially when my bonus kicks in. I may have screwed up my life but I can contemplate the yawning chasm that is my future from the comfort of a spacious Victorian villa or quirky Fifties semi, rather than my sad little shithole.

I even see a house I like, just south of Hove Park. Nothing major needs doing to it, there's no chain and it's within my price range. But what's the point? Who is it for? I'll only rattle around it like a sad pinball, kicking myself for being so monumentally dense. I can do that in my current place; its shabby grimness is the perfect setting for self-pity.

Apart from putting myself through long, punishing runs along the seafront, I go nowhere and see no one. I can't even rely on Andy for a pint and a whinge. He and Gillian have picked up where they left off and he's too besotted to realize that he's abandoned me. He's a great guy and he deserves to be happy. I'm not and I don't.

The only social engagement I have on the horizon is a 'do' at Tanya and Julian's. He and Dora are sharing a birthday party. My heart sinks at the prospect of yet another smug gathering in their smug house. Still, it's my daughter's special day and I won't miss that. What would be my excuse? 'Sorry I can't be there, but I'm going down with a nasty dose of despondency and I'd hate anyone else to catch it.'

Tanya was officious as ever when she rang to invite me. I can't believe I put up with her control-freakery for as long as I did. Poor old Julian.

'You needn't bring any food or drink, Ned. We've asked Dora's favourite restaurant to do the catering. And we can't move for Cava. Julian's cousin gets it for us wholesale.'

That's me told.

'The cake, then,' I say, surprisingly firmly. 'I'll bring Dora's birthday cake and I won't take no for an answer.'

Tanya reluctantly acquiesces. 'It'd better be special though. Not some nasty pink thing you grab in Aldi.'

'It will be. Any other orders, while you're at it?'

'I'll ignore the snarkiness. As it happens, we've gone for

another fun theme. You know how much Dora loves polka dots?'

'Still?'

'Still. Please come wearing something spotty. She'll be thrilled and it'll look so great in the photos.'

My turn reluctantly to acquiesce. If I've been permitted to provide the cake, I'll do as I'm told. I'm all ready to hang up when Tanya's nosey gene kicks in.

'And which of your many lady friends will be your plus-one? Ooh, bring Gemma. We liked Gemma.'

'She's busy. Sorry.'

I can't tell Tanya that Gemma was not my 'lady friend' and now she never will be. It still hurts. Beating yourself up inside your head 24/7 is guaranteed to have that effect.

The day before the party, I drive over to Ros's to collect the cake. She's been rushed off her feet with lots of big orders but said she could definitely knock up something spotty and special. I'm glad I asked her. It's good to hear that her business is taking off.

I don't, however, expect Gemma to open the door. She looks as shocked as I feel.

'What are *you* doing here?' I mumble, trying to keep my cool.

'I work for Sweetcakes now. Didn't you know? What are *you* doing here?'

'I'm collecting a cake.'

She frowns. 'Sodding Ros,' then beckons me in, leading the way to the kitchen. 'She asked me to hold the fort while she dashed out to meet Dan, to check out some half-price marble worktops. She said someone was coming over to pick up a cake but she carefully forgot to mention who.'

I try to process all this: Ros is out with Dan; Gemma works with Ros. It's like I've missed a week of *The Archers* and lost the plot.

'I had no idea you'd left the care home. You *have* left the care home?'

'It was always on the cards. You didn't know because you didn't ask. You were with Nancy and I never got the chance to tell you. Ros and I are going to be partners. I inherited some pearls which turned out to be worth a couple of grand, so I'm buying into Sweetcakes.'

'I didn't think you could bake.'

'I can't. I'm ace at admin and marketing and sourcing suppliers. Who knew, eh?'

'I'm not surprised. Good for you, Gemma.'

We smile politely at each other. We can still be civil. We can still be friends.

'The cake,' she says, suddenly remembering. 'Ros has done an awesome job.'

She whisks the cover off a cake stand and there it is. Lemon fondant icing, a mad rash of multicoloured polka dots and 'Happy Birthday Bub' in edible bunting.

'Dora's "Bub"?' Gemma asks. 'I didn't make the connection.'

'Short for "Adorabubble". I asked Ros to put it on the cake, to show Dora it came from me. Wow, it really is awesome.'

'Hang on a minute.' Gemma pulls a little box from her bag on a nearby chair. 'For Dora. It's a necklace, from the same friend as the pearls but sadly, it's not worth two grand. I've been meaning to pop it round to her but I thought it might be, I don't know, awkward. Now I can call it a birthday present. Give her my love, will you?'

Her thoughtfulness goes straight to my chest and I can feel my heart thumping against the linen of my shirt. She is a truly wonderful woman. 'It wouldn't be awkward at all. I'd love it if you gave Dora your gift.'

Last time I tried to tell her how I feel, the words came out all wrong. What possessed me to bring up that ridiculous 'fuck-ups' thing? No wonder she knocked me back. I have to get it right this time. 'I'm so sorry, Gemma. I've behaved like a total plank. At work, I manage things, anticipate things, see the bigger picture. I don't screw up. I see now how badly I managed our friendship and my feelings for you. I'll always be crap at this relationship stuff, but I can't bear that I hurt you.'

I keep going, scared to stop. 'You were right. I couldn't see how I felt about you until Nancy dumped me. I just knew something was missing between us. Her and me, I mean. So it was a relief in the end, when she pulled the plug. And then I knew what was missing. Who was missing. You. That doesn't mean you're second best. Anything but. You're first best, Gemma. Definitely. Completely. There. I've said it badly. I've said I'm sorry. Twice. Now I'll take my cake and stop embarrassing you.'

She shakes her head. In sorrow? In anger? Probably both. 'You can't just recite your speech and scuttle off. Apart from anything else, I need to pack the cake.'

She expertly flips a sheet of card into a sturdy box and lowers the cake into it. 'You *were* a total plank, Ned. I'm fairly sure you still are. Will that change? Probably not. But you're also a kind, decent man and you deserve to be happy.'

'You too. Not the "man" bit obviously.'

'Let's face it, we're both crap at this relationship stuff: making bad choices, not having the sense to see what's staring us in the face. If we know that, maybe we can try harder from now on. Can't we? I really want to.'

'We can. We'll be fine. We can do this.' I don't know what else to say. I think she's suggesting that we can be friends again. In the absence of anything more, I'll settle for that. 'I hope it all works out for you and Kelvin: Sweetcakes, your life, making good choices.'

'You too.' She knots a ribbon round the box and hands it over. 'I meant to ask: why polka dots?'

'Dora adores them so it's the dress code. All the party guests have to wear something spotty. Tanya can't resist line-managing every last detail.'

'Just like her other party.' Gemma grins. 'When I blended right in and you stuck right out. What are you going to wear?'

'A white shirt with red spots. I look like a nosebleed. It actually doesn't matter because I plan to drop the cake off, give Dora her present – I got her a bike – and slip away. I don't need Tanya gloating about my lack of a plus-one.'

'I've got a polka-dot dress. White with yellow spots. I look like a plate of fried eggs.'

I nod. So . . . neither of us suits polka dots. I guess that's that then. I feel sad.

'Oh, for fuck's sake, Ned. This is me asking to be your plus-one. If I can bring Kelvin.'

'You are? Seriously?'

I study her face for clues. I don't want to get this wrong . . . again. She gives a little sigh of impatience and gently rubs the confused frown off my forehead with her fingertip. Then I know, I really know that this will be all right.

'Unless you think you and me is a bad idea.'

Typical Gemma, she's already preparing the ground for

disappointment, waiting for the second shoe to drop. I can't let that happen. I want to give her all the reassurance I can.

I won't push it. I won't hug her or overplay my hand. Apart from anything, I'm holding £50 worth of cake. Then she smiles nervously at me, in a way that fills me with hope.

I smile nervously back. 'I think it's a fantastic idea. You and me. *Us*. I really, really do, Gemma.'

She suddenly puts her hand to her mouth. I bet she's changed her mind. She's realized that 'us' is an appalling prospect and she needs to extricate herself fast, before I dare to think we have a future.

'I've just had a thought.'

'Yes?' I reply, steeling myself for disappointment.

'What if we rock up in stripes, instead of spots? You, me and Kelvin. That would really yank Tanya's chain, wouldn't it?'

'She'd hate it. You are a bad person. Let's do it.'

'Will Dora mind?'

'When she's centre of attention? I very much doubt she'll even notice.'

And then I *do* put the cake down. I *do* hug her and, tentatively, she puts her arms around my waist. I can feel her face on my shoulder and I know she's smiling. 'I would *love* you to be my plus-one, Gemma.'

'Good. That's sorted then.'

'Not just for the party. You know that, don't you? I'd hate you to think—'

'Of course I know that, you idiot.'

We are. Idiots, I mean. For a year of wrong turns, false hopes and bad choices. I can live with that if it means Gemma and I are together. Maybe we had to get it wrong to get it right. To be here, now.

Gemma invites me to supper; apparently Kelvin's cooking his signature baked bean and bacon bake. 'If you're there too, that's one portion less *I* have to eat.'

I couldn't be happier. In fact, we're both so dopey and distracted that, as we get into my car, she realizes we've forgotten Dora's cake and has to go back for it.

I love her calm presence alongside me, cake box cushioned on her lap, as I ease my Picanto onto the Lewes Road and head us north to Bevendean. We don't talk. We don't need to. We catch each other's eyes at the traffic lights by Sainsbury's and smile in unison at the road ahead.

What seems like a million years ago, I thought I had a future with Tanya. I didn't. When Nancy dumped me, she asked if I could see us together five years from now. I couldn't.

Gemma gives me a nudge, to alert me that the lights have changed, and we set off. Can I imagine a life without her? I can't.

And I won't.

Acknowledgements

Ned and Gemma have been with me for decades. I invented them at a City Lit playwriting class, taught by the legendary Olwen Wymark. Many years after that, they appeared in a BBC radio comedy-drama called *soloparentpals.com*, about an online support group. I have David Hunter to thank for producing five series, starring Maxine Peake, Kris Marshall, Liz White and Julian Rhind-Tutt.

I always felt that there was much more story to explore, barely touched upon in my fifteen-minute scripts. How were Ned and Gemma dumped? Who were their ex-partners' *new* partners, their friends, their bossy bosses and disastrous dates?

With encouragement from my book agent, Gaia Banks, I wrote some chapters of *Pre-Loved*, now set in Brighton & Hove. I quickly found that I enjoyed moving from one form of storytelling to another, and my script agent, Lucy Fawcett, cheered me on. Thank you both.

I was so lucky that my work-in-progress landed on the desk of Sam Humphreys, Associate Publisher at Mantle Books. Sam has been the best kind of editor: laughing at the funny bits, while always pushing me to dig deeper for the big emotions buried below the surface. Her suggestions were invaluable and this book has benefitted from every single one of them.

I'm grateful to the Mantle team for their know-how, skill and support: Rebecca Needes, Philippa McEwan, Alice Gray, Eleanor Bailey, Jessica Cuthbert-Smith, Mary Chamberlain and cover designer Melissa Four.

Big thanks to my writing friends. It's so helpful to compare notes, either when you're on an exciting writing roll or when you've, quite literally, lost the plot. Kate Harrison, Laura Wilkinson, Frances Quinn, Janice Hallett, Donna Hay, the marvellous Material Girls, and many, many more, I salute you.

I wrote this book in 2020, the first year of Covid. Like so many authors, I found it strangely comforting to describe a world where people still went to packed pubs and parties, busy shops and restaurants. A heartfelt thank-you to the key workers who kept us going through lockdown and beyond.

I didn't think, when I moved to Hove in 2013, that it would become a character in a novel. Can one thank a city? I don't know. So, instead, I'll thank all the shops, cafes, pubs, bus routes, restaurants and walks that feature. Some appear under their own names; others are invented amalgams of existing places.

I've made so many wonderful friends here. Thank you all for being the non-speaking 'extras' who pop up on every page.

A huge hug to my sister, Ruth Teddern, who read an early draft of *The Pre-Loved Club* and gave me the best kind of feedback; firm, but fair; insightful and always encouraging.

Finally, there's my husband, Edward Crask. He brings larks and laughter, tea and biscuits, warmth and love. We met in our 'middle years' and are living proof that it's possible.